THE UNSEEN PLAYER

M.A. Senft

THE UNSEEN PLAYER

By M. A. SENFT

Published by DREAMSPACE PUBLISHING LLC,

Cover Illustrated by: Patrice Becker

www.masenft.com

Copyright © 2021 DREAMSPACE PUBLISHING LLC. and the Author M.A. SENFT. All rights reserved. Printed in the United States of America. Excerpt as permitted under United States copyright act of 1976, no part of this publication may be reproduced or distributed in any form, or by any means, or stored in a database retrieval system, without the prior written permission of the copyright holder, except by a reviewer, who may quote brief passages in review.

Neither the publisher nor the author is engaged in rendering advice or services to the individual reader. Neither the authors nor the publisher shall be liable or responsible for any loss, injury, or damage allegedly arising from any information or suggestion in this book. The opinions expressed in this book represent the personal views of the author and not of the publisher, and are for informational purposes only.

ISBN - 979-8-9899829-0-5   Paperback
ISBN - 979-8-9899829-1-2   Hard Cover
ISBN - 979-8-9899829-2-9   E-PUB

Revision 2 (JAN 2024)

THE UNSEEN PLAYER

By M. A. SENFT

"Every man is put on earth condemned to die. Time and method of execution unknown."
—Rod Serling, The Twilight Zone

"During the day, I don't believe in ghosts. At night, I'm a little more open-minded."
—Unknown

Dedication

The Unseen Player is dedicated to Walter E. Johnes. At ninety-nine, a World War II veteran, and a prolific writer, my dad delights in my gift of imagination. In his daily writings, he proves words have weight, and can transcend the page.

A special thanks to Patrice Becker, Cover Illustrator, for her excellent freehand artwork. What I imagine in my head she somehow magically converts to a book cover. Thank you for seeing what I see.

Historical Prologue

The Legend of the Reno Gang Missing Treasure of 1868

The American Civil War (a.k.a., the War between the States) was a conflict of opposing forces. Mutual distrust flared when disagreements over states' rights, commerce practices, and tariffs came to a boiling point on April 12, 1861. Slavery, the most contentious of the disputes, fueled the flames of conflict for four years. On April 9, 1865, after the Battle of Gettysburg, the Confederate troops surrendered, and the war ended.

However, in the aftermath of the war, unrest persisted. Unemployment skyrocketed and poverty spread. Skills acquired during the war became valuable resources to those unable to make ends meet. Lawlessness and guerilla strategies of stealing, evading capture, and plundering—encouraged during wartime—infiltrated postwar life. Bushwhacking and rowdiness increased, and public fear escalated. While desperados pursued easy money, vigilantes pursued the desperados.

One of the most infamous outlaw gangs to rise to fame during this period was Missouri's Jesse and Frank James. Lesser-known today, but just as notorious then was the Reno Gang from Indiana. Four out of six Reno siblings comprised the gang, plus additional members. Born on July 27, 1837, Frank Reno was the gang's oldest member and their leader.

During the war, the Renos resorted to bounty-jumping, an enlistment practice of collecting military incentives, ranging from fifty dollars to three hundred dollars as a sign-on bonus, and then deserting days later. They would then reenlist at another military command, under a different name, and repeat the deception.

Frank, accompanied by his brothers John, Simeon, and William, were born two miles north of Seymour in Rockford, Indiana. First

Historical Prologue

to be referred to as a "Brotherhood of Outlaws," they were also the first to rob a moving train. The country was shocked at their brashness, including famed outlaws like Jesse and Frank James, who applauded the Reno Gang's success.

Rockford, Indiana, became headquarters for the gang when the war ended. Reduced to a ghost town by a string of mysterious fires, suspected to have been started by the Renos years earlier, residents were forced to leave.

Inciting terror wherever they traveled, the Reno Gang held Seymour hostage. Swaggering an air of untouchability after each arrest, they reappeared in gambling halls and bars, boasting of their influence over the town's officials. The state paid notice as the gang's reputation grew.

An Indiana newspaper once wrote, "Jackson County contains more cutthroats to the square inch than Botany Bay." The columnist compared the Reno brothers and their gang's crime spree to the first Australian penal colony of lawbreakers that housed 736 convicts.

Unsuspecting citizens were ambushed and robbed by the gang. Or worse yet, killed for their meager belongings. A guest at the Radar House in Seymour was found beheaded and floating in White River. Witnesses claimed that Frank Reno often toyed with his bowie knife for sport, tossing it at innocent bystanders. It was a knife used for evil. Witnesses and local law officials dared not speak or report what they had seen in fear of the gang's retaliation.

Subsequently, *The Seymour Times* ran an editorial on August 3, 1865, forewarning readers that, "Nothing but Lynch Law will save the reputation of this place and its citizens."

According to history, on October 6, 1866, the brothers' first train robbery was staged. The train messenger, held at gunpoint, turned over twelve thousand dollars in cash ($188,000 in today's money.) A large safe, insured by the Adams Express Company, was thrown from the train. The brothers successfully escaped. Other gang members, who lay in wait, attempted to retrieve the safe but were caught by vigilantes and later lynched at a spot now referred to as Hangman's Crossing.

Soon thereafter, the railroad hired the Pinkerton National Detective Agency, the largest private law enforcement organization in the world, to investigate and hunt down the outlaws. With their stolen plunder stockpiled in a secret cave, the Reno's headed north to Canada. Trailed by a sheriff's posse, the brothers once again successfully evaded capture.

The gang eventually returned home to Seymour, where their next raid was schemed. Frank and the gang stayed at a fellow member's home but were tracked down by the Pinkertons. William Pinkerton led the raid. They arrested the outlaws and recovered over fourteen thousand dollars. The bandits were jailed, but on April 1, 1868, they broke out through a cavity in the cell, leaving a note on the wall that read, "April Fools."

Then on May 22, 1868, the gang robbed their fourth train, seventeen miles south of Seymour, in Marshfield, Indiana. Attracting national attention, this time, they made off with cash and government bonds totaling ninety-six thousand dollars (the equivalent of $1.7 million in today's currency.) William and Simeon were soon captured by the Pinkertons in Indianapolis and taken to the Al County Jail in Lexington, Kentucky.

Vigilantes had successfully hanged some of the Reno Gang and threatened to also hang William and Simeon. Alas, Laura Reno, the brothers' sister, had to pay to have them transferred to a sturdier jail in New Albany, Indiana. On July 29, in the middle of the night, Sheriff Thomas Fullenlove moved the brothers to Floyd County, Indiana.

Meanwhile, Frank Reno was tracked down in Canada, where, on October 6, 1868, he was extradited and placed in Pinkerton custody. The next day Frank was reunited with his two brothers Fullenlove to send the trio to a more secure jail in Indianapolis, but Fullenlove rejected the recommendation. Instead, the Sheriff made

Historical Prologue

a public announcement.

> "We do not believe that there is any danger of the Jackson County Vigilance Committee extending their visit to New Albany. They would be sure to meet a hot reception here, and they had better keep at a safe distance. These men were sent here for safekeeping, and they will be safely kept if it is in the power of the authorities to do so."

Irrespective of the forewarning, at 4:30 in the morning, on December 12, 1868, the jail was stormed by an army of fifty to sixty hooded vigilantes. The telegraph wires were cut, and the guard was seized outside before charging the sheriff's residence. When Sheriff Fullenlove refused to turn over the keys, he was shot and beaten. Mrs. Fullenlove surrendered.

Minutes later, at the top of an iron staircase on the second story where the Fullenlove's resided, the vigilantes hanged Frank. The other two brothers were subsequently hanged. One other gang member, who had been incarcerated with the Renos, was hanged twice because the original rope failed. History shows the lynchings were never legitimately investigated.

The bodies were displayed in pine coffins at the jail door, where thousands of people streamed by to get a glimpse of the notorious Reno Gang. Wagons, buggies, and persons on foot and horseback jammed the roadways into town. Later a Chicago newspaper described the event as: "One of the most violent nights in the history of our country."

In a six-month period, the Vigilance Committee lynched ten Reno Gang outlaws, including all but one Reno brother, John, who luckily happened to be serving a twenty-five-year prison sentence in the Missouri State Penitentiary.

The treasures the Reno Gang had stolen were never found. Little

Goss Cave, in southern Indiana, three miles off US Highway 150 near Greenville, is rumored to be where the Renos stashed caches of gold and silver, other people's treasures and precious jewels. Never retrieved, the brother's loot remains to this day, hidden in an undisclosed location.

The Unseen Player

Chapter 1
The End of a Dream
April 22, 1997

From the back of a black limousine a mahogany casket was wheeled. Beneath a Carolina-blue sky, the chest was meticulously carried over dew covered grass to its final resting spot by six pallbearers. Steadily they released the coffin onto a lowering frame atop a two-and-a-half-foot by eight-foot plot of ground where in less than an hour, the earth would reclaim the soulless body the casket cradled.

Unseasonably chilly for April, daybreak had ushered in the promise of a spectacular day. The sort rarely associated with funerals. In layered clothing, mourners, including the deceased's two boys and their families, crowded under a canopy that had been erected to shield them from the brisk morning breeze.

As the committal service was about to begin, a cold gust of wind surged through the crowd, punctuating the stark reality of the moment. In full bud and bloom, a nearby lilac bush had released its aromatic perfume into the air as a peculiar reminder that spring was a season of birth and renewal.

For the man seated closest to the casket, the smell of lilacs was bittersweet. One of the first plants to bloom in the spring, the flower was a favorite of the deceased. With hands clasped, a stone-cold realism coursed through his veins. Pinned to a shattered heart, from this day onward he would wear the label of a widower.

The man's vacant stare gazed past the spray of lacey, pink-fringed white roses that covered his sweetheart's coffin into a future devoid of warmth, silken hands, and the smile of the lady who loved him. Adorning the lid, the bouquet beautified the one person Clint had no idea how to live without–Elise.

The End of a Dream

Any other time the gentle caress of a cool morning breeze would have been welcomed. But not today. Still dazed by the tragic events that had unfolded only days before, Clint was numb to the core with grief. The root of regret had pierced his notion of being the perfect husband, causing him to withdraw from those who loved him most. Ill-equipped to handle irrational guilt for not having been with Elise in her final hours, despair turned to blame. *Had I only…* he imagined. *I might have saved her.*

No one looked around. They just looked down at their feet, out into the cemetery past the grave markers, or at the large blanket of roses centered over the coffin between the gatherers. When the bible was opened and a marker removed, all eyes turned toward the vicar who had just cleared his throat, ready to address the crowd.

When Pastor Jim began to speak of a promised land, of which his wife was now a part, Clint stopped listening. Breathing in the fragrance that reminded him of Elise, Clint could not bring himself to accept the preacher's meaningful words. Though they were intended to impart peace of mind, Clint had moved beyond being comforted. He drifted away to a place where joy still lingered, back to a time before his world had come crashing down.

As tangible as the ceremony felt at the graveyard, Clint saw in his mind and felt in his heart, Elise sitting by his side. They were in a lawyer's office, and he had just finished signing a contract with Orange County and the State of Indiana for a portion of the escheated property. Below his name, Elise had scrolled hers. Their eyes locked when she placed the pen on the desk, euphoria beaming on their faces. The deal was sealed.

Since no heirs had stepped forward to contest the reversion of land, which had been entrusted to the state, Clint and Elise were able to share in the good fortune of appropriation. A sizeable unpaid tax lien qualified the property for repossession. After a lengthy red tape jump-through-the-hoop-ordeal, the State of Indiana eventually annexed ten of the twenty-acres and put the

Chapter 1

remaining ten-acres up for sale. The state's acreage was absorbed into the national forest while the other portion that butted up to that acreage was sold at public auction.

Grateful to have purchased the residual ten-acre parcel, this fortuitous event had turned the page on a new chapter in their lives. A modest home surrounded by an idyllic white picket fence had become more than a mere pipedream.

In Clint's head, the ink had not yet dried on the last page and line of their purchase agreement with the state. It had been the most desired thing either one of them had ever yearned for in thirty years of marriage. They had become joint landowners. Their new home was situated off Highway 150 on South CR 550E in southern Indiana, southeast of Trotter Crossing. Seven miles from Salzburg, the nearest town, Clint and Elise's new property bordered the Indiana Hoosier National Forest.

Little did he know at the time, but Clint's future had a different story to tell that did not include Elise. Unfortunately, on April 20, 1997, just one week after they'd moved in, Elise collapsed onto the kitchen floor, never to regain consciousness. Their lifelong dreams abruptly ended. The trips they had envisioned to Montana to visit Wade, Clara and Lily, driving up to Alaska, gardening and harvest time filling Ball jars and making jam to store in the cold cellar for winter use were all erased. Those dreams would now never come to fruition.

With the fragrance of fresh lilacs saturating the air, Clint continued to flip through the pages of time. Walking down memory lane, he recalled how Elise often arranged vases of fresh lilacs in their Seymour, Indiana, duplex each spring. Symbolic of first love, Elise had tucked a sprig into Clint's lapel the day of their wedding. On March 2, 1967, she had proclaimed him to be her first and forever love.

For a thousand years and more, she often wrote at the bottom of her cards to Clint.

A voice reentered Clint's cognizance as Pastor Jim concluded the committal ceremony with a reading from 1st Corinthians 15:51–57. "But let me reveal to you a wonderful secret. We will not all die, but we will all be transformed," he quoted dolefully.

Clint closed his eyes, unable to listen to any message of finality regarding his wife. With his two boys and their families at his side, showing their concern and support for one another, Clint went through the difficult motions of civility as friends and family zeroed in on him. While unintended, their well-meaning gestures of reassurance and concern only managed to agitate him.

Pastor Jim took Clint's hand in his as the crowd meandered back to their cars. "I'm truly sorry, Clint," he said, probing Clint's eyes to see how he was holding up, "for your loss. You know I am here for you anytime, day or night. Rest assured Elise is in God's hands now," he prophesied. "She was an earthly angel and is among the heavenly ones now! We all loved her. A precious soul, she was…" his words trailed as he shook his head in sorrow. He seemed unsure whether he should add much more, given the blank empty stare he saw on Clint's face. "God's grace and time heal all wounds."

Cocking his head to the side, Clint gazed into the benevolent eyes of the preacher, wondering if he really believed what he was selling. "I don't mean to be rude, Jim," he replied coldly, "but that's not a lot of comfort. Not for me anyway."

Clint took a deep breath and counted to ten. With more distance between them, he glanced up and said, "No disrespect, sir, but I guarantee you some wounds don't heal. Not this one." He tried not to sound as callous as he felt, but within the dark recesses of his soul, a storm raged.

In his opinion, God was nowhere to be found. Elise was the believer, not him, and all the prayers in the world would not alter that fact or bring her back. They hadn't helped when Elise was discovered unconscious on the kitchen floor moments before her

Chapter 1

death, nor had they been answered at age five when his dad had abandoned him. They also weren't heard when his best friend Gary failed to return from Vietnam. In Clint's experience, God was not in the business of responding to prayers, at least not his. Not then, not now, not ever.

As Clint dredged up the past—amid two mausoleums at the back of Three Pines Park Cemetery—a mysterious presence stood silently observing the crowd. The activity at the grave and roadside was scrutinized as the folks visited and eventually moved toward their vehicles. The middle-aged man with black hair, who stood at the center of the commotion after losing his wife, was the spectator's primary focus.

Clint had been lured to the property he now owned by the entity who studied him. A restless soul, the gaunt-faced man in suspenders and a fedora was not seen by the naked eye but was present in spirit as he waited patiently for the service to end.

The forsaken countenance worn on Clint's face as he stood by the roadside appeared mindful. He had followed the crowd back to the road to suggest he too planned to return to the church, which in truthfulness, he had no intention of doing. As the cars and trucks slowly drove past, he dutifully acknowledged each one with a nod or a wave until finally the last vehicle had vanished through the gates onto the boulevard.

South Creek Assembly of God Church, where the funeral had been conducted, was the group's destination. A generous smorgasbord of warm foods and desserts had been prepared by the ladies of the church and awaited the funeral-goers. Elise had visited the church twice, both times without Clint. When he called to make her funeral arrangements, the minister graciously offered their services which included a meal in the assembly hall following Elise's committal ceremony.

Clint breathed a sigh of relief when the last vehicle motored through the gate. He then turned and scaled the steep hill back to her grave. He could not bring himself to leave Elise. The thought

The End of a Dream

of her alone without him was inconceivable. After thirty years of marriage and never being apart, Clint was drawn to Elise like a moth to a flame.

A host of conflicting emotions welled inside Clint. *They can carry on without me,* he thought. *I'll see Rusty and Wade and the rest of the crew in the morning on their way out of town.* He paused, thinking about his kids. *They have each other. I'll be there for them later, but not tonight.*

Like a child, when he reached Elise, Clint broke down and sobbed knowing the mahogany casket was ready to be lowered into the earth. He hugged his body tightly as he leaned against the bier, no longer able to hold back the floodgates of grief he had been masking for the family's sake. A reservoir of pent-up anger turned a valve that released a torrent of tears. The weight of his agony drew him into a place darker than the darkest night.

The observer from the mausoleums approached Elise's burial vault. The folding chair Clint had used during the service, now behind him, became occupied. Although not seen, the watcher from another realm lingered while Clint worked through his layers of emotions.

As strange as it may have sounded to the ordinary person, in that moment, Clint made the decision to spend the night. Exhaustion had waned the energy required to drive home. He knew the cemetery crew was standing at a distance, waiting on him to leave. As he walked down the hill back to his truck, he nodded at them, indicating they could finish their work.

The hour had grown late, and a cast of long shadows lengthened over the park grounds, producing silhouettes of headstones. A symphony of spring peepers swelled as nightfall descended over Three Pines Park Cemetery.

At last, the grave diggers tossed their tools aside, and with the last bit of topsoil deposited, they used their shoes to pack the soil tightly. While they strolled to their cars, Clint waited in his truck.

Chapter 1

After the two-man crew drove away, their red taillights enveloped in darkness, Clint grabbed the sleeping bag he kept stashed under the seat of the F-100. He climbed the hill back to the grave, his breath visible in the gradually falling temperatures.

Leaning against a nearby tree, Clint watched as the sun lowered in the west. As twilight descended, sounds played in his head—indeterminate whispers and sighs evoked from a distant past.

Memories flickered from the pages of time, reminding Clint of what it felt like to be passionate and in love. As the sunset and the minutes ticked by, the stark reality of separation grew stronger.

Although Clint assumed it was just the two of them—he and his Elise—on their final night together, he was mistaken.

Invisible to human sight, Clint had no idea that a third presence—the observer—had joined the wake.

Chapter 2
Josie's Diner
Six Years Later

At 5:23 a.m., the cock crowed. Its familiar alarm of *'cock-a-doodle-doo,'* ricocheted inside Josie's Diner as the staff hustled about preparing the start of a new day. The crimson sky, rising in the east, cast rays of sunlight through the front windowpane onto the booth centered below. Last-minute preparations required completion before the early morning crowd arrived and a new week began.

Sailor take warning, whispered Patrick, the Diner's owner when he saw what the day had in store.

After-hours the night before, Drury's Family Farm had delivered the restaurant's standard order of hams, bacon, and sausages, of which the diner was in short supply. Thirty minutes later, Shoemaker Creamery and Poultry Farm had also unloaded chickens, eggs, cream, milk, and butter to balance out the café's depleted inventory.

With the shelves and pots now filled with breakfast offerings, the four-person diner crew was ready to serve customers. The minute hand on the grill timepiece pointed upward to twelve while the hour hand rested on the six.

The welcome sign was flipped from CLOSED to OPEN as Patrick began greeting the high-spirited clientele who had been gathering outside the locked door.

Through the café blinds, sunrays crisscrossed the sit-down bar Julie Eileen Jenkins stood behind. Better known as Jules, since moving away from her hometown of Beech Grove, Indiana, her patrons were always greeted with smiling eyes as they came in or exited the diner. In her gingham red-and-white uniform and matching hair bow, she added authenticity to the establishment.

Chapter 2

A pail of bleach water, placed out of sight, was used one last time to wipe down the Formica laminate 1950s retro countertop. She watched as the diner's regulars were steered single file to their preferred stations. Lively conversation followed the Easter holiday in a diner of Coca-Cola, Elvis Presley, Marilyn Monroe, and James Dean decor.

Today's April 21st forecast called for balmy temperatures but stormy skies. After a bitter-cold winter, springlike temperatures had raised the spirits and attitudes of Salzburg's townsfolk. Signage mirrored this transformation, showcasing change-of-season items in store windows everywhere.

Jules busied herself topping off coffee mugs and wiping down tables of customers who had come and gone. All the while, she waited, watching the door for the one customer who had yet to arrive.

Four and a half years had passed since Jules had moved to Salzburg from her hometown of Beech Grove. Following her husband's fatal collision with a tanker truck on I-465's inner loop in Indianapolis—referred to by locals as the "Spaghetti Bowl"— Jules' brother, Randal, and his wife Anna had convinced her to take up residence in the southern part of the state. Near Greenville, they lived off Highway 150, where they had settled twenty years prior.

The decision had been a good one. Whereas Josie's Diner reaped the benefits of Jules' infectious disposition—seeing an immediate uptick in business—she, likewise, settled into a new life without constant reminders of the tragic affair and the sequence of events that followed.

New management and digital signage, coupled with Jules' upbeat personality, had become a winning combination for the restaurant. In the black for the first time in five years, additional European-style items had been added to Josie's menu offerings.

Profiteroles (a puff pastry filled with fresh cream and covered in warm chocolate sauce) from France, Banoffee pie (bananas and toffee in a graham crust) from England, and Black Forest Gateau (chocolate sponge cake with rich cherry filling) to represent Germany, headed the list.

Often Jules joked that Patrick was adding around-the-world menu choices as polar-opposites to downhome, country-style meals. She personally thought them strange bedfellows.

Along with the neighboring towns of French Lick and Paoli to the west and Hardinsburg and Floyds Knobs to the east, people would come to Salzburg to enjoy Josie's Southern dishes or pick a meal with European flair. From as far away as Salem and New Albany, patrons traveled to delight in the throwback atmosphere and the chef's original and tried-and-true creations.

The café had begun to attract several repeat customers, encompassing a large radius of locals. Many ate at the café daily, especially during the breakfast hours. However, Jules had singled out one specific patron above others.

Each morning she eagerly awaited his arrival, looking forward to their morning conversations with heightened anticipation. A special table was routinely reserved for the same time each day. During one of their many chats, she discovered he too was a widower, which made it easier for them to identify with each other's unique station in life.

Seven miles from town, rifling through the house for his car keys, Clint was running late. Misplaced somewhere inside the keys were never where they ought to be—hanging on the wall rack built specifically so he would not lose his keys.

Probably in the kitchen, he decided, aggravated with himself for his lack of attention to detail.

Confident they would resurface sooner or later, he headed for the bathroom to begin his morning ritual. Last night's dream shadowed him.

Chapter 2

Surprised to have dreamt such a weird scenario of events two nights in a row, and once the week before, he was confident the reoccurrence was somehow connected to his preoccupation with the treasure hunt he was beginning to formulate in his mind. He was aware dreams often reflected what a person was thinking about before falling asleep.

A special treat for his grandchildren, this year's treasure hunt would be scheduled in late September, which broke tradition to prior years when Elise was alive. When summer temperatures dropped mid-September, an exact date would be set. Clint figured one weekend in September would do perfectly.

In prior years, before his late wife's passing, the event would have been scheduled for the latter part of October, typically closer to Halloween. But not this year. The treasure hunt always coincided well with fall break. Nonetheless, if he were to have the event again without Elise, that date would have to be reset to something more palatable.

Clint realized since travel time was a consideration, extra days would need to be factored in for the visit. Given enough warning, he hoped his boys would indulge his request. The family lived a considerable distance from Salzburg. One son had laid roots down in Flathead Lake, Montana. The other dwelled in Crothersville, Indiana. Neither was around the corner.

This year's treasure hunt could be my one, and only, he reckoned. For Clint, age had become a factor. *My budget isn't set up to afford indulgences like what this treasure hunt will entail,* he warned himself. *With rising food costs and the price of treasures, it would be a taxing undertaking.*

From where he stood, the grandkids were close to outgrowing such frivolities anyhow. Hence, one of the reasons he had decided to host the event this year rather than wait. Clint knew his grandkids loved him, but teenage years produced less communication, not more. Friends would be on their radar, not parents and grandparents.

Their attention would naturally be directed toward things like girlfriends, boyfriends, sports, and school-church activities.

In last night's dream and just like dreams before it, Clint had been collecting numerous antiques. He had been taking them from a curio cabinet and placing them into a logo-imprinted bag. The dream had given him reason for pause due to the type of items he was gathering. In his foggy memory, the dream lingered, leaving him with more questions than answers. Like what might be prompting the repetitive dream?

Though the dream made no sense in the morning's light, at the time he was experiencing it, it felt perfectly natural.

As Clint showered, the smell of freshly brewed Columbian roast seeped through the air duct of his tiny bathroom, its rich aroma intoxicating. With a towel tied around his waist, Clint leaned in to rub away a section of the condensation-covered mirror so he could see his reflection. Time to shave his overnight growth of whiskers.

Clearheaded, Clint had yet to recollect the logo he had seen in his dream. The bag was made of paper, that much he recalled, but it wasn't an ordinary bag. He pondered the thought and location but came up lacking on the lettering, now lost to the ether of day.

The irresistible scent permeating the house inspired Clint to get a move on. *Put the dream aside for later analysis,* he decided. The Mr. Coffee machine, set to brew at 5:53 a.m., was nearing the end of its cycle. He glanced at the key holder on the wall.

Where are those stupid keys? he grumbled.

He went to look in the usual spots where they were typically deposited, bedroom nightstand, living room table, foyer stand.

"Dang it," he said. "Is there ever going to come a day I train myself to put them on the hanger in the kitchen where they belong?" He combed the back part of the house to no avail.

An early riser his entire life, Clint frequently dragged himself out of bed ahead of his alarm clock. With a circadian cycle set to 5:47 a.m., it didn't matter what the season, Clint's eyes popped open at the same time every day.

Chapter 2

The hour was now 6:03 a.m., and his brain fog had lifted, along with his mood. Clint knew he would soon sit down to breakfast at Josie's Diner. With a clockwork routine that included breakfast in Salzburg, he had noticed more pep in his step of late. A mere twelve-minute drive, Clint figured he would walk into the diner before the larger crowd hit. That was… if he could find his keys. He poured a cup of joe and eyeballed the room thoroughly.

"Where are those blasted things?" he grumbled, still aggravated with himself for not having put them on the rack when he came in from the field the evening before.

Clint's meager home, which encompassed ten-acres, required serious work. In need of repair, the place was badly run down. Now that the weather had changed, he'd direct his efforts toward the most neglected areas first, those that begged the most attention.

Recently, he had unearthed renewed inspiration to restore the place. Things Elise and he had discussed had been put on the backburner six years ago. Ideas they shared were shelved on April 20, 1997, the day of her unexpected passing.

The house was pretty much a fixer-upper from the start, as they had been aware. Bought as is, with "lots of potential," Elise's death had taken the wind out of Clint's sails. He had no desire to fix anything. Crippled by the shocking turn of events that had caught him off guard, he'd retreated from life. He literally stopped caring about the little things that would have brought most people joy. On the heels of her death, if he'd had the resources to walk away from the house, he would have. Trapped in a house of lost dreams, it was time to fix some of the damage to both his life and the property.

He easily recalled the first time they drove past the land. It was on a Saturday afternoon and an indelible memory. A pleasurable day, they were out house hunting but not in the Salzburg area.

They passed it driving west on Highway 150. With no destination in mind, other than lunch in the next town, they turned around for a second pass after seeing a FOR SALE sign by the side of the road. Inexplicably drawn to its location, despite its rundown appearance, the gears in Clint's head began to churn.

The realtor who had answered Clint's call while he and Elise sat in their idling car at the edge of the property informed him the county had seized a twenty-acre parcel, including that location. The State was selling off those ten-acres, which included the abandoned structure erected on the property.

Jonathan McClusky, the realtor, held nothing in reserve about his opinion of the rundown dwelling. He made it perfectly clear the structure needed to come down and a new house built in its place.

With few funds in the bank, the opposite decision came easy to Elise and Clint. They had enough to cover the earnest money and closing cost, if accepted, but nothing more. No new structure would be built. Where most other properties they had considered pushed their comfort zone, this one fell within their budget handsomely. They figured with some imagination and a lot of elbow grease, the house could be salvaged.

Having sat on the market for nearly two years—drumming up little to no interest, according to McClusky—the house and land's listed price had been dropped well below market value for a quick sale.

Clint and Elise's luck could not have been more well-timed. Or so it seemed. The deal was sealed on April 8, 1997, and they moved in on Sunday, April 13. Sadly, one week later, Elise's life suddenly ended.

Understandably Elise's death brought Clint's world to a standstill. Not only did his appearance become secondary, so did the condition of their fixer-upper project. Any desire to patch up the neglected dwelling they had purchased together and planned, as a team, to restore was put on the back burner. Still, his late wife's essence filled the place, and at times, he would have sworn she remained on the property. Some moments made him question

Chapter 2

if indeed she had moved on to a better place, certain that his movements were being watched.

The feeling arose primarily indoors, yet on occasion, Clint sensed something unnatural when working at the back of the property or around the barn, specifically, near the division line that separated the state forest land from his own. That area was unlike anywhere else. So much so, Clint became convinced his late wife's spirit remained bound to the property.

What other explanation could there be? he asked himself each time the peculiar sensation surfaced.

Clint reckoned Elise wanted him to be aware that she had stayed behind and was near. Out of reach, around a corner, she lingered.

The sensation had been occurring since the day of Elise's aneurysm. Later, at the conclusion of her funeral and when everyone had left the cemetery, Clint felt her presence. He had been sitting on the ground next to her casket when the phenomenon became so strong, he would have sworn he'd caught a glimpse of her in his peripheral vision as she passed by. In the faintness of a fading sun, he had observed her.

But when it came right down to it—in his heart of hearts—he knew better. The incident was invented, wishful thinking on his part and nothing more.

This year, 2003, had ushered in a better attitude toward the place Clint called home. He once again became inspired to complete the projects Elise and he had placed on a to-do list before the bottom fell out of his world—like fixing up the house—and now they had become a priority. The first order of business was to build a gazebo in her memory.

Elise loved to rock and read, recalled Clint comically. Once the soil was turned and the vegetable garden and berries bushes were planted, he would draw up plans and get to work.

Having given up on locating his keys, Clint walked to the bedroom. *At some point,* he declared, *they'll surface. I can always fix breakfast here.*

On the side of the bed, Clint pushed one leg into his trousers. Then, in an enlightened moment, he recalled his keys' whereabouts.

They are in my pants pocket, he yelped throwing his hands up into the air.

He felt the heavy ring of keys against his bare leg when he reached in to retrieve them. From the front right pocket of his jeans, he pulled the truck keys, tossed them on the bed, and continued getting dressed.

The thermometer, attached to the outside window of the house, registered forty-one degrees. *Not bad,* Clint considered. *It should hit sixty by late afternoon.* Ready to depart, he poured coffee into the thermal mug he kept by the door.

The smell of sodden earth greeted him when he stepped off the porch. The sweet-smelling fragrance of lilacs and honeysuckle, planted by Elise days before the tragedy, registered as he ambled toward his 1974 F-100. He opened the door and slipped inside, placing his large stainless-steel tumbler into the handcrafted cup holder specially designed for the truck.

The ignition turned over on the first try. Surprised and pleased the engine decided not to be obstinate for once, Clint pulled a Lucky Strike from the pack, tapped it on the dash, and stuck it between his lips.

He grabbed his plaid thermal lumberjack shirt from behind the seat. He kept it there for days such as this. The window was rolled halfway down for ventilation. He grinned, remembering he'd read somewhere that secondhand smoke might be hazardous to his health.

Chapter 2

The bumpy dirt road beneath the tires jostled him around on the seat. A trip to town, generally ten to fifteen minutes depending on the weather, was the perfect distance to relax into his first smoke of the day, which always tasted better than any that followed. Seven miles west, he could have driven the route blindfolded.

Clint pondered the dream from the night before. On the edge of his recall, he barely recollected entering a shop and hearing a bell jingle. Although he had heard somewhere that smells and colors were generally not a part of dreams, in this case, they were.

The aroma of musty books and stale cigar smoke was potent, permeating the air. Plus, a maroon curtain was noted, draped unattractively behind the counter. He assumed it was there to separate a private room from the main area. Then his mind catapulted him forward, like flipping through the pages of a book, he had entered another snippet of the dream. Facing a curio cabinet, Clint found himself in a different part of the store.

Reminiscent of a bed chamber, he saw an old cabinet with glass doors. It resembled furniture perhaps constructed in the 1800s, sturdy and made of walnut from what Clint could ascertain.

With the door open, Clint saw himself take a dagger from the inside shelf positioned next to a leather sheath. They appeared to be part of a set.

In Clint's hand he held a hand-carved Olivewood Bowie knife baring the initials F.R. At that moment, the dream faded from memory.

Chapter 3
Jules

Navigating noisily through the narrow streets of Salzburg, Clint's F-100 drove to his typical parking spot behind Josie's Diner. He closed the lid to his travel coffee mug before stepping out of the car and snuffing his cigarette on the hood.

With the butt tucked into his pant pocket, he ambled toward the front of the building. Clint hated to see cigarette butts scattered over the pavement and sidewalks. In his opinion, it made all smokers appear lazy and inconsiderate.

At the side of the building, he stuck two quarters into the newspaper stand and withdrew a copy of *The Vincennes Sun-Commercial News*. Tucking it under his arm, Clint entered the restaurant.

Wearing a shy smile, directed at Jules, he proceeded to the table she recently started reserving for him. She was aware he liked to sit a distance from the crowds, so every morning, she held the booth open as long as possible, hoping an overload of patrons would not require its release.

A mug of hot coffee sat on the table. Clint tossed his jacket on the seat, along with his cap, and placed the folded newspaper beside his drink. If nothing else, Clint was predictable, as was Jules. He glanced out into the diner where she was taking an order and mouthed a friendly, "Thank you."

Jules mirrored his greeting. With generous eyes, she nodded and said, "My pleasure."

Born into the same Baby Boomer generation, though she was twelve years his junior, Jules and Clint enjoyed conversing about things other than the weather and politics. They both often reminisced about the "good old days" when the world was far less complicated.

Chapter 3

Each year, it appeared, an alarming number of open fields were paved over and made into parking lots. While the information highway buzzed in and out of everyday life, influencing people's attitudes and opinions in whatever direction the fickle wind blew, Clint and Jules were content to be labeled old-timers. They kept their feet solidly set in the past.

She'd placed a three-egg, over-easy breakfast order ten minutes before Clint's arrival. As a prelude to the main course, she set warm biscuits on the table. Country fried steak and hash browns, smothered in sausage gravy, with a side of pancakes was Clint's standard.

Sitting side-saddle across from Clint, Jules casually crossed her ankles, patted the table, and asked, "So how is it going?" She turned toward the window to peer at the overcast skies outdoors. "A fine morning!" she grinned. "Life treating you well?"

"As well as can be expected." Clint grinned charmingly. "And you?"

A mane of black hair framed Clint's handsome face. With deep blue eyes and a square jaw reminiscent of Robert Norris, who depicted the Marlboro Man in 1965, Clint didn't give his appearance much notice.

At fifty-five, he looked ten years younger than his actual age would indicate. And, despite his huge appetite, he never fluctuated much from a buck seventy. Considered a reasonable weight for a man five-foot-eleven, his high energy kept his weight at bay. Never labeled lazy, where most men at his age carried a pot belly, Clint did not.

"Doing great!" replied Jules. "You were a little later than usual."

"Yeah, my keys seem to grow legs every time I go to look for them! Always somewhere they shouldn't be."

Jules' puzzled expression made him laugh. He put up a hand. "Don't worry, those suckers have met their match. I built a key rack to hang by the kitchen door." He grinned. "Except that hasn't worked out so well, at least not yet. Now all I have to do is hang them on the pegs."

Clint searched the crowd. "Enough about my keys. Looks like business is starting to pick up. Think it has to do with the time of year?" he asked, figuring the cold, hard winter might have kept customers away.

Behind Jules' kind face, Clint could see a packed diner, all seated and served. "Keeping you busy, I see." Clint was humored by the image that popped in his head, knowing the townsfolk stood waiting by the doors every morning at 6 a.m.

She turned toward the restaurant. "On any given day, they're out there waiting impatiently for Patrick to open the door." She snickered, "I prefer a steadier flow but don't want to look a gift horse in the mouth!" Her face brightened. "Right?"

Their eyes met, acknowledging the old proverb and its meaning. Clearly humored, Jules caught sight of Clint's empty mug. "Man, you drained that fast! I'll go grab the pot. And," she gently smiled, "to answer your question, it's the time of year. Nothing like warmer weather to bring in clientele!"

Giving a quick wink, she got up and headed for the coffee machine, passing the adjoining table where two truck drivers had just sat down. Moving with purpose, she called over her shoulder as she passed. "Good morning, gentlemen! I'll be right with you."

On her way back, with carafe-in-hand, she placed two mugs, menus, and napkin-wrapped flatware on the trucker's table. Simultaneously, she rattled off the breakfast spiel she knew by heart as if it was the first time she'd ever recited it, word by word.

"Don't know if you noticed today's special on the menu board when you entered, but for $8.99. you'll get hotcakes, waffles or biscuits, two eggs, and a side of ham, sausage, or bacon. Served with your choice of potato—hash browns or home fries. Includes coffee or hot tea, your choice." The men glanced over at the display board as though checking the accuracy of her words.

Clint grinned with insider knowledge. The so-called "special" was not so special. It had been on the board for as long as he could remember. Only the price had changed.

Chapter 3

None the wiser, first timers felt pleased when Jules suggested the myriad of tantalizing options Josie's Diner had to offer. Routinely ordered, Clint was certain the special's popularity had more to do with Jules' effervescent personality than what was on their plates. Full of charm, she was hard to refuse.

Clint read the paper cover to cover before placing it with the segmented copies that had accumulated on the bench next to the entrance. He looked for Jules before stepping out. He couldn't help but notice she had one eye focused on the customers and the other on the door. He fancied she was watching him but felt foolish for entertaining the thought.

"See ya tomorrow!" called Clint with a wave of his hand.

Jules' smiling eyes caught his as she hustled over to a table that had indicated her services were requested.

Standing outdoors in the moisture-laden air, Clint took a drag from his newly lit cigarette. Determined to smoke half and save the rest for later, his plan was to ration the pack. Smoking half at a time for one week had proven Clint's life-long vice had a stranglehold on him. Plain and simple, mind over matter wasn't cutting it.

While on a prescription designed to help people stop smoking, Clint's dreams had turned whackier than ever. Vivid, disturbing dreams had caused him to consistently awaken with night sweats. After only a few doses, Clint had tossed in the towel. The last thing he needed was more whacked-out dreams. The current ones were crazy enough.

The next stop was Hound Dog Feed Supply. He would walk down for the exercise but keep an eye on the weather. He always bought fifty-pound bags and had a routine of not allowing his chicken feed to drop below ten pounds.

Last year, early in the spring, he bought a chicken coop from Hound Dog's. He figured watching chickens run around his property could be entertaining. Fresh eggs were a bonus. However, he could never bring himself to kill one of them. Animals, like possums, racoons, red tail fox and coyotes roamed his land. Because it was their home too, the chickens were protected.

The plan was to gather his supplies and come back with the F-100 to collect the haul. A heavy workday lay ahead. Splitting wood, preparing the soil for the spring garden, driving stakes into the ground, and separating netting were all on his list of things to accomplish.

Early mornings were Clint's favorite time of day. Walking the streets of Salzburg appealed to his free spirit. Savoring a typical spring day kept him from being a slave to his work. He had had enough of that when he worked at the sawmill in Seymour when his day started at seven and lasted an easy twelve hours.

Clint's idea of retirement consisted of walking off breakfast. Always on the lookout for good gift ideas for the treasure hunt, he examined the display windows closely for noteworthy items that could be squirreled away until September.

Throughout the year, he made a point of finding worthy gifts for the treasure hunt. The event took a lot of preparation and foresight, which he suspected was lost on the family. More effort was expended than the grandchildren could possibly imagine. Hosting an event as involved as the treasure hunt took an enormous amount of planning and resources. The surprises he had tucked away were the tip of the iceberg.

At the intersection of Grandview and Ridge Crest, Clint took a breather. A new structure, at the far end of the street and a few blocks off the main drag, came into view. He wondered what the building might be and made a mental note to check it out. Tomorrow after breakfast, he'd take a gander.

Inside the feed store Clint gathered his provisions. They were rung up and stacked by the door while he went back for the truck. When he got home, he would change into his overalls and get to work. Rain was predicted to roll in between 3 and 4 p.m., so he needed to work fast.

Chapter 3

After filling the truck, he lit up a cigarette, rolled down the window on the passenger side, and drove home.

Before he knew it, the day was coming to an end. Pleased to witness a magenta sunset, Clint relaxed. Tomorrow promised to be as beautiful as this one was not. He'd be able to accomplish more chores. In no time, he would have his place in tip-top shape.

Moving inside, out of the nippy evening temperature, Clint instinctively hung his keys on the rack. Proud he had remembered, he said, *Good boy!* as he walked by.

The day had been a full one. Log splitting and stacking wood, not to be used for two years, was the first thing he had done. In the pole barn he had organized his tools and cataloged his garden seeds and supplies. Other duties like cleaning out the chicken coop, gathering and washing eggs, and burning trash were all part of his daily chores.

His sore muscles screamed for relief. A hot shower always helped. He'd rub his muscles down with Bengay directly afterward, which always worked best, helping him sleep more soundly. Clint hated to admit it, but his age was catching up with him.

After his shower, he planned to heat up a bowl of homemade chili, carefully concocted on Wednesday afternoon. The recipe had been in Elise's red metal file, where she kept her handwritten recipes on three-by-five cards. Chili he could replicate. However, his last attempt at her famous pot pie failed royally. He had mixed it together exactly as she had instructed, but it fell well short of expectations.

Even with following her recipes to the tee, nothing ever came out for Clint as well as they did for Elise. She had a magic touch when it came to throwing ingredients together. Clint had become somewhat proficient at cooking, but he'd be a dreamer if he thought he could ever match her God-given talent.

When they were first married, if she had flour, sugar, milk, eggs, onions, and a bag of potatoes at her disposal, a meal was possible.

His meals, on the other hand, merely kept him alive. Two things he could make to perfection—French toast and pancakes.

Elise's aneurism had stunned everyone. The changes Clint was forced to make were unfathomable, like learning to clean, cook, and pay bills—ordinary things Elise had always done. The memory of walking in and finding her collapsed on the kitchen floor was indelibly etched in his mind and never far from his thoughts.

For that reason, his meals were consumed anywhere other than the kitchen. Often, Clint sat in front of the fire in the living room, where he felt at ease. Or he watched television in the bedroom as he ate his dinner. It felt less lonely in other parts of the house. The kitchen was a solemn reminder, so he avoided it as much as possible.

Elise and Clint were married on March 2, 1967. He was nineteen and she was twenty-one. Thirty years had passed since they'd tied the knot. At age fifty-one, Elise moved on to her heavenly home and left a hole in Clint's heart the size of Texas. Worst of all, there was no warning to soften the blow. No last kiss to say goodbye. No final hug to carry him through the rest of his life.

Clint had been living in the aftermath of that day. For nearly six years, he had struggled to put one foot in front of the other. But now, at fifty-five, he had made peace with the fact he had no other choice but to accept his plight. Elise would be disappointed if he gave up. He knew that. Besides, Wade and Rusty, their two boys, needed him to stay engaged.

Wade, the oldest, was currently living in Flathead Lake, Montana. When his high school days were in the rearview mirror, he took a job on a cruise ship. His intention was to save money for engineering school at Purdue University, but fate made a course correction. While docked at port in Aruba on the Caribbean Sea, Wade met his future bride. Wade and Clara married and had one daughter, Lily. Trailing in his father-in-law's footsteps, Wade became a rancher.

Chapter 3

Two years later, Rusty married his grade school sweetheart, Molly. Running a farm in Crothersville, Indiana, they gave Elise and Clint two additional grandchildren, Trey and Dylan.

Clint's boys were a source of pride, chips off the old block, proving the apple didn't fall far from the tree. Both were hard workers and devoted family men.

In the living room, he watched the news. An hour later, he took his bowl to the kitchen. Stuffed and tired, he washed the dishes and placed them in the strainer to dry. From a canister that contained coffee, Clint measured grounds into the coffee pot for the next day before he turned off the lights and went to bed. It had been a fine day.

Chapter 4
Not an Ordinary Bookstore

Clint awoke at dawn to soft sunlight filtering through the east window. Rays barely visible, he knew the time—5:47, or thereabouts. Tossing the covers to the side, he pivoted on the mattress, his legs hanging, ready to start the day.

The first thought that crossed his mind was Jules and her Irish green eyes. She had a charismatic smile that he found appealing. It was no wonder business at the diner had picked up since her arrival. He wondered what she was doing at that very moment.

On her way to Josie's, I bet, he grinned, visualizing what it looked like each morning outside the diner before the doors were unlocked. *She'll be trying to get ahead of the waiting crowd.*

Clint liked that his mornings began with a hardy breakfast and adult conversation rather than the way it used to be—mumbling nonsense to himself as he aimlessly walked through the house, not always remembering what he was doing or why he had ended up in the room where he'd found himself.

To this day, when Elise's funeral crossed his mind, Clint felt a twinge of embarrassment for his irrational behavior that evening. The idea of staying at a cemetery past dark denoted outright lunacy, even to him. He had waited for the cemetery crew to finish their work so he could sit by her casket in an unrolled sleeping bag to keep his body warm, which now seemed a little over the top.

The dipping temperatures had eventually forced Clint to go home. His empty house, once so full of joy, punctuated his feelings of misery and shame. When he crawled into bed that night, Pastor Jim's words of solace rang in his ears. *"She was an earthly angel and is among the heavenly ones now."*

The last several years had been rough, and just when Clint had become convinced any semblance of normalcy would never return,

Chapter 4

his life had begun to turn around. Making repairs to the house had given him something to do. Transforming the homestead into what Elise had always envisioned filled his idle hours. He'd made a conscious decision to no longer withdraw from the world around him.

Into a dim room, Clint stared. Still in a brain fog, the scent of brewed coffee had filtered down the hallway from the kitchen. Enticed by its aroma, he located his house shoes at the end of the bed and slipped them on. In a half-stupor, he lifted his robe from the bedpost and shuffled down the hall to the restroom.

Finding himself in a better place emotionally, Clint felt renewed energy when he thought about his future. He visualized the house in better condition than its current state of neglect. Motivated to make upgrades, he decided to stop accepting its run-down appearance and put a hammer and some nails to the problem, along with a few coats of fresh paint. Some elbow grease toward its collective repair was part of the plan.

Finishing off the last bit of coffee, Clint put his cup in the sink. It was time to drive into town. He locked the door behind him and made his way to his truck, which felt like an extra appendage.

When the F-100 rumbled to life, he detected a disturbing sound—one that had been present for the past two months but steadily getting worse. She was a fickle machine and deserved better care. Pushing thirty years old, Clint knew the F-100 was well past her prime. If he did not take the truck to the garage soon, the entire engine could be compromised. It always came down to money because mechanics and truck repairs were not cheap.

Since he could not afford to replace his vehicle, Clint would take the truck to Joe's. It was not uncommon for Joe, the owner, to barter repair work in exchange for firewood or garden foods. Clint was hoping that would be the case this time.

The dashboard was patted with tender loving care. "When I'm in town, I'll take you by to see what can be arranged," promised Clint. Together they chugged toward Salzburg. Arriving several minutes later, he pulled into his usual spot behind Josie's Diner.

He removed the newspaper from the newsstand and tucked it under his arm as he always did. He advanced indoors and strolled over to his usual booth. To his surprise, another customer was seated there. Adding insult to injury, no hot coffee awaited anywhere he could see.

Clint sat two booths down, feeling disappointed that Jules had not come to his rescue. Searching behind the counter for her presence, he saw no one in the kitchen. He opened the paper and started to read.

Patrick came to the table with an empty mug and a pot of coffee. "Sorry, bud," he apologized, sitting down opposite Clint. "She's not in today," he volunteered knowing Clint expected his usual table. "She left a voicemail last night saying she needed to return to Beech Grove, her hometown. Said she'd be gone a couple of days." He splayed his hands, "Back on Thursday. That's what she said." Patrick looked worried. "I sure hope so." He grimaced. "Sounded urgent."

"Really?" Clint replied, not happy with what he had heard. "That doesn't sound good. I hope everything is okay. The diner wouldn't be the same without Jules."

"Yeah, tell me about it," agreed Patrick. "That lady is my greatest asset." He grinned anxiously, knowing the statement was undeniably accurate. "She's an easy one to grow accustomed to," he inserted before becoming contemplative. "Did you know some of our patrons actually drive fifty miles every day just to eat here? Jules' infectious personality has a lot to do with that. She's a people person, no mistake about it." He looked at the crowded restaurant behind him, "I'm totally aware our menu is not the only thing that draws customers in."

Patrick's brows lifted, "Everyone has been asking about her this morning." The look on his face revealed his uneasiness over her absence. "I guess she'll fill in the blanks when she gets back. Or when she calls." Holding an angst expression, he scanned the café's high-spirited mood. He had a full diner of happy customers. "To

Chapter 4

tell you the truth, Clint," Patrick's eyes narrowed, "I'm no fool. I'd be in big trouble if Jules wasn't here, especially when you consider how hard it is to find good help these days. Half the time, people don't show up, or worse yet, quit without notice. This place relies on her. *I rely* on her!"

"I have to say," Clint noted, having never heard Patrick talk about Jules with such fervent appreciation. "It does appear business has picked up since she came on board."

"It has," Patrick agreed, extending a huge smile. "Absolutely! I hired Jules because of her bubbly personality. She reminds me of my mother. She, too, had an infectious smile. The diner is named after her. Everyone called my mom Josie, but her real name was Josephine." Clint saw humor behind Patrick's smile. "Jules and Josie's, has a nice ring to it. Don't you think?"

Patrick glanced around. "When I offered Jules three days a week at the start, it was a gamble because the place was barely breaking even. But I decided to take a chance and boy did that turn out to be a smart move."

It dawned on Clint just how little he knew about Patrick, or Jules for that matter. He had taken for granted she had always lived in the general area. He had no idea where Beech Grove was or if it was even in the state of Indiana, but Clint made a mental note to ask Jules the next time he saw her. If there was a next time.

From the booth, Clint called Joe's Garage to make an appointment. When the call ended, he was scheduled to bring the truck in on Thursday for a tune-up. "We'll work out payment arrangements later," Joe suggested amiably. "If it gets too involved, I'll give you a part-time job to work it off," he joked with a deep hardy chuckle.

Outside, under a cloudless, sunny day, Clint followed the sidewalk north until he stopped a few feet from the last storefront on Grandview. A fair distance from Highway 150, at the last intersection before leaving town, a well-worn footpath appeared, running parallel to an open field on the west side of the street.

Had Clint not seen the structure the previous day, he would have thought the path led nowhere. The building was almost characterless in comparison to how it appeared the day before, especially from his current vantage point. More curious than ever, as to why any shopkeeper might set up shop so far from their desired clientele, Clint felt compelled to find out.

Not much foot traffic out this way, he reckoned as he glanced over his shoulder toward town. *How could a store this far away from the main artery stay in business?*

From afar, Clint observed the building's entrance. He waited for fifteen minutes before moving further along the path. Baffled not to have seen a single person go in or come out, he pondered, *I wonder if the store is even open for business?*

Although he had lived in Salzburg since his retirement in 1997, he was curious not to have noticed the storefront before, despite the fact the building was difficult to see from Grandview. He would have thought at some point he would have stumbled upon it, if for no other reason… by happenchance.

"I'm not shocked I didn't see it," he said, straining his neck to satisfy his curiosity. "That place is a far piece out."

Stepping off the curb, the thought crossed Clint's mind, *The scenery around here looks peculiar.*

Bizarrely, he then noticed the distant edifice had become hazier and slightly out of focus. The meadow area, on the other hand, appeared more pronounced than at first glance. More expansive than he believed, Clint viewed the terrain with a discerning eye. A strange feeling washed over him, one that would have been difficult to articulate.

"Everything feels strangely out of kilter," he mumbled under his breath. He took a few more steps closer to his destination but then stopped again. He cast a glance past the storefront and was taken

Chapter 4

aback by the lack of at least one farmhouse. All he could recognize was woodlands and fields. The undeveloped acreage was out of place. To not spot a single cornfield anywhere was remarkable, especially in Indiana.

The stillness of the footpath, and the odd locale of where the structure stood felt both familiar yet unsettling. It was as though Clint's awareness of his surroundings had expanded to an amplified version of awareness.

The scenery and fresh breeze felt exhilarating. Nonetheless, Clint's reverie faded fast because a frigid gust of air assaulted him, whooshing in from the meadow. The temperature took a nosedive, and for a split-second, Clint would have sworn he'd spotted snow in the field, which he instinctively understood had to have been an optical illusion.

Clint buttoned his jacket to his neck and forged forward. As he walked, Elise's wise words of advice came to mind. "Stop and smell the roses every day, my dear. We never know when it could be our last." A lump formed in his throat.

The journey down the path took longer than expected. He'd misjudged the distance, but at last, Clint found himself standing outside the building. A great deal smaller than he'd anticipated, the place reminded Clint of a turn-of-the-century barbershop. A large awning shielded a display window that showcased several random items. None of them appeared to hold much value. The place gave the impression of a thrift store or a next-to-new shop.

A sign swung marginally. Hanging above the entrance, when the wooden plague swayed, it creaked gently in the breeze. Clint was taken by surprise to see a hand-carved plaque, especially since they were so rarely used in modern times. He thought it was a nice touch.

Rod's New and Used Books, it read. *How did I not know this place existed?*

Wondering how long the store had been in operation, Clint admitted, "Nice to see a regular bookseller for a change, something other than a big-box retailer or online seller."

Clint found himself traveling down memory lane, recalling how it felt in his youth to rummage through bookstores. When he lived in the orphanage, the nuns would periodically have the children bused from Vincennes, across the state, as a special treat. Everyone excitedly looked forward to those days, he recalled. For him, being away from the children's home was a stellar event.

Routinely the trips were scheduled on Saturday or Sunday afternoons. They were taken to museums, libraries, and bookstores, which was a particular favorite of his. The excursions steered them through small Indiana towns or nearby cities. And, on occasion, they would visit an ice cream parlor or root beer stand.

Some of Clint's earliest memories entailed flipping through books that had made their way into the orphanage's library after an outing. He dreamt of far-away places, exotic locations and of traveling to foreign shores. Often the pages leaped to life as he read about distant lands never seen.

Always excited to escape the confines of the orphanage, Clint remembered with clarity how he felt back then at the prospect of a road trip. He didn't cherish the bittersweet memories but instead preferably forgot them. Too much pain was associated with his childhood to recall it kindly. The past was not a pleasant place to visit. Clint had worked hard to erase his early recollections of childhood. Anything that happened before Elise had been shelved, like the books he had once read, safely stored out of reach, never to be opened again.

However, his walk from Grandview had inexplicably prompted an avalanche of dark emotions buried deep inside. Surprised to have recalled so many of them at once, he was forced to sit down on the wooden slats in front of the building. He turned to see if anyone had witnessed his bizarre behavior and was convinced no one had.

Chapter 4

A faint, cutting wind brushed past.

One thousand and one, one thousand and two, one thousand and three, he counted.

Still surprised to not have noticed the bookstore before today, Clint fought hard to regain his composure as he stood and peered into the store's remarkably clean display window, where a variety of odds and ends were on exhibit. None held any interest. If for no other reason, other than to satisfy his curiosity, he went inside.

When he entered the establishment, a trace of his reoccurring dream surfaced. Unsure if it was the smell of cigar smoke wrapped in the distinct scent of leather or the interior's layout, something triggered his recent dreams' recall.

The place felt strangely familiar. Especially when the bell jingled above the door as he walked in. He stopped in his tracks. He'd heard the sound before—*in his dreams*. A weird vibe showered over him, cascading from his head down. Penetrating his mindfulness, he knew he had been in this shop before!

Not possible, Clint reminded himself in a flash. He scanned the room. *I couldn't have! I didn't even know this place existed,* his brow creased from confusion, *before yesterday.*

The feeling of déjà vu was strong. Images were taking form in the recesses of his consciousness but were quickly lost. Somewhere in the back of his mind, alarm bells sounded.

The shop resembled a cross between an antique shop and a bookstore with general merchandise mixed in. Clint noticed a diverse combination of this and that sitting here and there. Behind the counter, jars of candy, apothecary items and dark glass containers were neatly lined. A variety of handmade soaps and other items were shelved and displayed on a sidewall.

This was not a typical retail store. Outdated items were stacked against the walls and in the corners. Moving toward the front window display, Clint decided to take a closer look at the Underwood typewriter he had noticed from the other side of the pane. Interested, he wanted to check the price, hoping it was affordable and not antiqued-valued.

As he approached, the display appeared altogether different from the inside. Items were lying around, many not seen from outside. To his dismay, the Underwood was nowhere in sight.

He leaned in, peering across the street. He found the view, to some degree, altered. Distorted slightly, Clint's heart quickened. As his stare deepened beyond the window, out into the field, he became unsettled. He would have sworn he recognized snow on the ground.

"It has to be a trick of light," he murmured, unable to shake the feeling that everything, inside and out, was slightly misaligned.

The window glass must not be of good quality, decided Clint, unsure if there was any significance to the peculiar tint of light streaming through it.

A mirror hung in the center of the display window, fastened to the ceiling. The reflective side was turned inward as opposed to the street direction as Clint would have expected.

Why wouldn't the owner have that thing facing outward so people would know what they are looking at rather than the backside? wondered Clint, feeling baffled at the reasoning behind the decision.

He bent inward to price check the mirror, thinking it extraordinarily beautiful. It was suspended from the ceiling by a puffed 18K gold mariner's chain. Clint assumed the heavy chain was needed to control the mirror's weight distribution yet questioned why such an expensive chain would be required. In his estimation, it felt like overkill. Surely something of less value could have accomplished the task

Clint gingerly pulled the mirror toward him, and when he did, immediately realized the ornate piece had two reflective sides, which explained his confusion. It didn't make a difference which way it hung because they were both the same.

Chapter 4

The mirror appeared ancient yet in very fine condition—almost mint. A tincture of excitement tingled through his body at the thought of owning such a grand piece of history.

Clint could picture it showcased in his foyer. *A real conversation piece,* he fancied with hopes of cutting a deal, maybe do some bartering, a few ricks of stacked firewood in exchange for it.

He visualized the mirror hanging where everyone would see it first thing when they entered the house. It would be his first attempt to upgrade the décor and make the place more presentable, more like Elise would have wanted.

Wonder what she will think when she sees it? he wondered comically, pretending Elise would still be offering her opinion.

He took a step closer.

He felt a strong desire to examine the mirror. The frame was labeled as "Hand Crafted from Variegated Andean Walnut." Clint felt pensive as he pondered the claim. Unfamiliar with that specific species of walnut, he wondered where it was grown.

He twisted the mirror slightly, hoping to find a price. Distraught by the absence of a label or tag, he took it as a bad sign. To ask would be embarrassing, especially if it was beyond his means. Gently Clint released his hold, and it swung back to its original position.

The last thing I want to do is break the dang thing, joked Clint, thinking then he'd be forced to buy it no matter the cost.

When it settled into place, Clint was aghast to see a man in the mirror wearing a straw fedora Stetson hat. His cheeks were sunken and his eyes haunted. Withdrawn and scrawny, the figure stared out, observant and fixed.

Instinctively Clint turned to speak to the gentleman, presuming him to be the owner or store manager. When he pivoted, he apologetically offered, "I guess I should have asked before handling something so rare. I apologize."

Before Clint had finished his remark, his attention was diverted. Positive he had seen a man, Clint's eyes darted in all directions expecting to catch a glimpse of the person he was certain had been behind him.

But no one was there.

Chapter 5
The Antique Room

Clint combed the store thoroughly, checking all the aisles, but his search revealed no trace of the stranger. As Clint moved about, he became distracted by the sheer volume of books lining the shelves. Crammed tightly together, there were hundreds if not thousands of volumes. Organized alphabetically, rather than by author or genre, each hardback was neatly stacked from floor to ceiling.

Clint eyed the works of art—fiction and nonfiction—and became baffled. "There isn't one paperback on these shelves," he said in surprise. "And none have dust jackets!" He rewalked the aisles, searching for either one but was unsuccessful.

Likewise, his search for a clerk to assist him yielded no results. So, Clint decided to go up front and ring the bell. If his memory served him correctly, he had seen a service bell positioned beside the cash register when he entered the store.

Convinced of the man in the mirror's existence, Clint assumed he had gone to do a price-check. Clint's interest in the piece suggested a possible sale, he supposed. And, since the place wasn't exactly crawling with consumers and had an inventory bursting at the seams, Clint figured the sale of the mirror might be vital.

He lightly tapped the bell. When no one responded, he backpedaled to the closest aisle for a second peek at the sheer volumes of books. To his surprise, he noticed an 1851 first edition of *Moby Dick or The Whale*. Inquisitively, he lifted the jewel for a closer inspection. Amazed by its condition—pristine—he thumbed through its pages carefully, appreciating its worth. Shocked at the preservation of the book, he slipped it back into place with extreme reverence.

He removed and examined another book, *Great Expectations* by Charles Dickens, published in 1860. It, too, was a first edition.

The Antique Room

Then another book was taken from the shelf. Likewise, an original: *The Picture of Dorian Gray* by Oscar Wilde, published in 1890. The ages of the hardbacks were perplexing, especially when Clint factored in their condition. Most were astonishingly old but showed no signs of wear.

Before Clint could remove another hardback, he heard a clicking sound echoing off the wood-planked floor somewhere inside the store. With his attention diverted, he slid *The Picture of Dorian Gray* into the proper sleeve where he had removed it and headed to the common area, fully expecting to ask how a small shop in a tiny Indiana town could possess such treasures. When he arrived, however, he could not have been less prepared for what he encountered. Behind a cloth-drawn curtain, a snappy-dressed clerk emerged. The soles of his leather shoes had generated the sharp clacking sound Clint had heard minutes before.

"Morning, sir," the young man said gleefully, pulling the divider up and walking through to the other side.

Challenged not to gawk at the attendant who addressed him, Clint did not want to appear rude but was seriously distracted by the young man's expensive clothing. His Italian deep grey pinstriped, double-breasted silk suit, and burgundy and sapphire-blue floral tie stood out with stylish flamboyance.

His swanky wine calf leather, double monk strap shoes clicked on the floor as he moved about. The clerk's back was turned toward the door, accentuating the sun's rays that glistened on his slicked-back sandy blond hair. His hazel eyes sparkled from the light streaming through the window. Taken by surprise, Clint was not accustomed to seeing the likes of someone dressed so formally, especially in an unrefined town like Salzburg.

A city slicker, laughed Clint inwardly, shocked at what a fellow like this would be doing in a bookstore in his neck of the woods. Not just at this location but anywhere in southern Indiana. The man looked like he had just walked off the cover of *GQ* magazine. A popular British men's magazine since the late 1950s, Clint had

Chapter 5

only seen one copy in an airport but speculated the clerk resembled the type of gentlemen the magazine featured.

"Good morning," Clint responded rapidly, his real sentiments censored because what he really wanted to say was, "*Jolly well done!*" He refrained from expressing his inner dialog in lieu of something more civil.

"How may I assist you, sir?" the man asked, full of charm.

A firm hand was extended, which Clint hesitantly shook. Tongue-tied, he finally responded, "I didn't realize there was a shop this far down on Grandview, certainly not a bookstore." Clint didn't want to sound hypercritical, but against his better judgment, he expressed his opinion. "Set back a ways from any foot traffic. Don't you think?"

Clint tried not to overreact to the clerk's appearance but could not deny his blue-collar upbringing and influence. The man's expensive clothing made Clint feel like a country bumpkin. Embarrassed by his scruffy "good ole boy" work shirt and jeans, he added, "I don't really need anything. I was simply curious."

The young man responded as if he had not been listening. "I'm not surprised you haven't come across our store before," he said with a smile. "We're off the beaten track, but you were bound to find us eventually."

Clint hesitated. *What was that supposed to mean?* For reasons unknown, he felt uncomfortable. A sudden urge to leave to go home and work on his projects surfaced.

"Sorry, sir. I'll let you get back to whatever you were doing," he said, wondering what that might have been. Clint took in his surroundings again and then casually addressed the clerk's comment. "I've been too busy to have noticed this particular side street, but you've got a nice place here. Thought I knew every inch of this town. Guess I was wrong. My age must be catching up with me." Clint grinned awkwardly, not sure how to politely end the conversation. "Once planting season is done, I'll make a point to pay another visit."

"Don't let me run you off." The man's brow furrowed into a frown. "Browse a tad bit more. I guarantee you will find a diverse collection of items sitting about. Please, take your time," the clerk said encouragingly.

"Hey, I saw a man when I was up front," Clint stated offhandedly. He locked eyes with the young man, seeing something in them that was disturbing, but he cast the feeling aside. "He was behind me when I was looking at that mirror in your display case. Thought maybe he was checking on the price. Is he here?"

An odd expression crept onto the clerk's face, and his eyes narrowed to slits. "I'm sorry, sir, but no one other than me works here. If you want, I'd be glad to check on it." His stare seemed vacant and distant when he added, "The price, that is."

Clint knew the man he had seen in the mirror was someone other than the guy he was speaking with. They were not one and the same. In fact, they were total opposites. Had his brain played a trick on him? A distortion in light or a simple mistake? He supposed it was possible. *Maybe it was a reflection captured from somewhere else? A wall hanging, maybe?* Clint contemplated, glancing toward the display window.

Clint was aware the brain attempts to make sense of things, like seeing a face in the clouds. Or a face on Mars, which later had turned out to be nothing more than an ordinary Martian mesa and a natural geological formation. The images captured by NASA's Viking 1 Orbiter spacecraft created a worldwide buzz when they were initially released. Granted, the formation looked uncannily like a human face, and whereas conspiracy theorists would disagree, the face was nothing more than an optical illusion.

"I couldn't help but notice you have a lot of first editions on the shelves," Clint casually commented. "That's extremely rare. From the looks of it, I'm certain your inventory is outside ordinary means. None of the books were price-marked." He chuckled. "That usually signals higher priced items."

Chapter 5

"Oh, you'd be surprised," the young man replied with confidence. "Money isn't a priority around here. The truth is, the owner is very picky about who he sells to. Our books necessitate a good home, as you might imagine. They need the right owner," his eyes widened. "He'd cut you a bargain, without question."

Clint was surprised at the clerk's assertion. "That's a praiseworthy attitude in today's environment. Respecting property, especially antiquities like the items you have sitting in your store, probably isn't as common as it once was."

"Books are crucial to history. They mark the passage of time," the man responded swiftly. "Please, take your time. Enjoy your visit. If you need anything, I'll be in the backroom working on the company ledger. I was making an adjustment when I heard you come in."

Thinking a ledger was a strange thing to be working on, especially in a day when most businesses used QuickBooks, Clint assessed the man to be more than a little peculiar.

"I'm sorry. I didn't catch your name."

"Oh, my apologies. My manners fail me. The name is Rod, and yours?" The answer came with a glint of irony, knowing his name was carved on the custom-designed signage out front.

"Clint… Clint Reeves," Clint replied recalling the overhead sign. "Glad to meet you. So, you own this bookstore. You must be proud."

Not certain how to follow up his remark, he uttered, "I'll check the store out again. You can count on it. This will not be my only visit. Now that I know where you are." Clint smiled and shook Rod's hand again. "I'm surprised I haven't seen you in town before." Again, Clint scrutinized Rod's fancy attire. "A good-looking fellow like you. I'm sure I'd remember."

"Pleasure to meet your acquaintance, but I'm not *that* Rod. I'm his son. Rod, Jr. When my father isn't here, I'm in charge."

"I'm so sorry," Clint replied, slightly embarrassed at his deduction. "I just assumed."

46

"Don't be," Rod said with a tilt of his head. "I keep to myself pretty much. Not surprised our paths haven't crossed until now." Rod pointed to the shelves. "Please, take a gander. I'll go look up the cost of that mirror. Like I said, we have a lot of interesting items sitting on our shelves. This place is meant to attract the curious." Rod's face brightened as he turned to go back the way he had come.

Clint elected to accept Rod's offer, thinking the man eccentric but entertaining. While he waited, he wandered the five aisles of volumes, strolling the double-sided walkways. Glad Rod had gone to check on the price of the mirror. Secretly he had high hopes it was within his comfort zone. Nothing had ever baited him like it had. Rarely did he feel so compelled to purchase an item he didn't need.

In his head, he tried to rearrange his bills to cover its purchase. Scheming, he doubted a deal could be haggled, not like Joe and he always made. There would be no bartering here, especially with an item as unique as the mirror.

In no time, Clint was immersed in the classic titles at his fingertips. With each step, he felt more at ease with the store and its merchandise. More than once, it occurred to him how much at home he felt walking up and down the aisles. It struck Clint that it had been forever since he had this much fun. Getting engrossed in stories was one of his favorite pastimes. He enjoyed nothing more than a well-written tale.

A bookworm from an early age, at day's end, Clint often would sit down with a book and a cup of espresso. Once started, he'd read late into the night. Hours would slip by as he immersed himself into the characters and situations as they unfolded, the stories taking on a life of their own. Uncommon these days, he especially liked the classics, of which this place had no shortage.

Visibly he felt enchanted. He beamed. *I'm a kid in a candy shop.*

As he rounded the corner, it dawned on him what an enjoyable experience his little escape had turned out to be. He hated for it to end but also knew it was time to get home.

Chapter 5

The display window was only a few steps away. His aim was to take another look at the mirror and make certain he was willing to fork over the extra dollars. That was when he noticed a recessed area that led into another space he hadn't noticed before.

Slowly Clint moved toward the room, carrying two books he planned to purchase, *Moby Dick* and *The Call of the Wild*. *Moby Dick* was a short novel, only 104 pages. The thought was it was perhaps less expensive than lengthier novels like *Gone with the Wind* with its thousand-plus pages. The other book he had slipped from the shelf, *The Call of the Wild*, was a mere 232 pages. Both, he assumed, were reasonably priced.

When he moved past the entry to the additional space, he had to carefully negotiate the tight passageway that led into the semi-darkened room. Dimly lit, the tiny space was softly illuminated. In the corner of the room, he saw a cabinet shoved up against the outer wall. A small round table and Tiffany lamp were also seen, lit by a forty-watt bulb. The room was slight but cozy. The room reminded him of a person's living quarters.

When a youngster, Clint had been taken to a house with a room such as this, albeit not nearly as warm and inviting. He remembered it well. Off the kitchen, at the back of the house, the cramped room was grim, at best.

On the ceiling had been a stain in the shape of a human body. Though he could not recall the exact details, his impression was that a woman had fallen through the attic slats, thus creating the outline. At least that was what he thought he had been told.

Clint grinned. *That sounds ridiculous. Something only a kid would come up with.*

He recalled that in an armless rocker, he had been instructed to wait while the adults conversed. *The entire house seemed cold and frightening*, he remembered. He closed his eyes. *It was a scary place.*

In the dining room, in the middle of the house, the grown-ups had gathered. He could still see them at the table talking in low voices so they would not be overheard. And even though Clint wasn't told that the meeting was about him, he instinctively knew it was.

I was a little guy. Clint grimaced. In his mind, he could see the tops of his muddy black shoes and scruffy pants as he rocked vigorously in the room where he had been quarantined.

Why was I there? He deliberated. It was a memory he had all but forgotten until this very moment. Something about the bookstore had prompted those dark emotions to resurface. The dismal circumstance Clint had braved was underpinned by memory.

"A terrifying house," he whispered under his breath. A sudden urge to escape, to get as far away from this room where he had wandered, entered his mind. Too many uncomfortable memories had resurfaced for no good reason since entering.

Clint was fully aware he should not have ventured somewhere that was not part of the main area. He started to leave but stopped when he saw the cabinet on the far wall. It was a piece of furniture he had seen before. Sitting in the corner, Clint was stunned at what he was looking at. The exact curio cabinet he had seen in his dreams was five feet away.

His pulse quickened. For reasons that made no sense, Clint wondered if he was in a waking dream, and none of this was real. He inched closer to the glass case. In the distance he identified the deep tones of a windchime. Clint became certain he had wandered into a private section of the store.

The cabinet was every bit as beautiful as it had been in his dream. The shelves full of knickknacks were uniquely displayed. Though he was drawn toward it, a foreboding feeling washed over him. There inside the case were multiple items he recognized. Ones he had already purchased… in his dream.

"That's a one of a kind," said a voice behind Clint. The shopkeeper put a hand on Clint's shoulder.

Clint flinched. "I'm terribly sorry," he said apologetically. "I had no business coming in here. I thought it was connected to the store."

Chapter 5

"Don't worry. This room is part of the store," the clerk assured him. "Everything in here is for sale. I call this the Antique Room. Most items are circa mid-eighteen hundreds. Are you in the market for an antique curio cabinet? If you are, I can shoot you an exceptional price."

"No, no," Clint avowed. "I was simply admiring the craftsmanship. I have never seen anything so intricate. It's impressive." He regarded the items on the shelves. They were remarkably familiar. "A lot of uncommon trinkets in there."

Clint tried to reconcile what he was experiencing. He did his best not to overreact, but he found it next to impossible to curtail his emotions. No way was he going to tell this guy he'd seen the cabinet and the items inside in his dream, not once, but numerous times.

"Like I said, matchless collectibles. They all have an amazing story. Help yourself," he said. "Inspect them closer. You never know. There could be something in there you can't live without." A flicker shown in Rod's eyes as he spoke. "You know where to find me. Oh, and I have a price on that mirror. Dad says you can have it for $25.50. Wants it to go to a good home!"

Clint turned in shock. "What? It's worth ten times that!"

"Well, it's like I said, we aren't about the money. Who we're dealing with and who needs our wares is the important thing to us."

What a strange way to talk about sales, Clint thought, feeling a little stumped.

"But your father doesn't know me. We haven't met." Clint stared suspiciously. "Besides, I thought you said he wasn't here." Feeling confused by the conversation, Clint knew the mirror was worth much more than the price he had been quoted.

"He's not—now. Only comes in now and then. I suppose you looked like a nice enough guy to cut a deal to." Rod shrugged, like what other explanation could there be?

The man in the mirror! The one in the straw hat? thought Clint. *That is who I saw, the older man who disappeared in a poof.*

The Antique Room

"I can't believe that price. It is very charitable of him," responded Clint, grateful the mirror was in his budget. "I have the perfect spot for it—a place where everyone will admire it. I'll take good care of it. I promise."

Rod turned toward the case. "I believe you might find an item or two inside there that may well appeal to your adventurous side." His hand waved toward the cabinet of curiosity for Clint. When he opened the door, he said, "Please, help yourself."

Behind the glass, a collection of unusual items was layered over four crystal engraved shelves. Clint found it difficult to draw his eyes away from the objects. "Thank you," he said, turning to face Rod. To his disbelief, Rod was gone.

How did he get out of this room without me noticing? questioned Clint, examining the exit. Rod and his dad seemed to move about inexplicably. *Rod, Sr. was remarkably light on his feet,* thought Clint sarcastically, *and now Rod, Jr. abruptly departs without a sound.*

Clint sloughed off his unease. Turning around, he opened the glass door a smidgeon wider. The last thing he wanted to do was break anything. He took extra precautions when touching each item. The sheer uniqueness of them was mind-boggling. Then he saw one piece that stood out from the rest—a sheath and a knife.

In his recurring dream, he had seen an inscribed handle of a Bowie knife. Out of wonder, Clint lifted the sheath from the shelf and pulled the knife from its case. There, just as in the dream, the initials F.R. were engraved. Trembling, he lowered the knife and sheath back onto the shelf. Finding a knife with those exact initials was literally an impossibility.

As he sought to put pieces together that didn't fit, without warning, Clint's ears started to ring, and he became light-headed. Sitting on the stool behind him, which he had not noticed when he walked in, he waited. Many minutes passed before he was able to regain his composure.

Visibly shaken, Clint wondered why Rod had not come back to check on him. After much consideration, the catalyst, he construed,

Chapter 5

that connected this whole affair was the treasure hunt. There was no other explanation for it. The only link between his reaction, he reasoned, was his preoccupation with the hunt. Somehow, he had glimpsed into the future. As unlikely as that sounded, it was all he had to fall back on.

As he attempted to reconcile what was happening, his eyes zeroed in on a pile of paper bags stacked next to the exit. He walked over and removed one from the top. Rod's New and Used Books was boldly inscribed an inch from the bottom.

Weak-kneed, and still a little unsteady, he recalled from his dreams each time he had placed items into a bag with an unusual logo printed at the bottom. A portion of that logo he was able to recreate in his mind's eye. The lettering on the bag he was holding resembled what his memory evoked. Shakily, Clint walked over to the stool and sat down for a second time. Breathing deeply, he felt desperate to pin down an explanation for what was otherwise an improbable situation.

What other surprises lie beneath that vast assortment of strange objects? Clint wondered, speculating on the cabinet's contents. Feeling calmer, he got up and moved toward it.

Moving things about on the shelves, he found what he believed were several perfect pieces for his fall party. Processing his quandary, Clint deduced that what had transpired was nothing more than a curious coincidence on an eerily remarkable scale.

Plain and simple, a premonition had occurred. Nothing like this had ever happened to Clint, but he was aware of such things. Having encountered it firsthand, he could now relate to past discussions with Elise about her strong feelings of portent and foresight.

Thinking it astonishing, especially since he always marginalized things of that nature, Clint found humor in the irony and wished Elise could have been here to witness it. She would have been delighted, having had more than her fair share of the unexplained.

He discovered a small trunk-like box bearing a resemblance to a pirate's chest on the second shelf among other childlike relics. Perfect for his treasure hunt, it went straight into the bag. He lowered a small locomotive and snow globe he thought his granddaughter, Lily, would love inside as well. Next, he examined a toy replica whip that seemed to speak to him, along with several masked figurines, a conductor to go along with the locomotive, and a toy pistol. Then a miniature signed document, made of parchment, drew his interest. Keeping with the theme, he dropped it into the bag.

Clint accumulated many prizeworthy gifts and headed to the register. The bookstore showed no sign of the clerk he had been working with. He dinged the bell. Drumming his fingers as time ticked by. He soon became irritated. When it was apparent no one was coming to assist him, he hit the bell harder.

"Anyone here?" called Clint in a raised voice, feeling exasperated at the lack of service.

A few more minutes passed without any sign of the clerk. *Putting all this stuff back will annoy me to no end,* thought Clint. *Not to buy them after spending all that time will make this my first and last visit here. That would be wasted time I don't have.*

Apprehensive of the individual cost of the items, Clint decided maybe it was best to put them back. He had probably overspent anyway. Then, just as he was ready to give up, he noticed a folded note tucked under the register. Out of curiosity, he pulled it out from beneath. To his shock, he saw his name written on the top.

The note read: Had to step out. We can settle up later. Don't worry about the cost. Our prices are extremely reasonable, as I said, a good home…you know, so don't fret. The mirror is wrapped and ready. Help yourself. I placed it behind the counter.

Clint was dumbstruck. It was like the man had read his mind, and the note appeared. Not only had Clint not heard the bell sound above the door when Rod departed, which meant he exited by way of a rear door, but he also left the shop unattended. Clint could

Chapter 5

not imagine such irresponsible behavior or, even weirder, telling a customer to help themselves to the store's merchandise without paying for it. Nobody did things like that in 2003.

What kind of a nutcase am I dealing with here? scoffed Clint, shocked at the behavior he had been participating in.

He concluded his detour that morning was beyond bizarre. Having never done anything like it prior to this occasion, Clint wrote a response on the bottom of the note and placed it under the bell before pushing it to the side of the register.

"Thank you for your kind offer," it read. "I did find many fine pieces for an upcoming treasure hunt I'm hosting for my family in the fall. Tomorrow morning, around 9 a.m., I will stop in to pay my bill. I have listed each piece taken. In case they are outside my comfort zone, I'll bring them with me when I return. Thanks for wrapping the mirror. Tell Rod, Sr. I appreciate his kind generosity."

Outside in the fresh air, with the mirror clutched tightly in his hands, Clint stood at the storefront observing the fields across the street. They appeared unnaturally tall. The view bothered him, but he couldn't say why exactly.

Slowly he walked the dirt path back to the sidewalk, turning around twice to look at the street from where he had come. He walked over to his truck that was parked on Grandview. When he got there, he unlocked the door and slid inside. His head was in a tizzy at the wacky morning. Significant time had lapsed—more than he had anticipated. He swiveled in the seat to place the mirror securely on the bench beside him.

I lucked out on that one, he chuckled.

The time was 3:12 p.m. when he pulled into his drive. He placed the mirror, wrapped in brown paper, inside the mudroom until later when he could hang it in the foyer. He kept the other articles locked inside the cab of his truck behind the seat. They would stay there until he could settle his debt. A tinge of excitement stirred at the prospect of including them in his collection inside the gray cabinet in the pole barn.

The Antique Room

Clint could not get the young man from the bookstore out of his mind while working in the yard. Drifting in and out of his thoughts, never had Clint met anyone with such a professional appearance who behaved so incompetently, certainly not in Salzburg. Such a man would certainly stand out in rural America.

An upper northeast or possibly European influence I heard in his voice? Wearing fancy leather shoes and a silk suit, no way was that guy from southern Indiana. On the other hand, the man in the mirror… that guy fit right in, with his straw hat. Clint chuckled. *Not Rod, Jr., though. It's hard to believe the two men are even related.* Clint felt perplexed by the difference he witnessed.

Once dusk waned into the night, Clint decided he would go inside to read. Rarely did he watch TV. In his opinion, with so many channels there should be more to watch, but he had found the opposite to be true. He was of the mindset that watching television was a huge waste of time, especially when he had bookshelves stuffed with literature not yet read.

The bookstore inventory had put Clint in the mood for a classic. And, luckily, he had the perfect one. Maybe not a classic, but close enough. One that spoke to him. He went to the bookshelf and removed *Bid Time Return*, Elise's favorite.

From what he could recollect, the story was based on true events. One night, only two days following the move into their new place, Elise and he were sitting by the fireplace drinking coffee and making plans. She described the book and summarized its storyline.

And while Clint found what she had to say intriguing, the book sounded a bit too fanciful for his taste. The tale, as she conveyed it, had a paranormal premise where his preference typically fell toward biographies, nonfiction, and historical genres. Then again, after what he had recently encountered, nothing anymore was outside the realm of believability.

Clint laid the book on the end table, not quite ready to begin reading. Instead, he glanced at the ceiling, going through the

Chapter 5

events of earlier and the strange goings-on at the bookstore. He was having a hard time shaking the episode from his thoughts. The items he had taken without payment crossed his mind, and a pang of guilt made itself known. Never had he done anything like that before, and it wasn't setting well.

Lying comfortably in the chair, his eyelids grew heavy, and his head bobbed. From out of the blue, his eyes sprang open. Something or someone was in the room.

Chapter 6
A Walk in the Woods

The haggard man Clint had seen in the mirror at the bookstore the prior day had repeatedly crossed his mind, which he assumed was the explanation for why he had awakened with a start the evening before. He'd felt a presence in the living room after dozing off by the fireplace. The incident prompted him to retire for the night, and ultimately, he chose to ignore the whole affair. However, his questions continued to mount. Many, in fact.

Surprised he had not noticed the storefront before yesterday, or at least heard scuttlebutt about it in town, especially since Rod claimed to have set up shop years ago, Clint contemplated what he had been told. Perplexed at the claim, he considered, *How could that be?*

He pictured the salesclerk and his outlandish attire. In a small rural town like Salzburg, Rod was an oddball. *What kind of a person leaves their shop unattended with a customer still shopping?* Clint shook his head incredulously. *People could walk right in and steal things! But, on the other hand, he told me to help myself!* He snickered. *Shopkeepers just don't do things like that! Trying to look like a city slicker. Someone raised in these parts wouldn't dress that formally either.*

Clint crawled out of bed. In the kitchen he poured himself a cup of fresh brew, hoping it would clear the cobwebs from his mind. He set the cup on the cabinet to cool. He filled the sink with hot sudsy water where last night's dishes remained unwashed, which for him was a rarity. He spread a towel on the countertop where he could stack the rinsed items to air dry.

He walked outdoors and lit a cigarette. The rule was never to smoke inside. Weary-eyed, Clint stared into the field across the road. He had slept like a log after stumbling off to bed. No disturbing dreams were recalled… thank goodness.

Chapter 6

Later he would drive into town to grab some grub. The priority before Josie's, however, had to be to settle his debt. Nothing about walking out with unpaid purchases felt right. Contrary to his principles, his moral compass was spinning in the wrong direction.

His mind churned, questioning the rationale behind his actions. *To take the risk of someone else coming along and snatching those things up would have been stupid,* Clint argued inwardly. *They fit perfectly with my pirate theme! Can't let them slip through my fingers, now can I? One of a kind pieces, like those? No way!*

Passing through the foyer on his way to the kitchen, Clint glanced at the wall he intended to hang the mirror. *Why would anyone construct a mirror with two reflective sides?* he mused. *Seems rather senseless.*

Clint grinned. *Maybe Jules would enjoy hearing about the bargains I found.* Then a thought crossed his mind. *Someday, if I can garner enough nerve, I could invite her over to see the mirror and the items I'm buying for the treasure hunt.*

According to Patrick, Jules would not be at work for the next couple of days. Clint was concerned she might not return at all. "Beech Grove," Patrick had stated, "is a suburb of Indianapolis." He remembered something in Patrick's tone felt worrisome like he was leaving something out.

Jules' first visit would hinge on projects being completed. Just the idea of asking her over made him nervous. Uncertain if he could follow through, Clint had always been shy when it came to girls. *What if she says no or puts me off?* his negative side argued. Those thoughts were kept at bay while he worked on building his courage.

He lugged a shovel and pick from the shed along with other miscellaneous garden supplies and tools he would need later. The seedlings he had started indoors during the months of February and March were ready to be put into the ground.

The stage was set for the planting season, a time of year Clint enjoyed tremendously. Sprouted kale, beets, broccoli, carrots, lettuce, and spinach plants were the first to go in. After that…

seed-potatoes, onions, and yellow squash. By late May, some of the fruits of his labor would be ready to harvest. Asparagus, first to pop through the soil in spring, was picked from early March through mid-May.

Clint drove his tractor from the pole barn and left it idling in the driveway while he hooked the cart to the back. Several bare spots in the yard, front and back, required seeding before making his way to town. He was glad spring rains had been steady because now the moist soil was ideal for seeding. He climbed onto the seat and braced himself for a bumpy ride. Steering the tractor around the yard, he filled in the areas that required the most attention. After that, Clint parked the tractor next to the barn, killed the engine, and jumped down.

He proudly walked the property, admiring the fullness of the land. A red bud tree, planted immediately following possession of the house, had grown significantly. Lush, purplish blossoms contrasted with the green of spring and added delicate color to the lawn.

The dogwoods had matured into beautiful trees, and the open-faced orange and yellow lilies that lined his property brought spring to life with their light fragrance. He considered the many projects he hoped to accomplish. Since he had topped off his chicken feed, all that was left on his list was to purchase this year's peeps. Most of his projects, however, had been on the drawing board since day one.

It was painful to remember the days following Elise's aneurism. His inability to find pleasure in the smallest of activities had put everything on hold. His life had come to an abrupt halt, along with his desire to care about the simplest of things. Now six years later, with a renewed passion for his garden, Clint was ready to rejoin the living.

Whereas the house and property were far from presentable, they had started to take shape. The fact the land butted up to a state forest had been a huge selling point when he and Elise were out house hunting. Now, with trees in bud, following a long, harsh

Chapter 6

winter, he felt grateful to have come across such a fortuitous piece of land.

Since moving in, Clint had never wandered into the national forest that bordered his property. He often looked at the woods with curiosity but always set them aside for a later date when he had time to explore. Until just recently, he had been content to just work in his yard, sit indoors, or listen to nature. In 1997 his spirit of adventure had been broken. At some point, although Clint couldn't say when, things had begun to change.

Lately, Clint felt beckoned to the land behind his property, possibly because his heart felt lighter and less burdened than in years past. He didn't have a great deal of time to hang around the house because of his long chore list, but Clint figured another fifteen minutes wouldn't hurt. Until this morning, he simply had no interest. A renewed sense of fascination filled his spirit as he moved past the opening into the forest.

The first thing Clint noticed was May flowers poking up from the forest floor. Buttercups and bluebells speckled the terrain. Light rays streamed through the canopy overhead, down onto the decomposing leaves and debris left behind from winter. The air, saturated with the pungent smell of rotting undergrowth, produced memories of yesteryear.

He reminisced back to a time when the orphanage, where he lived as a child, would organize daytrips to Nashville, Indiana, or excursions to places such as Spring Mill State Park, Mammoth Caves, the Indiana Dunes, and other touristy locations. He recalled how the picnic tables the nuns would set for them would offer tantalizing foods never seen at the dinner table at the children's home.

He held bittersweet memories of scampering through the woods and up and down hills tightly to the vest. Rolling from the top of the hill down to the bottom in Brown County, cascading through layers of autumn leaves… these images had taken residence in the recesses of a discarded past. Filed far from recall, Clint remembered lunches served with Kool-Aid, potato chips, pickles wrapped in foil, and tuna fish sandwiches. These were some of the better memories of a childhood Clint chose to forget.

Several feet in from the shared boundary line, between his property and the state forest, Clint noticed a trail. Intrigued where it would lead, he advanced deeper into the thickness of changing colors and fragrances. Spongy emerald green moss squished beneath his feet as he wandered deeper into the woods. The smell of honeysuckle and wild ginger hung in the air. More diverse and expansive than Clint could have ever imagined, the forest had an enchanting atmosphere.

Clint decided he would transplant a half-dozen saplings to his yard. The same applied to some of the wildflowers. The thought occurred to him, as he walked the forest floor, that he might relocate everything to the side of the house where he needed a fresh look. Inspiration at the prospect made him smile.

The landscape continued to transform itself as he moved along the path, having no idea the direction it had taken. Wild morel mushrooms poked from beneath exposed earth, causing Clint to hesitate. Growing beside a dead tree, a patch of mushrooms was illuminated by the sun's rays escaping through the gaps in the forest canopy.

Delighted with his discovery, Clint squirreled as many mushrooms as he could muster into his ball cap. Later he would return with a larger vessel to house his pickings. This current sampling would be fried up and eaten for an evening meal.

Layers of pine needles showcased tiny violet blooms of trout lilies and wild geraniums as he journeyed deeper into uncharted territory. He marked trees to assist him in recapturing this pristine spot for a return visit. Although bragging rights were in order, no way would he divulge his secret spot where prize mushrooms abounded.

Chapter 6

Clint heard a gurgling somewhere off in the distance, lifting him from his reverie. *A pleasant prospect*, he thought. *A great place to have a picnic, maybe. I could bring Jules back here.*

He'd identified the perfect spot for solitude. As he sat in stillness, his back propped against a Sycamore tree, his body began to relax. To the music of nature, he drifted. Breathing in the fresh clean air, Clint sank into a deep slumber.

When he awoke, he was startled by the dimness of light. Aware that he had lost track of time, he jumped to his feet. Since he didn't wear a watch, Clint had no idea the time of day, but he could tell more minutes had lapsed than he'd wanted.

Clint aimed his attention toward the trail. Something didn't feel right. At that moment, a faint sound rustled through the branches above him. A distinctive sound carried through the budding leaves of the forest where he detected a soft, methodical, and nearly inaudible pitch.

Clint frantically searched the grounds, feeling he wasn't alone. When he saw no one, he scolded himself. Not liking the alternative, he chided verbally, "That's nonsense! Get a grip, Clint."

But Clint was not mistaken. It was not a figment of his imagination. The proof came when a hushed voice breathed: "He's here."

Beads of sweat formed on Clint's brow, and his hands trembled. The voice was familiar, he thought, as a feeling of terror coursed through his veins. He felt a fight-or-flight reaction as he zigzagged through the trees, trying to find the path he had taken to get there. He sprinted as fast as he could to safety—far away as possible from the clearing.

From the safety of his yard, Clint stared into the dark forest, disbelieving what he had experienced. He desperately wanted to ignore the reality of what he had heard.

No way was that real. He chastised himself for behaving childishly. *Two back-to-back strange occurrences in two days? That's silly!*

Clint sat on the grass, trying to compose himself. He pulled his legs to his chest and buried his head between them. As he took deep breaths, his heart hammered. Fear, the antidote for annihilation, surged through his muscles and brain as he scrambled for explanations of what had just occurred.

This was not the first time since moving into the house Clint had undergone the inexplicable. But never had he been confronted with something as tangible as what had transpired in the forest. On occasion, at the fringe of his peripheral vision, he believed a presence trailed him but never had he heard an actual voice.

"All people think things like that from time to time," mumbled Clint in explanation.

A strong memory from childhood, scary moments of climbing the staircase in the orphanage up to his sleeping quarters, came to mind. The same sort of creative thought process that had caused him as a child to fly up the stairs to the safety of where the other boys slept. His overactive imagination had been fertile back then and, from the looks of things, hadn't buried itself too far from reach.

Considerable time had passed before Clint could regain a proper perspective on the matter. He stood to his feet and hastened his step back to the house. Feeling ridiculous, he thought about the weird happenings at the bookstore.

"I imagined the voice," he stated, trying to soothe his frayed nerves.

Clint admitted that several unusual abnormalities had occurred of late, which might have added to the situation. *First the dreams, then the man in the mirror and the vanishing store clerk, leading up to an imagined voice in the forest.*

His thoughts traveled to Jules. *Bringing her to the house would be a mistake. Jules would infringe on Elise's space if I did. It wouldn't be right.* Clint felt terrible when he thought through his lapse in judgment. A touch of remorse had affected his mindset. That was his best guess for imagining a voice.

Chapter 6

Nightly he yearned for his wife to connect with him. Since her passing, Clint had been petitioning Elise to appear in his dreams. He beseeched her forgiveness on what he perceived were his shortcomings, regretting not to have been a better husband.

Guilt? Yes, he felt guilt and remorse he hadn't been there in her final hours. He had been carrying it like a manitou over his shoulder since April 20, 1997. He was also guilty of praying to her instead of God, asking her to watch over him. Not God. She would not approve of how far he had fallen since that dreadful day.

But he did believe that through a doorway in time, Elise was able to travel transient roads to reach him if he prayed hard enough. Clint had once read a quote by Nikola Tesla that predicted, "The day science begins to study non-physical phenomena, it will make more progress in one decade than in all the previous centuries of its existence." Believing this to be true, Clint became convinced at twilight from another dimension, Elise visited.

The night she died Elise was there when Clint confessed to a broken heart. In a space between consciousness and dreams, unbarred barricades dissolved. She lay beside him, wrapping him in her embrace. Her soul returned through the astral plane, crossing the threshold into his deepest dreams where suspended time existed. Across a thin veil, she slipped, moving through echoed sounds of distant places. At dawn, when the silvery light of day broke the horizon, whispers of promise were spoken as she departed back into her ethereal realm.

Clint had to confess, to imagine that Elise had been watching over him was one thing, but to hear her voice during daylight hours, well...that was an altogether different matter. *That bordered madness.* It was possible guilt had breached his awareness and fostered the scene. In recent days he'd offered up fewer prayers because his mind had been wandering in different directions, and he'd decided to let it go.

For the rest of the morning, Clint piddled in the garden. Too restless to stay engaged, he went to the barn to organize his tools for the second time that week. After fighting his lack of interest, he settled on remaining idle. Lost in thought and drained of energy, he grew weary. Uninspired to drive into town to pay his bill or stop by Josie's for an early dinner, he bagged both in lieu of taking a long walk.

"Crud, why can't I just move forward instead of always living in the past?" Clint mumbled in disgust at his unwillingness to let go. *One step forward and two steps back*, he chided, feeling flustered at his lack of contentment in the simplest of things.

Be patient. Tomorrow will be a better day. He grinned when a saying he once read on a t-shirt at a festival came to mind. "*Yesterday is history. Tomorrow is a mystery. Today is a gift. That's why they call it the present.*"

After returning from his walk, he leaned back in a lawn chair, watching the day unfold and making a mental note of plants he wanted to purchase for the yard. *Viburnums could be nice*, he speculated, *maybe three of them to the left of the door and one on the right. A magnolia pink tulip for the back would give it the color* he visualized.

When he entered the house, it felt painfully still, so he turned on the stereo to play instrumental music to help negate the loneliness that had come to call. Feeling melancholy, Clint switched gears to the voice of John Denver and Country Roads while washing and stacking dishes before his shower.

But now, the time had come to call it a night. He opted to retire early with a book he had received for Christmas—choosing not to start Elise's suggested hardback. He wasn't in the mood. He switched on the lamp beside. The cozy atmosphere it radiated felt comforting. He laid the book on the bed and went to the kitchen for a cup of hot chamomile, sitting at the kitchen table while his tea steeped.

Walking back to the bedroom, he thought of a rule Elise and he had endorsed. *Everything outside is your doings… Everything inside is mine,* he heard her say. Consequently, in the six years since

Chapter 6

her passing, inside nothing had been disturbed. The ambition to change décor or move one thing had never entered his mind.

Clint sank below the down comforter that covered his queen-sized bed. Before crawling in, he opened the window a smidgeon to let in a hint of fresh air. He'd changed the sheets the night before, making everything feel inviting. Because Clint enjoyed reading in bed, he changed his sheets frequently, just as Elise had done.

He welcomed the peacefulness that accompanied reading and the relaxation it inspired. He'd stashed snacks—usually licorice sticks, M&Ms, and potato chips—in the nightstand beside the bed. He lifted a bag of M&Ms from the drawer and placed them beside him. Elise hated it when Clint ate in bed, especially popcorn or chips. Now he did as he pleased.

Propping pillows behind his neck and shoulders, he decided it was time to return to the world of John Grisham and his Christmas book *The Broker*. The book had sat untouched, gathering dust, since December. Only into the second chapter, he found the story enthralling.

Clint read well into the night, drawn into the cast of characters and plot twists until, at last, his eyes grew too heavy to keep open. He briefly awoke when the book hit the floor at 2 a.m. He leaned over and turned off the light.

Chapter 7
The Accident, 1998

At 2:16 in the morning, the bedroom was silent until the telephone's shrill ring pierced the night. Waking her from a sound sleep, Julie Jenkins sat straight up in bed. One side lay empty. She looked at the clock and understood something was dreadfully wrong.

Lifting the receiver, she answered in a quiet voice, "Hello."

The inflection of the person on the other end of the line sounded apologetic when he spoke. "May I speak to Julie Jenkins."

"This is she," Julie responded as a knot formed in her stomach.

"Ma'am my name is Sargent Daniel McConnell from the Indianapolis Police Department. I am sorry to disturb you at this hour," he said.

"What's wrong?" she asked, wondering why an Indianapolis police officer was calling rather than someone from the local police department in Beech Grove.

"I am afraid I have some bad news. I need you to come downtown. Do you have anyone there with you?" he regretfully questioned.

"No," she answered with a quivering chin. She put her hand on his side of the bed, looking out the black window that faced the east and fearing why her husband had not come home. A couple of hours earlier, before drifting off, James had phoned. Everything was fine then. Nothing was out of the ordinary for a delivery truck driver to come home later than expected. It often happened that way following the final drop of the day.

"Okay, I'll send someone to pick you up," the officer gently informed her, perceiving her shaky voice on the other end of the line. "There's been an accident, and unfortunately, your husband was involved."

Julie stared at the wall, understanding what his words implied. "Oh no," she cried. "Please tell me he's uninjured."

Chapter 7

"Ma'am, Officer Lewis has been dispatched. He's on his way. He should be there in ten minutes or less. He'll escort you to the hospital."

Julie was paralyzed with fear. Her mind raced, trying to make sense of the conversation. Her heart quickened, pounding so hard it felt like it could explode in her chest. When she stood, the phone dropped to the floor, and she did not bother to hang it up.

She withdrew undergarments from the dresser drawer and slipped an oversized sweatshirt belonging to James that hung on the bedpost over her head before going downstairs to wait for the imminent knock.

In the half-bath, she ran warm water over her face and a brush through her tangled auburn hair but did not take the time to apply makeup. She removed a pair of sweatpants from the laundry room. Nowadays, because of her expanded waistline, they were the only pair that fit. Tears streamed from her chin to the floor below. She glanced at the woman in the mirror, not recognizing the terrified eyes that stared back.

When she heard the thump at the door, Julie could barely move. She slowly opened it and was greeted by a gentle, solemn face. "Mrs. Jenkins?" Officer Lewis inquired. When she nodded, he offered, "I'm here to accompany you to the hospital."

"I'll lock up," Julie said with her head low, weeping. Shutting the door behind her, she followed the policeman to his car. He opened the door and helped her in, noticing her unsteadiness.

The police described how the roads had turned icy. An oil tanker had spun out of control, triggering a five-car pileup on I-465. James' truck hit an embankment causing it to flip over on its side. Although multiple people had been seriously injured, including the tanker driver, James was the sole fatality.

Later that evening, because of the extreme strain Julie had undergone, the child she was carrying aborted. Sadly, not only did James lose his life that night, but his unborn daughter did as well.

The Accident

2003, Nearly Five Years Later

When Jules departed Boyner and Ellington law offices, she traveled down memory lane to the night her husband died. She recalled the wee hours of the morning that cold, snowy November day. As it turned out, bad weather and icy roads indeed contributed to the accident, as initially alleged, but were not the reason behind the tragic event. In fact, James' faulty brakes had failed and were responsible, which surfaced after an extensive investigation exposed the truth.

The report read that James' delivery truck had been following a tanker that had triggered the initial collision. The driver had fallen asleep at the wheel, according to witnesses, and was swerving on the roadway. James apparently hit his brakes before spinning into three other vehicles, causing them to careen into each other. The scene unfolded like bumper cars at an amusement park.

James was forced to the side of the highway where his truck smashed into an embankment, generating a ricochet effect. The tanker that was at fault, transporting six thousand gallons of fuel, had snaked across the highway into the guardrail and down into the ravine below. Onlookers reported to local TV stations how they watched the man sprint from the cab, just in the nick of time, seconds before the tanker exploded. Only one fatality was reported, but multiple injuries. It made sensational television.

Channel 6, late-night news, had covered the crash in detail. Julie witnessed the recap on the television as she walked the halls of the hospital on her way to the morgue. At Wishard Memorial Hospital in downtown Indianapolis, Julie Jenkins was taken to identify her husband's body. Although James Gerald Jenkins had been immediately life-lined to the hospital, he did not survive. He was pronounced dead on arrival.

Chapter 7

The traumatizing sight of identifying James had caused Julie to miscarry. She was six months pregnant at the time, carrying their first child. Having not informed the police or hospital personnel of her pregnancy, the damage was irreversible by the time she realized her err in judgment.

Before departing her father's home on 12th Street in Beech Grove, Julie visited Washington Park Cemetery on the east side of town. Hours slipped by as she lingered at the gravesite. Late that afternoon, sitting on a blanket, she updated James about her new life. She told him how her family had stepped in to take care of her following the accident. Her dad, brother, and sisters had all helped her move to Greenville, where her brother, Randy, and sister-in-law, Anna, lived.

She confessed to James that living in Beech Grove had turned out to be too difficult to remain in the apartment. The constant reminder of the memories was too painful. She voiced how proud she believed he would be of her for securing respectable employment. She was waitressing at a place called Josie's Diner and loved the fifties-themed uniform she was required to wear. Though James had been a good provider, she was delighted to report she was managing as well as could be expected on her own.

At six that evening, instead of waiting until daybreak, she hugged her father, Walter, goodbye. She gathered her bags and hit the road, headed to Greenville, where a modest nine-hundred-square-foot existence awaited—much smaller than the dwelling where she had lived in her previous life.

On her way home, she stopped at Sellersburg for a bite to eat. Since James' passing, Jules always carried a book in the car, taking her latest paperback into restaurants when she dined. At her therapist's recommendation, the practice had been a huge help in adjusting to her new status as a widow. Eating alone never felt good, but with a book at her fingertips, it felt less awkward.

The settlement she had received provided the necessary funds Randy and his construction company needed to begin Jules' new house three miles west of his residence on US 150. If all went well, the crew would break ground midsummer.

A bittersweet reality, created by her new reserves, caused Jules to weep at how the funds had come into her possession. She played songs that reminded her of James and their life together in his memory. Music she cherished more than ever touched the core of her being. No longer would she let the heartache of James' untimely death and the loss of her baby impede her happiness. She would celebrate what had been and move onward with anticipation of a brighter day.

When she arrived in Salzburg, shortly after 8 p.m., she called Patrick. On the third ring, he answered. "Hello, Jules!" he cheerfully chirped.

"Yes," she laughed. "I take it you have Caller ID!"

"I do," he confessed with a chuckle. "Give me some good news, girl!"

Jules' jubilant voice replied, "You mean like when I can come back to work? I could be there first thing in the morning. Normal time if you like."

"Man, is that music to my ears," he responded, not missing a beat. "We have really missed you. The place is falling apart. It's missing your bright smile. Customers have been asking about you all week. I hope everything turned out okay in Beech Grove. Whatever took you home on short notice, I assume things worked out okay. Nothing serious. Right?"

"No, just something that required my presence. Tying up loose ends, that sort of thing. It was a pleasant visit with my family. My dad and I had a nice lunch at Beech Grove Park yesterday. Just like when I was a kid. Dad and I sometimes would eat our sandwiches on a picnic table back behind our house on 12th Street. We would walk through some beautiful woods at the end of Dad's property, and when we reached the other side, was the park. I spent a lot of time there when I was young, with classmates and friends."

Chapter 7

She grinned, adding, "He's not getting any younger, and neither am I. It was nice spending some one-on-one time with Dad."

"I bet it was. You've earned some downtime, Jules. It's overdue." Patrick admitted knowing she'd worked an excessive number of hours since being hired.

"I must say seeing the family was nice." It was clear Jules was keeping an important piece of information in reserve. "But I need to get back to work."

Patrick offered, "Keep in mind you don't have to come in tomorrow, but if you do that would be wonderful. If not, I'm on board with whatever works best."

"No, tomorrow is fine, I'd rather stay on schedule. I'll plan to see you at 7 a.m., sir," Jules pleasantly replied.

"Wow, super!" Patrick was thrilled. "Hey, it's good to have you back."

"Thanks Patrick," Jules replied with heartfelt gratitude. When she hung up, the volume on the CD she had been playing was increased. She sang along with her favorite Jim Reeves tunes the remainder of the trip. When she pulled into the driveway of her small rental, a feeling of relief washed over her. She was on Highway 150 where she belonged. Her new, permanent residence was soon to be constructed. It was on the drawing board which brought extreme joy.

Jules was building a new life in southern Indiana.

Chapter 8
Settled Debt

That debt is getting settled, today! was Clint's first thought when he opened his eyes to an overcast sky. *Pay the bookseller. No excuses, Clint,* he barked.

It was disgusting to him that he had let his emotions stand in the way of duty. Especially when his reason was something as foolish as believing he had heard a voice in the forest.

After a good night's rest, refreshed and ready for whatever the day had in store, Clint filled his thermos to head into town. The sky, laden with rain clouds—lazily drifting in from the southwest—did not dampen his mood. His bill, squared first, would take precedence over dropping in at the diner for a late breakfast.

Turning left on the side street that he had ventured down two days ago, Clint eyed the route inquisitively. It seemed different somehow, altered, although he could not say how. Unable to identify what had changed, he parked his truck at Dillman Shoe Store, an outfit still giving little children Red Goose eggs from a vending machine with each purchase. There appeared to be no parking at the bookstore, from what he could tell, which Clint thought seemed counterproductive to business. A solitary footpath was the only way to reach the establishment.

As he moved closer, he noted the signage appeared more weather-beaten than the first time he viewed it. It was not as brightly painted as it had been on Monday. Still shocked that he had not noticed the bookstore before this week, Clint walked through the door with high hopes. Was the owner in, or was the son still in charge? This time, Clint couldn't help but notice the place felt empty.

What is it with this guy? Clint wondered.

The overhead bell on the door had aroused no one. Clint cleared his throat loudly enough to be heard two counties over. He

Chapter 8

considered the call bell sitting on the counter, designed to alert the staff that someone was up front and required assistance.

It's a good thing they have a backup, thought Clint sarcastically. He hit the bell three times, so there would be no doubt it had been used. He waited.

"Hello… is anyone here?"

"Good morning!" the dapper man said in the way of a greeting as he rounded the corner from behind the curtain. "Sorry, I didn't hear you come in."

"That's all right," Clint expressed with a touch of irritation. "I'm here to pay my bill."

"Oh, great. Sorry I had to slip out the other day." Rod searched the countertop, "Dad's note was right here." Then at the edge of the cash register, he found what he was looking for. He opened a creased piece of paper. "He says you owe him $27.45."

"What? No way," protested Clint, not believing the quoted price on the paper. "That's highway robbery."

"No, sir, it's written in black and white, right here…" the younger man stated. "See?" He turned the note toward Clint.

Uncertain what to say or how to react, Clint's attention was redirected to the room where he had found the items already in his possession. "Are you sure? I feel like I am stealing your inventory. Those things are worth considerably more than the owner is charging. And what about the mirror? You shot me a quote of $25.50! This doesn't make any sense."

Rod, Jr. shrugged his shoulders. "That is how he priced everything. The mirror was more than likely misquoted to start with. Not as much as first quoted." The young man looked extremely stunned by Clint's response to a fair price.

"Look, maybe you two are just trying to be nice, I get that, but the mirror alone is worth considerably more. Not chicken feed." Clint used a term he was familiar with and hoped the younger man understood his meaning. Not that Clint wasn't pleased with the cost of his purchases, but he felt reluctant to leave without doling out more bucks.

"I don't feel good about this," Clint admitted openly, "but I'm not going to argue with you. I'll bring by some garden deliveries during the summer to counter your deal." He chuckled and reached into his pocket. Pulling out his billfold, he put two twenty-dollar bills on the counter and said, "Please, keep the change. It'll make me feel better. Buy yourself a hamburger and coke or something." He felt a little embarrassed.

"Gee, thanks. That sure is kind of you," Rod smiled. "By the way, how does the mirror look in your foyer?"

"Oh, it is going to be an eye-catcher. Not hung yet but will be soon. I'll be putting a fresh coat of varnish on it. I feel fortunate to own it. Your Dad was generous to sell it to me at that discounted price. I do appreciate his kindness, though. Guaranteed to be admired."

"Good, that's all we could ask for."

Clint's eyes flashed, and red flags went up. "Wait a minute, how do you know I have a foyer? Or that I plan to hang it there?"

The man's face wrinkled as though thinking. "You mentioned it the other day."

Clint thought about that, completely forgetting the conversation. "I did?"

Rod grinned. "Yes, you must have."

Clint looked past the windows, feeling perplexed. "Sorry I can't stay. I wish I could. You have so many exceptional books, and I'd love to comb through them. That'll have to wait until I have a tad more time." He turned toward the door, but before stepping through, he turned round. "I'd also like to meet your dad sometime. I was hoping to run into him today. I'm sorry he's not here."

Quickly Rod, Jr. responded. "He's rarely here. Not anymore." His eyes took in the display case. "Only comes round when needed."

Chapter 8

Clint's forehead creased, wondering when that might be since he had not seen one person on either of his visits. "I'd like to personally thank him for the mirror and the other things I found in the curio cabinet back there." He became pensive when he looked over his shoulder to the room where the pieces were. "Those will be the highlights of my fall treasure hunt for the grandkids. Very well-made pieces. Authentic looking replicas, that for sure."

Rod's face glowed. "I'll pass the message along; he'll be glad to hear it. Your paths are bound to cross at some point by then."

What an unusual guy, thought Clint as he walked up the path back to his truck. He felt a fissure of excitement. His prizes were exceptional gifts, unlike anything he would have ever expected to have found.

The engine roared to life. He backed out into the street, all the while, wondering how Rod's New and Used Books ever turned a profit. He steered toward the diner, contemplating how Jules would react to his ordeal at the bookstore and the clerk who worked there. Thinking about it made him laugh at how unorthodox the whole affair had been.

When Clint walked through the door of Josie's Diner, he was greeted by his favorite waitress. Relieved and shocked to see her, he was not going to admit he had been worried she may not return.

"Good morning," Jules said, a sweet smile attached to her welcome.

Clint saw his regular booth was waiting. He grinned. "Good morning! Good to see you. You returned early! Patrick said you mentioned something about hopefully coming back on Thursday."

"Yeah, well, time to hop back in the saddle again!" She chuckled. "I saved your regular booth in case you stopped by. Coming in late today. Aren't you? I was expecting to see you earlier. Didn't give up your booth, though." She giggled.

"I had something to attend to. Figured I might have lunch instead of breakfast for a change. But I haven't quite decided."

Settled Debt

Customers came and went as Clint read the paper and drank his coffee. Settling on breakfast instead of lunch, Jules brought him his "*usual.*" Some habits died hard. Once the diner emptied, Jules sat down across from Clint for some small talk.

"It's been a long two days," she admitted with a sigh. "I'm not from here." She raised a brow. "I had some legal issues that required my attention. I will admit, going up north after being in Salzburg made me realize just how much I love this area. Less hectic than Indianapolis and has a ton less traffic. Too much cement for my taste. It's the country life for me. I didn't expect to feel this way in such a short time, but I do."

"I know what you mean. I used to live in Seymour and that was bad enough. Small town life has its charm." Clint tilted his head to the side with a grin. "What brought you down this far? If I may ask."

"My brother, Randy. He and his wife, Anna, live in Greenville, east on Highway 150. He felt moving closer to them could be just what the doctor ordered." She flashed a smile in return. "And, before you ask… no, I'm not sick."

"I know where Greenville is…" he snickered. "Well, that's a relief. You don't look terminally ill!" With inquisitive eyes, Clint asked, "So, you live by them?"

Jules' smile widened. "What a dummy. Of course, you know where Greenville is, being from around here. I live in a rental a few miles west of him. It sits on three-acres, which is nice."

Just then, Patrick called from the kitchen. "Jules, we could use some help back here. I sent Ivan on a store run."

Cutting the conversation short, she announced, "Back to work we go!"

"I understand." He winked. "Chores don't do themselves." Clint folded his newspaper and dropped a five-dollar tip on the table. He picked up the take-out Styrofoam coffee cup Jules had brought with her when she sat down. Beside the door, he placed the paper

Chapter 8

on the bench and, with a wave of a smile, walked out into the bright sunshine. The storm that was expected later in the day had passed over, leaving a beautiful day behind.

Clint parked his truck next to the barn, and behind the antique John Deere he had picked up at auction a year ago. Before leaving for town, he had pulled the tractor into the driveway.

The day had flown by, which left several tasks undone. The only thing he felt pressured to accomplish was the construction of the chicken coop. Even though he was having a hard time getting motivated, now that he was home, he did manage to haul the lumber from behind the barn to the far corner of the property. That project would begin tomorrow.

Though not exactly hungry, he had ordered and picked up a large cheese pizza on the way home. He had put it on the kitchen table before going outside to haul lumber. It was sitting on the table when he came into the house. The kitchen smelled like an Italian eatery, and an easy meal was always a welcomed sight.

The kitchen felt void of warmth, driving home his loneliness. He went to the woodstove to empty the ashes from the firebox into a copper bin he kept sitting by the glass door. Carefully he placed logs in a crisscrossed fashion and lit a match to the fatwood he had inserted between each log.

As though a light switch had been flipped, the room burst to life from the sound of the crackling tinder. Clint's preferred way to heat his house, the woodstove saved on the heating bill, plus he liked the way a frisky blaze transformed the ambiance of his small place into a cozier home.

He placed two slices of pizza on a plate and carried it to his favorite chair in the living room. There he stared into the flames, transfixed by the glowing embers. He was thankful that he had made a fire. Otherwise, the emptiness would have engulfed him, as it most often did in the evenings. For reasons he could not explain, his sense of isolation had grown stronger over the last year. It was hard to describe in words how listening to a crackling fire could make him feel less alone, but it did.

Gazing into the fire, the items Clint had purchased at the bookstore two days prior entered his mind. To have walked out without paying had been against his moral compass. In hindsight, though, he was glad he had taken them. Rare items, he was proud of his purchases. They remained tucked behind the seat, inside the truck.

Clint took his empty plate into the kitchen and placed it in the sink before setting the coffee pot for the next day. He organized the dishes on the countertop back into the cabinets before grabbing his jacket from the pine-oak hall tree and heading outdoors.

Heavenly bodies above a full moon illuminated a nearly cloudless sky. Casting moonlight onto the ground, under starry skies, crickets chirped, and owls hooted from somewhere deep in the forest while dogs barked their familiar change of command. From all appearances, it was an ordinary night.

He loved nights like these, not too hot or cool. Occasionally, he slept outdoors where he could observe an occasional meteor shower. Stargazing had always instilled a sense of belonging to something greater. With his telescope near at hand, he listened to the sounds of nature—one of his other preferred pastimes.

How could anyone ever get used to this? Clint reflected, telling himself, *Earth puts on a show every night."* He put his hands behind his head and looked upward, *I bet cavemen enjoyed their undisturbed celestial theater, too. No city lights to block their view.*

Frequently, Clint speculated about the pinpricked night sky, wondering if any stars harbored alien life and if intelligent beings existed like on Earth. If they looked like the little green men depicted in movies or like us. Were the aliens gazing up into the cosmic ocean of infinite possibilities, asking the same question as he was, "Are we truly alone in the universe?"

Chapter 8

He walked over and wrapped his fingers around the door handle of his truck, getting ready to reach inside to retrieve his purchases, when a curious sound caused him to hesitate. He heard steps close to the barn, which had drawn his attention. *What animal made that sound? Possum… or a raccoon?* He moved to the corner of the barn to investigate. In the moonlight, he searched for a possible culprit but didn't detect one. He knew they were out there. Nocturnal animals foraged for the table scraps he tossed out.

A nearby tree moaned in the wind—a delightful spooky sound Clint loved. When he didn't detect anything, he returned to his vehicle and pulled the seat forward. He reached behind the seat for the items he had stashed there. The sack was awkward and heavy, so he removed just one object at a time.

He pulled out the knife first, and the leather sheath was more tattered than he remembered. Guardedly he slid the blade from its case. The initials F.R. were rudimentarily carved into the knife handle.

Wonder what they stand for? mused Clint.

The texture of the handle felt velvety to the touch, worn from years of use. The blade's sharpness surprised him. When he gave it as a gift at the treasure hunt, he would make it clear this was not a toy. Before including it in Trey's treasure chest, he would first speak with Rusty and Molly to get their permission. Trey was not old enough to own a Bowie knife, not yet, but at twelve years old, it wouldn't be long. Clint would suggest "for display purposes only." Rusty could put it up until Trey was old enough to appreciate its true value and potential harm. He slid the knife back inside the sheath and placed it on the bench.

He withdrew the next piece, a small, ornate wooden box. He knew what was inside—a skeleton key. He'd selected this item for his granddaughter, Lily. A perfect gift, it was just the sort of thing she would treasure. Not like anything Clint had ever seen, the key was lying on a mossy green patch of organic material. The golden key sparkled as he moved it about.

Settled Debt

Clint retrieved more things but decided they could wait until tomorrow morning. He picked up the knife and the box and walked back to the house. As he did, a weird sensation came over him as though he was being observed. Again, he turned but saw nothing. He hastened his step and hurried inside.

Chapter 9
An Unrivaled Gift

Sitting in his oversized rocker, sipping on an espresso, Clint decided to read. He'd started a fire, but he didn't feel like hanging out in the living room. His favorite place to read was in bed. That way, when he dozed off, all he had to do was lean over and flip off the light.

Six years ago, the book Elise wanted him to read was yet to be started. It wasn't normal for him to read two books simultaneously, but he would make an exception. After all these years, he felt like he owed it to her, especially when she had declared it her favorite. He lifted the book from the table and headed to the bedroom.

Back in 1997, while driving west on Highway 150 a few weeks prior to putting an offer on the land, they had taken a break at Josie's Diner for a cup of coffee and a dessert. They'd hoped for a decent pie selection, which they pleasantly found. Afterward, Clint crossed the street to Ace Hardware while Elise wandered off to investigate other stores.

On her walk, she meandered through a retail shop where she purchased *Bid Time Return*. Clint recalled her telling him excitedly the clerk had sold it to her at a "bargain-basement price." He smiled at the memory. All in all, it had been a delightful afternoon, pretending the little backroad town was their home. The experience would have been even more enjoyable had they known their dreams were soon to materialize.

Now, in hindsight, Clint was ashamed of himself. It was high time he started the book. *Bid Time Return* had an unusual storyline, according to Elise, centered on the concept of time travel. Chances were, he would like it, if for no other reason than she had.

When he walked past the kitchen, on his way to the bedroom, he noticed the objects he'd brought in from the truck sitting on the table. Fancying one last assessment of the knife, he removed the blade from its protective covering. Oddly warm and inviting, it had an almost irresistible energy—tantalizing yet repulsive.

Both items were old, which in his mind made them that much more valuable. When he'd purchased them, he believed them to be replicas, but now he wasn't so convinced. An extra special treat for the grandkids, these keepsakes, in his opinion, could not be duplicated. Tomorrow he would deposit the remainder of the gifts, along with these two, out into the gray bin where other bags of party supplies were shelved.

He crawled into bed, pulling the cotton linens over his legs and stomach. With a cup of decaf espresso on the bedstand and pillows piled behind his back and neck, Clint began to read. He felt the written word come to life at his fingertips, forming pictures and situations in his mind that he could only dream of—to reverse time and travel back to the woman he loved.

In the room, Clint could feel Elise's presence watching over him, or at least it felt that way. The deeper he got into the plot, the more he believed she was keeping a close watch on his reaction to the story.

Chapter after chapter, the tale unfolded, drawing him in—just as Elise had suggested it would. Clint found the page-turner impossible to put down. A time-travel fiction of persevering love and devotedness had turned out to be an excellent read. He found it a captivating concept, and Elise had been right to recommend it. Besides, his wife bore the same name as one of the characters in the book, Elise McKenna, which made it even more enchanting.

When the clock in the living room struck 1 a.m., Clint decided it was time to turn in for the night. He laid the book on the nightstand and leaned over to turn off the light. Just seconds after his head hit the pillow, he was sound asleep.

Although he went to sleep visualizing Elise McKenna and Richard Collier, the two main characters in the story, bizarre images of mayhem and murder crept into his subconscious. Thus, at 3 a.m., he awoke abruptly in a cold sweat, his heart pounding

Chapter 9

wildly. Sitting up on the side of the bed, several minutes passed while he calmed his rational mind, reminding himself what he had experienced was merely a crazy dream.

Disturbingly, it had a tangible quality to it that was hard to shake. Once his foggy head cleared, Clint went to the kitchen for a drink of water. He sat at the table contemplating both the terrible dream and the book he had been reading before bed. He wondered why, after reading such a captivating story, he would have a dream so violent. Darkness, running in the forest, a strand of pearls at his fingertips falling from his hand, and a sense of evil pursuing him.

By the break of dawn, his uncharacteristic nightmare had been chalked up to one of the items he had handled prior to bed. Guessing his dream had been specifically sparked by the Bowie knife, he recalled visualizing the type of individuals that may have owned it before him. He remembered feeling both drawn and repelled by the weapon.

A fascinating reaction, he thought, in retrospect. Fatigued from his restless night, Clint filled his mug with fresh coffee and slipped out the back door into the coolness of the morning air.

"Why in the world would I dream something so farfetched?" he mumbled, feeling disgusted with himself for having concocted such a repulsive dream.

Concerned about his state of mind and recalling the last chapter he had read in John Grisham's book two nights prior, he deduced, "I really should read only one book at a time. *The Broker* isn't exactly a relaxing bedtime story. I'll read that during the day and stick to *Bid Time Return* in the evenings."

Never a warm-and-fuzzy morning person, Clint felt especially out of sorts. He needed—not wanted—more coffee to put his head straight. He glanced toward the wooded acreage that butted up to his property. A serene sight, he thanked the powers that be for his good fortune to have a forest situated behind his house, which eliminated potential neighbors.

He went inside to top off his mug. Years ago, he noticed if he skipped his morning coffee, he would develop a headache. Clint figured there was a logical scientific explanation for why that happened but never bothered to find out why.

The remaining items from the bookstore were to be stored in the gray bin in the barn before he started building the chicken coop. Clint figured with such an early start, he'd make good progress before the sun went down. On the porch, he breathed in the aromatic scent of pine and lilacs. Two of his favorite fragrances.

The door of the truck creaked opened when he tugged on it, and the familiar sound brought a smile. Clint marveled that the thing was still running, which was nothing short of a miracle. Almost thirty years had passed since he bought it from his neighbor, and he admired the vehicle's tenacity to persist, overcoming all odds.

He pulled the seat forward and removed the bag containing his gifts. He placed the Bowie knife and key case back inside the bag. When entering the barn, he glanced over at the right-hand corner of the structure where a vehicle was covered. His belly tightened, and he felt a pang in his gut, as always, when he thought about how the car came into his possession. Gary Walden, his best friend, had willed it to him thirty-five years earlier.

Rusty, Clint's youngest son had diligently taken care of the car prior to his move to Salzburg. But with Rusty nearly fifty miles away, the car sat neglected, and the cover hadn't been removed in over a year. The thought had occurred to Clint he should simply transfer the title and car over to Rusty, but he just could not bring himself to give it away. It had become part of Clint's identity and was all that remained of Gary—the car and his memories.

Occasionally, in 1968, Clint would take the car out for a spin to clean the exhaust walls and burn off any fuel buildup in the system. He knew the catalytic converter needed to reach full operating temperature in older cars, which translated to heating up the engine. The change between before and after driving it at high speeds made a quantifiable difference in its performance. In those

Chapter 9

days, maintenance was a dutiful effort. Later Rusty was given the pleasure of performing the task.

He moved closer to the car to yank the protective cover off, and it tumbled to the floor. After all these years, Gary's Tahoe Turquoise Convertible Camaro still had the ability to take Clint's breath away. This was not just an assembly line Camaro. It was a 1967 Yenko, 427 Big Block. Don Yenko, a former race car driver, was legendary for replacing original Camaro engines with 427-ci L72 crate ones, like Gary's. The same legendary powerhouse engine was offered as an option in the 1966 Corvette.

Clint eyed the Yenko hood scoop and emblem, recalling the first time he saw it. Rusty had informed him merely fifty-four Camaros had been converted with the Yenko upgrade. Clint could not believe he was looking at one. A rare specimen of sportscar fame, the Camaro had been a shared investment between friends. Short of funds at closing, Gary had phoned Clint for the extra cash to seal the deal. Clint willingly put the balance on his charge card. Gary drove away in the car of his dreams. At a time when twenty-eight hundred dollars was the average price of a muscle car, Gary's was a third more expensive than any basic model.

Two months after the car's purchase, Gary received a draft notice. Always the tough guy, he chose to enlist in the Marines rather than be drafted into the Army. Later, when he was sent to Vietnam, he asked Clint if he would store the Camaro at his place until he returned stateside. Unaware at the time, Clint discovered Gary had sold all his possessions, along with applying every paycheck he received from the government to pay the loan. A few months after Gary was deployed to Vietnam, the car was paid in full.

Raised together in the Vincennes Orphanage, their friendship was a bond stronger than brothers. Abandonment had been the glue that sealed their allegiance, not blood. But, in 1968, Gary was killed. Just another Vietnam casualty of war—a name on a list printed in the daily paper.

An Unrivaled Gift

Never far from his thoughts was the day Clint got the call that Gary would not be coming home. It was another grief-stricken, life-altering event in Clint's life, and he remembered it as if it were yesterday. It was 7 a.m. on a Tuesday morning, and Clint was preparing to leave for work when the phone rang. Terry, a mutual friend of theirs—his words still as clear as the day they were delivered—asked, "Hey, Clint, did you hear about Gary?"

When Clint stated that he had not, Terry's unfathomable words were spoken. "Gary's dead! Killed in Vietnam. He's listed in the morning paper, under this week's casualties." All Clint remembered after that was dropping the phone and falling to his knees. Shaken to the core, he covered his face and cried without shame. Elise lifted the phone to finish the call, and then she called work to say that Clint had fallen ill, not far from the truth.

Sick at heart, it took several minutes for Clint to process the news. A half-hour later, he arose and went to the spare bedroom, shutting the door behind him. He refused to let Elise in. No way could she or anyone else ever grasp the impact of his loss. Gary wasn't just a friend. He was the closest thing Clint had to a brother, a circumstance only an orphan could fully appreciate.

Two days passed without one word regarding the call. But when the subject did arise, no matter how much he loved Elise, Clint refused to discuss the matter further. The numbness Gary's death caused was filed alongside two other unspeakable disappointments buried deep below the surface—the memory that Clint's mother had died during childbirth and his father deserted him.

But then, a half-year later, Clint received a letter from McKinley & Matthews, a law firm in Louisville, saying he had been named in Gary's Last Will and Testament. Unbeknownst to Clint, the paperwork had been filed prior to Gary departing for Vietnam. He had willed the Camaro to Clint as a precautionary measure—a wise move for a guy Clint believed didn't possess a lick of sense for joining the Marines, knowing he was guaranteed to be sent to Vietnam.

Chapter 9

Clint cleared his memory log, filing the sadness back to where it came from. He peered at the back wall and sat down on the bench across from the Camaro. The sad recollection of the phone call made him melancholy, but he was equally as determined to put a new slant on the incident. With a heart full of gratitude, he made the decision that should have come years earlier.

"By God, it's time," Clint announced loudly, in a voice that declared his resolve. "I am going to enjoy this thing! Rusty has been faithful in keeping it in good running shape all this time, and I refuse to let his care of the car be honored."

No longer would Clint hide from the hurt. Instead, he would embrace Gary's gift wholeheartedly as his friend intended. In doing so, Gary's life would be celebrated, not hidden in a dark corner of Clint's buried past. He would allow their kindred spirits to soar together. Gary's memory would accompany Clint in the front seat as his sidekick, joking and laughing, just like in the old days. At last, Gary's Camaro would be admired for the extraordinary machine it was. *She will be revered for the beauty she is. A marvel in craftsmanship.*

May 20, 2003

The season was in full swing. Spring-green trees and colorful flowers were budding everywhere. Projects on Clint's to-do list were being checked off one by one. The house was receiving a fresh coat of paint, and the barn had been reorganized: tools sorted, grouped, and categorized made them easier to find.

Inside the house, the hardwood floors were given a fresh coat of Bruce's Floor Wax and polished to perfection, just as Elise would have done. The drapes had been dry cleaned, rehung, and pulled to the side to create a picture window effect. Elise would have approved.

The wall between the kitchen and living room had been whacked until it finally gave way. Clint had started the project last spring and had now replaced the old wall with a stone half-wall, creating a bar area between the rooms where he could eat or place food. Elise had mentioned the request when they considered the property. She had suggested Clint connect the two rooms to give the illusion of more space, and she was right. Clint liked the way the see-through area made the place look larger. Proud of his efforts, he knew Elise would have congratulated him on a job well done.

"A lot of tender loving care will be required to fix this place up," Elise had said with a grin when they walked through the house back in 1997. "We'll be forced to make some initial improvements, or we won't be able to live here. When the funds present themselves, we will direct them toward the most important upgrades first." On that, they had agreed. Six years later, here Clint was, at long last, checking off the highest priorities from the list.

In bed at night, during renovations, and before slumber, he would consult Elise, asking her what she thought of his progress. Yearning for their connection, as always, Clint prayed she would visit him in his dream, where their special bond, once again, could be felt.

Sadly, he was starting to forget the distinct lines of her face. He felt disturbed the specific aspects of her appearance were beginning to fade from his memory, but the sound of her voice lingered in his head. Sadly, he realized his daily thoughts did not always revert to her as they once had, which was troubling. Over time Clint made a conscious decision to make peace with his station in life. His love for Elise would live on, but his life would never be what it had been. Joy in the little things was starting to return, and for that, he was grateful.

The fact was he was a widower. After six years, he would accept what he *could not change*. The cards that had been dealt to him could not be put back into the deck or reshuffled.

Chapter 10
The Wait
Christmas Eve, 1953

With his knees on the davenport, leaning into the window, the small child watched heavy snow fall. Rarely did snow enter the picture in southern Indiana, so the event was monumental in his little world. He was thrilled to see it, although today, no snowman had been built from the blanket of white.

Nearing the end of the day, twilight had settled in as late afternoon faded. Silence filled the house, along with a dreadful feeling something was terribly wrong. Long shadows crossed the floor as the young boy tried to make sense of his father's absence.

"Why isn't he here?" he whimpered as he moved away from the dark window.

Never had anything like this happened before. Hours past his father's normal routine, the boy felt scared of the emptiness that hung over him. In the corner, he rocked as he often did when fear engulfed him. It wasn't the first time his father had been past his time but never to this degree. His young child-sized brain could not wrap itself around the situation.

Each time he was left alone, there was a strict rule for him to lock the doors and play with his toys until he recognized their secret code at the door—two knocks followed by a long pause before one final rap. This morning, however, he had awakened to an empty house. Surprised to find his father gone, he had been expecting him to walk through the door since early morning.

Five-year-old Clint thought about the day. "Christmas Eve," he said in a small voice. "Maybe Dad went to the grocery to make a special breakfast." That was at eight o'clock that morning. But wishful thinking hadn't brought his father home.

In Clint's ear, he heard his father. Eli's words stayed with him as he wandered the hallway on his way to the bathroom. "Do not answer the door. Under no circumstances!" He'd commanded the words in a stern voice. "Be a good boy until I get back." Those were the typical words of warning.

His current situation was different than any before it. Fear seeped into his awareness with each passing hour. The house felt frighteningly empty by nightfall.

Clint inserted the plug to the Christmas tree lights into the outlet. He had been directed never to plug the tree in without Eli there, but he could not help himself. It was the only company he had to keep the monsters at bay. He scanned the dark recesses of every corner before the idea occurred to him to light the tree. Instantly the illumination filled the room with bubbles and bobbles. Twinkling Christmas tree bulbs imparted hope that he'd soon feel his father's presence.

On the floor, he sat cross-legged and transfixed on the door. In the afterglow of bubble lights and garland, he waited. A long while passed before he went to the kitchen to look for something to eat. When the refrigerator door swung open, he saw nothing but grape jelly sitting on the top shelf and on the inside door a jar of pickles and two eggs. One stale pancake covered with parchment paper lay on the bottom shelf.

Taking the leftover pancake from the refrigerator, Clint set the plate on the table. He removed the pickles and pushed them beside the plate. His pudgy little fingers reached for the sugar bowl. He lifted the lid and, with a spoon, covered the pancake until it was as white as the snow that lay on the opposite side of the door.

He took one bite and then another. Licking his lips of the sugar that lined them, he pulled the pickle jar to the edge of the table. He opened the lid and reached inside with his fingers, using them like scissors, he captured two slices and stuck them in his mouth.

His gaze landed on the blackness of the windows above the sink. Afraid someone was watching, he left the empty plate and pickle jar on the table and lumbered over to the chair he had pulled to the wall. He climbed up, flipped the light off, and went into the living

Chapter 10

room, where he curled into a ball next to the tree. He buried his head into a pillow he had laid there, taken from his dad's bed. The scent comforted him. Minutes ticked away along with any hope of hearing the anticipated knock he had been expecting.

Tonight, Santa Claus comes, thought Clint. *What will I do if Daddy isn't here? We were going to bake cookies.* He sighed. Clint looked toward the kitchen, questioning how they could make cookies with so little food. His tummy tightened. Then the floodgates burst. Although he had stayed at home, alone, many times in the past, this felt different. Tears streamed down his cheeks and over his quivering chin to his lap.

Daddy? Where are you? he sobbed. *Maybe Santa will help me when he gets here*, Clint reasoned, trying to stay calm. *I'll stay up and wait for him, catch him and ask for help if Daddy doesn't come back.*

He peered at the wall where in other homes, a fireplace was typically built. Then he glanced to the front door. *What if he doesn't know the secret code?* considered Clint but then realized Santa knew everything. He was magical.

Standing on the couch, he stretched his short neck as far as he could manage. With his face touching the windowpane, he struggled to see the porch, not quite catching sight of the area he needed to monitor. If his dad did not come home soon, Clint would wait on Santa to unlock the door to bring his presents in. That was the plan.

Scared and frightened at what his dad's absence perhaps meant, Clint curled into a fetal position on the couch. Under a blanket, he imagined Santa's arrival, no longer waiting on his father. He pulled the wrap to his neck. Shortly, he found peace of mind in a dreamscape children alone wander.

Surrounded by festive lights, Clint waited for a sound that was never to be heard. Fully expecting Santa to save him from his gloom, his little eyes grew heavy, battling the line between wakefulness and drifting into slumber. Late that night, listening for the door to unlock, he lost the battle.

December 25, 1953

Morning crept through the window and over the coverlet Clint had cloaked himself under. The minute his eyes opened, he tossed the throw to the floor. Sitting upright, he started to cry. He had not been rescued—by Eli or Santa. No presents sat under the tree. In Clint's mind, Santa had also deserted him.

He slipped off the couch and went to the kitchen. Additional snow had fallen overnight. Tons of it, in fact, created a picturesque Christmas Day by all accounts. Outside the world depicted a Norman Rockwell portrait, perfect in every way. But inside, in Clint's little space, a storm raged.

Fear consumed him when his bare feet touched the carpet. He tiptoed into his bedroom, where he withdrew a pair of pants from the dresser drawer. A dirty shirt was lifted from the floor and pulled over his head. In the bathroom, he combed his hair but did not brush his teeth.

In the kitchen, he polished off the pickles and spooned jelly from a jar until it only held faint traces of what it had once been. Clint had licked the glass clean. No more food, other than flour, sugar, and a few boxes of things he could not identify. Otherwise, the cabinets lay bare.

In a confused state, Clint walked the house, lost for things to do. Time moved quietly past while he colored, played, and fretted. He had cried, laughed, screamed, and pleaded for rescue. None of his tactics worked.

Hours earlier, at the crest of dawn, when he'd found no presents under the tree and the door remained locked, Clint bawled his eyes out, certain he had been disowned. Not only had his dad failed to return, but Santa Claus had also decided he was not worth his time. Darkness had not merely set on the house that night. It grew inside

Chapter 10

Clint's being as well. Soon it became clear no one was coming for him. He had been forsaken.

Over and over, in the depth of night, he asked, *What should I do?* Clint had never been encouraged to pray, or he would have. He had not been taught to go there in times of need. Eli never knelt by his son's bedside with enlightening words about God. The prayer: *Now I lay me down to sleep. I pray the Lord my soul to keep. If I should die before I wake, I pray the Lord my soul to take,* had never been uttered. In the current situation it might have been wise he did not know the prayer because Clint had shifted into survival mode, and his soul being taken wasn't part of the plan.

Whereas God had not been part of any father-and-son conversation, Clint was convinced, the night before, that an entity stood stationary at the edge of the sofa by his feet. He felt love radiating from the being. It kept him company until he fell asleep. Clint believed that same presence protected him from the monsters that lurked in the shadows.

Rummaging through every cabinet and drawer in the kitchen, hoping to ferret out a nibble or two of food, Clint could hear his stomach growl. With nothing left to consume, except bird seed in the mud room, it was time to take matters into his own hands. Things were about to get worse if he didn't make a move. His child brain was forced to shift into adult problem-solving gear.

His father never kept money in the house, other than what was in the cookie jar—a small amount but enough to buy a small amount of food, Clint guessed. Tomorrow he would go into town. By that time, hopefully, the snow would have stopped. At least, that was how the scenario was expected to play out.

He pushed a kitchen chair over to the counter and climbed on top. He finessed the jar to the edge of the cabinet. Removing the lid, he looked inside—two pennies, a nickel, and one dime lay on the bottom. He hoped it was enough money to buy food to hold him over until his father showed up.

As the day slipped by, he frequently eyed the door and looked out the window, hoping for signs of his father's return. The day and shadows lengthened. The only thing that brought comfort was the Christmas tree lights and the red wreath hung in the small side window.

In the late afternoon he thumbed through the pages of *The Night Before Christmas.* Unable to read, Clint savored the colorful pictures, imagining himself in the scenes—a better place to be. To pass the time, he played marbles on the living room floor until the sun went down, and he lost interest.

Exhausted from bawling and wishing, Clint fell into a deep sleep.

Saturday, December 26, 1953

After removing his coat from the rack, Clint snapped his rubber boots over his shoes. He pulled on mittens and clipped them to his sleeves as his dad had taught him before wrapping a scarf around his neck. After layering his clothing, he knew what to do—exactly what his father would have instructed had he been there.

Clint was ready to face the grueling hike into town. The blustery winds had died down, making it easier to brave the elements that lay ahead. His tears had dried, replaced by sheer determination to fill his belly.

Trudging through the snow, he quickly realized by no means was the walk going to be painless, largely because he had short legs and the snow was high. It was essential, nonetheless, to locate food. The mittens that covered his small hands had let him down. Wet from falling face-first in a snowdrift, they had to be removed. His hands burned from the freezing wind that assaulted his skin.

Chapter 10

At last, Salzburg came into view. Rod's General Store—his destination—was a place his father frequented often. The owner and Eli were best friends. Clint reckoned Mr. Radcliff would furnish food and help him locate his dad. The plan was to buy a loaf of bread and maybe some peanut butter and jelly. If Mr. Radcliff happened not to be at the grocery, the bread would provide enough nourishment to get through the day. With a dime, nickel, and four pennies in his pocket Clint was ready to shop.

He entered the store from the side street and recognized the cashier behind the counter. In his eyes, the older lady looked angry.

When he turned into the baked goods aisle, she kept a close eye on the lad.

Clint pulled a loaf of Sunbeam bread from the shelf. Turning it over, he noticed the orange price sticker revealed twenty-five cents. In his head, Clint counted what he had in his pocket. With lots of coins to buy the loaf, he carried his prize to the register, figuring with what was left he'd buy a jar of peanut butter and then the jelly. He placed his nineteen cents and the bread on the counter.

The cashier regarded the coins and bread, unsure what he expected. "What's this?" she asked with a smile.

"Bread, please," Clint courteously replied thinking he had more than enough money.

"You're six cents short, sweetie." The lady laughed apologetically. She looked around the store. "Where's your dad?"

With a face that revealed volumes, Clint responded, "He's next door. I'll go get some more money." Shakily he apologized, "Sorry."

The woman watched as the small child took the bread from the counter and mumbled, "I'll take it back." Something felt off. Admittedly not a mindreader type, she could still discern a lie when she heard one. She walked to the window to see if Eli was anywhere to be seen.

"Aren't you Eli's kid?"

"I'm putting it back," Clint volunteered in a voice that sounded like he might cry.

"That's a good lad. When your father gets here, we'll settle up." She extended him a gentle grin.

Clint disappeared down the aisle, fearing the clerk had caught on his dad was not next door. He pressed the loaf to fit inside his coat, flattening it the best he could as his young mind plotted his departure. He would wait until the clerk was busy with another customer and then make a run for it.

When he had disappeared around the corner, the cashier picked up the wall phone receiver and dialed a number. As she spoke, she kept an eye peeled on the exit.

Hiding behind a display stand, Clint patiently waited for a customer to come in. When one finally did, he tiptoed to the front of the store, waited for the cashier to turn her back to him, and when the coast was clear, hightailed it out the door. Running down the street as fast as his little legs could carry him, what he had not anticipated was that the lady had called the police.

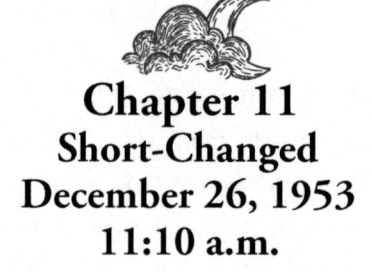

Chapter 11
Short-Changed
December 26, 1953
11:10 a.m.

"What do yah have there, son," the police officer questioned.

"Nuttin'," Clint responded with his chin puckering.

"I wouldn't call stolen property… nothing! Would you?" With a worried brow, the policeman watched Clint's body tense.

Then Clint burst into tears, sobbing uncontrollably. "I'm sorry," he bellowed through his hiccups. "I have money." He pulled the nineteen cents from his pocket.

"It's okay, kid. You're not in trouble. Just tell us where your parents are, and we'll get this straightened out in no time." The officer knew he had frightened the child and felt bad for scaring him. He supposed the kid was no more than five or six years old. "Do you know your phone number? Or address?"

Clint wanted to tell them, but his brain had gone numb. "No, sir," he cried.

"What's your last name," the policeman calmly inquired.

"Reeves," he replied.

The two policemen looked at one another. "You're Eli's kid?" the senior officer asked.

The youngster nodded, "Yes, sir."

"Well, this is your lucky day!" Alex Freeman, the man in charge, declared. "We'll drive you home and have a nice chat with your dad." He reached for the little boy's hand and directed him to the police vehicle.

Situating Clint in the back seat, the two officers shut the door and traded expressions of shock. Once in the car, they turned back to ensure the lad was all right before heading out. It took skill to master the slippery, snow-laden streets of town.

"How did you get to Salzburg, Clint?" Ed, the other officer, inquired.

"I walked," sniffed Clint. His head was in his lap, so his face couldn't be seen.

"Goodness, that was a long walk! There's a lot of snow out here!" Ed looked at Alex, his eyes expressing disbelief at how Clint could have managed the treacherous snow-covered road they were barely navigating.

"Yes, sir, it was."

When they got to the house, the windows were dark. Faint lights shone through the side window.

The two officers followed Clint to the door. They knocked, but Clint stepped in front, turned the knob, and walked in without waiting.

Sitting on the davenport, Clint put his fingers over his face. "My dad's not here," he spoke in a shaky voice. "He always comes back, but not this time." With eyes that communicated panic, he shrieked, "Daddy didn't come home! He left me. Santa didn't bring me any presents!"

Ed jumped to his feet. "Ah, come here, son. I understand you're afraid. Don't worry. We are here to help. I am sorry your dad didn't show up. Santa sometimes makes mistakes. He has a lot of children to take care of in just one night."

He put his arms around Clint until the sobs finally subsided. "When did you see your dad last? he asked, looking into Clint's glazed-over eyes. Something tragic had taken place. Ed could feel it. No father leaves his son alone on Christmas Eve, or anytime for that matter.

"I don't know," Clint muttered. He crinkled his forehead. "He wasn't here yesterday."

"Now think, Clint. What about the day before? On Christmas Eve? Was he here then, at any time?"

Chapter 11

"*No!*" he shouted. Tears streamed down his cheeks. With terrified eyes, he said, "Daddy tucked me into the bed and never came back."

"When did he tuck you into bed? The day before?"

Clint dipped his head with the saddest eyes Ed had ever seen. "I was hungry!"

Neither man was equipped to respond to the shattered heart of a petrified little boy. Nonetheless, they were certain of a serious problem looming.

"I know you were," Ed soothed. "And you are not in trouble for taking the bread. You tried to pay for it. Pearl said you tried to pay. That was the right thing to do, Clint. Not steal. We are going to take you to get some lunch… if you feel up to it. Maybe you could bring the bread along. We could have the waitress toast us some! Would you like that?"

Clint stared at his feet, bobbing his head to the affirmative.

"Good," stated Ed. "After that, we'll take you someplace special. Pearl's house. She said you could come spend the night with her." Ed instantly saw terror arise in the little boy's dark eyes. "Don't worry, son. It will only be until your dad returns. You can't stay here by yourself, Clint." Ed's kind smile was meant to reassure his young companion, but from the look on Clint's face, it hadn't worked.

Clint spoke so quietly Ed found it difficult to decipher his words. "Do I have to?" he asked.

Sorrowfully, Alex addressed the question put before him. "Yes, son, I'm afraid you do. You can't stay here. It's not safe. We understand you're afraid, but it'll only be for a short while."

Clint looked petrified. "I can't. I gotta be here when Daddy comes home."

"We will find your dad. Don't worry, Clint. The minute he arrives, I'll call you at Pearl's house. I promise. No matter the hour."

Alex's last words didn't hit his target. From the expression on the little boy's face, they were meaningless. Alex fretted he had made a false promise, scared he had made an unkeepable vow to a child who depended on his words to be truthful.

Clint wriggled off the couch and moved to the door, resigned to his fate. He opened the door and walked through.

Just as he did, the wall phone in the kitchen rang. It was Rod Radcliff, Sr. on the other end.

"Hello," answered Alex.

"Hey, Alex! Rod here!" he stated. "Pearl told me Eli's boy was in the store. Stole some bread. Is that right?"

"Yeah, I'm afraid so." There was an extended pause because Alex realized Clint was listening on the step by the door. "We've got a situation."

"What kind of situation?" Rod responded with concern. "Where's Eli?"

"Don't know, that's the snag. Look, Rod, we are taking the boy to get some lunch."

"Good God, Alex. Eli would never let his kid come into town unchaperoned. Especially in these conditions. It's cold as crap out there." Rod's raised voice sounded close to yelling.

"The problem is worse than that, I'm afraid." Alex lowered his voice to a whisper. "You available to talk in a little while? Now isn't a good time." He glanced at Clint, who had come back inside and was paying keen attention to what was being said.

Alex stepped behind the door, putting more distance between Clint and himself. "It would appear Eli has gone missing."

Rod took a sharp breath. He quickly thought back to an earlier conversation he had had with Eli only days before. "What did you say?"

"Sorry, Rod, I know you two are close friends," Alex offered.

Rod considered what Alex had reported, and a deep sense of alarm rushed over him. "Look, could you call me as soon as you get somewhere private?" he asked Alex. "I've got something important I should share. Could shed some light on the subject."

Chapter 11

A long silence preceded Rod sharing a supposition. "This is no time for secrecy," he boldly admitted and then cleared his throat. "Eli shared some news with me that you'll find startling. I sure did. I believe it could have a bearing on his disappearance. He made an important discovery."

A troubled frown crept onto Alex's face. "You think there could be a connection?"

"Yes, I'm afraid I do. After hours, if you could ring me, I'll fill you in."

Alex held his hand over the phone. To Ed, he mouthed, "You have time to call on Rod this evening?"

Ed nodded his head agreeably. "Will nine work?"

"Is nine too late?" Alex asked Rod in an apologetic tone. "Sorry for the late hour, but paperwork needs to be filed on Eli's…" he looked over at Clint, who was staring at him, "situation. Is it all right if I send Ed? Tonight I have the Boy Scout troop coming over to my place to discuss Valentine gift ideas for their mothers. I have paperwork at the station I have to finish before that."

Alex moved as far away from Clint as he could pushing the kitchen door almost closed yet leaving a few inches so he wouldn't upset the boy. "Heard you were under the weather."

"Nine works fine for me, and so does Ed," Rod agreed without hesitation. "Nothing more than a cold."

"I'm glad to hear it," stated Alex. "Pearl said to drop Clint off at her place. He can stay there until we sort this out. I'm certain Eli will resurface soon," he glanced at the fearful youngster leaning against the wall in the living room and lowered his voice even further, "I sure hope so."

"So do I." Rod further emphasized, "Alex, I've got a bad feeling about this! Pearl is a good egg. She'll take good care of Clint. I have her scheduled until five, but I'll send her home early when I get there. Carl works the night shift. Between the two of us, we can handle the store. I feel ashamed, because I had planned to drop by

Eli's house yesterday for Christmas. I have a gift for the kid. But I fell asleep in my chair and forgot to call."

"Don't blame yourself, Rod. You couldn't have known?" Hesitation lay in Alex's voice. "Hey, you should be aware, plenty of people around town have contracted the flu. Could be what you've caught."

"Maybe." Rod agreed, reluctant to accept he might have the flu instead of a simple head cold. "Pearl is filling in for me. Always will if I ask. If not her, I have another backup. But I'm hoping it doesn't come to that." Rod coughed, "Better get off here and get some rest. If one of you guys could just call me, whenever convenient, I'll explain in more detail. An actual visit isn't necessary, I suppose, especially if I am contagious."

"Will do," replied Alex.

He returned the receiver to its holder before stepping back into the doorway. With his back to Clint, he said to his partner, "Listen, Rod says he has information that could affect our investigation. Says it is relevant." Alex glanced into the kitchen as if recalling the conversation with Rod.

"I guess Eli disclosed some information with Rod he believes could shed light on the situation."

"Is that right?" Ed responded with heightened interest. "Sounds intriguing."

"That's what I thought. Rod made it clear he didn't want to talk about it over the telephone, but being under the weather, might have to."

Alex's brow furrowed in puzzlement about what Rod knew that could be so vital. "Well, I suppose we'll find out soon enough," he said in a fading voice.

The two men escorted the boy out of the house and into the car. When they closed the partition between the front and back seat, Alex turned to Ed, "Man, this has the earmark of something bad."

Chapter 11

"I agree," Ed responded, sounding worried. "I wonder what Rod will say. At best, he sounded cryptic."

"Whatever it is, it is going to be a confidential conversation, or Rod would have just said what it was while we were on the line. I just hope it gives us a solid lead."

Chapter 12
The Accused
Later That Day

Outside Rod's General Store, later that afternoon, a hostile conversation was taking place. Face-to-face with Luke McCauley, a comrade of Eli's, Rod was angry. He had been leery of the man since their first introduction. Two opposing forces stood, challenging each other.

In the alleyway, adjacent to Rod's General Store, voices escalated into an angry exchange.

Luke was doing his best to convince Rod he had no idea where Eli had vanished, but Rod was not having it.

"So, when did you speak to Eli last?" Rod asked, skeptically eyeing Luke.

"Can't say for sure." Luke shrugged. "Been at least two weeks, I guess. Being the Christmas season and all, we haven't talked much. Why do you ask? Is something wrong?"

"They found his boy stealing bread this morning from my store. The child was starving. Apparently, Eli hasn't been seen since the twenty-third."

Luke took a step back. "That's terrible news! Eli is usually so attentive to that kid. I can't imagine Eli letting the boy walk to town on his own." He shrugged and lowered his head to break eye contact. "We don't really see each other all that much during the winter."

"How do you know he walked?" asked Rod suspiciously.

"Dunno," Luke slurred in a lazy drawl. "Hey, I'm just makin' an educated guess. Get off my back."

Rod sized up his adversary. "Eli told me you two discovered a promising place in Goss Cave where the Reno Gang treasure might be hidden." Rod watched Luke's pupils closely for signs of dilation, knowing this information was private and not to be shared. He had

Chapter 12

promised Eli never to mention it, but it was the only card Rod held that might lead to the truth.

"Odd you say you hadn't seen him when he told me you guys were going down into the cave to check a specific location on Christmas Eve. What do you say to that?" The unexpected question was tossed out to catch Luke off guard, and from the look on his face, it had.

"No! There was no such place. Not that I know of. We had *no* plans to go down there again. Not until the weather broke. We decided to wait until the holidays were long gone, maybe start up again in March. That is what we discussed." Luke gave a lopsided grin and squinted over Rod's head into the sun.

"Well, that doesn't match what Eli told me on Wednesday." Rod scowled. "He said the plan was to go down the hole early Thursday morning—both of you. He felt confident he'd located the Reno plunder."

"Well, that's news to me!" Luke blurted out, sounding outraged and agitated. Fury flushed his face. "I hope the bastard wasn't trying to con me out of my fair share. We are supposed to be partners! That find is half mine!" Luke spat angrily. "We've been working for years on this, trying to locate the Reno Gang loot. Better not have done that, or Eli will have to answer to me." He planted his feet and cocked his head in defiance.

Rod stared at Luke, knowing an act when he saw one. "I was wondering where that coin came from? The one you paid for your groceries with. Pearl said you gave her a Liberty Head twenty-dollar gold piece dated 1861. She called to ask if she could accept it."

"Oh, that… It was my grandfather's." Luke looked away. "I'm running a little short of cash these days. You know, being Christmas and all. Wanted to get my Ma something, so I took Granddad's coins out of the safe." A smirk appeared on his face. "Can't spend 'em in heaven. Now, can ya?"

"Really? Seems a little odd. Don't you think? Seriously, Luke, you expect me to believe it's just a coincidence you happened to use a rare coin to purchase your groceries today for the first time ever? The day after Eli's gone missing. Three days after he informed me the two of you were going into the cave because he was optimistic he had, at last, figured out where the treasure was hidden. As a matter of fact, if I remember correctly, he said it was stashed behind a heap of geodes at the entrance between two rockfaces. He mentioned the entry was difficult. Does any of that sound familiar?"

"Listen to me. Eli was pulling your leg! He didn't mention a word about the treasure to me." Luke stomped about like a mad bull, showing signs of aggression.

When he spun to face Rod, he was visibly hot under the collar with fire in his pupils. "Besides, why was he telling you all that stuff anyway? Who are you? Just some dumb grocer. The location was supposed to be kept secret. We made a solemn oath not to tell a soul. Right there shows Eli couldn't be trusted!" Luke raised his voice an octave. "Looks like he lied to me! The snake! So you two were planning on cutting me out of my part of the riches?"

"We *made* a solemn oath not to tell a soul? Eli *couldn't* be trusted?" Rod said, repeating Luke's exact words. "What's up with that? Past tense?" Rod moved closer. "You make it sound as though Eli had kept you in the dark—on the one hand—but discussed the location with you on the other? You can't have it both ways, Luke. Either you were aware of it, or you weren't."

Luke zeroed in on Rod's language, suspicious he was outed. "I meant in general," he barked. "We were supposed to keep it between us two partners. No one else. That's all." Luke paced around like a wild animal. He clearly saw red. "I bet he told a shit load of people. Now, the whole damn town will be looking for my treasure."

It was easy to read Luke's gait. Agitated, he whipped from one direction to the next, always just missing Rod as he passed by. His actions of jabbing at the ground were obvious. A fight was at hand.

"Not just anybody, buster! Let me make that clear," Rod spat venomously at Luke on one of his passes. "Me! Eli told me! I alone

Chapter 12

know the truth! And don't you think for one minute I am not prepared to share what I know with the authorities."

When Luke circled back, this time he bumped directly into Rod. With a hiss, he jeered, "I smell a *rat!*"

In a raised voice, Rod took his low opinion of Luke one step further. "Eli has more smarts in his little finger than you have in your entire body, you idiot! To blab it all over town, like you insinuated, would be foolish—dumb as dirt." He acidly added, "Why would Eli gamble or take a risk like that, you bungling fool?"

Rod struggled to regain his composure, realizing Luke had pushed him to his limit. Speaking in a much calmer tone, he stated, "The reason Eli shared his breakthrough news with me, besides the fact I'm his pal, is because *I can be trusted.*" He stared daggers through Luke. "The question is, *can you be trusted?*'" His eyes grew dark. "Am I missing something here? Isn't it Eli's and your treasure, not just your treasure?"

"Stop twisting my words! Of course, the treasure is mine and Eli's. What kind of fool do you take me for? It belongs to both of us! I'm not stupid!"

Rod rapidly became watchful when he spotted Luke's temple visibly pulsing. Using a more relaxed tone, Rod expressed his thoughts. "So, let me get this straight. Eli disappears after you guys agreed to return to the cave. According to Eli, that is."

When Luke tried to interrupt, Rod raised his hand, signaling Luke ought to hear him out. "Let me finish," he insisted.

Flashes of anger ignited in Luke's eyes at Rod's condescending voice.

"Then, on Saturday," Rod's eyes narrowed, "you come into *my* grocery, handing over a *rare* 1861 gold coin to purchase your groceries. T-bone steaks, potatoes, beer, and cigarettes. Really Luke?" Rod put a finger to his mouth. He frowned. "I find that all a little fishy. I bet the local police will too."

"So, what are you trying to say?" shrieked Luke. "You think I killed him?"

"Killed him?" Rod enunciated with alarm. "Is that what you think I'm implying?"

Rod's eyes grew leery. "I didn't say I thought Eli had been killed. I said he was missing, not dead. My concern has been he was involved in an accident or is trapped in Goss Cave and can't get out."

"Get out of my face!" Luke said, shoving Rod hard to the side of the building, nearly knocking him over. "I told you I haven't seen him, and I ain't! Sounds like an interrogation to me, and I've had enough." Luke spat out a warning, "You'd better stop accusing people of things you don't have any idea what you're talking about. Not wise to threaten me, Mr. High-and-Mighty Business Man. You might be important in this here town, but you ain't to me. To me yer a waste of a human being."

"Is that what I'm doing, Luke?" Rod countered with his fists clenched. "Well, when Edward Joseph stops by later tonight, which he will because I asked him to, I'll be sure to tell him you said hi!"

"Shut the hell up! I'm done talking to you. You've got no proof I did anything." With his departing words, Luke stomped away, headed toward his truck with dark images running rampant through his thoughts.

5:20 p.m.

Quitting time for Pearl had already come and gone.

Rod apologized for his tardiness the minute he walked through the door. "Sorry, Pearl. Got hung up." When Pearl moved in his direction, he held up a hand. "Don't get too close. Not sure if I've got a cold or the flu."

"That's okay, boss!" She laughed. "If my little ones haven't passed it on by now, I'm more than likely safe." Pearl had two daughters and a son and was about to have an overnight visitor.

Chapter 12

When the phone call came in, confirming Clint's predicament, she readily agreed to house him until his father resurfaced.

"An ounce of prevention, Pearl," Rod advised, keeping his distance. "I hear you offered to take Clint Reeves in for the night. Thanks, Pearl. That means a lot to me. I don't need to tell you how worried I am."

"I understand. It is the least I could do under the circumstances. Hope things turn out." Pearl stood by the door. "Is Carl due in?"

"Yeah, should be here any minute. I tried to call him to say not to come in, but no one answered. He'll be sent home as well since I seem to be feeling worse, not better. Replenishing the shelves can wait until tomorrow. I'll do some this evening before calling it a night. Rest is the best thing, I'm told. At 9 p.m. I have one short appointment, and then it's lights out!"

"Got my vote," joked Pearl. "I'm out of here!" She reached for her coat from under the counter and pulled her gloves up and her hat down over her ears. "I'll be here in the morning to open. Harry can take the kids over to his mother's, including Clint."

"That would be great. I'd like to have at least one more day. I can restock shelves in the morning."

"Consider it done. You might want to turn your fan on to help block the noise in the morning."

"I use a fan every night," replied Rod. "White noise helps me sleep. I like the way it feels on my face."

"Get to feeling better, boss," Pearl said as she held the door on her way out. "I'm not used to you being sick!"

"Pearl… leave!" Rod laughed. "I don't want you to get sick too. You're my fallback gal."

After Pearl bid him goodnight, Rod believed he heard a sound in the back room. He assumed it was Carl shuffling about. "Hey, Carl, is that you?" he called.

No one answered. Rod didn't want to spread his germs to Carl any more than to Pearl. "Carl? Are you there?" he said louder.

"Yeah," Carl replied. "I'll be right up."

"No, I don't want you anywhere near me. I think I've caught something. If you will sort through today's deliveries, that will be it for the night. Stay no later than 8 or 8:30. And don't come up front."

"Sorry you aren't feeling well. Okay, I'll let myself out and lock up." Carl said as he disappeared back into the storage room.

Rod retired to a part of the store not seen by customers, where a living quarter was used on the nights he didn't want to trek home. During the busy seasons, he worked, ate, and slept in this room. To the right of the display window, he slipped behind the door. Rod flipped on the fan, just as Pearl had suggested he should. Going through the cash register receipts and other paperwork, he worked for the next two hours. When he opened the door and went out into the main part of the store, he was pleased to see Carl had gone. The hour was later than he thought.

He glanced at the clock. The display showed 9:09. Ed had not stopped by as Rod had hoped he might. Considering how he felt, he figured it was best not to speak in person anyway. *It can wait until morning*, he told himself.

Just then, the phone rang. "Rod's General Store," he answered.

"Ed, here," the voice declared. "Rod, I apologize. I had more work to do at the office than I realized. Is it too late to stop by now? Say in thirty minutes?"

"Don't worry," Rod replied. "I'd rather wait until later anyhow if that's okay with you. It's nothing that can't wait another twelve hours. I think Alex was right, I could have the flu."

Being a perceptive police officer, Ed asked, "Can you give me an idea what this is about? You sounded rather cryptic when you spoke with Alex earlier."

"Ed, like I said, I'd feel more comfortable if we spoke in person rather than over the phone. I am ready to call it a night. I don't suppose you've heard any news about Eli?"

Chapter 12

"I don't like this one bit!" Rod moaned. "Hey, I don't mean to sound so vague. I have a hunch, is all." Rod thought about his confrontation with Luke that afternoon. "More now than ever. Something has come up that, for me, raised a red flag. Not something I want to discuss right now, though. I'm pretty beat. I'll be restocking shelves early tomorrow. I could meet you at the café when I'm done. Across the street, say 12:15. We can talk then. That is, of course, if I feel better. If not, I will call and share my concerns. I'd rather speak in person but will explain over on the phone if I must."

"That works for me. To tell you the truth, I'm exhausted as well. It has been a long grueling day. I'm ready to get home and have some dinner. The wife keeps it in the oven most nights."

"Like I said, I could be off the mark. It's just a gut feeling that I have. We can chat over a cup of coffee."

"Sounds good. I'll see you then," Ed agreed. "If you change your mind, please call me at home. I'll be up a couple more hours. Feel free to call. WALnut 7-4955."

Rod crawled under the covers, knowing he would not last long. His body ached, and his throat hurt. After popping a Smith's Brother cherry cough drop into his mouth, his coughing soon subsided. It wasn't completely gone but enough to invite slumber.

He began to relax with the dose of Miles Nervine potion he had taken as a sleep aid. As he began to drift, Luke's words floated across his mind. *You think I killed him?* In and out of consciousness, Rod became convinced Luke knew more than he was letting on. A strong inkling gnawed at him, growing in intensity that Eli's partner was directly involved in his sudden disappearance.

The police will figure it out, he breathed deeply. As the pill did its magic, regret over not reporting the knowledge he possessed hit him hard. It felt like a blunder. But he was so groggy he couldn't get to his feet to make the call. *Ed will be up*, he thought as he fell fast asleep.

Two blocks away, parked in an abandoned lot, Luke watched as Rod's General Store went dark. After-hour lighting had replaced the bright glare of normal daytime appearance.

Luke had been waiting for Carl's shift to end, aware that the man worked at night. Pleased to see him lock up earlier than expected, Luke watched as Carl disappeared around the side of the building carrying a thermos and smoking a pipe. Listening closely, Luke detected the sound of Carl's truck when it fired up and rumbled out of town. Luke slipped from his vehicle and quietly latched the door.

To the other side of the street, he carried a crowbar that had been tucked under the front seat. A trusted tool used more than once for cases that required more than brawn, it could serve many purposes. He carried a metal can topped off with gasoline in his left hand and the crowbar in his right.

The door splinter with little resistance, and Luke silently moved inside. Painstakingly he scattered gasoline in strategic locations that he assumed would ignite easily: the range, the congested storeroom, places where junk had accumulated. It was paramount not to overdo. The fire had to appear to be the result of faulty wires. Not arson.

At Rod's door, Luke sprinkled a thin layer of fuel. The liquid flowed down the frame and onto the grooves of the wooden slats under the door. He could hear Rod snoring on the opposite side as well as the sound of an oscillating fan. He took the lighter from his shirt pocket and flicked a flare. The gasoline ignited instantly. Clumsily he slid the lighter back into his pant pocket. It was all so picture-perfect.

"Nice," scoffed Luke, a curl to his lip. "Fan those flames," he said to the fan on the other side of the door. As he retreated, he snubbed what was soon to be the remains of Rod Radcliff.

Chapter 12

"Burn baby burn," he mocked the grocer, "I warned you it wasn't smart to threaten me. Now see what you've made me do?"

Luke's mania had been channeled to Eli's one and only friend. No way on earth was Luke going to allow this man to spill the beans founded on an unsupported gut feeling. Rod would have stirred up a hornet's nest. To expose Luke's fortune or his potential involvement in Eli's desertion of his kid was not in the cards. Luke had no trouble stacking the deck in his favor. Rod simply had to be silenced before his suspicions found a listening ear.

It is a simple case of survival of the fittest, Luke thought as he drove home. He remembered some guy named Darwin had said something to that effect. *Must have been one tough hombre.*

"A necessary evil, I'm afraid," Luke uttered in defense of his actions. "Someone was going to have to level this playing field. Rod or me, one of us was going to have to go. and it sure as hell wasn't gonna be me. I couldn't let the police get involved."

On his porch, Luke sipped his last can of Pabst Blue Ribbon. Smoking a cigar, he anxiously awaited the fireworks to start. It was only a matter of time before the fire engines would encircle Rod's General Store.

"A waste of effort," Luke voiced sardonically. He thought about his luck. *Next time, idiot, be more careful,* he reprimanded himself. He had not considered such a simple matter like using a twenty-dollar gold piece for his groceries would raise such a ruckus. Next time paper bills would serve as his only means of payment.

With the coins being minted in the late 1800s, he decided it was wise to cash them in a few at a time. *At various pawn shops in the area, I'll exchange them for up-to-date bills. That way, I can move about freely, spending dough discreetly and cutting deals under the radar.* Luke felt proud of his use of such big words.

Sirens from the fire department would soon split the night with their shrill sound. Luke felt drained from the energy it required to stay self-indulgent. The grocery should be a raging inferno by now, he expected, destroying every trace of its structure until it was reduced to ashes, along with the expendable occupant inside.

In the aftermath, every attempt was made to save the building, but with a gasoline-doused interior, the blaze would not be contained until the damage was complete. Rod's General Store, and the *Keeper of the Secrets,* were no more.

Rod had been caught off guard to the dangers that threatened his existence. Caught in a sleep that would lead to the grave, the truth would expire under layers of blackened rubble. In its place, the blame would land at Rod's feet. Newspapers would report he presumably fell asleep while smoking in bed. "He was a heavy smoker," everyone agreed. The investigation quickly tilted to tobacco smoking as the root cause of the disaster.

In the wake of misinformation, Rod would take Eli's exceptional discovery and Luke's involvement in his missing person investigation to the grave along with a case of murder. Not one but two unsuspecting souls had been killed by this ruthless killer.

Chapter 13
The Date
September 5, 2003

As years have roiled beneath the sea, lazy sailors made shark bait feed

Avast—no worries! Dead men tell no tales,
Cap'n Reeves says he's ready to sail

Older and bolder, Mattes yea be,
Need to weigh anchor, head out to sea

Fortnight past six, the hour we meet,
A nighttime venture Scallywags compete

September 20, the adventure to begin
For treasures so great, only a Seadog shall win

    Clint set the rough treasure hunt invitation draft aside, planning to read it again later. He pushed his chair away from the table and arched his back. Stretching his spine, he worked his tight muscles caused from hovering over the poem and laboring on what to say.
    Striving to construct a poem that necessitated correlation made his brain hurt. Writing was not his strong suit, and creating words designed to rhyme was grueling. Nonetheless, Clint was determined to put forth a handwritten invitation for his family.

The Date

The treasure hunt mandated something exceptional. Not a store-bought, cookie-cutter card with generic wording.

"They will not see this one coming!" Clint chuckled humorously. He topped off his mug and popped it into the microwave to be reheated for the third time. *The kids are going to be ecstatic,* he thought, waiting for his coffee to warm. *Especially the big ones because they know what to expect.*

The last time he had hosted a treasure hunt for his grandkids was on October 18, 1996. For the last six years Clint had been trying to mend his life. He figured it was time to do something fun like arranging a family reunion. What better excuse than a treasure hunt?

Clint was the type of man who loss cut deep. A bit emotional, from an early age, he had learned to turn inward when forced to accept what he could not change. Often, he would crawl into a shell, at least temporarily, when he felt overwhelmed.

Still, when it came to his most current heartache—losing Elise after three decades of an ideal marriage—he found himself unable to crawl out of the abyss he had fallen into. That pain was too great to absorb.

Now, here he was six and a half years after that life-altering event, able to breathe again. He was tired of hiding behind the pain. He was ready to join life and the rewards it had to offer.

The grandchildren are at perfect ages for a treasure hunt, he deduced, wondering if they even remembered the last party they'd hosted in Seymour, Indiana. That was in the fall of 1996, only months before Elise and he relocated to Salzburg.

Last July, Lily, Wade's daughter, turned fifteen. The two grandsons, Rusty's boys, Trey and Dylan, were twelve and eleven, respectively. Ideal ages to search for treasure and transform into imaginary pirates. Clint realized he was having as much fun preparing for the party as they would almost certainly have participating in it.

Chapter 13

I'll start searching for pirate costumes. Check out what Amazon sells. They usually have things like that. The whole experience will be more authentic if the kids are wearing costumes! Lily may or may not think that is a great idea, but I'll buy her an outfit anyway, just in case.

With the event less than two weeks away, Clint pictured the supplies he would want to have on hand. Plastic utensils, paper plates, party-themed tablecloths, etc.

The party supply store in New Albany will have everything on my list, he figured. *Especially since the release of the movie* Pirates of the Caribbean: The Curse of the Black Pearl *last July. The kids should be pumped after seeing the movie. It will be an easy theme to find.*

He picked the invitations up from the table and slid them into the kitchen drawer, deciding he would revisit his handiwork later in the day. Maybe his head would be less foggy the next time he read the stanzas. Believing his vocabulary was limited, rhyming words had always been a challenge. Several people Clint had known over the years worked crossword puzzles, but not him. Those took way too much brain power.

Clint went to the bedroom to get dressed. Last week he had picked up a lumberman shirt at Cabela's for the fall party. He believed it made him look more manly. Plus, he needed some new clothes anyway. His standbys were outdated. With his hair combed and his new shoes tied, Clint felt proud of the way he had cleaned up.

On his way to the kitchen by way of the hallway, he passed by the antique mirror. He paused, often delighting in how exceptional it was. He had never seen anything like it before or since his stroke of luck at Rod's New and Used Books five months ago. The odd fella who had assisted him that day came to mind. *He was as peculiar as the store itself,* Clint snickered, recalling the man's strange appearance.

After nearly five years of small talk, abbreviated conversations, and exchanged pleasantries at Josie's Diner, Jules and he had become great acquaintances. As a result, Clint's overall appearance mattered more to him than it once had.

These past few years of Jules' employment at the diner, coupled with his routine visits, had turned their trivial conversations into meaningful discussions. Clint was aware of their age difference, but on the other hand, Jules and he had much in common. As a result, she had become the closest thing he had to a best friend.

He revisited in his mind a day last June when he eyed her singing in the diner's supply room, "Small Town," by Johnny Mellencamp. She confessed with a smile that Johnny was one of her favorite musicians, volunteering that she owned all his albums. The memory of that day made Clint smile. Especially since he revealed to her Mellencamp was one of his favorites singers as well.

After much deliberation, Clint decided no harm could come from asking her over to share a meal. She could see where he lived, and he could show her the progress he had made on the property. It would be fun. They'd had numerous conversations over coffee at the diner, so he guessed to have her out would simply be an extension of those chats. In truth, he had talked so much about his repairs and upgrades, it would be nice to share his endeavors in person.

Following multiple failed recipes that had bombed miserably, one, at last, became foolproof. Spaghetti and meat balls with a salad from his garden along with garlic bread on the side would be his meal of choice. The sauce was made yesterday and placed in the refrigerator. All he had to do was warm it up. Of course, a shared meal hinged on Clint mustering enough nerve to extend the invitation. Considering he had chickened out three times before, the verdict was still out. If Jules did agree to dinner, Clint had decided he would use the Camaro to pick her up in Greenville.

The F-100 fired up on the first try. When Clint turned into the café parking lot, just one spot remained. He extinguished the first half of his cigarette on the hood and put the remaining half back into the pack before retrieving a paper from the stand, as

Chapter 13

usual. Clint waved as he walked through the door. His eyes caught a glimpse of the steaming hot cup of coffee already poured and sitting on *his* table. His inner self smiled. Josie's felt like a second home.

As Jules scurried about, Clint studied her movements from over the morning newspaper. He noticed instantly that she was donning a new red and white cap and matching apron. Notably attractive, he inspected her twisted hair, mushroomed into what resembled a flower decoration. Jeweled bobby pins pinned it in place. Surprised to see her wearing a tiny bit of makeup, which Jules normally shied away from, he could not help but note how pretty she looked. Typically, she went for the fresh-scrubbed, natural look. This was a nice change.

She floated from booth to booth until, at last, she stood at Clint's table without removing her pad. She knew his order by heart and had put it in five minutes before he had arrived.

"Top of the morning to yah!" she jovially greeted.

Clint's face brightened. They often used that phrase. "How are you today? he responded.

"Doing great, as always."

"Business appears to be picking up." Clint scanned the diner, noting the uptick in customers. "I bet Patrick is one happy camper. He struggled for a few years, but it is clear to see he's struggling no more. You guys keep this up and Josie's Diner will need to expand."

Jules beamed with pride, knowing she was partially responsible for Patrick's success. "Yeah, he mentioned last night before leaving that he was going to give me another raise. Said I deserved it." Her eyes sparkled with glee. "Didn't want to lose me, he claimed. Kind of funny because there is nowhere else I could go and make these sorts of tips. People are so generous and kind around here. Keeps my head above water."

"Hey, he knows a good thing when he sees it," stated Clint matter-of-factly. "Has a knack of hiring the best. The whole crew seems well-suited and that new cook he hired a couple of weeks ago is terrific. Ivan is a natural! Never a bad dish. I don't know how Patrick does it, but his staff is as good as it gets."

Jules giggled. Playfully she retorted in a heavy southern draw, "Ah shucks, Clint. Yah really mean it?"

"Jules, you crack me up. How many accents do you keep under that hat of yours? And, for the record, I like the new uniform."

"Really? I wasn't too keen on it at first, but it's starting to grow on me. Red, white, and blue, reflect the message Patrick wants people to picture when the diner's name comes to mind. American, European cuisine, and local foods. Everything we buy and sell is made in the good ole USA."

"All I can say is whatever he's doing, it's working," Clint agreed.

Patrick called out, "This ain't no social club, Jules!" He smiled at the two of them, knowing their friendship was maturing.

"Don't you have some fish to fry, old man?" Jules countered with a chuckle.

The table behind Clint's burst into laughter.

"I'll catch you later," Jules said as she glanced around. "He's right, I missed a table. They must have slipped in while I wasn't looking. Your breakfast will be here in a sec. Shouldn't be long."

"That's fine. I'm in no hurry. Take your time." Clint did not mind waiting because it afforded him more time to work up the courage to ask Jules his dreaded question.

But serendipity would soon play its hand, making the situation easier to tackle. Patrick moved from behind the counter and turned the menu board to the other side to reflect today's lunch specials.

When Clint checked his watch, he was shocked to learn he had been at the café for close to two hours. With an empty plate and a full belly, he wondered just how long he could continue to nurse his visit without making it noticeable he was delaying his exit. Then, just as he was about to leave and save his invite for another day, he saw Jules headed his way with a carafe of coffee and a small piece of pie.

Chapter 13

"Let me get those plates for you," she suggested pleasantly as she neared Clint's table. "How about a fill-up?"

As she spoke the words, Jules lost her footing as a spot of grease from a slice of bacon that had fallen from a plate earlier caused her to sway. Forgetting to wipe it up, in one quick, fluid movement, Jules landed where the ham had fallen. Dishware sailed from the platter she had been cradling. Everyone watched in horror as shattered cups and glassware spewed across the checkerboard tile floor. Humiliated, she buried her head in her hands, realizing exactly what had occurred and why.

Clint jumped to his feet in a flash. "Jules, are you all right?" he inquired, afraid she may have broken something considering how hard she fell.

Initially, she tried to sidestep any concern put forth, but in truth her ankle had twisted under her and promptly started to swell. "I think I turned my ankle," she answered in a youthful voice. She viewed the gawking crowd and felt like crawling under Clint's table. "Other than my pride and ankle, I believe those are the only two injuries," she teased. Her ankle had grown twice its size. She couldn't slip it out of her work shoe.

Patrick and Clint rushed to assemble the broken pieces of glass as onlookers ogled the activity. Patrick, who had sped to Jules' side the instant she went down, pitched the broken pieces onto the serving tray and sat down on the floor beside her.

Clint moved back, wanting to give Patrick and his employee some space. Jules put her hand out for Clint to lift her to her feet. "Patrick, you are a dear," she said with a generous smile. She sat down in Clint's booth. Beside her, Clint shielded her from staring eyes. With a lowered head, she moaned, "What a klutz!"

Patrick had her elevate her leg. In the kitchen he prepared an ice pack. When he returned, he laid it on her ankle, hoping to stifle the swelling. Now, here she was without a thing to do other than wait for the swelling to ease.

"Glad you didn't do any more harm than you did," stated Clint.

"Yeah, only a bruised ego." Jules grinned.

Clint swallowed hard. "Well, since you have been forced into a break, I have a question for you." He could feel his heart pounding in his chest, the fear of being rejected hovering in the air. "I was going to ask if you would like to come over to my place tonight for a bite to eat. Show you where I live, but considering what just happened..." he literally was backing out of his invite when he continued with, "I guess it can be placed on hold for another time."

Jules' eyes grew large, and their eyes locked. She had been looking forward to this day for so long. When Clint felt comfortable enough to ask her to go somewhere other than the diner. She had always respected how guarded he was because she, too, lived a similar life.

The thought ran through her mind, *Had I only known all I had to do was make a fool of myself, I would have done it sooner.*

A smile crept onto her face. "Yes," she answered without hesitation. "I'd love to."

"Great!" Clint gleefully retorted. "Tonight?"

"Yes, tonight!"

"I will warn you, I am not a great cook, not like Ivan back there." Clint glanced over at the tall, handsome man behind the grill, "but I can make a mean plate of spaghetti and meat balls." He chuckled. "It's my specialty!"

"I bet you can!" Jules cackled. "I hate to break it to you, Clint, but all guys can make spaghetti." When his expression drooped, she giggled. "But not meatballs! Guys cannot make meatballs. That's awesome!"

"All right, smarty pants!" Clint said, rolling his eyes.

Observing her swollen ankle, she expressed her concern. "It's my left ankle so I should be able to drive without much difficulty. I'll sit with ice on it before trying to stand. If I ask, Patrick will let me go home early." She gave him a fleeting glance. "What is your address."

Chapter 13

"I have a better idea." Clint suggested with a sheepish grin, "I will follow you home, make sure you get there safely, and then I'll swing by at 6:30 and drive you to my place. How does that sound?"

Jules reached out and brushed his hand. Instantly she felt better. "Thanks for the extra effort," she said gratefully.

Chapter 14
A Trick of Light

The spaghetti warmed on the stove, and he'd placed the garden salad in the refrigerator to chill. Clint hustled about, making certain everything was in its proper place. He wanted it to look perfect.

After giving the house a once-over, he made his way to the restroom. He'd cleaned the cramped space with a discerning eye. He switched out the dwindled toilet paper on the spindle for a fresh roll, making certain the sheets dropped from underneath as opposed to over the top. When he was finished, Clint washed his hands in hot sudsy water before returning to the kitchen. He had not felt this alive in years. The prospect of inviting a lady to his humble abode was beyond anything he could have imagined a few years back—totally out of the realm of probability.

More so, the woman who was soon to pay a visit wasn't just any lady. Jules Jenkins was stopping by. He had never felt comfortable meeting new people, especially ones of the opposite sex. He hoped the comfortableness they shared would carry over to time spent away from downtown. If he was honest, Clint would have to confess to his loneliness. Spending one-on-one time with his friend from the café was something he looked forward to.

He turned the back burner of the stove off before going to the foyer to grab his jacket from the hall tree. When he passed by the mirror, for a split second, he would have sworn he saw a flash of movement. He detected an object at the edge of his peripheral vision, and he swiftly turned. But, of course, Clint saw nothing other than his own image reflected.

Clint had a problem. He hated to admit it, but he had been seeing and hearing things for some time. They were commonplace nowadays, and Clint could not say if the unusual occurrences started before or after Elise's death. Things were a blur nowadays

Chapter 14

when it came to his feelings. When he thought back over the past several years, it felt like strange things had been happening since the first day he walked the property with Elise and the realtor. He distinctly remembered being drawn to it like a magnet, as if the land was beckoning him somehow.

Clint moved to the mirror and took a hard look at his reflection. For a moment, he considered the idea that guilt had raised its ugly head. A twinge of remorse showered over him for inviting a woman into their home. He would not lie. The thought had crossed his mind more than once that maybe, just maybe, he was conjuring up things that go bump in the night to convince himself he was not alone. Wishful thinking, he supposed, that Elise might be near.

He stood stationary for a moment considering the likelihood he saw something and then drew a conclusion. *That's silly. Elise would want me to move on—not stop living! She will always be my first and only love. She knows that!*

Truth be told, Clint wasn't so certain. The house had never been the same since Elise had passed. It felt as if the place had taken on a life of its own with an energy that felt unnatural and sounds he couldn't explain away as he had at the beginning. *The house is merely settling*, was what his sensible side told him.

To make matters worse, he had seen things on the property that defied explanation. He had heard a voice in the woods earlier that year, which had shaken him to the core. Not able to distinguish the voice as a woman or man, Clint toyed with the idea Elise could be trying to make contact. It wasn't like these occurrences happened often, but when they did, they were disturbing.

He slipped his jacket on and headed for the car. Not his truck… the car! Gary's, 1967 Camaro. He thought about his friend and wondered what he would have thought about him cruising around in his hot rod at the age of fifty-five—an old man driving a young man's car.

Thanks to Rusty's tinkering, the car had not turned into a rust bucket but instead was kept in pristine condition and maintained with tender loving care. Handled with kid-gloves, the car looked and sounded new.

At the turn of the key, the engine rumbled alive. Listening to the engine purr, Clint laughed with gratitude. With a touch of his foot on the gas pedal, the motor roared like a beast lay under the hood. Clint had become quite fond of that sound. To show the car off would be delightful. In Clint's mind, he saw Jules sitting beside him with the top down and the wind blowing in their hair. The daydream made him feel like a young man again—a teenager with not a care in the world.

When he pulled up outside her home, Jules was standing at the door. Soft curls fell around her shoulders. She was wearing a green chiffon blouse with white slacks. She closed the door and walked toward the car.

Clint was taken aback. Trying not to stare, he had never seen Jules in anything but a uniform with her hair tied up. What he saw now was nothing short of heaven on Earth.

"Hey, nice wheels," she said, wearing a generous grin. "I didn't know you owned a Camaro. What a beautiful car. 1967… right?"

"Yeah," replied Clint surprised she would know the year. "How did you know?"

"No vent windows for one. Or lights on the fender or the rear," she stated matter-of-factly as if it were common knowledge.

"Holy cow, girl! You know your cars."

"Back in the old days, I owned a Firebird," she snickered. "What can I say? I like cars!"

"How's the ankle? You seem to be walking fine."

"Good to go. The swelling went down. Aches just a little, that's all."

He had inserted a CD into the new unit he had installed. Jules was surprised by the tune that started to play. One of her favorites. "Rain on the Scarecrow," by John Mellencamp. To Clint's delight, she began to sing along.

Chapter 14

A feeling of freedom blew with the breeze as they chimed in with Mellencamp. Jules seemed to know every word to every song that played, which made the trip back to his place entertaining.

When Clint turned off the car and the music, Jules reached over and said, "Thank you so much. That was a blast!"

Following Clint's excellent spaghetti dinner, they retired to the backyard. Clint made a fire in the brick fire pit he had constructed over the weekend. Midway to the forest, they sat on lawn chairs, talking and watching the flames flicker.

As darkness fell, Clint told Jules how he had come into possession of such a timeless classic car and about the loss of his friend Gary. He felt self-conscious divulging the truth about his past—that he was raised in an orphanage—but he also wanted to be honest with her and not keep secrets.

He chronicled his life, telling her what it was like being raised by nuns. That he and Gary were like brothers. Both were abandoned. Gary's mother had given him away…literally, by leaving him on the doorstep of a church, whereas Clint's father, he suspected, had chosen a more carefree life that did not include a kid.

Jules held back, at least temporarily, from talking about her happy childhood and what a great family she had. She did recap James' accident and even told Clint about her settlement and how it had afforded her the house where she lived. That her brother had purchased building materials at his cost, which allowed her more home than she would have had otherwise.

By nine o'clock, she reluctantly admitted it was time to go.

"I should leave," she softly said. "I have to be at work the same time the roosters crow." She chuckled, thinking about the chicken coop. "Clint, I can't believe you have chickens! What a wonderful evening it has been. And that meal was really good. You did a fine job. I can't remember when I've been this relaxed. Next time, we'll have dinner at my place." Jules patted Clint's knee and stood. They walked toward the car, carrying the promise of better days.

When they arrived at Jules' home, Clint walked around to the passenger side and opened the door. He extended his hand to assist her from the car. On the porch, he expressed his sentiments. "I enjoyed this evening. I hope we can have a repeat performance sometime soon. If you are up for it."

"I am." She smiled, leaning in to give him a quick hug before opening the door. "Thanks, Clint. See you tomorrow!"

When Clint turned to face the Camaro, his heart swelled. "Thank you, Gary. It's a great ride." He could have sworn he felt Gary in the passenger seat on the way home.

Saturday Morning
September 6

At the post office, Clint bought a sleeve of stamps. He used two on the envelopes he carried addressed to his boys. September 20 was the official date of the treasure hunt. He had talked to them on the phone to verify the specifics of the event, but he wanted the grandkids to have personalized invitations.

The plan was for everyone to come early so they could play games and roast hot dogs before the hunt. Clint deliberately set the big event to start at six in the evening, figuring later in the day would make it more exciting. They would hunt for treasure near sunset. As a gardener, he understood dusk would fall close to six. He figured the grandkids could use flashlights if necessary, which would make the treasure hunt more exciting.

Clint had not recently taken inventory of his total prize count, but he decided today would be that day. At Hobby Lobby in New Albany, he had selected treasure boxes to hide the major gifts in. He'd purchased simple things like candy, compasses, eye patches, and plastic swords several months ago and added them to the other items stored in the gray bin.

Chapter 14

The part he had to concentrate on was clue creation. Treasure hunts were fun but coming up with clues took a great deal of brain power. He would walk the land to find secret places that would challenge the children but not make the hiding spots so difficult the clues were not discoverable. Clint figured the clues could be more complicated now than back in 1996.

On the sidewalk, in front of the post office, Clint took in the beautiful, bright sunny day. Encouraged about the treasure hunt and feeling more at ease with its direction, he crossed the street to Josie's. Seeing Jules this morning, especially after last evening, would be different. They had connected on a fundamental level. She was as enlightening and authentic as he had hoped she would be. After her slight mishap the day before, he figured she would take extra precautions.

The night before, she confided in Clint that three years after her husband's fatal accident he had appeared to her in a dream. James had told her that he loved her. Just knowing he was all right had lifted her spirits. Jules' description of her dream was captivating. She expressed to Clint from that day forward, her grief had lessened. It was as if James was conveying to her that he was at peace and she should be happy too. He had let the air out of a balloon full of sorrow, allowing her to enjoy the richness of life.

She also shared a dream she'd had of her unborn child. Her little girl was playing in a field of flowers with other children. The child paused when she saw Jules. Then she ran toward her. The little girl put her arms around her neck. Her sweet little face looked up and said, "I love you, Mommy! Don't worry. We'll see each other again!" Then she returned to her playmates, waving as she joined them.

To share such deep emotions with him had given Clint a sense of closeness with Jules. The only reluctance he had was his experiences had not been as uplifting. His story was one of confusion. He could not share with her that he believed he was being observed. That he had researched his property to see if there was a history that could explain the unusual happenings he had been experiencing. He had decided a spirit was living in his house. The consolation in his certainty was who or whatever it was, the entity did not want to harm him.

A car passed before Clint had a chance to cross the road. When he finally crossed, he walked to the newspaper stand and inserted fifty cents, and withdrew a paper from the stack. As he did, he glanced over at the post office. To his surprise, a man was standing where he had been standing only moments before. The thing that took Clint off guard was the man resembled the man he had seen in the mirror at Rod's New and Used Books. The owner of the shop.

Wearing a hat and overalls, the man stared straight ahead as if in a trance.

Clint straightened his spine. Moving toward the figure, he felt obliged to speak to the man and thank him for the deal he had given him on the items from the bookstore last April, especially the mirror. But, just as Clint came to the edge of the sidewalk and stepped into the street, another car drove between them.

To Clint's shock, when the car passed, the old man was gone. Clint looked up and down the street but saw no one moving in either direction.

Not this again, Clint groaned. He took a deep breath. *Would you please get your act together? The guy simply went into the post office. Does it have to be something paranormal? Come on, Clint!*

He walked inside the diner but not before looking one last time at the spot where he had seen the man. No one stood on the far side of the street.

Sitting with his back to the door, Clint decided to let it go. It was a trick of the imagination—nothing out of the ordinary. The man simply resembled the old man, he assured himself.

He would be mistaken.

Chapter 15
Remnants of a Dream

Tired of his fertile imagination running wild, Clint decided no longer would he show indifference to his property or ignore the forest behind it. True, the last time he walked the woods, a quirky situation arose. The land seemed to have beckoned Elise and him to it from the start, and he felt beguiled by the house. True, he had been experiencing odd phenomena since taking possession. However, all those things did not constitute something ominous going on.

I am a grown man, for cryin' out loud, Clint grunted. *Not a kid anymore. No monsters live in my closet or hide under the bed! Grow up!*

Clint chastised himself as he strode toward the woods, determined to give his fears marching orders. He had not been in the clearing since the day he had heard the voice. It was time to put his fears aside and prove once and for all nothing really took place that could not be explained in natural terms.

The leaves on the trees had begun to fall. The branches were half the fullness they had been a mere month ago. September was the turning point where the weather changed. It would dramatically switch from hot to more comfortable temperatures. Typically, by mid-month the summer season ended, beginning its reversal toward winter. With the treasurer hunt only one week away, he was expecting favorable conditions to host his event.

The forest floor was covered in leaves, acorns, and walnuts as he made his way through the underbrush. As he shouldered through, a sense of calm came over him, and he moved deeper into the forest. It was a different world back here, and his body told him as much. He was drawn to the clearing and was ashamed he had let his fears keep him away.

Clint identified countless locations to hide clues and deposit treasure. The grandchildren, he deemed, would be ecstatic with the locations and the sense of adventure it held. The ground was evaluated for acceptable hiding places, not too hard or simple. He found a murky hollow that reminded him of a pirate's lair. He pushed debris to the side and thoroughly examined the area for the best place to hide the final treasure chests. In a hollowed-out log, near a small creek that ran through the property, the treasure hunt finale would wind down.

"What a great place to hide the chests," Clint said aloud. "I'll have to bring Jules out to see what she thinks and ask her opinion."

The idea of including Jules in his treasure hunt gathering felt right. The notion popped into his head, *There is no good reason not to invite her.* He hesitated. *Better make sure Wade, Rusty, and the girls are okay with it beforehand.* He sat down on a log, taking in the freshness of the woodland. The sun shone through the branches, as it had on the first visit to the clearing. *What is it about this place that feels so familiar?* he wondered.

In a short while, he stood to his feet, ready to head out. Pleased to have put his reservations behind him, he contemplated what a mistake it would have been not to have returned to the woods. By the time he had reached the house, his brain had shifted into overdrive, planning and solidifying his final to-do list.

He'd checked the perfect place to hide the treasure chests off the list. The hard part came next, constructing the last dreaded clues. Writing poems was not his strong suit. He envied Jules. She had done it so easily. The strategy was to walk the land, jotting down notes as he went along. That way, he figured, the task may perhaps be less painful.

The thought had crossed his mind on the way to the diner that morning to invite Jules to help him with the task—a great lead-in to asking her out to dinner.

"Sounds like fun," she agreed readily. "I enjoy writing poems."

"Music to my ears because I am not good at rhyming words. To tell you the truth, my spelling is seriously flawed." He chuckled. "Wasn't my strong suit in school."

Chapter 15

"Well, it's your lucky day. You are talking to a spelling bee champion!" Her eyes glistened with humor.

"I was thinking," Clint said in a more reserved tone. "On Tuesday, if you have no plans, I could take you someplace more formal for dinner, like the BBQ joint up in Paoli."

Jules giggled. "I don't know, Clint, if I have the clothes for something that upscale."

Clint wagged his head, half-expecting her sarcasm. That was one of the things he appreciated about Jules, she had a dry sense of humor, and it always caught him off guard.

"No, I'd love to," she responded sweetly. "I have no plans." Jules patted him on the shoulder. "Sounds like fun." She walked away, ready to check on her other customers. "Pulled pork is one of my favorite meals!"

During dinner, Clint figured he would extend an invitation for Wednesday afternoon as well. Together they could walk the property a second time to decide where to hide the clues. They could order a pizza and, if time permitted, they could watch a movie.

The next two days, Clint worked at the house, tidying up the place. He hung fall baskets on the porch, power-washed the patio, and tossed trash that should have been discarded years ago. He weed wacked areas close to the house and barn, removing all unsightly growth.

He placed lawn chairs by the firepit and set up the additional tables he had purchased at Walmart in New Albany, beside the barn, to accommodate the meal. He expected the smaller of the two to hold desserts while the larger one displayed the real food. He planned to tuck soft drinks into ice in the old wash tub and set it at the far end of the table on the ground.

Clint calculated the lawn would require one additional mowing prior to the season's end. The gutters looked better now that they had been cleaned, and the extra wood he had stacked at the side of the barn could be used if they ran short. He'd already hauled a tracker wagon full of logs to the firepit area. He used his wood-splitter the greater part of Sunday afternoon getting ready for winter and the party.

Perhaps I'll use more wood than in years prior, he contemplated, thinking about Jules coming over more often.

When Monday rolled around, Clint was exhausted to the bone. He decided to take the evening off. A used telescope, purchased on Craigslist, had been delivered by UPS on Saturday, and Clint was eager to start its assembly. Fascinated with the heavens, he often stretched out under the stars at night and, on occasion, slept outdoors. Listening to owls and other nighttime critters had always been a favorite pastime.

The telescope was a vintage refractor style from the late 1950s. According to the reviews, his newly purchased Mayflower was known for its amazing optics. He had set the padded hard case in the yard. Something was psychologically pleasing about operating an older quality telescope. The hands-on viewing experience brought him immeasurable joy. On Wednesday, if Jules was able to drop by, he figured together they could check out the range of view.

Clint went indoors and started a fire. He opened the windows so the house wouldn't get too warm and uncomfortable. With a book in hand, he made his way to his easy chair. *Bid Time Return* had developed into a captivating tale. As a result, he had put his other book, *The Broker*, on the shelf for a later read. Elise's book had become so enthralling he found himself setting time aside each evening to see what happened next.

With an opened bag of M&Ms on the side table and a cup of decaf espresso cooling, Clint opened the text and started reading his next chapter. Later, with three new chapters under his belt,

Chapter 15

Clint felt powerless to throw in the towel, so he got up and went to the kitchen to pour a second cup of brew.

Absorbed in its pages, Clint was struggling to put the book down but vowed to finish the chapter he had begun and then call it quits. When he lifted it from the stand, he noticed an earmarked page he hadn't seen before. As he turned to the page, a slip of paper fell out on the floor. It was a receipt.

Clint was shocked to see Elise had purchased the hardback from Rod's New and Used Books. He wondered how Elise would have encountered the bookstore and when? Amazed at the coincidence, he recollected their visit to Salzburg back in 1997 and the coffee break they'd taken at Josie's Diner that day.

After that, they ventured out to do a little sightseeing. He walked into the old Ace Hardware that gave the appearance it was straight out of the 1940s—and still there—while she took off the other direction. She must have purchased *Bid Time Return* that day.

Unbelievable, Clint mused, slipping the bill of sale back inside the page. He pulled the bookmark he had been using out and set it on the table, replaced by her receipt. He started chapter twelve. Not a large volume, only 321 pages, he was nearing the climax. With the windows open and a cool breeze wafting through the rooms, the house felt cozy.

I can't believe one of the main characters in this book is named Elise. Clint beamed. *I bet she couldn't wait for me to see that! How cute!*

Richard Collier, a screenwriter, was the other main character in the story. A tale about time travel, Clint had become quite fond of the plot. He could see himself playing the part of Richard and Elise as Elise McKenna, a stage actress from the late 1890s. It was as if Clint had rewound time to meet his Elise—a delightful prospect.

"No wonder she had thought I would appreciate the story," he breathed.

Clint read late into the night, falling asleep to the thoughts of how to self-hypnotize and travel through time to find his lost love. When he awoke at 2 a.m. in the chair with a jolt from not remembering where he was, he got up and stumbled off to bed.

When he shut his eyes, Elise appeared in his dreams. It was as though she moved quietly alongside him, whispering, "All is well." Her words of solace, "You're not alone," lingered. Other voices echoed, words not fully formed when the sun arose, faded behind the thin blue line that separated dreams from reality.

On Tuesday morning, when he stirred to consciousness, her essence was still with him. At 5:45, his eyes opened. No matter what time he fell asleep, he was programmed to awake on the hour and minute. He hated that his brain refused to let him have extra shuteye, especially on Sunday morning.

Clint sat on the side of the bed, tears burning inside. The feeling was so strong it was as though he could have reached out and touched her, closer than any other time prior to that night.

It took some time before his feet hit the floor. But when they did, he heard the words, "All is well." Followed by… "You're not alone."

Clint did everything in his power to push last night's dream out of his mind as he wandered through the house. He desperately wanted to believe Elise's message was meant as encouragement for him to embrace his direction and not to worry. He knew in his heart of hearts she would want him to find happiness. She loved him, yet he had this feeling of uncertainty that weighed heavy on his heart.

Headed for the restaurant, Clint automatically withdrew a cigarette from the pack and stuck it in his mouth. Then he hesitated and put it back inside the sleeve again, determined to quit. With the windows down, Clint sang along with David Lee Murphy. He

Chapter 15

had put a CD on and was playing "Pirates Cove" on a loop. He laughed at himself because the song reminded him of his upcoming treasure hunt.

The crowd at the diner was a lively bunch. When Clint walked through the door, Jules winked. She had never done that before. To a freshly poured cup of coffee, he sat down and began reading his newspaper, knowing full well bacon, eggs, and a side of biscuits and gravy would soon follow. The robust atmosphere and chit-chat with Jules and Patrick perked up his day.

Nevertheless, an early departure cut his diner visit short. A few stops were on his radar, with one of them being the bookstore. He had not been there, regrettably, since last spring and, no matter how elusive the owner was, he still wanted to thank him properly for the discounted items he had walked away with. He also wanted to share with him that his late wife had been in his store and had purchased one of his books. After that, a short run through the grocery was in order.

When he entered the bookstore, as before, the bell sounded. It came as no surprise when no greeting was extended. *How does this place stay open?* Clint asked in his head, humored by the consistency. At the nearest aisle, he waited. Arranged alphabetically, the leather-bound manuscripts smelled intoxicating as he moved down the aisle.

Taking a hardback from the shelf, he deliberated on whether he really needed another book. Other than the off chance of getting to speak with Rod, Sr., he also wanted to enjoy the ambiance and antiquated feel of the place. Clint found titles from English-born Shakespeare to French author Voltaire. Both were hard to fathom on the shelves in Salzburg. Or anywhere, for that matter.

"Anybody home?" Clint called out impatiently.

Receiving no response, he walked over to the counter and dinged the bell three times. He waited, and just as he was about to leave, the same young man walked out from behind the curtain.

"Hello there." He welcomed Clint. "Haven't seen you in a minute."

"I was beginning to think you weren't here," Clint replied with a frown.

"I don't always hear the call," Rod, Jr. replied. "Sorry. I wouldn't have wanted to miss you."

Clint's face squinched, finding his terminology strange. "You mean bell, don't you?"

"Yes, right… the bell!" The sharply dressed man's eyes glinted. "So, how can I help you today? Don't see anything in your hands. Do you have a question?"

"No, not really. I just wanted to see if I could speak with your father. If by chance he was here today." Clint remembered seeing the older man on the sidewalk a few months ago. "I saw your dad at the Post Office a while back," he said casually. "I tried to approach him, but he slipped away before I could catch him."

"Is that right?" Rod responded in an astonished tone. There was silence for a moment, then he said, "Nah, he's not in."

"I know," Clint replied. "Only comes in when needed." He laughed, thinking by the looks of the place, Rod's father would never be called in to help.

"Maybe next time." The younger Rod answered in the way of an apology.

"That's all right. I suspect at some point our paths will cross."

"Yeah, I suspect they will."

Clint moved toward the door, "I'll stop in again." He hesitated and then noticed the man was staring at him too intently. "I noticed you have Shakespeare novels and poems on your shelves as well as some other highbrowed authors and dramatists. Around here, I bet you don't sell many of those." Clint laughed inwardly thinking he was clever. The clientele in southern Indiana was not exactly an audience for playwrights and poets.

Chapter 15

"Oh, you'd be surprised who we cater to. Different strokes for different folks. History always sells."

"Yeah, I suppose it does," said Clint, tilting his head and thinking about what was said.

Then, just as he was about to walk out the door, he heard the man mumble, "*Yeah, O call back yesterday, bid time return!*"

The minute Clint heard the phrase, he froze. Pivoting around, he asked, "What did you say?"

Rod's eyes brightened, knowing Clint would react. "You mean, '*Yeah, O call back yesterday, bid time return.*'" He smiled. "Folks are drawn to yesteryear."

"How odd," Clint stressed with a puzzled expression on his face. "I'm reading a book called, *Bid Time Return*. My late wife bought the copy here in your store. I meant to mention it but got sidetracked. Perhaps you sold it to her."

"Never know. I could have." Rod tossed out, looking rather smug. "Wasn't that script made into a film?" Putting a finger to his lips, he declared, "Yes, I believe it was. *Somewhere in Time*, if I recall, starring Christopher Reeves and Jane Seymour. Right?"

Clint looked stunned. "I wouldn't know. There was a movie made from the book?" He thought back, "The copy I have, which of course was my wife's, was written in 1975. I don't recall her ever mentioning they made a movie of it. Did you say, *Somewhere in Time?*"

"Yeah, it was one of those movies they considered a *sleeper* at the box office. No one really went to see it when it was playing at the theater, but later it became a cult flick. The book, if I remember correctly, was set at the Hotel Del Coronado in Coronado, California, but the movie version was staged at the Grand Hotel on Mackinaw Island, Michigan." Rod added, "Filmed in 1980, I believe."

"How coincidental. I can hardly believe this! You know so much about the book. And the movie!" Clint's eyes drifted toward the ceiling. "My deceased wife's name is Elise! She said *Bid Time*

Return was her favorite book and wanted me to read it. For years it sat on the shelf. It took me some time, but I'm very close to finishing it. A great premise for a story."

"You should rent the movie sometime. I think you'd find it fascinating." Rod's face looked reflective. "There's another book I think you'd find fascinating," suggested Rod. "Along the same lines as *Bid Time Return*. The author is H. G. Wells, the book is titled, *The Time Machine*. It was written in 1895. Only eighty-four pages, a relatively short book by today's standards. Have you heard of it?"

"Sure, everyone knows that book!" chortled Clint. By the look on Rod's face Clint was afraid he might have offended him.

"Well, not everyone," reacted Rod with a twisted smile. "Hang on," he said. Rod disappeared around the corner and was back in a flash. "Here," he said. "My gift to you in appreciation of your business."

Clint looked at the book face and then opened the cover page. *The Time Machine*, by H.G. Wells. "I can't accept this! It's a first print."

Rod gazed into Clint's eyes. "I have a question. Do you believe time travel is possible? Visiting the past, I mean, or the future? Even for a split second? Or maybe longer?"

"Not hardly," Clint snickered cheerily, thinking their conversations had a way of jumping the rails.

"Life's full of little surprises," mumbled Rod as he walked away, leaving Clint holding the book. "Isn't it? Better get back to work. A busy day ahead! Have a good day, sir."

Clint, rather shocked at Rod's quick retreat, spoke to his backside, "Sorry, I didn't mean to keep you." Rod disappeared behind the curtain like he had been called to an emergency. Clint said, "You too."

Outside Clint stopped at the bay-style window that displayed a wide range of knickknacks. None seemed of much interest. Eyeing his gift, Clint was uncertain more than ever how they were able to keep their doors open.

Chapter 16
A Reason for Pause

From the darkest part of the yard, Clint and Jules gazed up at the stars. He'd hoped she had an interest in that sort of thing, and it turned out she did. Surprised to hear as a child her family owned a telescope and even used it in midwinter when stars were at their brightest due to long nights and less humidity, her infatuation turned out to surpass his own.

Dinner in Paoli had lasted close to two hours, shedding more light on their past lives and future goals. At home, before adjusting the settings on the telescope, they sipped coffee and shared a slice of pumpkin pie Clint had bought at the store.

Through the telescope, they took turns viewing the moons of Jupiter. Time passed too quickly, and before they knew it, eleven o'clock had rolled around. They gathered their things and walked to the house, reluctant to bring the evening to a close.

"What time do you want me to come over tomorrow?" Jules asked in a sweet voice.

"I was thinking maybe around 2 p.m. We could grill out in the afternoon, and if you are still up to the challenge, afterward, we could write clues."

"Sounds like a plan," she agreed, remembering his unease with poem writing. "I'm not any better at rhyming words than you are," she said, hoping to make him feel better. "Two heads are always better than one." She touched his arm, "Hey, I could make my famous fudge. Do you like fudge?"

"Seriously, Jules? Who doesn't like fudge? Excellent, we'll make that our dessert. I have hamburger meat in the freezer, plus I can put foiled potatoes on the grill."

"All right! You'll see me at two," she said agreeably.

Clint opened the car door and helped Jules get inside. He felt naively optimistic about the future but a little dazzled by all the changes that had developed in his life over the last six months.

The next day at two o'clock sharp, Jules was standing on Clint's doorstep calling through the screened door. "Company's here!" She chuckled.

"Hey, hello," Clint called from the kitchen. He looked at his watch. "Right on time." He opened the door to allow Jules to scoot in with the bags she was carrying.

She placed a decorative tote on the kitchen table and unloaded three containers. She removed a covered nine-by-thirteen metal pan of fudge along with a container of chip dip. The third tub held the remainder of the sour cream that had not been compromised by garlic, cream cheese, or Hidden Valley Ranch dip mix.

"It's nice to have you here," said Clint. "I'm looking forward to the day. The party is just one week away, so I've got to get those clues done. Like you said, two heads are better than one," he laughed.

"All hands on deck," Jules joked. "The cavalry has arrived!"

They sat at the table conversing and eating potato chips and dip. Something to take the edge off until dinner.

"I think that is the best dip I've ever tasted," Clint said, finding it difficult to stop eating the creamy, rich concoction. Not wanting to appear like he was starving, he pushed the bowl closer to Jules. "Man, that stuff could become addictive!"

Jules, who had been shoveling it in as well, chortled. "Yeah, I know what you mean. I could make potato chips and dip the main meal."

They both got up from the table at the same time as she smiled.

"I'd like to show you what I've gathered so far," he said, humored by their timing. "The stash is in the barn." Inside, he led her over to the gray cabinet. Clint lined the gifts on the table and put the treasure chests out for display.

"What a haul!" Jules said enthusiastically. Then her face turned more serious. "Don't you think the boys could be a tad bit young for that?" she asked, pointing to the knife. "That thing looks lethal."

Chapter 16

Clint liked the fact that Jules would speak her mind so freely. "It is lethal," he replied without hesitation. "I want Trey to have it, but not until his dad feels he's responsible enough. I'm going to put it in a wooden or glass display case. One with a lock. The leather whip is for Dylan. Don't want him to feel left out. You know how boys are." The moment the words were out of his mouth, he regretted them. Jules would not know because she had lost her only child.

"I'm sorry, Jules. That was thoughtless of me," Clint said apologetically.

With a wave of her hand, Jules brushed the oversight off. "Never you mind, I've been around enough boys to know how they are about weapons. I have siblings and cousins, you know. When will you have the treasure chests ready? Before Saturday, I assume."

"Yes, I plan to fill them ahead of time. The more I have ready beforehand the better." Clint faltered before he asked the most pressing question of all—one he had been carrying on his shoulders for days. "Jules, I've been meaning to ask, would you like to join us next Saturday?"

She turned, surprised at what he had asked. "I'd love to join you, Clint. Do you think the family would be okay with it? There'd be a stranger in their midst," she said, supporting a broad smile.

"As a matter of fact, I talked to both boys this morning, and they said they'd love to meet you." A sheepish grin appeared on his face. "I confess, I've mentioned your name a time or two. I do believe you'll like my family, Jules. They are a friendly bunch."

"I'm excited. What can I bring? I refuse to show up empty-handed."

"Well, to start with, I'd love a repeat performance of that chip dip. And another pan of fudge. The entire family likes fudge, and yours is outstanding."

"Since it's a cookout, I may bring another surprise dish. One you haven't had."

Clint's eyes beamed with the idea of Jules cooking for the treasure hunt. "I want to show you the areas I plan to hide the treasure chests in before dark," he excitedly said. "There are three grandkids, so putting them all in the same location won't do."

"Where did you say you got the main gifts from?" Jules asked inquisitively, thinking how extraordinary they were.

"Oh… a bookstore in town, off the main drag."

Jules looked unsure where that could be and stated, "I didn't know we had a bookstore in Salzburg."

"Yeah, me neither," Clint responded quickly. "Not until last spring. Apparently, it's been there for ages."

"Really, I'll have to check it out. I love to read and really like wandering around in bookstores. It mustn't be too big of a place, or I would have known about it before now."

"It's not. As a matter of fact, you'd swear it was built a century ago. Reminds me of a general store. Constructed to appear old-fashioned, I imagine." Clint hesitated. "It's a really cool place with lots of uncommon things. Some of the candies I haven't seen since I was a kid, like Slo Poke suckers." He laughed. "Don't expect to be waited on. At least not in a hurry. It's a father and son operation, and they are as laid back as they come."

"Ok then, I won't set my sights too high, at least on customer service."

"Don't!" Clint joked, "If you do, I promise you'll be disappointed. But, if you like to read, they have an amazing assortment of books. Many extremely rare editions. Ones you'd never expect to find around here."

They walked toward the woods, and as they did, Clint explained how he had come in possession of such a superb piece of property.

Under an awning of forest trees, the atmosphere seemed to change. Jules sensed a faint melody carried through a gentle breeze. "This place is enchanting," she asserted, trailing behind Clint through the decomposing underbrush of vegetation. They skillfully mastered fallen branches and shrubs as they progressed

Chapter 16

deeper along the path. "It's picturesque, like something you'd see in *National Geographic*."

Clint turned. "That's what I thought when I first ventured in. A perfect place to hide treasure. Wouldn't you say? If I time it right, the kids will start reading the clues around dusk." Clint raised a brow. "It will be considerably darker inside the woods, but enough light left in the day to find their treasure chests before nightfall. I want them to feel like they are hunting for real treasure."

"Sounds like a blast!" Jules responded. "You say you've done this sort of thing before?"

"You bet! Several times when I lived in Seymour when the boys were just little tykes and even once when the grandchildren were young. This will be my first event to host here. I doubt Lily, Dylan, or Trey remember the last one we had up that way, but they certainly have heard about the hunts from Wade, Rusty, and the girls. Everyone is super excited. Sorry to say, I have not had any get-togethers for a long time. Not since Elise. Family outings are important, so I will definitely be having more."

When they reached the clearing where Clint planned to hide the chests, Jules asked, "How far into these woods have you explored?"

"No further than here," Clint answered, thinking of the first time he encountered the area and how unsettling it had been. He gave a slight chuckle. "The previous time I was here, it almost felt haunted."

Jules' eyes widened. She had ignored a sensation she had experienced earlier, upon entering the forest when she'd detected an interesting vibe. "It's funny you would say that because it has a completely different feel back here as opposed to in the yard or up by the house. It's almost as if we entered another dimension. Like people resided on these grounds at some point, and their energies have remained behind." She shrugged with a girlish gaze. "You up for some exploring?"

Clint had it in his head clue-writing would follow their excursion. Reluctant to dampen Jules' sense of adventure, he replied, "Sure!"

Clues can be done another day, he reminded himself.

"Maybe we'll find other great spots to hide clues," Jules called out excitedly as she took off in the opposite direction.

They had not gone far when Clint spotted an outhouse. Shocked by its presence, he remarked, "Didn't expect to see that. You're right. Sometime in the past, someone must have lived here. Interesting." He looked to Jules, wondering how she was able to pick up on such a thing. "You didn't tell me you were psychic."

"Didn't know it myself until now," she chuckled. "a pretty good guess, huh?"

"I'd say. Let's check it out."

Clint and Jules could tell by the barbed wire fence they happened upon that at some point, a person, or persons, indeed took up residence on this parcel of land. A tin plate lay on the ground along with a wrought iron chisel and wooden mallet, which made no sense to Clint. A pitchfork, hammer, or ax he would have understood, even a saw, but those items seemed odd, especially since there didn't see any furniture or items where woodworking would be involved.

They had walked the area only briefly before Clint admitted he was ready to turn around. "I'm getting hungry. Maybe we should head back." He said in the way of a question. He reached out for her hand, which she gave freely.

Jules' heart skipped a beat. He had not done that before. "I'm hungry too," she admitted. "I think we've explored enough. Plus, we have clues to write. If you fire up the grill, I will put some verses on paper."

Jules' words were music to Clint's ears. That meant she planned to stay longer than he had expected and would start the process of clue writing. "You're on!" He agreed eagerly.

Chapter 17
The Unobserved

The evening passed pleasantly. Under the stars, for a second night, they discussed the mysteries of the universe and life in general until finally, Jules had to call it a night.

"I hate to mention it," she reluctantly said, "but I'd better be getting home… 5:30 a.m. rolls around way too soon." She stood. "I've had a wonderful time. And those steaks were out of this world. You sure know how to grill the perfect sirloin."

Clint beamed with pride. "Thank ya, ma'am! My pleasure!"

A smile crept onto her face. "Tackling the lion's share of the clues should be a relief. Only three days before your big event. The last couple of clues leading up to the finale I left for you."

"Great, I can handle that!" He flashed a sheepish grin knowing she had done the bulk of the work. Time sure seems to fly. Doesn't it? The older I get, the faster it evaporates!" The corners of his mouth turned up. "These last few months have zipped by. Last spring, the treasure hunt felt like forever away, and now here it is."

They walked to her car. Before she got in, Clint leaned in and gently kissed her on the cheek. "It was a great day, Jules. Thank you for coming into my world. It's a brighter place because of you."

Jules almost cried. "Clint, I feel the same way. I was so lonely until I met you. Two wayward souls drifting in this sea called life." Her eyes twinkled. "Thanks for inviting me to the party. I'm really looking forward to it and to meeting your family."

As she vanished into the darkness at the end of the street, he waved a final goodbye before heading back indoors. He gathered the few unwashed dishes sitting about and placed them into the sink. They could wait until morning. Before turning in, Clint intended to finish his book, *Bid Time Return*. It had been such a pleasurable evening he wanted to squeeze every second from it before calling it a night. A cup of decaf in the living room at the end of an idyllic day was the proverbial "cat's meow."

However, when he went to the foyer to hang his jacket on the hall tree, a noise generated from the back part of the house caught his attention. He looked down the hallway, past the arched entryway where he was standing.

Assuming something had fallen, Clint started for the back part of the house to see what had caused the noise. As he passed the mirror, his attention was arrested as he registered a glint on his left side. Stopping on a dime, he backpedaled.

Startled by another flicker of movement, Clint peered hard into the antique mirror but saw nothing other than his own reflection. Then he spotted a faint wraithlike substance, standing behind his right shoulder and did an immediate about-face.

He had stopped resisting what he had come to accept as fact. Utterly convinced a presence followed his every move, of late, the entity seemed more engaged and insistent on making itself known. With each passing day, that realization of likelihood had put Clint on guard. Prior to this event, he was of the mindset he could be behaving immaturely and a wee bit delusional. That presumption was now debatable.

He decided the sound had come from outdoors. Clint stepped out onto the porch. Everything appeared perfectly normal. Did he dare act on his instinct, which was to investigate further? Without being baited by some abnormality, Clint decided to check the barn. Never did it cross his mind that to proceed on an impulse—inspired by an anomaly—was unwise.

He moved across the lawn until the barn door latch was at his fingertips. He walked through to the inner space where he scanned for anything out of place. With great care, he inspected each dark gap and recess. Nothing remarkable stood out. Everything was as it should be.

When he unlocked the gray cabinet doors, Clint expected the same, but upon repositioning the various gifts, something felt off-kilter. Unable to pinpoint what it was, he stepped away. Then he saw the blade on the shelf above where the other treasures were

Chapter 17

gathered. The initials, F.R., instantly grabbed his attention. The Bowie knife had been taken from its sheath and laid onto a different shelf.

Lifting the knife from the shelf, Clint struggled to recall if he had put the weapon in its proper place after showing it to Jules when they were in the barn earlier. He felt positive he had not left it out and carelessly exposed!

Clint shut his eyes, trying to recall. *Could I have failed to lay it with the other things?* He had a hard time believing that he had been that negligent, yet it appeared that he had been.

When he closed the door behind him, the sound he had heard that originated from the bedroom or mudroom area came to mind. On the way back inside to investigate, he told himself repeatedly that he was dramatizing events. Things like ghosts and hauntings did not exist. Always the skeptic, his eyes simply had to be playing tricks on him.

"There must be a logical explanation for these things," Clint said aloud as he hastily retreated indoors.

In the foyer, looking at the mirror, he oscillated back to his original opinion of it. That the materials used to make the exquisite antique were inferior. A more reasonable explanation for why he kept thinking a figure was seen in its reflection. It was not a *someone* he was catching a glimpse of, after all, but more likely an imperfection in how the glass was fashioned.

For a moment, he considered taking it to the pole barn but then thought better of it, not wanting to pacify his fears. Besides, he enjoyed the statement it portrayed when people entered the house. It was a classy addition to his décor, one that had not previously been present.

Clint walked down the hall to the bedroom. Curious about the noise, he checked the mudroom first to make certain nothing had fallen from one of the shelves. Nothing of consequence was detected. That was not the case when he entered the bedroom.

Scattered on the floor next to the bed, he caught sight of the clues Jules had prepared for the party, the ones he had stacked on the table to reread when he got into bed. A marble he kept on the bedstand, saved from his childhood, was also on the floor.

What the heck, thought Clint, surprised at what he was looking at. *How did those get down there? Like that?*

When he bent down to pick the clues up from the floor to put them back in order, a frown appeared on his face. He glanced at the window and saw it was cracked a smidgeon. *Okay, now it makes sense*, he reconciled with a sense of relief. *A gust of wind must have blown them all off the table.*

He scratched his skull, fed up with assuming every time something strange happened, a sinister motive fueled it. It was like borrowing trouble. *I've managed to turn a perfectly fantastic day into a fiasco.*

"Enough!" Clint yelled, throwing his ballpoint pen onto the mattress. He felt disgusted with himself for attempting to sabotage his own happiness. "Let it go, for God's sake! She's not here hanging around expressing her displeasure with me. Elise is gone!"

Clint covered his eyes with the palms of his hands. From the depth of his being, tears formed and flowed. Afraid he could be mistaken, and Elise was trying to make contact to express her displeasure, Clint reminded himself, *it is our hous*e! Although consensus, in general, stated paranormal events were nonexistent, his personal resolve was starting to crumble, and think otherwise.

Taking a deep breath, he said, "I need a drink!"

Back to the kitchen, he went with the intention of mixing Crown Royal in a small amount of soda. This situation called for something stronger than decaf coffee. *Whiskey will dull my troubled mind*, his inner chatter promised.

With a drink in hand, he reentered the living room ready to pick up where he had left off in the book. Except the book was not on the table where he expected to find it. Initially, he assumed he

Chapter 17

had carried it someplace else, set it down, and forgot to put it back. But then, to his surprise, he saw it beside the chair, open with the pages exposed. His bookmark lay beside it as though it had been thrown to the floor.

Clint could not believe his eyes. *How did that happen?* he questioned himself, not remembering having dropped it. If he had, he knew he would have picked it up. Confusion ricocheted through his thoughts as his stomach knotted. Then his eyes traveled the length of the room. It had to be Elise.

With tears in his eyes, he cried, "What do you want from me?"

Attempting to come to grips with his emotions, Clint raised the book from the floor and placed it on the table, thinking maybe, just maybe, it was the sound he had heard earlier in the evening. Not a noise that had originated from the bedroom or from outside, but instead, from the living room.

How could it have fallen off the table? Clint posed, feeling desperate for answers. *I must have set it too close to the edge. With the door being opened and closed so often today, that must have caused it to vibrate and topple over the side.*

Several scenarios played out in his mind as he tried to determine how the sequence of events might have unfolded. Once again, he settled on natural causes rather than otherworldly interference. Thinking otherwise would not be conducive to a restful night's sleep. No way was he was going to let his imagination run amok any more than it already had.

On his way to bed, he sipped more whiskey. Determined to finish *Bid Time Return*, he tossed the book onto the bed and got undressed. He slid beneath the covers and let the whiskey do its job.

Thursday, September 11

In the light of day, clarity of mind resurfaced. Last night was a tough one, but without question it wasn't his worst since Elise has passed. He'd had been many such nights. No doubt his discombobulated evening was tied to harboring guilty feelings over the kiss. The truth of it was, considering the misgivings he experienced afterward, he should have anticipated this.

For Clint, the impulse of displayed affection had been a monumental step in moving forward. The kiss was not a decision he had taken lightly. The sickening feeling that he had cheated on his deceased wife afterward, however, was disheartening. He supposed he would have to get used to the feeling. After thinking about it, he bet most widowers felt that way, at least until the newness of seeing someone else eventually wore off. Sooner or later, he trusted, the ghastly feeling of shame would dissipate.

Just be patient, Clint commiserated with his rational self. *Nothing changes overnight.*

He considered stopping by Rod's place to scan a few self-help books on how to cope with grief. Then the thought crossed his mind how embarrassed he would feel to put a book with that kind of subject title on the counter and then pay for it. Exposing his weakness didn't feel masculine.

No, I'll get it online. Find a forum to see how other widowers cope. Find out if anyone else has encountered the sorts of things I'm going through with seeing and hearing things that aren't there. Clint made a face. *Misery enjoys company*, he thought humorlessly.

Chapter 18
A Bad Omen
Friday, September 12

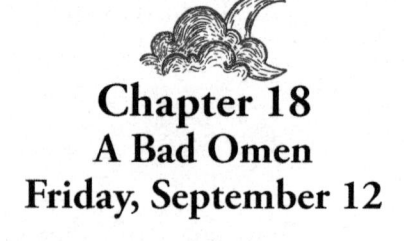

"So, did you ask about getting off early on Saturday the 20th?" Clint asked Jules as he took a swallow of his coffee.

Jules was smiling as she sat Clint's breakfast plate on the tabletop. "Yeah, Patrick said no problem. Sophie, our part-time girl, wants more hours anyhow. He didn't seem too bothered, but he did ask why I wanted off. I told him it was to join you and your family at the treasure hunt."

"Patrick liked the idea of a treasure hunt when I explained what I was doing," Clint inserted. "He wants my family to stop in before leaving town. Said breakfast was on him."

On Jules' face, Clint detected a question. "What's up?" he asked.

Jules replied, "Am I that transparent?" She laughed.

"I guess so." Clint shrugged. "I can see your wheels turning."

"Okay." Jules tossed her hands into the air. "Are we still on for this evening? If so, I have a surprise. Something you are going to get a big kick out of."

Clint's spirits skyrocketed. He could not remember the last time he had received a gift from a girl. "As far as I'm concerned, yes. Dinner at my place? Seven o'clock? Or is that too early?"

"I get off at six, so that works perfectly."

Clint responded enthusiastically, "I look forward to it."

"I'll bring dessert," she stated. "Patrick says we're going to start carrying cheesecake. Dillon's delivered a bunch of them this morning. I'll bring a slice of praline and Napoleon. We also have strawberry and carrot cake. Do any of those sound interesting? Do you even like cheesecake?"

"I love cheesecake," Clint answered, relishing the conversation. "I'll take a slice of carrot cake, thank you very much."

A Bad Omen

Clint felt like he was walking on air when he left the restaurant. The day was shaping up to be a good one. He had several things to do before Jules came over, so he went straight home, never giving a visit to the bookstore a second thought. With consistent cooler weather these days, he could build a roaring fire and not fret about the house getting too warm.

During an afternoon break, Clint enjoyed a half-smoke on his front porch while contemplating life. One thing he desperately wanted to do was stop smoking. Even though Jules had not said one word, he felt it was something he needed to do both for her and his health.

Life is good, despite my crazy pea brain antics. The boys and their families will be up in Crothersville a week from Friday, he reminded himself, *I'll drive up and take them all out to dinner at a nice restaurant. Knowing Wade, he will pick Cracker Barrel.* Clint smiled at the prospect.

When they came to Indiana, Wade, Clara, and Lily typically arranged to stay with Rusty and Molly in Crothersville. A few miles south of where Elise and Clint had once lived. Clara had expressed to Clint the grandchildren were really looking forward to seeing one another again and simply could not wait for the treasure hunt on Saturday. They were extremely excited and nearly bursting at the seams. It had been Thanksgiving a year ago since everyone had gathered.

Unfortunately, a sadness still existed when the family reunited. Like a heavy cloud hanging over them, things just were not the same. Clint was under no illusion, believing himself to be a good father but incapable of filling Elise's shoes.

This was Clint's first time to invite the kids to the house since Elise's funeral six years ago. Overdue for a pleasant get-together, Clint was anxious about introducing everyone to his new friend. Excited and nervous at the same time, he could not imagine how it was going to feel to have Jules here with his family—a stranger in the group. Nothing about that scenario felt natural.

Chapter 18

He dropped the first of the half-smoked cigarette into his front pant pocket. He had things to attend to, and they weren't going to take care of themselves. Most of his chores pertaining to the treasure hunt were completed. All he had to do now was to bury the treasures in their hiding places. He had been looked forward to this last phase of the setup.

Dinnertime was approaching, and Jules was due at seven. A pot of chili with spaghetti was warming on the stove, and a salad in the refrigerator was ready to be served. Of late, Clint had become quite the chef. Proud of his newfound talent, he had ventured beyond Elise's recipe file to the *Food Network* website on the internet.

Tomorrow night, according to Jules, they would have dinner at her place. At the diner that morning, she had mentioned a surprise. All day he had been anticipating what it could be.

He had burned the trash and hauled logs to the bin next to the woodstove. The box was ready to light. Clint felt proud of the improvements he had made around the house. The autumn air was refreshing, filling the house with a cool breeze. The smell of chili wafted through the rooms creating a homey atmosphere.

When Jules knocked on the door, music was playing in the living room, and the table was set.

"Hey, good to see you. Right on time, as always."

"Yeah, I have a thing about being punctual."

"Come on in!"

Jules unloaded a plastic bag onto the table. Withdrawing four slices of cheesecake, she declared, "Since your eyes lit up each time I mentioned a flavor, I went ahead and got us four of what I thought were the best ones." She folded the bag and put the boxes in the refrigerator, and then she reached inside a second bag and pulled out a video. "And, this is your surprise," she said, handing it to him.

"A video, great. So, we are watching a movie after dinner. Super! Which one is it?" he inquired.

A Bad Omen

"I'm not telling. That part is the surprise." The video was face down on the table covered by her purse. "I'll show you after we eat."

With smiling eyes, Clint replied, "Okay! So, let's eat! I tried my hand at chili. You will have to be the judge of how well I did. And, if you don't keel over afterward, I guess we can call this—*dinner and a movie*—like that program on television."

During dinner, they went over the menu and plans for a week from Saturday. She would show up ahead of the family to help set up. Her things would be dropped off Friday night while he was in Seymour having dinner with his kids.

After dinner, the two friends sat on the porch eating cheesecake and drinking coffee. They took turns recapping their day as the sunset behind the trees. Early evening stars and Venus, followed by Jupiter, had poked through the disguise that divided day from night when they finally decided to come indoors. The sounds of night filled their senses. A herd of deer had crossed the outer edge of the property, and they saw a red-tailed fox trotting across the driveway.

"Okay, Clint, you go find a seat, and I'll get the movie," Jules announced excitedly. "You are going to like this one. I guarantee. I can't wait to see your face!"

Clint headed for the living room where he lit the fire and took a seat, as instructed. Waiting for Jules to return from the restroom, he crossed his long legs and folded his arms behind his head. He couldn't remember when he had been this happy. At least not in a half-decade.

Jules joined him in the living room. She handed him the movie, *Somewhere in Time*.

Clint's breath caught in his chest. He could feel the walls closing in around him. His stomach knotted, and his face turned pale.

"What's wrong?" Jules asked, alarmed at the look she saw on his face.

Chapter 18

Trying to escape the terror that welled inside. "Nothing, Jules. I was thinking about something I had forgotten to put away in the barn. I left the Bowie knife on the shelf and forgot to put it back," he lied thinking back to yesterday. "It'll only take a minute." He stood and almost ran to the door.

Eyes wide, she replied, "I swear you look like you just saw a ghost!" She jokingly laughed but felt mystified by Clint's strange change in behavior. "Do you want me to walk with you?"

"Oh, no, that's okay. It won't take a minute. I'll be back in a jiffy." Clint was out the door before Jules could add another word.

Outside, his mind whirled. What was he going to do? Did he dare watch a movie based on the book *Bid Time Return*? This was the movie Rod had described, based on the book he had just finished reading. *Elise's favorite book.*

He could not recall ever mentioning the story or book to Jules and found it disturbingly coincidental that she would bring that specific movie over for *them* to watch, not knowing he had the original story in his bedroom.

Uncertain how to digest what had just happened, Clint stayed longer in the barn than expected. No way could he sit beside Jules and watch a movie based on a book Elise had asked him to read. He'd finished the book three days prior and placed it on the nightstand. In his mind, he could see it lying there.

After about five minutes he returned, still confused about how he should handle the situation. By no means would he tell Jules the truth. He tried to be honest with her, but not on this matter. The less she knew, the better.

He walked into the living room to find Jules standing by the window. She didn't turn when he came up to her. "Sorry it took a little longer than expected," he lied for a second time. "I'm not big on leaving my tools out. Habit I guess."

She turned to face him as he walked through the door, searching his eyes for the truth. "Are you sure you're okay? Honestly, Clint you are acting like something is wrong. Maybe it's my imagination, but I think I know you well enough by now to recognize when something is bothering you."

"No, no… I'm fine, really. Please excuse my rudeness. I got distracted in the barn plus I was upset with myself for not putting the knife away. That's how accidents happen."

"I see," she said suspiciously, not sure she really believed what he was saying. Although she couldn't explain why whatever had happened seemed major.

"Hey, let's get started," Clint suggested, feeling he had no other choice but to watch it with her. Otherwise he would have to explain why he didn't want to, and he wasn't going down that rabbit hole. "Is this a movie you particularly like?"

"I don't know," she hesitantly replied. "I haven't seen it, but you said a couple of weeks ago you were reading a book about time travel. This story is about a guy who goes back in time to meet an actress. He sees her picture in a hotel and can't explain why he believes he knows her. He becomes obsessed with her picture. That is all I know."

Clint's heart skipped a beat. "Really? That sounds intriguing."

Jules grinned. "Hopefully, it'll be worth watching. I don't know anyone who has seen it, though. But I can say, it came highly recommended."

"What do you mean?" Clint asked as trepidation filled his thoughts.

"It was the oddest thing. The other day I was talking to Patrick and I mentioned something about coming over here this evening. Said I wanted to pick up a movie for us to watch. I told him you liked sci-fi."

Her brows drew together. "There was this guy at the counter that apparently overheard our conversation. He insisted, *Somewhere in Time* was an excellent choice. '*The perfect choice*,' in fact. Those were his exact words. He said he had a copy at his shop. That he'd drop it by later that day. I must admit, he was a curious sort of fella. Terribly skinny!"

Chapter 18

Clint held a poker face as he tried to process the narrative Jules had just delivered. He was in all-out shock that a stranger might have brought this exact movie up in a conversation and then recommend it. Other than Rod at the bookstore, no one had ever spoken of *Somewhere in Time* before. And, to his alarm, the man's description sounded eerily like Rod Sr.'s.

"Did he say where his shop was located?" Clint asked in a controlled voice.

"No, not really and I was too busy to stick around to chat. A nice fellow, though. Wore one of those old-time straw fedoras. You know, the kind you see in the 1940s."

With trembling hands, Clint inserted the video into the player, not knowing if he should tell the truth about his situation. He sat down and started the movie.

"Thanks for bringing a movie over tonight, Jules."

She relaxed, but he did not. The lights were turned low. Clint was relieved because he did not have to hide his shock. They waited. The movie started. The music score filled the room, a hauntingly beautiful composition.

Christopher Reeve, playing the role of Richard Collier, came onto the screen. The scene was an opening night celebration of Collier's first successful play in college. An old woman approached him. Dressed in black, she laid her hand on his mid-back. When he turned, visibly surprised, she wrapped a pocket watch in his hand and said, "*Come back to me.*"

The video suddenly stopped playing. Clint's face turned ashen when the screen went blank. The movie, replaced by wavy horizontal lines squiggling in all directions, flickered across the screen. The player had malfunctioned.

"Oh no!" Jules said, visibly upset. "What happened?"

Clint jumped to his feet and rapidly ran over to eject the movie. "Not a good sign!" he mumbled with relief.

Turning to Jules, he apologized. "Sorry, Jules! Guess it wasn't meant to be."

Chapter 19
A Need to Step Back

Jules wandered up and down the sidewalks trying to find the shop where the old man worked. Salzburg did not have a ton of retail shops, so she assumed it would be an easy task to return the video at lunchtime.

She was looking for a place that sold or rented DVDs. The nice gentleman she had met had to work close by, she speculated, because of the short amount of time it had taken him to return to Josie's with the movie. It was almost instantaneous.

"I can't imagine where this store is," Jules complained as she crossed the street, feeling confused with the lack of options.

The movie was damaged, and she felt terrible. She tried to rack her brain if she might have caused the damage somehow but came up empty-handed. She simply could not account for any such mishap.

Unless it was a rental, she reasoned, *and was damaged by the people who rented it before me.* Jules considered the possibility. *I will simply tell the man the truth and hope he believes me.*

Earlier in the day, when Jules told her boss about what had happened and asked if he by chance recognized the man that had given her the movie, Patrick confessed he did not. He had no idea who the man was.

"Haven't seen him before," Patrick claimed.

With her half-hour lunch ending, Jules returned to the diner, mulling over what to do next. Then, it registered. *Maybe the video came from that bookstore Clint had mentioned. Off one of these side streets in town.*

She gazed out the window and wondered if she had not gone far enough. She had not come across anything that fit that description while strolling through town but figured maybe she had yet to amble down the right street. Clint had told her the store was off the main drag.

Chapter 19

I'll check with him when he calls, she told herself. *Get the exact location and stop by tomorrow.*

At the diner, before returning to work, the events from the evening before replayed in her mind, and a persistent feeling loomed. Clint was rattled but didn't want to admit it. She saw uneasiness in his eyes when he came in from the barn.

A sickening feeling bubbled up from deep inside. *Could the way he acted have been related to me? Maybe he feels we are moving too fast,* Jules reflected when she noticed him walk through the door. *Been seeing a lot of each other lately.*

Jules stood at the counter holding back the floodgates. Afraid her insights could be justified, she thought about her late husband, James, and wondered what he would say if he knew what was going on. That she was seeing Clint on a regular basis. The whole idea of her having a relationship with someone other than James seemed preposterous, yet that was exactly what was going on.

Until this very moment, she had imagined James as giving his blessings, but now she was no longer convinced. The thought crossed her mind that Clint was having second thoughts as well. Not a surprise. Maybe they both were.

After the treasure hunt, she chastised herself, *I'll pull back. Take a break to give us both some breathing room.*

The evening at Jules place went along smoothly, yet a cloud hung in the air. Clint was not his jovial self, but neither was Jules. Words were left unspoken and feelings ignored. They both knew it. Niceties were exchanged, but something huge was absent. Warmth.

Over a bowl of chicken and noodles, Jules asked one question she could not dodge. "Where did you say that bookstore is located?"

"It's off main, why?" Clint studied her face wondering why she was asking.

"I need to return the movie and suspect it might have come from there. I want to thank the kind man who loaned it to me but also advise him about the damage. What did you say the name of the place is?"

"Rod's New and Used Books. Not far from Main, at the intersection of Ridge Crest and Grandview you take a left."

Clint's guess was the video had originated from that location as well. Especially since Rod, Jr. had broached the subject, pointing out the connection between the book and the movie on one of his visits to the bookstore. He wanted so badly to tell her about their conversation but decided not to.

"How funny! I swear I glanced that way. Didn't see any shops, though." Jules tried to recall her steps but came up blank. "I'll try again tomorrow."

Clint chuckled jovially, shaking his head and remembering what it was like the first day he ventured down that way. "Don't give up. When I went that direction, it looked like a mirage." His face brightened as he began using his hands to describe his experience.

"Because of the way the light camouflaged it, the building appeared to be situated at a strange angle. Look for the footpath at the end of the sidewalk on Grandview. I know that sounds odd, but so is the store." Clint laughed nervously. "You'll be surprised. I guarantee. The place is like a walk down memory lane into the past. I feel certain that's where your video originated."

The moment the last words slipped off his tongue, Clint flinched. *Better change the subject,* he thought, not wanting to get into a discussion about the movie. "Was it busy at Josie's today?" he asked pleasantly, trying to redirect the conversation.

Jules searched his eyes. With great effort, she held his stare, thinking, *Since when did we get into small talk?*

"Yeah, pretty busy," she replied, not sure what to add. "A typical day."

Chapter 19

A heavy silence hung over them as they ate their meals. Finally, Clint brought up a topic he wanted to clarify. "So next Saturday, you're planning on being here before the gang arrives, correct? And bringing some things over beforehand next Friday. I could use your help with hiding the clues and setting up. Want to help me with that?"

"Yeah, if you still want me to," Jules replied. "Wasn't sure how much you planned to have done in advance."

"Oh, there will be plenty to do. I assure you." Clint reached across the table and took her hand. Instantly he felt a connection. He had noticed a sadness in Jules eyes that gave him reason to ponder, but he chose not to ask, figuring if she wanted to tell him what was on her mind, she would.

Jules smiled. "Will 9 a.m. be too early?"

"No, that'll work fine. It'd be nice to sleep in a bit." He laughed, knowing the chances of him sleeping in, with so much going on, was next to impossible. "Especially since I know I'll be up late that night."

Clint gathered the plates from the table and put them into the sink. "I'd be happy to come and get you," he said with a turn of his head. "We could talk afterward. Get your thoughts on the party and the kids."

More confused than ever, Jules nodded in agreement. "That would be nice."

The remainder of the evening was pleasant but cut short when Clint announced he had things to do before turning in. It sounded like an excuse to Jules, but no way was she going to pry and ask what they were. At the counter, she packed a small container of chicken and noodles and told Clint it was for tomorrow's lunch or dinner. Neither brought up seeing one another.

Jules tossed out, "Randy asked me to come visit tomorrow."

Clint stared into her green eyes. A wall had been building between them, and he sensed it. "I bet you'll enjoy that. It's been some time since you mentioned them."

A darkness fell over her when it appeared Clint seemed glad. "It has been."

"Give me a call when you return," Clint commented in an upbeat tone. "Being Sunday, I have a lot to do around here. Plus, I need to run into town to pick up a few last-minute supplies for the party, along with stopping by Ace Hardware for extra lawn chairs and another small folding table. Clint manufactured excuses for visiting the old-fashioned hardware every chance he got.

"Ace is only open from noon to six tomorrow." Clint fell silent then said, "Maybe we could hook up midweek on your day off. If not, we'll be seeing each other at the diner."

Jules walked to the refrigerator and put the remainder of the leftover meal onto the shelf. With her back to him, she said, "Will do." In her heart, she believed her suspicions had been confirmed. Clint was not the same person as before. What had gone wrong, she had no idea, but something had.

When the front door latched, and she heard the truck driving away, she cried. She felt hurt and angry at letting her guard down so soon, and her misery was written on her face. *Why would you let yourself get personally invested like that? Julie! How could you?*

When Clint climbed into the F-100, he put his head on the steering wheel. The night had not gone well. He was not able to identify what had gone wrong, but he knew something had. His best guess was it had to do with Monday night and the aftermath of the movie debacle. In his view, she had been evasive since that night.

Got to let it go, he said in his mind. *A bad idea to start seeing her one-on-one like that. How do we backtrack now? Return to being friends? That never works.*

To that, Clint had no answer.

Chapter 19

Friday, September 19

At 11 a.m. Clint got the call. The plane had landed. Wade, Clara, and Lily, after collecting their luggage, and picking up their rental car, would head to Rusty's farm.

The Camaro was packed and ready to fire up. He looked forward to the long drive to Crothersville. Just him and his emotions battling it out over how to proceed with his life. Everything had turned topsy-turvy since the movie malfunction ordeal.

That same night, after Jules went home, he felt haunted by his late wife's memory. He hated to admit it, but he wholeheartedly believed, more than ever, Elise was sending him strong messages. She had caused the video to fail. There was no other explanation.

No way was Elise going to allow me to watch Somewhere in Time *with Jules,* he told himself.

Last night's dream was an unsettling issue as well. The old man in the straw hat, of all things, was in it. Clint felt certain that Rod, Sr. had most likely given the movie to Jules. At the edge of Clint's dream, the old man stood, gesturing to Clint to follow him into the forest. There was an urgency to his plea. Clint was reluctant. The man's boney finger pointed at the dark forest.

There were different stages and facets to the dream, but none made any sense. At one point, Clint was standing at the clearing with the moon shimmering through the trees. The next frame had him digging in the ground at the place Jules and he had stumbled upon at the beginning of the week.

Through a lens of disorientation, Clint caught sight of a shack sitting off in the distance behind the barbed wire fence they had discovered. A dim light radiated from within the structure, and a dark figure stood at the door.

Clint had awoken abruptly. Sitting on the side of the bed, he stared at the wall wondering why he would dream something so fantastical. Thinking the man in the straw hat had somehow transformed into someone else—a person Clint remembered from his distant past or maybe the orphanage—he tried to put the disturbing dream out of his mind. He got dressed. During the day, however, the dream frequently resurfaced. Although he was unable to pinpoint why he felt as he did, the dream had the earmark of a memory stashed deep in his subconscious, as though a long-ago incident was trying to break through.

Before leaving his house, Clint dialed Jules. She seemed reserved, but he reckoned that could have been a result of being at the diner, making it difficult for her to speak freely. Only one two-hour lunch had been discussed. They made plans to drive to Paoli for pizza on Wednesday.

Clint could feel the strain building between them. He was convinced having downtime would provide perspective on if they should continue to see one another as frequently as they had been. He was equally convinced they had moved too quickly into a relationship.

He estimated his arrival time back home to be around ten or eleven. In other words, they would not be seeing one another again tonight. He had plans to take the family to Cracker Barrel in Seymour for dinner. After that, they would all hang out at Rusty and Molly's for a visit before heading south.

He told Jules she was welcome to bring her things over whenever convenient. She said she would. He was looking forward to Saturday and all the hubbub. The only *fly in the ointment* was Jules, and he appeared to be on shaky ground. Introducing her to his family felt like a huge mistake, but at this late date, he couldn't withdraw the invitation.

The hour it took to arrive at the restaurant on I-65 was just what Clint needed to clear his head. The windows were down when he pulled into the parking lot. Immediately the family, sitting outside on the rockers, jumped up to greet him. The grandchildren came running into his arms for hugs.

When Clint neared, Rusty was the first to speak. "Hey, look what the wind blew in? I can't believe you are driving the Camaro.

Chapter 19

Very nice!" Everyone laughed, including Clint, aware this was a *new Dad* they were talking to.

"Yeah, it was time. Gary wouldn't want his car turned into a rust bucket."

Trey and Dylan clung to Clint's waist. "We missed you, Grandpa! Can't wait until tomorrow."

"My goodness you boys have grown!" Clint rested his hand on their heads.

"Grandpa," screamed Lily when she turned the corner. She had gone inside to use the restroom.

Lily squeezed Clint's side. She had grown into a lovely young lady. Her long, strawberry blonde hair made her appear older than she was. Her fifteen years looked more like twenty. Her blue eyes reminded Clint of her grandmother. Long eyelashes were highlighted by sapphire eyeliner. She was wearing a stylish jean jacket and leather cowboy boots. Clint had to laugh. Lily favored Elise in more than her eyes and hair. No taller than the last time he saw her, she stood at five feet.

Trey had grown a half foot in the year since they were all together on Thanksgiving 2002. Dylan was close to the same size. He, too, had grown.

Everyone headed indoors when the overhead speaker announced: "Reeves, party of eight, your table is now ready."

At the table, amongst the chatter and activity, the family caught up on Wade, Clara, and Lily's lives in Flathead Lake, Montana, while Rusty, Molly, Trey and Dylan updated everyone about farm operations in Crothersville, Indiana.

Clint described to the family the improvements he had made around the house and professed he believed Elise would have been pleased with the efforts he had exerted to improve the house and property.

Wade instantly inserted, "Dad, she knows!"

Clint would have to agree.

"Tell us about the party tomorrow," Dylan said excitedly.

"It's a treasure hunt, young man. With real treasure! What more can I say?" replied Clint with a glint in his eye. "You *pirates* better have your thinking caps on."

"When do you want us to show up, Dad?" Wade asked. "I thought we would hit the road about 9 a.m. if that works. That would put us there a little after ten."

Immediately Jules entered Clint's mind. They had agreed that she would come over at 9 a.m. Perhaps he should call her and ask her to come sooner. Especially if everyone was going to be there earlier than planned.

"I'm okay with whatever time suits you kids. I'm home all day. But I will say, I'm hiding clues in the morning, and I don't want anyone watching me! So how about eleven? That will give me plenty of time to hide treasure and the clues before you get there. I'll have you boys help me set the tables up. Believe me, there will be plenty to do."

"Sounds good to me," agreed Wade.

Rusty concurred, grinning. "We can take our time in the morning. Maybe stop by here again for breakfast."

Wade injected his observation. "Don't have a Cracker Barrel anywhere close to Flathead Lake. I crave their homemade southern food. It's like Mom used to make." Everyone laughed, aware that his testimonial was spot on.

Clint took a deep breath, relieved the boys would be at the house after Jules got there. He wanted to have a little extra time with her before the family arrived.

"Okay, then! Eleven o'clock it is," said Clint. "Just so everyone knows, unlike the treasure hunts when you were little," he looked at his boys. "This one won't start until dusk. The cookout will come first. We'll play some games before the hunt, too if you wish."

They finished dinner and drove to the farm. The children played outdoors. The parents gathered at the table. Molly had baked a

Chapter 19

German chocolate cake for an afternoon treat. Everyone was talked out when Clint got to his feet and announced he was going home.

"See everyone tomorrow," he said as he went to the kitchen to collect his things. "I'm really looking forward to having you kids back at the house again. This time under better circumstances."

Molly made an offer. "Are you sure you don't want to hang out for a while longer? I have a fresh ham I sliced this morning. We could share some finger food, cheese on crackers, potato chips and dip, plus I'd be happy to fry up some ham and Swiss sandwiches."

Although tempting, Clint declined the invitation. "Sounds wonderful, but I want to hit the road before it gets any later. Nighttime driving is a little more challenging than it used to be."

Standing by the car, he said, "See you kids tomorrow!" As Clint pulled out of the drive, everyone waved.

On his way home, he wondered if Jules had made time to stop by with foods she had prepared in advance: fudge, baked beans, chip dip, and macaroni and cheese. He had purchased chips, salsa, hot dogs, hamburger meat, and condiments. Plus, the drinks and ice for the coolers.

He had to have a heart-to-heart talk with Jules and tell her the truth of what had been going on with him and why he was so spooked when the movie stopped playing.

If it wasn't too late when he got home, he'd phone.

Chapter 20
Pearls of Truth

The house was eerily quiet when she stepped through the door. She was met by a fresh breeze as she leaned the umbrella she carried against the coat rack and set her purse on the floor. The weatherman had forecasted light showers by early evening, so Jules had come prepared.

"The key is under the second rock, closest to the house, left of the porch," Clint had advised her the night before.

Being alone in Clint's house felt weird, despite the fact he had told her to let herself in. To be in someone else's home without them there gave the impression of snooping or breaking and entering.

A quick trip, in and out, was the plan. *Be here no longer than necessary*, she reminded herself. The lingering scent of Clint's cologne hung in the air when she unlocked the door. Regret washed over her. *This could be my last visit,* she speculated, *except for tomorrow's treasure hunt.*

Unable to pin down her suspicions, for some reason it felt like theirs would be a short romance. Neither had put *that* label to it, but the fact was they had become closer than mere friends. At least that was her impression. The notion of pulling back hurt. She had known Clint for more than four years and liked him a lot. Now more than ever. He was a good, decent man who held the same values she did. Nonetheless, for whatever the reasons, she could tell he was applying the brakes.

It took three trips to the car to bring everything in from the trunk. Food and groceries sat on the kitchen table, ready to be put away. Against her better judgment, Jules elected to go ahead and drop off her contributions for tomorrow's event this evening rather than wait until Saturday morning. She remained unconvinced it was necessary. However, on the other hand, she concluded it freed up more time in the morning to get ready.

Chapter 20

When she got home from work, she artfully designed treats for the kids. Iced sugar cookies decorated in fall colors: bats, pumpkins, autumn leaves, and ghosts. Proud of the results her efforts had produced, the festive table decoration would add a nice touch to Clint's September event. Centered on the table, the cookies were covered in plastic wrap. No doubt Clint would find them a pleasant surprise when he returned from Crothersville.

Should I make a cup of coffee? Take a breather before heading home? Jules weighed her options, then asked, *what harm can it do?* She grinned at her naughtiness. *Maybe eat one of my cookies?*

Unable to produce a reason not to rest her tired legs, she went to the counter and filled the coffee machine with enough grounds to make two cups—the equivalent of one for her. With Clint out of town, she made herself at home by putting her feet up on a chair. She grabbed a cookie and waited for the pot to finish its cycle.

Clinching a warm coffee mug in her hands, Jules walked into the living room. Immediately she noticed the DVD player had been pulled away from the wall at an odd angle. The thought occurred to her that maybe it had stopped working altogether.

Wonder if he is going to replace it? she curiously pondered. Then another thought popped into her head. *If so, does that mean the player malfunctioned that night and not the movie?*

When she recalled the weird incident, she cringed. *Our disconnect started that same night.* She sighed, unable to connect the dots between that specific event and anything other than that… where Clint might have taken issue with her. Everything between them had been going well until then. Jules had a hunch they were somehow linked.

But why? she pondered. She was still considering the question when a cool breeze stirred in the house, catching her off guard. Following its source, she realized she was in a part of the house she had never seen before.

What the heck? she thought, shocked to see the back door standing wide open. *Clint left without closing the door. Really?*

That's not like him! He is going to be upset with himself when I tell him what he did. Or didn't do! Jules smiled. *Should probably pass on making an old age joke.*

She and Clint had always used the front entrance when she visited, so Jules was in uncharted territory. From the looks of it, this room was a utility room. Pegs on the wall held caps, sweaters, and jackets. She grinned. *Not as presentable as the front entrance with that pretty mirror!*

She peered through the screen door at the forest and the colorful autumn trees that had started to turn. The temperature, a comfortable sixty-three degrees, was ideal for a short stroll. *This place is heavenly*, she thought, remembering the picturesque space Clint and she had visited a couple of days before. She glanced overhead. Not a rain cloud in the sky, despite the forecast.

Do I dare? She pondered, knowing she had nothing else to do. Clint would not be home until ten or eleven, according to him.

When she arrived at the mouth of the woods, the path that led to the clearing was easy to identify. She moved along the shaded trail, deeper into the forest. Not wanting to admit it, the image of Clint and her sharing a life together had crossed her mind on more than one occasion, especially the day he had shown her where he'd found the morel mushrooms last April. It was wishful thinking, she knew. From the direction, things appeared to be headed—a pipedream.

She pivoted toward the house, wondering if what she was doing was out of line. Without question, she was certain Clint would not care one way or the other if she revisited the two sites they had selected as possible hiding places for the treasure chests. They had yet to make up their minds, and this was her opportunity to weigh in.

If he does show, I'll tell him I'm playing scout, thought Jules humorously. *He'll see my car and know I'm here.*

She probed additional hollows to hide the final clue. Twittering birds, settling in for the evening, responded to her movements as

Chapter 20

she passed below them. Prompting a smile, she advanced farther. Then a startling sound caused her to stop and rethink. It was the bone-chilling howls of a pack of coyotes.

That's not exactly music to my ears, she thought frightfully, convinced it was time to get out of there.

"No!" Jules yelled loudly as she nosedived face-first to the ground. Feeling like a klutz, she reached for her face and saw blood on her fingertips. The scratch happened when the toe of her shoe got caught on a partially submerged branch poking out from the forest floor, which in turn had caused her fall.

Annoyed, she chastised herself, "That was brilliant, Jules!"

Swiveling to an upright position, she remained on her rear, looking around, thankful no one had seen her trapeze act. She was beginning to wonder about herself. Two falls in less than two weeks.

Better get out of here, she decided, standing to her feet swiftly.

That was when she saw it—a fragment of a solid object glistening from beneath the soil. A shimmering glint revealed its position. Excitedly she dug into the dirt until she unearthed something she would never have believed in a million years to have found.

Stunned by what she was looking at, she gazed at an ultra-pale blue pearl necklace, casting an iridescence of the highest quality from where it lay still partially buried in the ground. Shockingly she saw, edged alongside it, what appeared to be three diamonds of reasonable size. She carefully excavated the strand and gems.

Cradled in the palm of her hand, she speculated, *Did I just find real treasure?* Jules squealed, considering the prospect. *Must have been lost ages ago from the condition the pearls are in. Yet, they look new!*

Baffled as to why anyone would be carrying around loose diamonds, she was in awe of her discovery. *If they are real diamonds, they must be worth a fortune.* Ultimately, she concluded they could not possibly be the real deal. *They have to be fakes! Toy gems,* she determined. Then she wondered if they had that sort of thing back in the old days. The high quality of the stones, however, forced her to doubt her hypothesis.

She loosened the clumps of muck that clung to the strand, revealing the clasp with the name Monet engraved on a tiny oval gold plate. Having nothing to wrap the necklace in, she slid it into her pocket for safekeeping until she could hand it over to Clint, along with the diamonds. She felt like a little kid, unable to contain her excitement.

Her exuberance, however, did not last long. A presence loomed as darkness fell, and Jules sensed she was not alone. Her ears perked up. She could hear animals moving about over the dry leaves, but that was not what had caught her attention. She could see a strange shape off in the distance, through the gaps and denseness of trees.

Jules took one last glimpse into the thick foliage of uncharted territory, wondering what other mysteries that section of the forest held. *Apparently, people did live on this land!* A chill ran up her spine, and she walked briskly away from the forest and back toward the house. *I may have just seen one!*

Too close for comfort, a band of coyotes howled, filling the night with their terrifying echoes of torment. Jules had heard them before, but nothing like this. Some poor animal was being consumed or fought over from the sound of it. Dinner!

I wonder if different breeds of coyotes co-exist in the same territory? she questioned. *Each having its own unique cry that differentiates them from others.* The heavy steps she had heard earlier and chalked up to deer could have been these animals, she supposed.

Moving across the lawn, she studied her surroundings and decided it was time to leave. Later she would mention her find to Clint. She would hand it over but not without an explanation. The hour had turned late. Being in the forest after dark lacked common sense. She had never been afraid of the dark, but that place felt alive. Childish, she knew.

Chapter 20

Entering the rear of the house, she heard Clint's car pulling into the drive. It felt awkward to be in his house without him there. She reminded herself he had encouraged her to bring things over ahead of time. What she was doing was perfectly all right.

Clint knocked on the door. With laughing eyes, he asked, "Anybody home?"

They both snickered at how awkward the situation was, vice-versa from how it should be playing out. "This feels wrong on all kinds of levels," she confessed. "The intruder has been caught red-handed!" Her eyes grew large. "I promise I didn't scavenge through your desk drawers!" After making the offhanded remark, she wished the inappropriate joke could have been reeled back in.

"I wouldn't care if you did." Clint grinned. "Glad to see you. I was hoping I'd get home in time." He looked to the table and saw the cookies Jules had put there when she first arrived. "Man, aren't those something. Mind if I have one. Or are they off limits?"

Jules chuckled, "Are you kidding? I had one a bit ago. Made myself at home and helped myself to coffee! I bet the pot is still warm." She went over and felt the glass. "Yep!" She turned to face him. "Can I make you a cup?" With Clint in the house, Jules felt more relaxed. She noticed right away he didn't seem as uptight as he had been.

"Decaf, please," he replied with a big grin. "Feels like I'm at Josie's, placing my order. Cookies and coffee, what a great combination. They do look tempting. Did you make these?"

"Sure did, after work," she answered with a tilt of her head.

"Nice decorating job! The kids will love them. A nice touch for tomorrow."

The pot began to drip coffee for a third time that day. Clint had to laugh at its use. Once upon a time it only sprang to life at dawn, but more recently, he was firing it up on a regular basis. Jules drank as much coffee as he did, which was hard to believe. They made a good pair.

From the other side of the table, Jules reached into her pocket. Eagerly she announced, "I have something to show you." Then a quick frown appeared on her face. "Hey, you aren't going to believe this, but when I got here, your back door was open."

Clint looked behind her toward the back of the house. "That's odd."

"Yeah, that's what I thought. When I went to close it, I decided to take a walk. It was so beautiful outdoors. Hope you don't mind."

"No, not at all," Clint remarked pleasantly, noticing she had a cut on the left side of her face. He touched her cheek. "What happened here?"

Jules' eyes shifted away from Clint's. "Oh, that. I hate to admit it, but I fell flat on my face. Tripped and went down like a ton of bricks." She noted the surprised look on his face and immediately inserted, "I'm okay, just embarrassed." She withdrew the strand of pearls and set them on the table. "Look what I found when I was down and out. Treasure on state property! Do I need to declare it?"

Clint flashed a smile. "I won't tell if you don't. It'll be our little secret." He reached across the table and lifted the pearls. When he did, a strange sensation came over him. "Where did this happen?"

"Where we were the other day. That pretty open area. Something back in the woods caught my eye. When I moved that way, my shoe got caught. It's amazing what you see when you are face down in the dirt."

Clint moved to the other side of the table, cognizant that the scratches on Jules' face were deeper than he first realized. "You really did take a tumble. Didn't you?" He turned her face to the side. "One of those cuts is serious." Blood had pooled on the surface, making it obvious she had hurt herself to a greater degree than she was letting on. "Bet that shocked you."

"Yeah, it sure did." Jules put her fingers to her face.

"I have some ointment in the other room. I'll go get it." Before Jules could refuse his offer, Clint had disappeared down the hall to the medicine cabinet. When he returned, he handed her the tube.

Chapter 20

"Better play it safe. You can use the mirror in the entry."

Jules flashed a smile, pleased with Clint's concern. "Thanks," she said, getting up to apply the ointment. When she returned, she inquisitively inquired, "So what you do think about that necklace? I'm surprised I even noticed it, considering how deep below the soil it was. From its appearance, it has been there a long time."

Clint examined the pearls with a closer eye. "You know I think I've seen this necklace before. I don't know how that's possible, but I believe I have. They are elegant." At the sink, he grabbed the Dawn dish soap, filling the basin with lukewarm water. The necklace was given a good soaking before pulling it from the sudsy water. "That should do the trick." After a painstaking wash, Clint returned the necklace to Jules. "I hope you enjoy them."

"Don't know about that. They were on state property. Shouldn't I turn them in?" These were no ordinary pearls. Although small, they were exquisite. A surprised look appeared on her face. "Oh, I almost forget. I found these too." She pulled the stones from her pocket. "No doubt they are replicas, but they sure look real."

Clint was shocked when Jules handed the diamond like stones over. "Why would these be out there? Wow! At least a carat each. I'd lay money on they're genuine."

"Look at this," she said, handing the necklace back over to Clint. "The name Monet is embedded on the clasp."

"That's interesting," he remarked. "We have a mystery on our hands. You'll have to see if you can find out who or what Monet is." He turned her shoulders halfway round. "Here, let's see how they look on you. And, by the way, you absolutely should keep all of it, including the stones. Maybe you can make the stones into a nice necklace or a couple of rings. The state has nothing to do with this. They are your find."

The movie *Somewhere in Time* crossed his mind. The part where the old woman walked up and placed a pocket watch and chain in the playwright's hand. The watch would have been considered an antique in modern times.

When Jules turned to face him, Clint brushed her cheek with his hand. "Fits you perfectly! Man, those are gorgeous. Our first treasure on Reeves' property."

He corrected himself quickly, "Technically state property, but whose cares?"

Then the thought crossed his mind, *Jules could have easily kept the necklace and diamonds and never said a word. Instead, she innocently wanted to turn them over to the state.* Where Clint felt positive someone else would have pocketed the find, he noted, *Jules is too honest to do something like that.* Either way, her willingness to relinquish her discovery was a revealing insight into her character.

"I could put them into my jewelry box for safekeeping." She grinned charmingly. "They should be admired." Then a frown crept onto her face. "I can't quite explain why or put my finger on it, but when I hold them, it's as if they have a story to tell."

Clint looked down at the pearl necklace, certain he had seen it before. Thinking he had to be mistaken, he said, "I imagine they do. They look old."

They talked a while longer about Jules' find and the events of the day. An hour later, with a glance at the clock, she pushed her chair from the table and said, "I'd better get going."

Clint walked Jules to the door. When she turned toward him, he kissed her goodnight and gave her a hug. As she moved to the other side, he said, "I'll see you in the morning." His eyes sparkled with laughter. "A fine day it be, Matey."

Chapter 21
Searching for Treasure

At 5:45 a.m. the next day, Clint had slipped out from under the covers, had gotten dressed, and was sitting at the kitchen table drinking his first cup of whole bean Columbian roast. The glow of the sun's rays had just begun to break the horizon, not expected to show itself fully for another hour and a half.

The treasure hunt and the upcoming introductions were at hand. Though a bit awkward, underneath, Clint knew he sought the family's approval of his new friend. His thoughts traveled to the prior evening and how delightful it had been having Jules at the house when he returned from Crothersville. He thought it cute she had ventured into the woods without him at home, and she felt comfortable enough to do so.

From the freezer, Clint removed two pounds of bacon. He wanted plenty of bacon available for the hamburgers he planned to put on the grill later and this morning's breakfast when Jules arrived.

At nine o'clock, like clockwork, Jules was standing at the screen door holding a box of doughnuts. She had stopped by Donut Delights on her way, ordering a half dozen yeast, three jelly-filled, and three chocolate-covered cream—all favorites.

"Howdy," Clint called out.

"Good morning," Jules replied, handing the box of pastries to Clint. He set it on the table and quickly turned to help her with her jacket.

"It's supposed to be beautiful today," she noted. "The forecast calls for blue skies and a high of around seventy. Can't get better than that!"

"Yeah, I heard that on the morning news. Thank goodness for small favors. Treasure hunts don't work well in the rain." Clint grinned. "Hey, breakfast is ready. You hungry?"

"Sure," Jules answered. "Smells delicious." A plate of bacon and a bowl of scrambled eggs sat on the table along with a carafe of coffee." Clint had put them out when he saw her pull into the drive.

"Hope you came ready to hide prizes and clues!"

"You bet ya!" Jules chortled. "Yesterday, before I fell flat on my face, I saw several additional spots you might want to consider." Her eyes sparkled.

While they ate, Clint conveyed to Jules the grandkids' excitement over the treasure hunt, and the cookout in general, plus that Lily was revered by her two younger cousins.

Clint explained the history of why Wade lived in Flathead Lake, Montana. How his son and daughter-in-law had met on a cruise ship. Clint also laid out how it happened that Wade owned a three-hundred-plus-acre ranch. Clara's father, as a wedding gift, offered the couple a portion of his land. The only caveat was Wade would have to move away from Indiana.

Clint also filled Jules in on the farm in Crothersville and how Rusty and Molly loved the seclusion and had known each other since kindergarten. Her parents lived in the same town as Clint and Elise. The kids had gone to the same school. Both Clint's boys and their wives enjoyed country life and working the land.

By 9:45, Jules and Clint were out the door and moving toward the woods. Clint had put the treasure chests and prizes in plastic bags the night before. With more than an hour to plant the clues in the yard and woods, they got to work.

6:45 p.m.

At the open firepit the family enjoyed each other's company, visiting and catching up on current events. Clint had introduced Jules, and to his delight, she fit right in. The young ones kicked a soccer ball and then played badminton and bocce ball. Clint

181

Chapter 21

had taken them on a tractor ride down the road and around the property as the parents and Jules chatted.

The hour had arrived to start the treasure hunt. The children had changed into their pirate costumes and were sword fighting one another when Clint announced the hunt would start in fifteen minutes.

Clint had added some interesting items to his surprise package for the kids. Thursday, after breakfast, he visited the bookstore for the last time prior to the event. As usual, no one answered the bell, but Clint was used to that. He had selected extra items that fit perfectly with his pirate theme: fool's gold, assorted stones, play money, and coin candy. All of them lent a certain mystique to the hunt.

As he stood at the counter waiting for Rod to answer the call of the dinging bell, his attention was drawn to a slip of paper partially tucked beneath the cash register. Out of curiosity, Clint gave it a marginal tug and was shocked to see his name. He unfolded the paper. It read:

Clint, I saw your approach but will not be able to assist you. Please take what you wish. We will settle the bill later. Enjoy the hunt.

Rod

When he left the book shop that day with his items, he marveled at the strangeness of the store manager and his father. Both Rods were odd ducks. Yet to meet the old man, Clint presumed at some point their paths would cross. Rod, Jr. recollecting the actual date of the treasure hunt had surprised him. His memory was to be commended. Accustomed to their unorthodox ways of doing business, Clint had departed and never gave it a second thought, figuring he would stop in the following week to pay his bill.

The children were escorted to the front porch, where the hunt was expected to begin at any moment. The clues would take them through the house, to the vacant property north of Clint's place, and then to the forest behind it. Clues and small treats were hidden at several locations along the way, all adding to the thrill of the chase.

The adults heard giggles and laughter as the kids scrambled from clue to clue, progressing toward a more enticing triumph. Clint had their individual treasure chests engraved, leaving no doubt which one belonged to whom. Time had neared where the buried treasure would soon be found.

Lily had insisted the three cousins were all old enough to find their own clues. No parent should assist them. Once they were read, suggesting the rhyme's next location, off they went. The kids ran around searching for hints and signs, through clucking chickens loose in the yard, until only a few clues remained.

The adults sat by the open fire and could hear the whoops and hollers as the children bulleted from spot to spot. They screamed when clues were uncovered and solved. Charging off to new locations, the closer they got to the forest, the more excited Clint and Jules became.

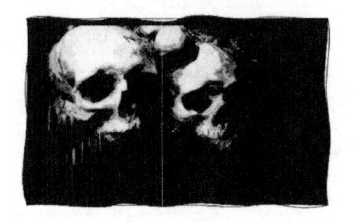

This next clue could give you trouble
Just like this picture, you will see double
Toward the south is all I will say
A repeat is where your next clue lay

Trey, Dylan, and Lily bulleted to the south after having uncovered their next clue. When they started the hunt, Clint had handed Lily a compass to help simplify directions.

The children stopped at where a joined, double stump was seen. They had reached the right location. The next clue was tucked between the *repeat* stumps.

Chapter 21

A little tougher thy next clue be
Not so easy, you might agree
Think of a pirate's favorite drink
That is where to find the next clue link
Used to create their special brew
This receptacle is not so new

The kids searched extensively, unsure where to find this elusive clue. Lily excitedly proclaimed, "It must have something to do with a container people drink from."

Dylan chimed in, "Yes, but it says receptacle. I don't understand!"

They scanned the area, and when Trey saw an oaken barrel turned upside down in the yard, he hollered, "Over here, guys!" Pointing in the direction of the barrel, the others quickly followed.

To the west, I would look
For a sad tree story, that nature took
Proud and tall, I once stood, but weep no more… will I
Instead, it is grandpa that does cry

Dylan clapped his hands excitedly, "I know what it is," he yelled jumping from the ground. "It's that dead tree over there. Wasn't that a weeping willow tree!"

Off they took in the direction of the dead tree at the side of the yard. There they searched the tree branches until Trey turned up their next clue:

To the secret trail, I would now head
Through thicket, by Lily, yea shall be led
Before you enter the woods, look around
Your next clue is somewhere to be found

Clint, Jules, and the older children were delighted with the adventure that was taking place. Finishing up their meals, they decided to pour some drinks.

"Hey, Dad, you okay if we rob your liquor cabinet?" Wade asked with a smile.

"Certainly," Clint responded without hesitation. "I'll have a drink too. I have Cabernet on the counter and Crown under it. Sweet white wine is in the frig." He looked to Clara, Molly, and Jules. "Would you ladies like a glass of wine? Or something a bit stronger?"

"I'd love a glass of red wine," Molly answered first.

"Ditto on that, except I'd prefer white," Clara chimed in.

"I'll join the girls. White for me." Jules grinned, savoring the moment. Not much of a wine drinker, she enjoyed opportunities to indulge, given the right circumstances.

Clint could not remember when he had been happier. The family was all sitting around, laughing and enjoying each other's company. The grandchildren were elated, and so was he. Everything seemed right as rain.

Jules walked over to the dessert table. Clint and the boys headed for the house to gather drinks. "Would either of you want some chocolate pudding cake?" she asked Molly and Clara while spooning herself some into a bowl.

Chapter 21

Both hands went up. Jules smiled and dished out two more helpings. She took them over and handed them out. "I'm not sure how good the wine will taste after eating cake, but I'm willing to give it a whirl!" She laughed as she sat down.

Molly agreed, "Yeah, coffee might have been a better choice!"

Sitting at the fire, everyone lifted their glasses in a toast, glad to be together again.

Clint watched the grandchildren head for the woods.

"Are you guys okay if I follow you? I promise I'll not say a word."

"Of course," Lily answered with a crazy little smile. "We just didn't want everyone deciphering our messages."

The clues had led them to the edge of the forest. Lily understood their next rhymes would take them inside. Scavenging around was going to be an adventure. She had always been an explorer at heart, and this was the height of uncharted territory. She looked over her shoulder at the adults sitting by the firepit and smiled.

With Clint at her side and her two cousins next to him, she read the next clue:

The land of the pirates you are about to enter
So, stay on the trail, exact to center
47 pirate paces I would make
About that many, give or take
On the left, a tall tree does hark
At the base, you will find peeling bark

"Heavens to Betsy, this is fun." Lily laughed, her blue eyes gleaming because she had used an old-fashioned slang phrase. "Sounds like real clues to a treasure. Grandpa, those maps you gave us at the beginning are awesome." She hugged Clint tightly. "I love you! This is so much fun!"

Clint's face revealed his pride, his life rounding another corner when he heard Lily declare her love for him. "I love you too, kiddo!"

Into the woods, they all went. Clint watched humorously while the grandchildren searched without success. They found nothing that resembled the clue they had been given. Then, in a shrill voice, Trey declared, "I think it might be over here!" Sure enough, they discovered the next clue.

You are now so very, very close
To the treasure, you desire the most
But first a new word you must learn
To find the treasure you so yearn
To hide the treasure, pirates used this special thingy
That they more often call a dinghy

All three looked around, staring at each other with confused expressions. "Okay, I'm stumped," said Trey, looking at the other two.

Yesterday Clint had dragged his Jon boat to the clearing. That was where he hid the treasure chests under the boat. The final clue made it more fun for him because he felt assured the grandkids would have no idea what a dinghy was…unless they figured it out from the image he had copied. This last clue was going to take some brainpower.

Chapter 22
A Misplaced Weapon

Trey and Dylan were completely stumped, unable to figure out the word dinghy. "Lily, what the heck is a dinghy?" asked Dylan, hoping she would know.

"Well, I say we look a little deeper because it's clear nothing that resembles the picture is around here." She smiled, not wanting to give away that she, in fact, did know.

"Do you think it's a boat?" asked Trey. "Is a dinghy a type of boat?"

"Could be," replied Lily, wearing a hint of a smile.

Trey's face contorted, "What would a boat be doing in the woods?"

"Maybe because we are having a treasure hunt," she said sarcastically. "Grandpa is pretty clever, you know." She could hear the grown-ups conversing at the firepit, their voices raised in laughter. It had been so long since the family had this much fun.

While the boys searched, Lily explored. She had already spotted the Jon boat and guessed the final treasure was hidden somewhere near it. She had only taken a few steps when something caught her eye. She wondered what she was looking at. A structure of some kind, she deduced. She was advancing toward it when her father's voice was heard.

"Lil, where are you?" her dad called. "Stop messing around. Get over here!"

"Sorry, Dad." Choosing not to disclose what she was really up to, she quickly answered. "I'm looking for the final clue."

"Well, I think you could be a little out of range," Wade said with a chuckle, surprised she had veered that far from Dylan and Trey. "Head back this way. Join the boys. I can't believe you are going to let them outsmart you!"

Lily, who had come across a run-down shack, carefully stepped over the low-hanging barbed wire fence that separated her from the dilapidated structure. When she did, her ankle scraped against its spiky points. With a pained face, she called out, "I'll be right there!" She looked down. Blood oozed through her white sport sock.

Curious about the building—now believed to be decades older than she initially thought—Lily was ready to turn around and head back to the family gathering. Then a flash of movement grabbed her attention. She would have sworn she had seen a figure standing at the edge of the forest near the shack.

Lily sidestepped so she could view the structure from a different angle. The area of interest revealed nothing out of the ordinary. Had she imagined something that appeared real?

Dylan screeched at the top of his lungs. "*I found it!*"

Laughter burst out. The entire family had entered the clearing area, knowing the big discovery was near.

Next came Trey, "Lily, get over here. We know where the thingy dinghy is!" he joked.

Okay, that was weird, thought Lily of the shack and figure she believed she had seen.

"Lily, where are you?" her dad called. "Stop messing around and get over here!"

"Dad, I'm on my way." Lily glanced over her shoulder one last time and saw nothing exceptional. Convinced she was mistaken, she returned to the group.

Clint was standing off to the side and enjoying the kids' reactions. Opening the treasure chests, they could not believe their eyes. But neither could Clint. Something was wrong. Terribly wrong.

"Where is the knife?" he asked, turning to Jules, aware that there was no way she would know.

"It has to be here. Maybe Trey turned it over when he pulled the chest out from under the boat." Jules guessed, hoping she was right.

Chapter 22

As curious as Clint was to where the knife and sheath may have vanished, she inspected Trey's chest. Open on the ground with all the other treasures accounted for, the one very crucial item was missing.

Clint searched every inch of the ground. He noticed Dylan's box had the whip he had purchased, and Lily's chest held the box and key. Both were where they should have been.

"Hey guys," Clint spoke up in a serious tone. "An important treasure that should have been in Trey's treasure chest isn't there." He gazed into Trey's eyes with a puzzled expression. "That empty container you are holding," Clint pointed to the box. "It was inside that."

Trey turned his treasure chest over and emptied the contents out on the ground. "Sorry, Grandpa, I don't see anything. What was inside?"

Clint did not want to answer, especially since it was an actual weapon. "I'd rather wait until we locate it. An explanation comes along with that specific item." He looked at Rusty, who was aware of what was missing. Clint had called to discuss the knife with him before adding it to Trey's gifts.

Lily could see the concern in Clint's eyes. "We'll find it, Grandpa. It's got to be here."

By now, everyone had gotten the impression that whatever was not in the box had been of great value. At least from the reaction Clint displayed, it appeared to be of great importance.

"Let's take all three chests over to the firepit and then unload everything and see if maybe they got mixed up somehow," Rusty suggested calmly. "There is an awful lot of things inside these treasure chests, Dad. By the way, having the kid's names engraved on them was awesome. That way, no one messes with the other person's things. Plus, they'll be keepsakes."

"Yeah, I thought engraving them was a good idea," Clint said with hesitation, not sure if he wanted to mention what was missing in Trey's box to the rest of the family.

At the pit the children unloaded their surprises. Clint had outdone himself. Most items were modern-day things found in any department store, but many were not.

Lily was especially thrilled with the snow globe she had uncovered in her finds. Another item she found was a small ornate box that resembled a miniature treasure chest. When she opened it and saw the skeleton key, she couldn't have been more delighted. It looked mysterious like a story was waiting to be told.

"Incredible," she exclaimed. "This box is so beautiful. Where did you find it?"

"At a bookstore in town," Clint readily replied. "The strangest place I think I've ever been. The store looks old, but it's not. Just built to look that way. Turn of the century kind of shop, only relatively new. Several things I bought you guys are from there, including the thing that is missing from Trey's treasure chest."

"So, what was it, Dad," Wade asked but eyeing Rusty, who appeared to be in the loop.

"I'm afraid to say," replied Clint honestly. "It was going to come with a warning."

"Whoa, that sounds scary," replied Colleen.

"No, what I mean is I was going to have Rusty and Molly keep it in a safe place until Trey was old enough to really appreciate its true value. I can't imagine what has happened to it. It was there this morning."

"Okay, you have my curiosity up for sure now," said Wade with a huge grin. "Spill the beans, Dad."

Clint looked sheepish, thinking that maybe he had made a grave error. "Well, the good news is it is not inside the box, so no one will get hurt. I guess it might not have been such a good idea. Seemed like it at the time." He looked to his son. "It was a Bowie knife in a worn sheath. I know how I was when I was Trey's age. I would have loved to have been given such a cool gift. But the orphanage didn't hand out weapons." Clint snickered, not sure his joke was that funny.

Chapter 22

"You are right about that. I can't imagine a nun handing a Bowie knife over to a kid. Would have been afraid it'd be used on them." Rusty laughed hard until he saw Molly staring daggers through him. "Just kidding, darling!" he roared.

Trey and Dylan lowered their heads, thinking their dad's joke was hilarious. Lily, too, hid a smile.

"It'll show up," said Jules. "When it does, Clint can show it to you both to get your opinions." She shrugged her shoulders. "Nothing says it can't be given to Trey later when he's a bit older."

Immediately, judging from the expressions on their faces, Jules realized she was out of line. It was not her place to say when Trey should take possession of a knife Clint clearly wanted him to have now. *Men and women view these things so differently*, she scolded herself. Unfortunately, it was too late to withdraw the comment. *That sounded controlling. Like I was overriding Clint's decision to give his grandson a knife as part of the treasure hunt.* She hesitantly turned to Clint, afraid he might be offended, but she was pleasantly surprised.

"She's right," agreed Clint. "I'll show it to you when it's found, and then you can give me your honest opinion." He turned to Jules, "I had described it to Rusty when I visited them, and he thought it might be all right, but seeing it is another matter." Then he turned to his son and his wife, "You won't hurt my feeling if you think now isn't the right time."

Dylan was playing with the multi-wheel, smokestack wooden train Clint had picked up on a recent visit to Rod's. From the look on Dylan's face, it was a winner.

"What'cha got there?" Clint asked walking over to his grandson.

"This is really awesome, Grandpa. I've always liked trains." Dylan beamed as he pushed the engine around on the grass.

"Is that right?" replied Clint. "I had no idea. Though I figured you might like it. It's different, that's for sure. Haven't seen one anywhere else." Clint looked down at the train in Dylan's hand. "It looks like the real deal, only miniature."

"This thing looks ancient!" Dylan said enthusiastically. "I have the perfect place in my room to put it."

Watching the sun go down, Jules and Clint enjoyed the robust fire burning in the pit. Fiery sparks disappeared into a starry sky. They listened while the family chatted about their lives. Occasionally Jules, who was wrapped in a sweater, asked a question but, for the most part, just observed.

Lily had pulled a chair close to her grandfather. When the hour drew near for the family to depart, she leaned in and whispered a question that had been weighing heavily on her mind. "Grandpa, do you mind if I spend the night?" Afraid that maybe she had been too bold, she tossed out, "I know Rusty and Molly live a long way from here, so if you would rather not, that's okay."

When Clint searched his granddaughter's eyes, he could see she really wanted him to say yes. "Sweetheart, if your parents agree, I'd love to have you. They fly out on Monday, right? I'd be driving up that way anyhow. I could drive you back on Sunday afternoon."

"That's great!" Lily squealed, popping out of her chair. "I'll ask."

She went over to her mom, and likewise, whispered in her ear. "Is it okay if I stay overnight here with Grandpa? I'd like to spend as much time as I can before we leave."

Clara replied without a second thought, "Of course, if it is okay with him."

"He said I could, but I needed to check with you first."

"Well, then I guess you are staying at Grandpa's this evening," Clara replied with a smile.

When Dylan and Trey heard that Lily was going to spend the night, they asked if they could as well. Clint had no qualms with all three grandchildren hanging out with him for an evening, but he made it clear they would have to bunk in the spare room. His second bedroom had been converted into a study.

Chapter 22

"Dad, are you sure about the kids all staying here?" asked Rusty with a concerned expression. "That's a big undertaking, especially with my two boys."

"Hey, if I could handle you two, I can manage these guys," kidded Clint. "I'm not that old!"

"All right," Rusty laughed. "Remember you asked for this!" Everyone had a good laugh. "That'll work really well for us too. Molly and I could take Wade and Clara over to the Off the Rails Bar and Grill. They have live music on Saturday night. Molly and I went there a couple months back. It's a fun place."

"You should go," encouraged Clint. "How often do you guys get to spend time without the children? Enjoy yourselves. I'll bring them to you tomorrow afternoon."

Rusty stood and made an announcement to the group, in a "ta-da" style. "We have a built-in babysitter. Grown-up fun begins in five, four, three, two, one minute!"

Wade responded with two thumbs up and quickly ejected from his chair.

They said their goodbyes and extended their appreciation for a wonderful day. Then the big kids made a beeline for Rusty's car, with the promise of a nice meal on Sunday afternoon, compliments of Rusty and Molly. One last meal before Wade, Clara, and Lily returned to Montana.

Chapter 23
Decision Made

As the adult children pulled out of the drive, they flashed their car lights before turning into the street. With all the grandkids having a stayover at their grandfather's, Clint's boys and their wives had a carefree evening ahead. It had been forever since the siblings had enjoyed a night on the town.

Clint, equally, was thrilled that Lily had asked to stay, which prompted all three of the grandkids to hang out until tomorrow when he would return them safe and sound to Crothersville. The five of them would play Spoons at the kitchen table, which Clint happened to know was one of Lily's favorite games. Jules had offered to make popcorn in the big iron skillet before the game began.

Spending time together had been loads of fun. At 9:30 p.m., though, Clint announced it was time for bed. He had been up since early morning and was slowly running out of steam. Jules stayed around until the children were settled in the den, the boys on the floor, and Lily in the daybed. Then she sat at the table waiting for Clint to return to the kitchen so she could offer a proper farewell.

"Wow, what a day," said Jules as she searched for her keys. "Your treasure hunt was a huge success!"

"Yeah, I'd say!" Clint huffed in agreement as he sat down, exhausted. "It's been way too long since we were able to relax and have fun." He wavered before adding, "The last time we were all here was after their mother's funeral." His eyes gradually lifted. "I'll invite everyone down again, and it won't take six years."

"Well, I say the day was a total success."

Clint frowned. "Yeah, everything except that stupid knife that came up missing. Where in the heck do you think it is?"

"I have no idea," said Jules with unease. "The fact it wasn't in the treasure chest when I distinctly saw you put it in there, is

Chapter 23

troubling." She stood, tossing her handbag over her shoulder. "It'll surface at some point." Jules walked through the foyer to the door. She gazed into Clint's eyes. "Don't worry. It'll show up sooner or later."

"But that's just it, Jules. I am positive that knife was inside the chest. I remember seeing it. There is no way for it to have fallen out unless it happened when Trey picked it up. It makes no sense. And, the truth is, I'm worried about someone finding it who shouldn't. It's not a plaything. If a kid got hurt or hurt someone else because of my negligence, I would never forgive myself." He leaned against the wall. "That would be devastating."

Jules hugged him goodnight. "Don't worry. It's around here somewhere. You'll find it." With a gentle smile, she added, "I guess I'll see you Monday at Josie's."

"Yeah," Clint responded, still despondent over the knife. "I'll give you a call tomorrow when I get home from dropping the kids off. Hopefully, I will have come across the knife by then."

With that, Jules was out the door.

From the hallway, Lily stood listening to Clint and Jules' conversation. She wanted to get a drink of water but did not want them to think she was eavesdropping. She tiptoed back to the den, having overheard how upset her grandfather was. Determined to be part of the solution, her brain shifted into gear. Her grandfather was worried about the knife, and she was worried about him. She was upset because it was unfair for bad luck to surface when he had put so much effort into organizing a successful event.

After her grandmother died, his involvement with the family had waned. She remembered hearing of his withdrawal and not wanting to leave the house. Lily cherished many good memories when visiting her grandparents' house in Seymour. She refused to allow the knife fiasco to have a negative impact on his current mood. In her heart, she felt the responsibility of helping solve the mystery of the missing knife instead of just sitting by idly. That one gift should not be allowed, in her opinion, to overshadow or ruin the whole treasure hunt affair.

From the den, she heard Clint moving about in the kitchen. He was preparing the following morning's coffee.

She rendered a decision to act. With her head propped onto the pillow, Lily waited for Clint to turn in for the night. When the house grew quiet, she made her move. Always the nervy one, she would recruit help from her two younger cousins. That was the strategy. Their willingness to participate in a daring rescue mission to locate the elusive knife was without question.

Together they'd carried out other such missions—not on as grand a scale as this, but escapades, nonetheless. Often, when she or they stayed over at each other's houses, they sought adventure after dark after their parents had turned in for the night.

They conducted meetings in secluded areas of the house where they would not be overheard. At Trey and Dylan's house, they often sat in the glider-rocker behind the house. Lily was a master storyteller, and the boys loved to listen to her imaginary tales. Eating leftovers, like cold fried chicken and drinking pop, they would stay awake well into the night.

This evening the adventure would be taken to a higher level. They would slip outdoors where she would explain the mission.

Lily declared in defiance, "That stupid knife will be recovered! Tonight!"

The minute on the digital clock beside her bed in the den clicked from 11:15 p.m. to 11:16 p.m. It was time to wake the boys.

"Hey… Trey, Dylan," Lily whispered, shaking them in their beds.

Trey was the first to respond. "Lil, what's up?" he said sleepily.

"Want to do something off the charts?"

Chapter 23

"What?" answered Trey, confused at her meaning.

"I want to know if you guys are willing to go out into the woods with me?"

"After dark, are you nuts?" Dylan spoke, thinking his cousin had lost her mind. "No way!"

"Fine," Lily snapped, "I'm going to the place where we found the treasure chests. Thought you might want to join me."

"Why?" asked Trey curiously, not sure why she would want to do such a thing. He looked outside, realizing it was late—very late.

"Because Grandpa is really upset over misplacing that knife. The one he thought was inside your treasure chest," she explained, looking at Trey with an expectant expression. "It's missing, and he's worried. It must be out there somewhere. Dropped on the ground when we opened our chests is my guess."

"I'd like to find it too," replied Trey. "Sounded pretty cool from how Jules described it to Mom, but I don't know about trekking off into the forest to go look for it at night."

"My intention, and I will go alone if I have to, is to locate the thing and then put it on the kitchen table. So, in the morning when Grandpa gets up and starts to make his coffee, he'll see it. Then he won't have to fret anymore."

Dylan, who had been taking in the conversation, grimaced. "But, Lil, it's dark outside. Couldn't we go look for it in the morning?"

"No. I want to surprise Grandpa. I'm not afraid of the woods. If you guys are, I'm okay with that. I understand." With conviction she injected, "But from where I stand, there is nothing in the dark that's not in the light." She pondered her own words, thinking them wise. "Maybe the reason I'm not afraid is that I'm older." Lily knew she was using reversed psychology on her cousins but didn't care. She wanted company.

Trey stood, "I'm in! I like horsing around outside after dark. And venturing in the woods will be a ton more fun. The stuff they make scary movies from!" He halfheartedly laughed, unsure that he hadn't lost his mind.

"Good! We have an adventure on our hands." Lily put her arm around Trey's shoulder. "Partners in crime," she proclaimed, "that's what we are. You can be assured real pirates roamed dark woods at night. They weren't afraid of anything!"

They both turned to Dylan, who looked as if he had just swallowed a poison pill. "Like I'm going to stay behind, and you guys go out there without me. No way!"

"Alrighty then! Our three-person motley crew is about to embark on finding lost treasure of the third kind." Lily expressed her amusement, patting both boys on the back while pushing them toward the door. Sounding braver than she felt, Lily said, "We'll be talking about this night when we are old and gray!"

Little did she know, her prediction was spot-on.

"We have to be out of our minds," mumbled Trey, chuckling under his breath.

He watched Lily remove the key from the wooden box that sat on the dresser. She had taken it out of her treasure chest. Intrigued by it, she threaded it on the chain that hung around her neck.

"I carry the key that unlocks the mysteries to the questions we seek," she declared triumphantly. "Don't you guys love the way it looks? It's so ancient. Like something right out of Indiana Jones!" She moved it around on her neck. "A skeleton key, full of mystery."

The threesome snuck into the mudroom. They switched into the boots they had brought for the treasure hunt and went out into the open air of the backyard. The moon shone brightly overhead, making it easier to navigate under a starry sky. Lily led the pack toward the dense forest, determined to accomplish her goal. She imagined the look on her grandfather's face when he realized what they had accomplished. True love held no boundaries!

In her bag, she also carried the snow globe. Removing it from her backpack, she asked, "Isn't this amazing?"

"Not like any snow globe I've ever seen. What is that on the inside?" asked Trey.

Chapter 23

"Sort of like a geode. Don't you think? Odd, huh?" Lily countered.

Trey reached for it, and she handed it over. He wanted to inspect it in more detail. "From this angle, it looks like the opening to a cave. Do you see that?" he asked, pointing to the mouth of the rock. "A perfectly formed cave entrance. Those crystals on the bottom are extraordinary." He put his face close to the glass. "Talking about an unusual snow globe scene! Where would someone come up with an idea like this?"

Lily studied the globe with greater interest as well. "You know, you're right. The amber color sets off the jagged quartz-crystal-edged bottom. The cavity does resemble a mouth to a cave." *Why would anyone put a cracked piece of rock inside a snow globe?* she queried.

"What's so strange about it," she said, in a puzzled voice, "is there is no liquid glitter on the inside like you would typically see. No snow in the snow globe?" she laughed curiously. "Just this pretty rock." She shook the globe to make sure she wasn't missing something. Under the domed glass, nothing but glycerin water swirled around a crystal quartz rock.

"True. Very odd indeed," agreed Trey.

Chapter 24
A Light in the Dark

Dylan grabbed the flashlight, tucking it inside his trouser pants. Determined to complete their mission and return to the den before anyone knew they were gone, the three would-be pirates eyed one another, not sure if what they were about to do was smart.

Outside on the lawn, in the brisk late-night air, they took a collective breath. Close to midnight, the prospect of their adventure felt exhilarating. The sort of thing all kids dreamed of when their parents were not around to say no.

Lily grinned. "Pretend we are real pirates on a secret expedition."

"Aye-aye, Captain!" laughed Trey.

Dylan said nothing.

Stars twinkled brightly, down from a cloudless sky as they moved toward their mission at the back of the property. The excitement of a true quest had their adrenaline pumping. The idea of putting the knife on the table before their grandfather awoke in the morning fueled their determination.

"Follow me," Lily instructed as she entered the worn path. With the woods darker than envisioned, she questioned her judgment but said not a word.

Behind her, Dylan carried the flashlight aiming it in all directions as though he expected something to jump out at him at any second. "Lil, I'm not sure about this," he complained.

"Hey, we won't be long," she assured him. "Don't worry, Trey and I are here. Nothing is going to happen," Lily stated confidently. "If we don't find the knife in a reasonable amount of time, we'll head back indoors."

"Okay," mumbled Dylan, still not hot on the idea of tramping around in the forest after dark. "What about snakes and creepy stuff crawling around back here?"

Chapter 24

When they came to the area where the dinghy rested, and the treasure chests had been hidden, Lily suggested, "Maybe it would be best if we split up. Each takes a separate section. Get on our hands and knees, retrace our steps, and comb the ground thoroughly. Just be careful!"

"Sounds like a plan," agreed Trey without hesitation.

On all fours, the three cousins scoured the ground. They turned over every leaf, rock, and limb. After a considerable amount of time, Trey pulled his knees up, facing his cousin, and dejectedly declared, "Lily, I don't think it's here."

"Yeah, I'm afraid you're right," she agreed. "The only thing I can think of is Grandpa did not put it inside your treasure chest like he thought he had."

Dylan, glad to hear they were of the same mindset, suggested, "Okay, can we go now?"

Lily and Trey grinned at one another, cognizant that Dylan was afraid, and rightfully so. They understood because it was spooky in the forest with owls hooting and things moving about that couldn't be identified.

Disappointed they failed to produce the Bowie knife, Lily sighed. "I suppose you're right." She faced her two cousins, "I really thought we'd find it."

Having joined forces, at least they had tried. As they retraced their steps, Lily, who led the way, came to a sudden halt. Trey and Dylan also stopped, almost colliding with her.

"What?" Dylan cried.

"Hold on," whispered Lily with her hand up indicating to be quiet.

"What? asked Trey inquisitively.

"I don't know, but I thought I heard something."

Dylan was ready to wet his pants. He was so scared. "C'mon, Lil… let's leave! Of course, you heard something. This place is full of creepy sounds."

"Not so fast, Dylan," she responded as an older sister might.

They stood at the mouth of the path, searching in all directions for what Lily found troubling.

After a few moments, in an astonished voice, she inquired, "Look, do you guys see that?"

Trey looked around but saw nothing. "No, what are you looking at?"

"Over there, deeper in the woods. There's a light." Lily turned Trey's head in the right direction. "I think someone is living out there. I didn't say anything earlier, but I thought I saw someone during the treasure hunt. There was this shack!"

"How odd," replied Trey. "How about we do a little exploring, Capt'n?"

"You and I think too much alike," Lily snickered. "But I think we need to take Dylan inside first." She turned to her youngest cousin and gave him a hug. "Hey, I know you're not keen on doing this," she admitted. "So, we will take you back inside the house to the den, and then we'll come back out."

Dylan sulked, not happy. "I'm not afraid!" He raised his voice, "So who cares if someone lives out here anyway?"

"It's not a big deal, really," replied Lily. "But I'd just like to investigate. My thinking is someone saw us today and came up here before the treasure hunt started and stole the knife out of Trey's chest. I'm not saying that's what happened, but it could have. To me, it makes more sense than the thing vanishing into thin air."

"Well, I'm staying. I don't want to go to the house." Dylan stood straight with his spine straight. "We're a team. All for one and one for all!"

"It's your choice, bud," Trey chimed in. "But honestly, what Lily said makes sense. We don't mind taking you to the house."

Dylan looked at his older brother, close to tears. He had no intention of letting Trey have an adventure with Lily that he wasn't part of. "No, I'm coming with you guys."

Chapter 24

"All right," said Lily. "We are in this together. I have this feeling that whoever that is, they may have watched Grandpa put the treasure chests under the boat and then snuck up here and opened them. At least Trey's. He saw the knife, thought it was cool, and took it." She turned to Trey. "You know it could have happened that way. That is why Grandpa was so certain the knife was in the chest, and you were sure you didn't drop it."

They trailed Lily deeper into the woods, following the flicker of light she was sure she had seen. Although, to her dismay, it wasn't as distinct as when she first noticed it. They had gone only a short distance when she stopped everyone.

"I was sure I saw something. Thank goodness the moon is bright enough to shed light through the trees." She looked at where she thought the glow had been seen and, to her surprise, it was there, only dimmer.

"Hey, I see it. Over there." Lily pointed.

"Yeah," said Dylan and Trey simultaneously.

"Weird... it has a bluish tinge," Trey added with a look of confusion.

"Sure does," agreed Lily. "Let's get a little closer and find out what it is."

Although no one said it, they were all thinking the same thing. This was not a good idea. Toward the object and the bluish light, they inched. When they reached their destination, Lily realized the light was emanating from the old run-down shack she had seen earlier.

She whispered, "I bet some homeless person is living in that shack."

"Could be," said Trey in agreement.

Closer yet, they noticed the door was open and the light had turned more luminous.

"Look, why don't you two stay here and I'll just take a peek inside," advised Lily.

It took no time for the boys to agree.

"After that," said Trey, "I really think we need to get back to Grandpa's. Something about this doesn't feel right, Lil."

"I know," said Lily, unable to squelch her curiosity. "I'll only be a minute."

Chapter 25
Double Take

Lying in the dark, staring up at the ceiling, Clint deliberated about the Bowie knife and how it could have possibly been misplaced. *Where could it have fallen? Did it fall out before or after Trey got into the chest,* he hypothesized?

In Trey's excitement, wondered Clint, *did he take it out and then got distracted? Maybe he forgot to put it back inside the chest? I bet it is in the clearing.*

The notion it could be lying on the open ground made Clint nervous. *That was the find of the century,* he reminded himself, not liking the idea of it being subjected to the elements. He was tempted to get dressed and walk to where he imagined the knife might have ended up, but his weary bones said it could wait until morning.

He thought about the gift Rod, Jr. had given him. A copy of *The Time Machine*. He chuckled inwardly, fantasizing, *Maybe, if I focus hard enough, I can reverse time and see where I put the darn thing. If it was inside Trey's treasure chest or if maybe he dropped it.*

The knife was on his mind when Clint's eyes grew heavy, and he drifted into slumber. A few hours had passed when, as he slept, he saw himself hovering above a small child who was asleep in his bed. But like in most dreams, it seemed perfectly normal.

Clint's essence floated to the ceiling. Wondering why he was there, a feeling of nostalgia struck him. Outside the window, he recognized snow piled high on the ground.

He watched the child turn on his side and cradle his arm under his cheek. Then an unnerving thought engulfed him. It was as though Clint had had this dream before. Been in this exact room, with this very child, on more than one occasion. Though he did not recognize the location, it did have a ring of familiarity.

Then a peculiar sensation came over him. He was being pulled toward the figure on the bed. Their dual energies were merging as a convection of transference took place between them. The sleeping child's spirit had awakened Clint's through a form of atmospheric telekinesis. Sinking deeper into his innermost self, both souls entwined in a frequency of fused energy.

Clint had become linked with the sleeping boy. He noticed the child had changed positions. No longer was he in bed sleeping, as he had been. The child had moved out into the hallway. Voices echoed in the corridor as Clint trailed behind him. They had entered a realm that clung to the edge of time, deeper than any ordinary dream. Then it turned from strange to stranger.

The boy was standing on a stool in what appeared to be Clint's own foyer. The little boy, barefooted and in his pajamas, tiptoed to gaze into the ornate mirror. It looked exactly like the one Clint had purchased at the bookstore. Somehow the two locations, Clint's and this little boy's, had become intertwined.

From the hallway, Clint curiously observed the child. Through the lens of his dream, confusion arose. The boy appeared to be talking to his own reflection. Then the reality of what was truly going on became obvious. When seen from a different angle, Clint could tell the child was not having a conversation with himself. On the contrary, from the other side of the mirror, a man was interacting with him.

A shudder penetrated Clint's awareness, charging through his body like a live wire. The discussion the boy was engaged in appeared to be instructional until suddenly, the old man Clint had encountered at the bookstore walked out of the mirror and straight through the child's body to the opposite side of the room.

Standing at the doorway, in a fedora hat, the ghostly figure motioned for the boy to follow his lead. Suspendered trousers over a worn-torn shirt open to the nape of his neck, the man's outstretched hand patiently motioned, waiting for the boy to obey.

Chapter 25

Into a wooded area, the man entered. The boy, like a robot, trailed behind. The yard they traversed seemed eerily like Clint's. From behind a tree, Clint observed the young boy on his hands and knees frantically scouring the forest floor as though he had lost something. The child was alone. The man was nowhere in sight. Then Clint realized the boy was in the clearing. It dawned on him the child was searching for the knife. His knife!

Clint watched the boy jump to his feet. Urgently he ran into the thickest part of the forest, clutching something in his hand. It appeared he knew exactly where he was going.

Seeing nothing but a dense black forest, Clint suddenly noticed a worn path beneath his feet—the same one the child had taken. Although he had not moved, a decaying structure, barely standing erect, came into view, nestled inside a grove of trees. He spotted the young boy running toward the shack as though this wasn't the youngster's first time to be there.

Standing with his arms outstretched, a ghostly figure waited for the child to join him. Clint watched as the boy moved through the doorway, disappearing to the other side.

By the time Clint reached the opening, the boy had vanished. However, Clint felt a presence.

Words echoed in the night, as though coming from deep inside a chamber, "*He's here.*"

Rarely do dreams make sense in the light of day. When they are being experienced, however, they feel perfectly rational. That is until we open our eyes. Then we think… *what nonsense!* This dream was not like that. A message of hidden significance had been delivered.

Clint shot straight up in bed. Cold sweat beaded on his brow. Trying to regain a foothold on reality, he took numerous deep breaths to calm his shakiness. "Good Lord!" he moaned. "What brought that on? Had to be the most convoluted dream I've ever had," he breathed, relieved it had ended.

With the dream at the edge of his recall, Clint scrambled for answers until he remembered the science fiction novel he found himself engrossed in before bed. He'd not read much, but he figured it had been enough to spark the dream.

"The book had to be what brought on that weird dream," said Clint, positive he understood why the dream had developed.

He distinctly recalled, before drifting off, how nice it would be if he could travel back in time like H.G. Wells had done in *The Time Machine*. If Clint were able to reverse time, he would then find the missing knife and put it inside Trey's treasure chest. Or better yet, if he concentrated hard enough, he might do as Richard Collier had done, retrace his steps to figure out where he had misplaced it.

Clint sat on the edge of the bed, rattled by the dream and trying to collect his thoughts. He thought about the little child and wondered why he would dream about a kid. The young boy's face was innocent and trusting to a fault when he followed the old man who had stepped out of the mirror without regard to his safety. Truth was, it felt as though they knew each other.

An image of the small boy holding something in his hand gnawed at Clint. It appeared the boy dug something up in the clearing. That *something* looked a lot like the Bowie knife. Then he handed it to the man in the straw hat.

But then again, it was only a dream and dreams are like that sometimes, Clint reconciled. *No rhyme or reason to their purpose or message.*

Feeling restless, he slipped his house shoes on and headed for the kitchen, figuring a nice warm glass of milk would settle his nerves. The house was dark and still as he moved through the hallway. He could hear the clock's minute hand ticking as he walked past the credenza.

Clint stopped when he got to the foyer, remembering the young lad from his dream who had been standing on the stool. He scrutinized the mirror in detail. "What is it about that mirror?" he questioned. "It's been full of mysteries from day one!" He inched

Chapter 25

closer so he could peer into its reflection. He half anticipated the ghostly figure he had seen in his dream to pop out from the other side.

"Now you're being silly, Clint," he said aloud with a chuckle as he turned back to the kitchen.

He went to the refrigerator, poured a half glass of milk, and put it in the microwave for thirty seconds. Sitting down at the table, he waited for the ding. In the silence, he thought about Jules. He wondered how she felt about the previous day's activities. What she thought of his boys and their family.

There had been measurable tension between them of late. He was not in denial about that. It was easily discerned, especially after the weird happenings at the house the night they had tried to play *Somewhere in Time*. He wondered if Jules was having second thoughts about their relationship.

Even though he was accustomed to the queerness of his property, that one evening when she came over with the movie was more disturbing than most. That night fell into another level of creepiness. The house had never been an easy place to live with sounds coming from this place or that. Peculiar occurrences could never quite be explained. To him, it was normal, but when the movie stopped, that felt like a warning and had upset them both.

If truth be told, Clint felt upset from the moment he had realized what movie Jules had brought over for them to watch. He was taken aback and blindsided when she recounted that an old man who sounded an awful lot like Rod, Sr. had given it to her and suggested they watch it. It was as though the two Rods had teamed up against Clint in a sinister plot to cause trouble.

Clint was convinced, more than ever, that it was not merely a coincidence that Rod, Jr. had pointed out to Clint a few weeks back that the movie, *Somewhere in Time*, was based on the manuscript *Bid Time Return*.

He had responded badly to the situation with Jules. He was aware. Becoming alarmed, when out of nowhere the movie stopped, Clint was disappointed with himself that he had not kept his emotions in check. He had worn his feelings on his sleeves, and that was regrettable.

"It wasn't Jules' fault! How could she have known the connection?" Clint asked out loud. "She was as upset as I was." He considered the situation, *how ridiculous to think that my late wife was opposed to me watching* Somewhere in Time *with Jules. That's downright idiotic!*

On his way back to bed, Clint decided to look in on the grandchildren. It wasn't every day he could see their precious faces sleeping at his house. That had not happened in years. Wasn't it just yesterday they were just little tikes? Now here they were, almost grown-up. Over the next year or two, Trey and Dylan would be his height or taller, he guessed.

Clint pushed open the door to the den expecting to see the children spread out on the bed and floor.

To his shock, the room was empty. The children were gone.

Chapter 26
Strange Disturbance

Jules felt confused when she looked at the jacket cover of the *Somewhere in Time* video in her hand. On the back was a small, printed label: Rod's New and Used Books. *Odd, I didn't notice that label when I examined it before,* she thought.

The name matched the shop where Clint had purchased gifts for the treasure hunt. Despite its vague location, Jules was determined to pay a visit to see for herself why Clint found the shop so remarkable.

When she picked up the case, *Somewhere in Time's* music replayed in her mind. Captivated by the melody, she later read on the internet that John Barry's soundtrack had been adapted from Russian composer Sergei Rachmaninoff's *Rhapsody on a Theme of Paganini*. Composed for both piano and orchestra, it was the perfect theme song for the movie.

Jules had set the video on the hallway table days prior, forgetting about it until she saw the case under a stack of junk mail yet to be discarded. Her intention was to return the damaged video the day after it had failed to play.

It wasn't possible to return the video prior to Josie's Diner opening its doors. No stores were open at that hour. The plan was to take it back on her lunch hour and hope the bookstore was open on Sunday. She set the video by the front door so she would not forget it when she left for work the following morning.

Getting ready to turn in for the night, Jules thought about her day off from work with the Reeves family and how pleasant it had turned out. Though she was nervous beforehand, having never met any of them, everyone had been gracious and friendly. Plus, her food contributions were well-received, which made her happy. The girls, Clara and Molly, were especially cordial. Clint had not left her alone much and Jules was grateful.

Pulling her cotton nightgown over her head, she thought about Clint and how fond she was of him. She wondered if their relationship would ever progress any further or reach another level. He was considerably older than Jules, but that did not bother her.

What mattered to Jules was how well she and Clint communicated. They understood each other on a deeper level than mere small talk, she believed. Granted, the twelve-year gap between them was nothing to sneeze at, but their similar personalities made up for the age difference. They were cut from the same cloth—born a decade apart. Their relationship had grown into being each other's confidants. The glue that sealed their initial attraction was tied to the loss of their spouses, but that is not what attracted them now.

From the restroom, where Jules was preparing for bed, she could smell the aromatic scent of Egyptian licorice and ginger tea wafting through the hallway from the bedroom. The coffee maker could be heard brewing from inside the small alcove next to her turned-down bed.

During construction of the house, Randy had hoped the extra amenity would add a special touch to Jules' pocket-sized abode. When drawing up the blueprints, she had asked him if such a thing was possible.

Without hesitation, Randy fired back, "Absolutely. Not a problem." At an arm's length, the built-in pot and rectangular-shaped surface held just enough room for a pitcher of cream and a bowl of sugar, plus a spoon rest. Used often, the coffee pot had become one of Jules' favorite features in the entire house. Randy had guessed correctly, making his sister happy. Having a nice warm cup of tea or a mug of Ovaltine while reading in bed was the perfect end to a day.

Jules climbed into bed and waited for the combo tea concoction to finish infusing its magic. Licorice and ginger were her standby remedies after overindulging in too many fatty foods and rich

Chapter 26

desserts. Licorice's natural sweetness warmed her throat, and ginger settled her stomach.

Tomorrow would be here before she knew it. Normally, lights were turned off by 10 p.m., but that hour had come and gone. She glanced at the clock, 11:12. Still wired from having such a high-spirited day, she had no idea how she was going to quiet her mind so she could get some rest.

She lifted a book from her nightstand. Borrowed from Ivan, Dean Koontz's *Odd Thomas* had come highly recommended. He'd told her to expect a quirky tale, saying it would make her both laugh and cry.

Jules read the first paragraph. A smile crept onto her face, thinking Ivan was right.

Saturday After Midnight

"Where would they have gone?" Clint mumbled worriedly, on the edge of panic, standing outside the den door. *If my boys ever did this, I would have knocked them into the next week.* Clint pulled a face. *Maybe they did do stuff like this!* His lip curled, humored by the thought.

Instantly he rushed to his bedroom to get dressed. He hated to lay down the law, but the grandkids were about to get an ear full. There was no excuse for going outdoors at this late hour if that was what they had done. Not to mention scaring him half to death.

I'm way too old for these types of shenanigans. Plus, I would think they'd show more respect. Clint's brow knitted. *Maybe they are just on the front porch. I'll check out there first.*

Clint pulled on his cap, went to the front of the house, and opened the door. They were not sitting outside on the lawn chairs. In his rush to the other end of the house, he glanced at the wall clock—12:52 a.m. A chill ran up his spine. Dread coursed through his veins. "Why would they do something like this?" he asked in desperation.

Outside he searched the grounds, fully expecting to see them at the campfire chatting as kids might do. *I do that sort of thing. Why not them?* he rationalized. To his disappointment, the children were not there. Frantically he ran off to comb the rest of the yard and out at the street. *Maybe they are just walking around,* he considered.

Again, they were nowhere in sight. To his chagrin, the only place left to check was the forest. Clint hoped they had the good sense not to have gone back there, but that was the only place left to look.

Why would they have ventured back there? considered Clint. The forest was not exactly inviting after dark. Having a hard time believing his grandchildren would take off in the middle of the night in the first place, Clint reluctantly went toward the woods.

When he arrived at the path, he hesitated, remembering the lost knife. A thought crossed his mind. *Could they have come out here for that reason, to find the knife?*

Turning toward the area where he had hidden the treasure, Clint called, "Trey, Lily, Dylan? C'mon, kids! Where are you?" He heard nothing but the sounds of the forest.

"Faith sees best in the dark," quoted Clint as he inched deeper into the darkness, all the while calling to his grandchildren to show themselves. His pleas were rendered, but nobody responded.

Thoughts raced through his mind. He wondered what his boys would think if they knew Clint had no idea where the children were. His grandchildren! Hoping they were safe and nothing awful had happened, his assumption was they were acting as any reckless teens might behave under the same circumstances. Taking risks and throwing caution to the wind!

The moon's light shone through the trees as Clint made his way into the creepiest part of the forest.

Chapter 26

"Lily, Trey, Dylan?" he called a second time. Other than the sounds of nature, silence persisted. Shadows on the ground from light trickling through the branches and limbs shed what little guidance he had to manipulate the impossible trickiness of walking through a forest at night.

The woodlands possessed a peculiar sense of presence. The panic he had been struggling with over Lily, Trey, and Dylan was placed on pause when a sixth sense alarm bell rang out. He was not alone! He could feel the vibration of another being.

He detected a sizeable animal as it crisscrossed the forest floor. Clint observed the object moving gracefully into a cluster of trees. Concerned it might be a coyote tracking him, he could not have been less prepared for what came next. The silhouette of a large black cat with the most haunting green eyes Clint had ever seen materialized out of nothingness.

Motionless, the black figure watched Clint with great interest before eventually turning in the opposite direction. One last full body rotation was directed at Clint, as if to acknowledge his presence before the animal's large paws slowly lifted and moved through the doorway of what appeared to be a shack.

Clint felt paralyzed with fear. The cautious cat appeared uninterested in him, which he found puzzling. Then a ghastly thought crossed his mind. Had this cat already caught a meal? One of the children?

The blue light dimmed to nonexistent. In total darkness, Lily backed out the door. "Hey, guys, I need the flashlight." She motioned for Trey or Dylan, who were standing a fair distance away, to bring it to her.

Trey handed it over, and Lily turned it on. She scanned the empty space where she stood, seeing only a tiny room with one closet. Nothing seemed out of the ordinary.

"I swear to heavens I saw a light in here," she said, confused how she could have been mistaken. "Seems I was wrong." She pivoted toward Trey and Dylan, who were now standing at the entrance. "I thought we all saw it. Someone could have lived here, but that's been eons ago from the looks of the place."

"We've been out here long enough. It's time to leave," Trey urged, sounding serious.

"I agree. Turned out to be nothing but a wild goose chase, I'm afraid." Regretfully, Lily admitted. "Coming out here to find the knife was a mistake." She laughed and quoted something she had recently read. "Best-laid plans of mice and men often go awry."

Dylan frowned, "What does that mean?"

Then, before she could answer, Lily's snow globe began to behave strangely. She looked down, sensing a vibration in her purse. Amazed at what she saw, she said, "Guys, look at this!" She squealed, "It's glowing!"

The large geo stone situated in the center of the globe had turned a soft shade of amber. The slivered crack in the rock had become more pronounced than when first noticed. This time it literally resembled an illuminated cave entrance. She shook the globe vigorously, wanting to see, if this time, any glitter would appear. Only glycerin swirled.

She passed it over to Dylan. With great care, he held it in his hands. "Lil, I think it's getting brighter." He handed it to Trey.

Trey took a hard look at the globe. He turned it over, expecting it to be battery operated. It wasn't. *Is there anything that could have caused the change in lighting*, he pondered?

"You know what's strange about this?" he said, glancing up. "This stone and broken pieces of crystal around it couldn't look less like a snow globe. Who would make a snow globe that looked so unlike a snow globe? With no glitter or floating flakes?"

Lily grabbed her neck. "Whoa, what's happening?"

"What do you mean," asked Dylan.

Chapter 26

"It's my necklace. The thing is vibrating!" Lily unlatched the chain allowing the key to fall into her hand. She examined it for a moment and then passed it over to Trey. "Can you feel that?"

"I sure can. It feels like it has an energy source," agreed Trey, astonished at the weird movement. "Here, Dylan. Tell me if you can feel it?"

Dylan held the key only briefly. There was no doubt he was uncomfortable with what had become apparent. This was no normal key. He immediately put it back in Lily's hand.

"Trey, I think you're right. We should go," she stressed. "I have no idea what time it is, but it feels really late." Lily watched her cousins flee outside faster than speeding bullets. Their exploration was over.

Then from out of nowhere, Lily felt a heaviness surrounding her, as if she were being drawn toward the closet. The feeling was so intense, it nearly sucked the breath out of her. She ran for the entrance as fast as her legs could carry her.

In her haste, she dropped the key. Before she could pick it up, a disturbing sight was encountered.

Chapter 27
The Message

"Grandpa!" cried Lily.

"What are you doing out here?" Clint questioned in a harsh tone. "You scared the living daylights out of me."

"Oh, Grandpa, I'm so sorry. We didn't mean to alarm you."

"You didn't answer my question. So why are you out here?" Clint repeated.

Trey stood at Lily's side. Dylan hid behind them, afraid of being yelled at. Assuming they were in big trouble, he volunteered an explanation… throwing Lily under the bus. "We wanted to find the lost knife. Lily thought it would be fun to surprise you. We didn't mean anything wrong."

Clint's brow knitted. "What would the knife be doing out here in this run-down shack?" He replied in a stern voice. "And how exactly did you find this place?"

Lily turned toward the shack as though it were communicating to her. "Well, at first, we only intended to look around the clearing area where we found the treasure chests, thinking the knife had to have fallen out. But it wasn't there." She shrugged. "Then we saw this light coming from back this way." She looked over at Dylan. "It was my idea to investigate. I thought maybe if someone lived here, it was possible they could have stolen the knife after you put it in Trey's chest yesterday."

Staring deeply into Lily's ocean-blue eyes, Clint could tell she had not meant to cause such aggravation. A foolish idea for sure, but her intentions were honorable. "Look, you kids made a bad judgment call. Never, *ever*, do anything like this again. When you spend the night at my place, you stay indoors, not running around like half-brains!"

"We're sorry, Grandpa," Lily apologized with remorse.

Chapter 27

"I'm not going to tell your parents, but you need to think twice before traipsing off into unknown territory without supervision. It could have turned out differently." Clint gave his words a second to sink in, not sure if he should tell them about the large cat he had spotted. He admitted to only part of what was on his mind. "Just so you know, on the way here, I saw a large animal outside this very shack!"

Clint could see the humiliation in Lily's eyes. Trey was looking down at the ground, avoiding eye contact. Dylan looked like he was ready to have a total meltdown.

Putting his arm around Lily's neck and pulling the boys close, he stated, "C'mon, let's get inside. No harm, no foul. Consider it forgotten. But stay close to me on the way back." Trey and Dylan couldn't wait to get into their beds.

At the opening to the yard, Clint realized Lily was carrying her snow globe plus another item. "What'cha got there? he asked pointing to an object under her arm.

"Oh," Lily yelped, forgetting about the book she was holding. "This was inside the shack." She handed it over to Clint. "On a bench," she said with her face contorted. "That was the strangest place. I swear we saw a light coming from inside the shack. But when we got there, it went dark. No light. If someone was there, they must have seen us coming and taken off."

Clint turned the book over to view its cover. Stunned, he was shocked at what he was looking at. An unusual title to find in a shack in the forest, and it just so happened to be one of his all-time favorites, *Treasure Island* by Robert Louis Stevenson.

"That's hard to believe," he said in a surprised tone.

"Yeah, that's what I thought," Lily concurred, surprised to have seen it sitting on the bench. "Clearly, people lived in that structure in the past. It's uninhabitable now but at some point, it must have been someone's home."

"It appears you may be right," Clint responded. He glanced at the book a second time. "You know, back in the old days, that was an extremely popular book. When I lived in the orphanage, in fact, I read it several times. I was about nine at the time." He gave her a lopsided grin. "I read a lot back then. Not much else to do in a children's home."

"Can I keep it?" she asked with a touch of sympathy to her voice. Then she reconsidered. "Or, since you liked it so much, maybe you should."

A big grin crept onto Clint's face. "No, I've read it enough. Of course, you can keep it. Finders keepers, losers weepers, my dear." He lovingly handed the book over to his granddaughter. "A souvenir and reminder of your misguided post-adventures at Grandpa's treasure hunt!"

They were laughing when they went indoors. Clint walked with Lily to the den. Both boys were under the covers on the floor, their eyes wide open. Clint sat on the edge of the bed and expressed to them how happy he was that they had stayed over and that none of them had been hurt.

"You guys have no idea how much you mean to me. If you promise never to pull a stunt like that again, I'll have you come spend the night as often as your parents will allow." He rubbed the top of Dylan's head with his knuckles. "Maybe we can talk Lily's parents into letting her visit before the end of the year, and you boys can join her."

After saying goodnight for a second time, Clint went to bed. When he glanced at the clock, the display reflected a ludicrous hour—1:28. No doubt, by tomorrow exhaustion would set in. Between the crazy dream he had experienced and the kids wandering off in the middle of the night, he figured driving to Crothersville and back home again was going to be a serious challenge.

His thoughts traveled to the sizable cat he had seen wandering the woods and wondered what exactly he had witnessed. It was as if it had entered from another dimension. Because, although the timing was nearly exact to his arrival of finding the children, they did not mention seeing a large black cat come into the shack.

Chapter 27

The powerful animal could not have done so. Otherwise, the kids would have screamed bloody murder. What could he make of that discrepancy?

Unquestionably, this had been one bizarre night.

Clint awakened at his usual time of 5:45 a.m. He tried to force himself back to sleep, but his brain refused to cooperate. Last night's capers had made him restless. He put his feet to the floor with the knowledge he would be dead tired by midafternoon.

He went to the kitchen to start frying the bacon he planned to serve at breakfast. Blueberry pancakes were on the menu, along with scrambled eggs and home fries. Clint was proud of the cook he had aspired to be and accomplished. Nowadays, he was much more confident of putting a suitable meal on the table.

Standing as if he was comatose, staring inside the refrigerator, he withdrew the carton of milk from the shelf and set it on the counter, nearly missing the edge. He'd start pancakes after the bacon and potatoes were frying. Once done, those would be set in the oven to be kept warm. "I'll make the pancakes last, fresh off the grill when those rascals show the whites of their eyes," mumbled Clint with a smile. "First things first, get the bacon started. The smell of bacon can allure the best of them!"

The smell of coffee roused his foggy brain, and the thought of Jules popped into his head. He wondered how she would have reacted to what the kids had pulled in the middle of the night. A smile arose when he recalled their shocked expressions. They were frightened when he appeared at the shack door. He, on the other hand, was thrilled to see them.

The morning sun streamed through the living room window, imparting its special style of greeting. A beautiful day lay ahead from all indications. The house smelled of hickory-smoked bacon and fresh brew. Clint had already stolen two pieces from the plate and was battling with himself not to take another.

Dylan was the first to walk into the kitchen and plop down. "Hi, Grandpa," he said sleepily.

"Good morning, sir!"

"Smells good in here."

Clint reached over and took a slice of bacon from the plate. "Here," he said to Dylan. "Don't tell."

"Thanks," said Dylan with droopy eyes.

Sitting at the table across from Dylan, Clint watched as Trey and Lily barely made it into the kitchen. "Good morning," he said, welcoming the two of them.

"Good morning," they replied in unison.

Lily was holding the book from the night before. "Grandpa," she said with an uneasy expression. "I think you need to see this!" Her tone was somewhat alarming.

"Why?" he asked, watching her slide the book across to the other side of the table where he was sitting.

"Just open it and look at the front cover page," Lily said with her eyes wide.

Clint did as he was told. The book was opened to the inside cover. His entire body withered.

Written on the blank left side of the open book, he struggled to absorb the words he had read.

> *Someday you will find this tale fascinating. Until then, pictures will have to do. When you are a bit older, we will join forces in the search for the Reno Gang's treasure.*
>
> *Merry Christmas. Love, Dad*

Chapter 27

At the top of the page on the right-side, Clint's full name was written in calligraphy, along with the date: *December 25, 1953.*

But, when Clint saw what was at the bottom, ROD'S GENERAL STORE, he buried his head in his hands.

Shocked to the core, his body was trembling when he said... teary-eyed, "If you don't mind, I'll keep this."

Chapter 28
Missing in Time

That same morning the mantel clock chimed 5:15 a.m. at Jules' place. It was time to get a move on. Not a far distance, she could get to Josie's Diner in less than fifteen minutes. The sun showed little sign of breaking in the east when she locked the door behind her.

As she got dressed, the previous day's activities replayed in her mind. What a fun time they'd had. Meeting Clint's family had been less stressful than she'd anticipated. They were delightful people. The grandchildren were extremely energetic, with the prospects of treasure looming over the activities and meal prior to the big event. The young ones had taken to her from the start. Like they had all known each other their whole lives.

The window was open on the passenger side of the car. She glanced down at the video sitting on the seat and began humming the theme song from the movie. Feeling especially content, she decided today had the earmarks of perfection.

When she walked through the rear entrance to the diner, Patrick greeted her cheerfully. "Mornin'!" he said on a high note.

"Back at ya!" she countered.

"Did you have fun at the treasure hunt?"

Jules grinned, giving him a look of approval. "Marvelously! Clint's family and the grandkids are lovely people. We had a blast." She rubbed her midsection, "I've not eaten that much in years!"

Patrick smiled. "Glad to hear the party went well."

Jules' eyes sparkled. "Yeah, it's nice to have met the family. Clint's three grandchildren spent the night. An unexpected development." She laughed. "I hope he survived it!" she giggled. "We played a few games before calling it a night. He's taking the kids to their parents in Crothersville later today."

Chapter 28

She parked her purse under the counter and wrapped her uniform apron around her waist before clipping her cap securely to her pinned-up auburn hair.

"Hey, Patrick, do you happen to know where Rod's New and Used Books is located? It's supposed to be somewhere here in town." She splayed her hands. "But for the life of me, I can't find it."

"Can't say I do. Don't think I've ever heard of it." Patrick frowned.

"You do recall the video the old man told me about and then later brought a copy by for me to take to Clint's place? Said he had a copy back at the shop. Skinny guy?" Jules said, feeling a bit guilty for describing him that way.

"Yeah, I remember." Patrick recollected the occurrence and said, "Odd fellow. Never came too close, if I recall. Kept his distance from both of us."

"Yes, that's him. The movie stopped at the beginning. Rod's New and Used Books is stamped on the jacket sleeve. Clint tells me there is a bookstore down one of these side streets. Apparently, they sell antiques there as well."

"You are full of surprises. Haven't heard of an antique or bookstore around these parts." He flashed a smile, taken aback for not knowing his town better.

"I tried to find it one day last week, on my break but ran out of time. Could not locate it anywhere. Clint said to turn left at the intersection of Grandview and Ridge Crest." Jules' eyes seemed deep in thought.

"Sorry, Jules. Can't say I've ever heard anyone mention that place before. A little puzzling. Don't you think? Let's look it up on the Internet. Chances are it's listed." Patrick went into his office to fire up the machine.

Jules made them both an iced tea and sat down opposite him. As she waited, she told Patrick about the treasure hunt and how excited the kids were when they found their treasure. She told him about the clues and how clever Clint had been in writing them.

That she had helped to a small degree, but Clint mostly had the ideas.

"Don't see it," he said, looking over the computer.

"Not everyone has a website. Or a listing on the internet." Jules looked confused. "Try Rod's, Salzburg, and see what pops up."

Patrick typed in the phrase and waited. He scrolled through the listings and stopped when he saw Wikipedia's History of Salzburg, Indiana. "Hey, can you imagine this? There is a history of our town."

Jules said sarcastically, "Must be a short recap. A thimble's worth," she giggled.

"Whoa, guess what I just found?" Patrick said with his brows raised.

"What?"

"There used to be a general store here in Salzburg called Rod's General Store."

Jules moved closer.

He clicked on the photo to enlarge the picture, turning the computer for a better view.

Jules stared at the scene. "Burned down in 1953. On December 26, only one day after Christmas."

A man who looked an awful lot like the one who had loaned her the movie appeared on the screen, rendering both Jules and Patrick speechless. A younger version of who she had talked with was standing in front of the general store, wearing a straw hat and suspenders. He had a solemn look on his face as they always did in that era. No one ever gave the impression they were happy back then.

"Who is he?" Patrick asked, now as curious as Jules.

"From what Clint described to me, that store bears a striking resemblance to the one he bought a few of his treasure hunt gifts for the kids from." With mischievous eyes, she added, "Of course, that can't be."

Chapter 28

They stared at the picture of Rod's General Store in disbelief, not sure what to say or think.

"No wonder I hadn't heard of it. It burned to the ground long before I moved to Salzburg. I didn't move here until 1969," offered Patrick.

"Obviously, it can't be the same place," Jules replied, somewhat stunned. "They must have rebuilt it," she stated skeptically. At lunch break, I'm going to find that bookstore if it kills me. This time I'll take the car and drive up and down every street until I do." Jules giggled. "No, Patrick, we aren't living in the Twilight Zone. We did not have a conversation with a dead guy." Her wheels were turning but hit a brick wall. Out of ideas, Jules said confidently, "My guess is, it's his son or another family member. That makes the most sense."

Jules got up and went to the kitchen to start her routine. Her head was spinning. She hadn't been able to find the store. They did find information about Rod's General Store on the internet. The original store no longer existed, however, one with a similar name did. More determined than ever, Jules was steadfast in tracking down its location.

Patrick agreed to let Jules take her lunch break at ten instead of eleven. She would not rest until the mystery was solved.

An Untapped Emotion

Clint's eyes grew huge in disbelief. His throat constricted and his eyes welled with tears. "This book was found inside the shack. Meant for me in 1953? How do I wrap my head around that?"

He had no words to describe the thoughts zigzagging from one side of his brain to the other-from the logical left side that said it was just a coincidence, to the creative, emotional right side that attached more meaning. Clint chose to bow his head in lieu of conversation, not wanting the grandchildren to see him lose control. Formless words clung to his lips. Inside, his body shook from untapped pent-up emotion.

Lily pushed her chair back and walked over to her grandfather's side of the table. Having heard the tragic stories of his childhood, she put her arms around his neck.

"That is why I waited until now, and not last night, to show you. I kept wondering how a book from your father got inside that shack. How is that possible? Without a doubt, he must have been there. From the date at the top, it was close to Christmas, the same year he disappeared."

The heartbreak was too great to absorb or share. Clint could not bring himself to raise his head. His heart felt shattered all over again, taking him back to a day he had worked his whole life to erase. He had stepped into December 24, 1953—to the moment he realized his dad was not at home. Crystal clear memories of waking up on Christmas Eve and his dad not being in the house ricocheted through his being.

"Grandpa, something else happened last night I haven't told you about." Mature for her age, Lily knew when things were not right.

Clint gazed into her eyes, wondering what she could possibly have to say that was more bizarre than giving him a book from his father. "What could be stranger than this?" he replied, tapping the top of the book.

"I don't know. This is some pretty weird stuff." She squirmed in her seat, eyeing Trey and Dylan before going on. "You know that snow globe you gave me at the treasure hunt?"

"Yeah."

"I had it with me inside the shack." She tilted her head and turned her hands outward, not sure how to explain. "I brought it along but now I'm not sure why." An incredulous stare appeared on

Chapter 28

her face. "Grandpa, it lit up. Like a light had been turned on. Only there wasn't any light source. It doesn't hold batteries." Lily's eyes glinted. "And that's not all."

Clint held a concerned expression, eyes not wavering, wondering what Lily could mean by her last remark. "What? Are you sure? I assumed it was battery operated."

"I'm positive, Grandpa!" she said with conviction. "Like I said, last night didn't feel like the right time to mention these things. But we *all* saw it. Didn't we?" Lily turned to the boys.

Both boys nodded.

Shaking his head in agreement, Trey added, "It's true. We all saw it. And there wasn't a switch of any kind on the globe. No batteries, like Lil said."

Lily pivoted around toward Clint. "It was crazy! I don't know how to explain it."

"You said that wasn't all! What else, Lil?" he asked, his voice trailing away.

Clint's lucid dream hit rewind. The boy and older man had disappeared inside a shack. It became clear as day, at that moment, that both shacks were one and the same. And to muddy the waters even more, Clint had also witnessed a large black cat enter the same shack.

His head was flooded with questions that had no apparent answers. But two kept rising to the forefront. *Who was the child? And who was the man in the fedora?*

Lily looked at her cousins as if to ask, do I dare add more fuel to the fire?

Trey shook his head.

Dylan lowered his eyes, not wanting to get involved any more than he already was.

"That key that was inside the box," she started out warily. "It was threaded on my necklace chain. I thought it would be fun to wear it." She looked down, remembering how it had taken on a life of its own. "I took it off." She touched the skin on her neck where the key had hung. "I'm afraid I dropped it when I saw you and neglected to pick it up."

Clint stood to his feet. "So, you are telling me it is still out there?"

He anxiously paced from the stove to the sink and back again. "Look, what has happened is a gross misinterpretation," he stated with authority. "Plain and simple. Especially with you kids traipsing out there in the forest after dark. Quite frankly, that is the only logical explanation for this. Let's keep our heads about us, guys. Don't forget the treasure hunt was on everyone's radar and could have affected your judgment. Everyone's judgment, for that matter, including mine."

Clint chuckled, "This situation has been a dilly." After a brief hesitation, he made a confession. "Okay, I'm as guilty as you three!"

Trey, Dylan, and Lily looked at each other inquisitively, waiting to hear what their grandfather was about to add to the strangeness of an inexplicable episode.

"I had a weird dream last night," he confided. "That you might say ties into your experience." Clint took a deep breath. "They have similar earmarks, and someday I'll be glad to share the detail. But for now, I say we put this whole ordeal behind us. I've got my money on a treasure hunt connection." He shifted his attention, "I'm telling you, kids, the mind absolutely has a way of playing tricks on us."

Lily moved to the refrigerator, ready to open the door. "I agree 100 percent," she stated, searching her grandfather's eyes for believability. "May I have some orange juice?"

"Sure, help yourself," Clint replied, puzzled by her cavalier response to his remarks. Nevertheless, he could tell her wheels were turning.

Lily volunteered, "We had the flashlight on, and that could have caused the snow globe to give the appearance of being lighted." Lily said all the right things but believed none of what she was

Chapter 28

saying. She shifted her glance to Dylan, who was paying close attention to her comments. "We were out expecting an adventure, and I guess we gave ourselves one. Especially me. I'm to blame. The boys weren't keen on the idea."

She wavered, adding one last, hopefully, convincing remark. "I'm sorry, guys, for scaring you. I think my fertile mind got the better of me. I saw what I wanted to see."

At the table, they sat eating breakfast in silence. After about fifteen minutes, Lily finally broke the silence. "Do you mind sending the key to me?" she asked Clint. "I'd rather not search for it today."

Clint reached over and took Lily's hand before turning toward the boys. "No problem. I'll mail it to you." A gentle smile caressed his face. "A pact… no more adventures at Grandpa's house. Unless he's with you."

They all laughed, but a shadow of skepticism lingered. What really took place the night before was without a true explanation. Even so, one undeniable fact remained. The book *Treasure Island* was found in a shack behind Clint's property with his name written inside. Intended as a Christmas gift from his father but was never received.

At 10 a.m. sharp, Jules removed her apron. She tossed it below the counter and grabbed her bag. Leaving through the rear entrance, she headed to the employee parking lot. The pressing errand weighed heavy on her mind.

From the driver's seat, she looked down at the package she was determined to return to its rightful owner. The video case was flipped to the back cover, displaying Rod's New and Used Books but no street address.

At Grandview, she turned left, just as Clint had instructed.

With great care, she examined every building until the street came to a dead end. Jules stared into a cornfield when she stopped to turn around.

On the return trip, she painstakingly examined every storefront but found no such place. Exasperated, she hung another left at Main and aimed her car toward the library. There she would consult with Bonnie to see if she could shed light on the Rod's New and Used Books mystery.

"Long time, no see!" Bonnie said in a way of a greeting when Jules walked up to the counter. "I've missed you, girl. What has it been… a whole two weeks?"

Both ladies laughed.

When Jules moved to Salzburg, Bonnie had been the first person in town to extend a helping hand. Jules' brother and sister-in-law had been diligent in assisting Jules with the transition; nonetheless, having a girlfriend to turn to during the dark days of adjustment had been a saving grace.

A week into her relocation, Jules shared with Bonnie the details of that horrific night she lost James—the telephone call she had received from Sargent McConnell of the Indianapolis Police Department to inform her of James' accident and the unbearable suffering it had caused.

Bonnie listened as Jules expressed what it was like losing James and their unborn child on the same night. Understandably, the aftermath that followed triggered inescapable agony. Subsequently, many late-night conversations had taken place between the two ladies. Jules had been dealt a tragic hand, and Bonnie had offered a shoulder to cry on, which created a lasting bond between them.

"Yeah, that sounds about right. A long dry spell for us," Jules interjected with a grin. "We should grab lunch sometime soon. I'm so busy at the diner these days there is barely time to think." She omitted telling Bonnie about Clint because she didn't want her to jump to any conclusions. Clint and Jules were just friends and

Chapter 28

nothing more.

"By the end of the day, I'm dog tired, but no excuses, we must make the time! Besides, I have some things I'd like to share, but not now."

Bonnie frowned, thinking what Jules had said sounded strange. "I'm on board with that. So, you must have come here for a reason then. What can I help you with?"

"Well, I have an odd request. I was given a video from a place called Rod's New and Used Books, and I'd like to return it. I'm told the bookstore is here in Salzburg, except I can't find it. Thought maybe you could help with the location."

"Sure, let me see what I have on file." Bonnie made a few quick clicks on her computer, scanning through listings of all businesses in Salzburg and the surrounding area. When she came up empty-handed, she stated, "Nope, don't see anything with that name. Could it be listed some other way?"

Jules looked dumbfounded. "It's the strangest thing. This guy came into Josie's one day and overheard a conversation Patrick and I were having. He ended up loaning me a copy of a movie that he said he highly recommended. He told me he worked at a place here in Salzburg." She handed the movie to Bonnie. "Check the back side. The name is on the label."

A frown appeared on Jules' face, "I've since thought it odd that he was so willing to go fetch a movie for me. He didn't know me from Adam, and here he was handing over a movie for me to tote to Clint's. He had no guarantees that I'd even return it."

Bonnie's face showed her surprise. "Did I understand you correctly? Did you say, *'tote to Clint's?'*"

Jules immediately realized her mistake. With a huge smile, she replied, "We'll talk about that later. I promise."

Bonnie glanced at the video. "You know I've seen that movie. It's very good. What did you think of it?"

"Don't know, it stopped playing after the scene where the old lady, the actress Jessica Tandy I believe, walks down the aisle and tells Richard Collier, 'Come back to me.'"

"Oh, I remember that part. That was creepy. She was dressed in black, and the people all parted as went by." Bonnie's eyes brightened. "Jules, you missed a classic. That man was right. It was an excellent movie. A real sleeper at the box office. It's a shame the player malfunctioned."

Jules' eyes narrowed, recalling the day the gaunt man placed the movie on the counter. "Yeah, he mentioned that." Ready to return to work, she gave Bonnie a hug and a promise to be back in touch soon.

Before Jules stepped outdoors, Bonnie yelped. She put her hand up. "Wait a minute, Jules!" she called out to the front of the store. "I just remembered something. There used to be a place called Rod's General Store here in town. However, that was a long time ago."

Bonnie walked briskly to the middle of the room, where another desk was located. She opened a metal file cabinet and began rummaging through folders of old documents.

Jules walked up and put her purse back down on the desk. "Yeah, I heard Salzburg used to have a general store. Patrick and I saw something on Wikipedia." She elected not to tell Bonnie what she knew. She would wait to see what the archived files revealed.

"Here it is!" Bonnie declared excitedly. "I knew I had seen an article on that place."

Her expression changed, turning grave. In a surprised tone, she said, "I didn't remember that! Apparently, it burned down in 1953. The fire started at the front part of the store, and according to this account, the owner was at fault. He fell asleep while smoking in bed."

Bonnie pursed her lips as she read farther down. "Damn cigarettes!"

"Patrick and I saw that on the internet," Jules confessed. "Sad, isn't it? Does it give the location where the store used to be?"

"Yeah, on Grandview, why?" Bonnie inquisitively replied.

Chapter 28

"Because I'm going over there. I understand the original store no longer exists, but I think maybe Rod's New and Used Books has been built in its place. To be honest, this whole thing is starting to drive me bonkers."

At the door, Jules turned, facing her friend. "Would you be available this coming Thursday? We could grab a bite to eat at the diner. Sit at that back booth—the one closest to the kitchen. Maybe squeeze a short visit in. Noon, our normal time?"

"Sure, Jules." Bonnie looked at her calendar and gave a thumbs up. "I have no plans. I'll make the time. Close the library for thirty minutes. Sounds wonderful."

"Great, see you then. I look forward to it!"

At the corner of Main and Grandview, Jules turned right. Proceeding through the Ridge Crest intersection, she slowly drove farther along Grandview, knowing this was where Clint had said she'd find the bookstore. The article indicated the general store had once stood in this area as well, but she spotted nothing that resembled what she was looking for.

Holding the newspaper account Bonnie had given her as a guide, Jules let the car idle. She picked up the paper for a closer look at Rod's General Store. In the picture, an awning overlaid a sizeable display window. The storefront matched Clint's description of the bookstore to a tee. Just as it had on the internet.

The man in the photo standing at the entrance area to the store worried Jules, and an unsettledness rushed over her. She had seen him in the photo Patrick and she had viewed. The hairs on Jules' arm stood on end. Although the picture was no more than four inches in diameter, it was easier to make out than on the computer. The fedora the man had on his head matched perfectly to that of the man who had given her the movie.

She brushed the idea aside, realizing it was an absurd thought.

Other than the fact the name Clint had encountered was Rod's New and Used Books, the image of Rod's General Store appeared to be uncannily similar.

She took a hard look at the empty lot across the street. Remains of where a structure had once stood were clearly defined. Everything came into focus. All that remained of the destroyed building site were two keystones, foundation supports, and remnants of mortar and chunks of concrete.

This was not what she had been searching for.

Chapter 29
Joined Forces

By the time Clint pulled into the drive, the sun had set. One of the most beautiful sunsets he had ever witnessed had dropped into the western horizon, fading into yesterday. A good visit with his boys and the family during the early evening had put things right. Once again, they had stopped in at Cracker Barrel and shared the last minutes of their day before everyone went their separate ways.

Amongst the laughter and love, one question continually crossed Clint's mind. *How did the book get in the shack?*

Clint had asked the children not to bring the subject up. He didn't want them to get into any trouble or stir up a hornet's nest of questions on how the book was found. Later they would bridge the topic but not today. The children had agreed it was best.

Clint went to the living room and plopped down in his recliner, tired to the bone. Keeping his eyes open on the way home had turned into a real battle. The events of the last few days were both delightful, unsettling, and exhausting. It had been an eventful two days. He would give it that.

He dialed Jules' number.

"Hello," she answered on the third ring.

"Hey, it's me," said Clint. "Just wanted to say hi before calling it a day. See how you're doing and what your day was like."

"Doing great," replied Jules. "How about you? Did you enjoy the grandkids' stayover?"

"Yeah, just barely," he half-heartedly joked.

Jules assumed he meant they were having fun playing games or goofing off like teenagers do. "What time did you get home?"

"Just a few minutes ago. I'm pretty bushed but didn't want to wait until tomorrow to speak with you. Something extremely farfetched happened with the kids. I can't get it out of my mind."

Jules could hear the seriousness in Clint's voice. "Tell me!"

"Last night Lily and the boys, like idiots, went to the place where we had hidden their treasure chests. They were hoping to find the knife. After I went to bed, mind you. They said they wanted to surprise me. Thinking maybe Trey had simply dropped it out there. They meant well."

"Are you saying they were all out in the forest after I went home?" Jules asked in disbelief.

"Yep, they sure were! I found them in a shack. A structure past the clearing. Who would have known? I suppose someone must have lived there in the past or homesteaded."

"Holy cow! That must have been weird." She started to chuckle. "No wonder you said you barely survived it. It was late when I left. What time was this?"

"I can't remember for sure, but well past midnight. I think I crawled back in bed around two."

"Clint, that's loony!" Jules responded empathetically but genuinely humored.

"You're not joking. Talk about feeling my age," he said with a snicker. "But I haven't told you the strangest part yet." A lump formed in his throat. "Lily found a book inside the shack… "

A long silence followed his comment. Finally, Jules said, "Clint, are you there?"

"Yeah, I'm here," he responded, trying to compose himself before continuing. "Jules, it was a book meant for me, from my father. *Treasure Island*. Dated Christmas, 1953. But, as you know, I never saw him after December 23. We had dinner that night, and it was the last time I ever saw him. On Christmas Eve, I woke up to an empty house."

There was another long silence. This time it was Jules who was not talking. "Do you want me to come over?" she asked. "I can be there in ten minutes."

"No, no… that's not necessary. You have to work tomorrow, and I need to digest this."

Chapter 29

Clint regarded the book on the table in front of him. "But you do know what this means. Don't you? He must have been in that shack the day of his disappearance. Either December 23 or early morning December 24. For what reason, God only knows. It's anybody's guess."

"Clint, promise me you'll come to the diner in the morning. I'll not rest until I see you." The truth was Jules wanted to tell him about her discovery but knew this wasn't the time. Her bombshell could wait one more day.

"Sure, no problem. As tired as I am, when my head hits the pillow, I'll be out like a light. Guaranteed."

"Okay. I'll be watching for you. Your coffee will be ready and waiting."

"Sounds good. I look forward to seeing you. I'd better go before I fall asleep on the phone." Again, he was attempting to insert humor in the situation. "Sleep well."

"You too, see you in the morning."

Clint disconnected the call and set the phone on the table beside the book. In the kitchen, with the lights off, Clint sat in darkness a while longer before getting up to go to the bedroom. He got undressed, replacing his heavy clothing with his Notre Dame lounge pants and shirt. The overhead light was turned off, and the lamp beside the bed was on. *The Time Machine* sat on the nightstand. He did not dare pick it up or try to read.

Slumber came gently and without incident.

Monday, September 22

At 6 a.m., Clint was out of bed, dressed, and ready to head into town to settle his bill with Joe, his mechanic, for what turned out to be a quick fix on the truck. The plan was to walk down to the garage after a relaxing breakfast and a few cups of coffee while reading the newspaper.

More than ever, Clint looked forward to his standard meal of chicken fried steak, home fries, scrambled eggs, and biscuits, which would be served to him in less than a half-hour. With the promise of a sidebar conversation with his favorite waitress, Clint's leisurely drive west on Highway 150 into Salzburg underscored his mellow mood.

Watching Jules scurry about, taking orders, and chitchatting with her customers, was comical to ponder. Monday felt more uplifting than the day before with all the earth-shattering revelations brought to light. Eight hours of shuteye rarely occurred in Clint's world. Last night's uninterrupted sleep of nine hours had improved his disposition greatly.

On the drive to town, Clint considered how he was going to convey, in its entirety, the episode involving the kids. He would welcome her assessment of the ordeal. The book Lily had presented him with lay beside him on the seat. *Treasure Island*, signed by his father, was meant as a gift fifty years in the past.

"I wonder what she'll say to that?" He spoke quietly, looking down at the book and thinking it would be nice to light up. It had been four days since he had smoked, and his body was telegraphing its deprivation loud and clear.

The realization that he possessed a Christmas gift his dad had intended to give him on Christmas morning when he was five was overwhelming. He smiled, wondering if his dad had meant to put any other gifts under the tree that year.

Memories flooded his senses. How he had stayed up waiting on his father to return on Christmas Eve. Snow was falling hard that night, he recalled. From the couch, he had watched it through the window. He remembered thinking, Santa would rescue him at midnight. Clint grinned at the innocence of his younger self.

Clint pulled behind the diner. He parked the truck in its usual spot and took the morning news from the newspaper stand. Tucked

Chapter 29

under his arm, he tipped his cap at Jules as he took a seat at the table reserved for him. A filled coffee cup and a biscuit awaited him. He took a deep breath, glad to return to normal life.

"Hey, stranger!" Jules cheerfully greeted him as she topped off his mug, more as an excuse than a need.

"Glad to see you," Clint greeted her in return. "The rest of your evening go well?"

Jules grinned and sat down. "I started a book called–*Odd Thomas*. Didn't get too far into it before I conked out." She chuckled. "Man, I was tired. Not used to so much activity nor eating up to here." She pointed to the top of her throat. I made some tea, but that didn't help." Jules' face brightened. "I know I'm getting old when I can't stay up an hour past my bedtime."

"Ditto. I felt like a train had run over me by the time I hit the sack." Clint guffawed at his old-timer's humor. "Two old geezers, that is what we are!"

Jules stood. "Better make my rounds. Before you leave, I have something I want to tell you. Don't want you slipping away before we speak one final time."

"I never leave without saying goodbye."

She nodded. "That's true, but this is important. Something you are not going to believe. I wish I could tell you now, but it'll take me a second or two to recap what I want to share." She glanced at the grill clock. "I could take a short break around nine. Do you have anything to do in town?"

"I can always find things to do in town," Clint admitted. "Truth is, I already had planned on stopping in at Joe's. I also need to run to the grocery to pick up a couple of loaves of bread and a gallon of milk." He smiled. "Should grab extra feed at Ralph's. Didn't realize how low I was. Don't want the chickens to starve! They provide eggs for my breakfast when I'm not here," he laughed. "Now you have my whole day's schedule! Oh, and there's always ACE Hardware."

"Sounds like a plan. I'll clock out at nine for fifteen minutes. I doubt Patrick will care."

Clint read his newspaper cover to cover. He worked the crossword puzzle before folding it and setting it on the table by the entrance for the next customer to comb through. He waved at Jules when he walked through the door on his way to Joe's Garage.

When their eyes met, Clint could tell something of importance was on her mind.

Chapter 30
Unvarnished Truth

At nine o'clock sharp, Clint was back at Josie's Diner. Disappointed that his normal reserved table was occupied by a mother and two rowdy children, he hightailed in the opposite direction from the commotion.

Jules walked over and sat down. "Right on time," she remarked with a smile. "If there is one thing about you, Clint, you're punctual."

"Yep, 'better never than late,' says Bernard!" Clint chuckled at the confused look on her face, obviously clueless to his reference. "It's a quote from George Bernard Shaw." When her expression remained the same, he said, "Forget it. That was goofy."

Jules patted his hand, "I forgive you!"

"Thanks," he said, feeling amused. "Hey, what did you want to talk to me about?"

Jules took a deep breath. "Well, this one is a little weird. And, truthfully, I don't know if you are going to like what I have to say."

"Okay, that sounds worrisome."

"I'll get right to it. You know that bookstore you've been visiting, Rod's New and Used Books?"

Clint looked puzzled, "Yeah."

"Well, it seems to be missing." Jules grimaced.

"What are you talking about? I was just there. Not that long ago." Clint crinkled his forehead.

"I know that's what you said." Jules sighed, reluctant to finish what she had started. "I concluded the guy who loaned me the video was the same man that owned the bookstore. The older guy you had been trying to connect with since day one."

"And…"

"The damaged video I brought over the other night came from there. I'll give you that! On the back of the case sleeve, a label was attached, Rod's New and Used Books. Well, it turns out there is no such bookstore here in Salzburg. Never was. I set out to return the movie with an explanation but couldn't locate the store—for the second time."

"Jules... that's impossible. I bought gifts there."

"I know. But, Clint, I'm telling you it doesn't exist. Patrick and I looked it up online, and the only thing we found was an article about Rod's General Store and the fire that turned it to ashes in 1953. Nothing was built in its place."

Holding his eyes steadfast, Clint tried to digest what she was saying. He shook his head, "That can't be."

"I'm sorry, Clint, but it is. I went to the library to check it out and, Bonnie, my friend who works there, retrieved a newspaper article and gave it to me." Jules pushed the article across the table for Clint to examine.

In disbelief, he stared at the man on the front cover. Standing at the entrance to a building he knew well. An awning to the right of the entrance. Rod's General Store appliqued onto the window. The same signage dangled above the door where the man in the picture stood. Just as it did at Rod's New and Used Books.

"What is this?" Clint asked, his stomach-churning.

"Like I said, it's an article about the fire. If you turn the page, you'll see another picture from a different angle. Apparently, Rod was asleep in the spare room he had rigged up as a living quarter for when he spent the night. A section of the building he converted into a bed and bath space."

Jules waited for the information to sink in. "That's where he was when the fire broke out. The arson investigators theorized that the fire either started in the kitchen and then spread to the storage room and eventually consumed the rest of the store. Or Rod was smoking in bed. The final analysis, albeit not conclusive, slanted to Rod causing the blaze." Her brow creased. "The article says he was survived by one son. Lived in New York with Rod's ex at the time of the accident."

Chapter 30

"Really?" he said, astonished at this latest revelation. In a flash Rod, Jr.'s attire came to mind. His silk suit, slicked-back hair, and fancy shoes. Clint was half expecting what came next.

"Do you want to look him up on the computer?" Jules asked. "Bonnie sent me a link. She accessed the archived files from the courthouse, which are more in-depth. But, to tell you the truth, almost anything can be found online these days."

"I do."

"Patrick already said I could use the computer in his office."

Jules led the way and Clint followed.

They scrolled through the pages of time, going back decades. The article she had highlighted leaped off the page. Rod's son, Rod Radcliff, Jr., was mentioned in an accident report.

Jules almost choked. "Apparently, he had secured a license to rebuild on the same piece of property that Rod's General Store had once been erected. The business name registered at the city county building lists the new site as, Rod's New and Used Books."

"See, I told you." Clint grinned, relieved to have been right. "I'm not bonkers."

"Okay, Clint," Jules replied quickly after seeing how agitated Clint had become. "Maybe I just wasn't thorough enough. I could be wrong."

Clint was aware Jules was attempting to pacify him. On more than one occasion, Clint had mentioned that the clerk's name was Rod, Jr. and that Rod, Sr. was his father. Though in Clint's estimation, the clerk did not look old enough to be Rod, Sr.'s offspring. His was a baby face compared to the senior Rod. Furthermore, from what Clint deduced, one or both gentlemen followed through with plans to rebuild on the identical property the General Store had once occupied.

Clint weighed the appearance of the man's face he had seen in the mirror, the thought crossing his mind... *Rod, Sr. must be older than I figured. If he owned the general store in 1953 and was an average of thirty-five to forty years old back then, that would make him eighty-five to ninety today.*

No way, Clint said in his head. *He doesn't look anything close to that. Maybe a little weather-beaten and undernourished, but he moves light as a feather.*

In a controlled voice, Clint stated, "It's not that I don't believe you, Jules. I'm sure you have tried to find the place. But I have walked around the store, and I know it exists. No, I have not lost my marbles. Some of the treasure hunt gifts were purchased in that store. So, Rod's New and Used Books cannot be a figment of my imagination! The gifts are real, and so is the store."

He took a much-needed reset. "Rod, Jr. assisted me. Even helped me select a few of the items. We discussed their origins and why they would be perfect for the treasure hunt."

Straight away, Jules recognized an edge to Clint's voice and how serious the conversation had turned. "I know. This is just one big misunderstanding. When I drove by yesterday, I must have seen a different location than the original build spot for the bookstore. I could tell a structure had been erected where I was. The foundation has an earmark of the past."

Clint did not know what else to say, but his mind stirred with unanswered questions.

They sat in silence, trying to stitch the pieces together. Neither side of the divide had an explanation.

Jules felt uneasy over the direction Clint and her conversation had taken. A fire had once destroyed the property and surrounding area of where she believed the bookstore might have stood. That was not debatable. However, she would not toss that piece of information out for Clint to grapple with. It could wait, considering the questionable and seemingly distant posture Clint displayed. Jules did her best to project solace into a situation born out of improbabilities.

Chapter 30

Chills traveled up Clint's spine. The hairs on his arms stood on end. "Jules, I don't understand," he admitted despondently. "What is going on? First the book, now this!" He sat beside her without saying a word. To Jules, it felt like an eternity. At last, Clint asserted, "I'm going to drive over there right this minute. It must be there. Either that or I'm ready for the freakin' loony bin."

Jules stared at Clint. He had never used slang like that in her presence. Not that she cared. She was just surprised at his uncharacteristic emotional outburst.

They walked back to the table, and sat down. Jules had exceeded her breaktime but didn't care.

He raised the book Lily had found, previously hidden from sight under the table on the seat. He placed it on the tabletop. Pushed between them, Clint had brought it in to show her. Hesitantly he said, "Here's the book I told you about." His eyes looked sad when he confessed, "I can't make heads or tails of this."

"It is a lot to take in, Clint, but there must be a logical explanation," offered Jules confidently. "All I can say is take a step back. We'll get to the bottom of it." Her tone was reassuring. "I'm sorry, Clint. I know this is hard." She pointed to the book.

"Yeah, no kidding. I'm not so convinced there is a logical explanation as you say," he confessed. "I feel like I've run into a brick wall. My brain is numb from all the strange things going on." Clint's brow creased. "Maybe it's coincidental, but it feels like everything started to escalate around the same time I happened upon the bookstore. Like somehow they are all connected."

Even the atmosphere had a peculiar vibe, he recalled. *The scenery felt altered somehow.* It was as though he had walked back in time. Oddly, the storefront felt both new and old, in harmony with years gone by and the current day.

Clint felt alarmed. *Could what Jules shared be true? There is no bookstore?*

He examined the direction his thoughts were moving. *The man in the article we saw on the internet is the same man I saw in the mirror's reflection that day. He was in the store. I saw him.* Clint froze at the truth of his words. He did not see him in the store, *only* in the mirror. The same mirror that currently hung in his foyer.

"I'm as dumbfounded as you are," Jules admitted, jarring Clint's concentration. "For heaven's sake, the man gave me a movie." Jules paused, questions and doubt written all over her face.

"Clint, I told him you liked sci-fi. He returned to his shop and came back with a copy of *Somewhere in Time*." Jules looked frightened. "There is a label on the video sleeve. It clearly says, Rod's New and Used Books." She turned pale. "That man looked a whole lot like this guy!" She placed her finger on Bonnie's article. I brushed it off when I first saw it, but now…"

Clint pointed to the book he had pushed across the table. "Turn it over," he instructed.

She flipped the book over. ROD'S GENERAL STORE. Her eyes widening in disbelief. "We have to get to the bottom of this Clint. Who is this guy?"

Clint grabbed his cap. "I'm going over there." Placing his hand on her shoulder, Clint offered, "I'll stop by before I head home. Tell you what I find. Buildings don't just vanish into thin air." With that, Clint made his exit.

Jules watched as the F-100 rumbled by the diner. She wondered what Clint would find.

He pulled the truck into an empty parking lot while he tried to pull himself together. He needed to regain a perspective on the situation. His head rested on the steering column with his eyes closed. *What if the store isn't there?* he worried. *Then what?*

There had been so many inexplicable occurrences, Clint could not decide which was the most alarming. Lily had told him they had seen a light in the forest that led them to the shack and the book. *What is the connection between these events?* he contemplated.

Chapter 30

He got out of the truck. *Fresh air will do me good,* he told himself. *The walk will help clear my head.*

Rod, Jr.'s words echoed through his thoughts, *Only shows up when needed.* A decrypted message, Clint now believed. Then another unusual comment that he'd made surfaced. *I'm sure your paths will cross eventually.* Could he have been given an omen?

He stepped off the curb and was caught off guard. Unlike the last time he walked the footpath with Jules, the landscape looked remarkably different this time. In the distance, he spotted a farmhouse that he hadn't noticed before. It looked out of place, as though a setting from a remote and shrouded past. Even though he could not precisely pinpoint the discrepancy of the change, he knew the current view of this end of town had been discernably modified.

The bookstore came into view—almost as though with each step he took, the store materialized out of nowhere. The same awning, the same signage–Rod's New and Used Books. He stood outside the door. To enter meant it was real, not an illusion.

Clint put his hand on the latch, opened the door, and walked in.

Chapter 31
As Above, So Below

When Clint walked through the Rod's New and Used Books entrance, no one was there to greet him. The store appeared unattended, and an eerie silence resonated around him.

Not surprised at the lack of service, Clint moved through the store, hoping to eventually locate Rod, Jr. Sooner or later, Clint figured Rod would respond to the bell that had jingled.

Growing impatient, he decided he would wait at the bay window. All new items were on display. None of them held much appeal, so he redirected his attention to the bookshelves where he knew he would find something of interest.

Glancing down each aisle, he stopped in the middle of the first walkway. From there, he had a clear view of the cash register. Taking a book from the shelf, he studied it closely. An unknown title and author. *Good Morning, Midnight* by Jean Rhys. He opened the book to the first page. Published by W.W. Norton & Company, Ltd., Castle House, 75/76 Wells Street, London W1T 3QT. Written in 1939. He slid it back onto the shelf. Not his cup of tea.

He then went back up front. "Anybody here?" he called loudly.

"Hello!" came a voice from behind the curtain.

Clint put his hands on the counter, ready to brace himself. "Good morning!"

"How can I help you?" asked a face Clint knew well.

"To start with, you can tell me who you are?" replied Clint aggressively.

Taken by surprise, Rod responded with the same level of brashness. "Sorry?" he responded tartly, matching the gruffness of Clint's voice. "What do you mean? We have had numerous conversations. Don't tell me you've forgotten."

Chapter 31

"I think you know what I mean, Rod." Clint's face turned stern. "Yes, we've talked, but I don't know who you really are. Do I? Or who your father is, for that matter. Or how it just so happens you work at a store no one other than me can find." Clint was blunt and to the point, tired of being polite.

"My, my!" Rod Jr. grinned. "A little testy today. Aren't we?"

"You would be too if you knew you were being messed with!" Clint's glare was disarming.

"Look, you came here looking for gifts for your treasure hunt. I sold them to you. End of story." Rod shifted his glance to the window display.

"We both know that is not what this is about," Clint countered. "Where is your father? I want to talk to him. Now! And don't blow me off with… 'he only shows up when he is needed.' He's needed, right this minute! Tell him to come out here!"

"He's not available," Rod responded swiftly, his eyes defiant and displeased with Clint's attitude. "He doesn't hang around the store waiting for you to come in demanding his presence! I told you he is seldomly here."

"I know what you told me, but that's not cutting it. Not this time! I want answers! And, apparently, he is the only one who will provide them. Because you sure as heck aren't! All I get from you is double-talk."

"That's not true." Rod's pale face grew dark. "Don't use that tone of voice with me." He saw red, and his eyes flashed. "I don't like it."

Clint examined Rod's threatening countenance. He looked different than Clint remembered. "Okay, I'll give it to you straight," he said, not backing off. "I want to know who your father is? And you.

Rod's expression softened to a rosy pink. "See, all you had to do was ask. I'll be glad to answer your questions. I didn't have to come out here, you know. And I certainly don't appreciate verbal abuse."

Clint's brows lifted, showing his surprise. "Okay, we'll do this your way," he said calmly. "I was shown a newspaper article with Rod, Sr., your father, standing outside this store, only the name wasn't Rod's New and Used Books, it was Rod's General Store. Explain that!"

"That's true. The store name used to be Rod's General Store. That's no secret. It's mine now. I changed the name to Rod's New and Used Books. I like books better than grocery and knickknack stuff, so I changed the inventory to reflect my personality! Not his."

Clint was having no part of Rod's manipulative explanation. "Stop screwing with me! I want answers," Clint demanded. "Is your dad alive? I want the absolute truth. This place doesn't seem to have a listing in Salzburg. Tell me, why am I the only one who seems to be able to find this location?"

Rod faltered, "What are you talking about? It does exist in Salzburg. We are interacting with one another; therefore, it exists."

"For God's sake, Rod! What the hell does that mean?"

"Okay." He put a hand up. "I can see you are upset." He pointed to the stool behind Clint. "Have a seat. I'll explain."

Clint was shocked to see a stool, not recalling it being there when he walked in. He was glad for the suggestion because otherwise, he might have been tempted to strike Rod in the jaw. Fed up with his word games, Clint gestured, "Fire, I'm all ears."

"Our relatives knew one another. Eli and Rod, Sr. A long time ago." Rod brushed the air as though he were painting a canvas.

Clint's heart nearly jumped out of his chest. A bit of bile climbed up his throat. "Rod, Sr. knew my dad?" he repeated.

"Yes. They were good friends, in fact. Palled around with each other from what I've been told. The old man would have given his life for Eli." Rod, Jr.'s eyes grew distant. Tears formed. He looked away.

"Rod?" Clint implored, not sure what had been said to cause such a strange reaction.

Chapter 31

"If it ever came to it," Rod replied, rejoining the conversation. "We Radcliff's are a devoted bunch."

Clint wanted to scream from frustration. The older Radcliff that owned Rod's General Store, couldn't be this person's dad. He and Jules had determined there was another Rod, Jr., who they deduced was this Rod, Jr's. father.

Rod's last comment hung in the air, stymying Clint's next thought. After a few minutes, he collected himself and asked the question he most wanted answered. "What about the fire? The article said Rod Radcliff died in a fire."

"Died? I'm sorry to dispute what you've read, but my father is very much alive." There was a twinkle in his eye. "As far as the shop, we rebuilt. Closed case." With a placid expression, Rod brushed a strand of sandy blond hair from his brow.

Clint's voice grew weary. "Rod, that's simply not true. You did not rebuild. There was an accident. It said he perished in the fire."

"Which one?" Rod retorted, shocking Clint.

"What do you mean which one?" he asked irritably. "Was there more than one fire?"

Rod didn't directly answer. Instead, he wore a blank stare, gazing over Clint's left shoulder as though he recalled something.

Annoyed at the lack of transparency, Clint claimed, "I think one of you has been in my house. I saw a reflection in that mirror you sold me. The one Rod, Sr. pretty much gave away for a song and dance."

"Wouldn't know anything about that," Rod swiftly replied. "All I know is the old man has an interest in you. Said you were a good lad. Wanted you to have the mirror. Mentioned something about a gateway. I can't tell you anything more than that. Can't tell you things I'm not privy to." He turned his back to Clint. "Now, if you don't mind, I have work to do." He twisted around, ready to leave. "That is unless you have something you'd like to buy."

Lad... he called me, lad? Clint smiled, finding the choice of words odd. "I came in here for information," Clint insisted.

Rod moved to where he had been before Clint entered the shop. "I have things to do. You'll figure it out," he said, holding the curtain that separated the back room from the front.

"And the items I bought from the curio cabinet? What about them? Did Rod, Sr. specifically want me to have those too?" asked Clint curtly.

The answer was written on Rod's face. He withheld most of what knowledge he possessed but gave a partial explanation, "Your guess is as good as mine, but if I had to take a stab at it, I'd say, most likely."

Putting his hands over his eyes, Clint felt like his brain was going to jump out of his skull and start running around screaming. He was no more informed now than when he walked through the door. The only gratification he felt was Rod, Sr. and his father knew one another.

Rod turned toward Clint one last time. "Be careful, Clint," his dark, beguiling eyes warned. "I believe Ben Franklin once said, 'Believe nothing of what you hear, and only half of what you see.' I suggest you heed his advice and pay close attention to the events that surround you."

With his parting words, Rod, Jr. vanished behind the curtain.

Outside, in front of the bookstore, an intense emotion washed over Clint. One he was unable to define in words. *Will I ever see him again?*

When Clint walked into the bright sunlight, he felt more befuddled than ever. Rod had not improved his mood. Not by a long shot. Retreating to his truck with unanswered questions—plus some new, fresh ones—he noticed the town was a little out of focus.

Chapter 31

Sauntering along the footpath, Jules came to mind. He could not wait to advise her the bookstore was right where he said it was. That was a relief. He would also impart Eli's close relationship with Rod Radcliff, Sr. And that Rod's father was indeed alive, which seemed hard to believe considering the article Bonnie had unearthed. The two accounts did not jibe. Clint intended to get to the bottom of it and look online for a death certificate if there was one. That would put an end to the controversy once and for all.

Then the lights came back on in Clint's head. He and Jules were right. It was the only thing that made sense. The original Rod Radcliff did indeed have a son. That would account for the age discrepancies between the first Rod Radcliff and his grandchild. The Rod Radcliff, Jr. Clint had been speaking with all along. The one that owned Rod's New and Used Books. He had picked up the torch and eventually built the bookstore. Clint contemplated the sequence of things. *Rod must carry an II behind his name. He's Rod Radcliff, Jr. II.*

Clint thought about their conversation as he came to the end of the footpath and near the sidewalk on Grandview. *That comment Rod made bothers me,* reasoned Clint. *What did he mean when he said, "second fire?" Could the original Rod Radcliff, Jr. also have been involved in a fire?* His head hurt from all the unanswered questions that hung in the air.

He knew his assumptions were a stretch, but it was all he had. Yes, he was reading between the lines, but three Rod Radcliff's filled in the blanks nicely. The young man who called himself Rod, Jr. was, in fact, the third Rod Radcliff. And *his* father was alive—the second Rod Radcliff. And he had survived a fire, unlike *his* father. The man in the article who died in 1953.

Feeling smug with himself to have tied the loose ends, Clint breathed a sigh of relief. *Everything adds up! A second Rod Radcliff explains why the kid and I were having trouble communicating. Now I understand why he was as irritated with me as I was with him.*

Aside from a slight headache, and aching bones caused by the cold temperature inside the store, Clint stepped a little lighter on his return trip. *Why would anyone keep their store that chilly?* he wondered, thinking it could deter customers.

One last time Clint turned to make certain the structure was in sight. It was. *Good to know I don't see things that aren't there!* Clint lamely joked.

Behind the wheel, he felt confident his presumptions were dead on. Jules would be brought up to date tomorrow since more time had lapsed than he had gauged. Best to wait, he reasoned, cranking the engine over, ready to leave town.

The antique mirror crossed his mind. He decided the moment he walked into the foyer, the thing was coming down. *Enough is enough!* He swore unwaveringly, *Until things settle down, I'll store it in the pole barn.* Clint couldn't bring himself to separate from the mirror. It connected the past to the present.

He was acting juvenile and felt embarrassed at his childishness. If he had to make an educated guess, he would say the treasure hunt had activated repressed emotions about his dad, and when the book was inserted into the equation, things rose to another level.

Clint had always believed precognition, and paranormal phenomena were nothing short of hogwash. However, after what had been taking place, he admitted the probability of such things was plausible. For him, the undelivered Christmas gift from his dad had been a real game changer.

Grateful to be enlightened, Clint ruminated on the meaning of current events in his life. *Maybe that is what this whole thing has been about all along. Some universal law arranged for me to have possession of the gift I was destined to have ownership of. Treasure Island—a book my father bought at Rod's General Store and intended to surprise me with on Christmas morning.*

Chapter 31

The image of Santa Claus having come on Christmas morning, presents spread under the tree, and among them, *Treasure Island* with Eli's endearing message painted a dreamy picture in Clint's mind.

Reaching behind the seat, Clint withdrew his emergency stash of cigarettes. He tapped one from the pack and held it between his lips. He tucked the half-empty pack between his legs in the event one wasn't enough. He told himself he deserved a smoke. The truth was, he did not want a cigarette. He needed one. For the first time in weeks, he gave into his impulses without remorse. In a flash, his nervous tension subsided. He thought about how the trajectory of his life was course corrected in the snap of a finger.

I wasn't abandoned, he breathed with relief. *He loved me and wanted me!*

The realization his whole life had been based on a lie was a hard pill to swallow.

Chapter 32
Night Whispers

The storm door latched behind Clint. He stared at the mirror across from him. Did he really want to remove it and leave a bare wall? Not really, but he would. Temporarily he would take it to the barn.

The mirror had been part of his journey and a catalyst that made one element evident. Clint was the boy in the dream. Everything had been neatly tied with an impressive bow. The mystery surrounding the strange episodes in his life could be laid to rest.

He went to the sink and filled the espresso machine with filtered water. He was convinced good water yielded a better cup of coffee. Buying bottled water as opposed to tap water was easily justified since a six-ounce shot wasn't much. After the day he had endured, a hot drink was in order. Soon he would pick up where he left off in *The Time Machine*.

Clint thought about time travel, a subjective premise of countless manuscripts. He considered the many signs he had experienced in his own life since moving into his house. Odd that all of it was linked to finding one solitary book.

Then a startling breakthrough emerged from a corner in his mind. *This house? Could this be my childhood home?*

Stunned by the thought, he rationalized, *that would explain why the book was sitting inside the shack. The shack was in the woods behind our house when I was a child. My dad must have gone there. Otherwise, the book would not have been found on the bench where Lily discovered it.*

Clint thought hard and knew in his heart he was right. A salad plate he was holding almost slipped from his grip when a faint memory trickled to the surface. *I remember those woods!*

Recollection cleared the path to greater clarity. Extensive repair work had been done on his residence, which had changed the

Chapter 32

home's general layout. An image of the original design clung to the edge of a distant memory.

The magnitude of his query generated a startling revelation. *This is where my father and I lived before he went missing? Before I was hauled off to foster care and the orphanage?* Clint gasped, "Is this my childhood home?"

He couldn't believe it had taken him this long to connect the dots. One by one, the levels of illumination became clear. Everything circled back to the man in the straw hat. Rod, someone who dearly cared about his father, had led the children to the shack where they had discovered the book and Clint to revelations about his past.

It became evident why he was drawn to the house and land it was built on from the start. With his adrenaline surging, he thought, *I lived here, and on some innate level, realized it. This was the house the policemen brought me to, and I was taken from.*

Surprised he had not made the connection before, Clint exhaled with joy to have discovered his roots. He lived in a house he had only recently purchased from the state at a bargain-basement price. *The house I live in is where I was raised until Dad disappeared!* Clint smiled fondly. *I was meant to find this place and property. And to think, all that time, the book was sitting in the shack, waiting to be discovered.*

Clint would have thought the mysterious episodes he had been encountering unrelated. But now, he understood otherwise. Rod, Sr. had been resolute in his desire to shed light on matters of monumental consequence.

Simple enough to understand and imagine, believed Clint. Although this was outside Clint's wheelhouse to buy into such notions, it had not stopped the powers that be to make it happen. The bottom line was he possessed a book, and not just any book—*Treasure Island*—that his dad once held. That was the long and short of it, and Clint could not have been more pleased.

Clint was elated to share his discovery of a lifetime. His was a true-life mystery that easily could have been aired on the new series, Unexplained Mysteries. The program had been piloted last Saturday, but he'd missed it because of the treasure hunt. Not this week though. He had already invited Jules over for a cookout. Later they would watch the second episode. He thought about the treasure hunt—one for the record book.

He picked up his cell phone and dialed Jules' number, hoping by this hour she would be home.

She answered on the fourth ring. "Hey there!" Jules said, looking at the caller I.D.

"Hey, yourself!" laughed Clint.

Jules was shocked to hear the animated tone of Clint's voice. She immediately knew something was up. And that something was big. "Where are you?"

"Home," he said. "Man, what a day I've had. You'll never believe it. Before I say anything more, I want you to know, the bookstore is right where I said it was. I talked to Rod, Jr., and he unloaded a wealth of information." Clint paused hesitantly, wondering if he had spoken accurately.

"Is that right?" Jules gleefully responded, wondering how that could be. "That's great. I was beginning to think we were both off our rockers."

"Nope… it's there."

"No way!" Jules shrieked. "Are you kidding me? I actually drove right by it?"

"Yep, I'm telling you it's right there on Grandview. Maybe you just didn't drive far enough."

"I'm flabbergasted, Clint. Not to say, feeling a little foolish. I'm sorry for upsetting you this morning." Silence reigned on the phone as she recalled their earlier conversation. "But what about Rod, Sr.?"

Chapter 32

Clint hem-hawed around, not sure how to answer that question. "Well, that's where things get a little messy. I'll save that story for tomorrow. Too lengthy and complicated to talk about over the telephone."

"Okay…" Jules responded, unsure why he would hold anything back. "Sounds intriguing."

"Believe me, it is," Clint replied mysteriously. "Can't wait to fill you in. A bounty of subjects is up for discussion." He laughed from deep inside.

Jules chuckled right along with him. "You do know this is going to drive me nuts until you tell me what's going on."

"Yeah, I know," he chuckled. "That's part of the fun. Sorry, but I just can't talk about it right yet. Would you like to come over for dinner before the show? I make a mean pot roast! Mashed potatoes gravy and sweet corn for sides."

"Wow! Now that is an invite. How could I refuse an offer like that? What time? Tomorrow is my day off."

"That's right. I forgot. Great… let's say 5:30. We have plenty of desserts left over from the party."

"I bet you do. Okie dokie, see you tomorrow." On a high note, Jules hung up. Stumped by what was left unspoken, she felt delighted that the controversy around the bookstore had been put to bed. She could hear the relief in his voice, but for her, the mystery remained. She would have to see the bookstore with her own eyes.

There was a chill to the evening air when Clint carried the mirror out to the barn. This time of year, the temperatures dropped quickly. The scent of fall permeated the air. It was his favorite season, hands down. In his mind's eye, he saw the two of them, tomorrow evening at the firepit, under the stars, roasting hot dogs and marshmallows—a comforting thought.

Clint could feel Jules and his bond shifting to a better place. So far, there had not been a cross word between them. However, he was aware that the way people dealt with confrontation was a sign of compatibility and the first argument was a tell-all in the way disagreements were settled.

On the way, Clint watched the overhead clouds drift lazily across the October sky. He wondered how to explain his chat with Rod, Jr. to Jules and the improbable facts of what he had come to understand. Never could he say he was a nonbeliever again. Some things were truly stranger than science.

He leaned the mirror against the wall and closed the door. Walking back to the house, the adage, water always finds its level came to mind. Life could return to normal now that the book had been retrieved and returned to him. No longer was anything out of balance. No more crazy happenings around the property or inside the house. The mystery of the misplaced book was solved.

Relieved to have the mirror stored in a safe place, Clint lifted his personal treasure from the table. He carried the book to the living room. *Treasure Island,* he thought, looking at the title. *An odd word, treasure. Means different things to different people. Having this book in my hands is a treasure in and of itself.*

As a kid, Clint had read *Treasure Island* dozens of times Tonight, he'd start to read it again. This time it would hold more meaning than the first time he devoured its pages. The memory of Gary and him sharing the worn copy, loaned from the library, entered his mind. A smile covered his face as he scrolled through the pages of time and the good times they shared: the late nights, the dreams of owning a business together, and discussing girls that lived in the orphanage.

A frustrating thought popped into his head. *The knife... I forgot all about it. I meant to look for it when I was out there.*

The fact was he had not thought about the knife since the night of the treasure hunt when the children went out to search for it. Sleep would not find him until he checked.

Chapter 32

It must be there, he told himself. *The kids didn't find it at the clearing, so it's got to be in the barn.* He shook his head disgustedly. *That stupid knife has been more trouble than it is worth. When I find it, I'm taking it back to the bookstore. Give the damn thing away to the cheapest bidder if Rod doesn't want it.*

He laughed at his reaction to an inanimate object. *It's only a knife! Not that special, other than it's as slippery as a wet noodle. I'll apologize to Trey and tell him it never showed up. A lie, I know, but it wasn't such a good idea in the first place. Maybe let him pick something else out. A replacement.*

For the second time that night, Clint went to the barn. The hour was late. Dampness hung in the air. He could feel moisture on his skin as he moved over the lawn. Nearby a tree swayed, creaking in the gentle breeze–an eerie sound. The moon shone brightly overhead through the passing clouds. By all accounts, it was a picturesque evening.

When he went inside the barn, something felt off. *Not again*, Clint grumbled. *It's that stupid mirror. When I'm near it, everything turns weird.*

Clint moved to the gray cabinet where he kept supplies—the same place he had stored the treasure hunt gifts prior to the party. Inside he searched diligently for the missing knife. He combed every shelf and reached to the back of each.

"Where the heck is it?" he shouted, uneasy thinking the blade would be lying about, and he had irresponsibly mislaid it. Clint was ready to spit nails when at last he located what he was looking for. On the third shelf behind a clay pot, he saw a sliver of the sheath.

"It's about time you showed up," he said, reaching back to retrieve the knife. "For Pete's sake, you aren't worth this much bother."

He soon felt disappointed when he realized the sheath was there, but the knife was gone. A chill ran up his spine.

"If the knife isn't here, and it isn't at the clearing, where the devil is it?"

Chapter 33
Goss Cave

Back out on the lawn, in the cool night air, Clint felt as frustrated as he had ever been. The view overhead was outstanding but fell short of restoring his peace of mind.

Sick and tired of anything that had to do with the knife, or Rod and his double-talk, for that matter, left Clint perturbed. Plagued by the goings-on around the time of the treasure hunt, Clint's dream of the little boy who had dug up the knife and darted into the forest crossed his mind. Of course, it was just a dream, but when he had it, the scenes felt real.

In his opinion, the treasure hunt had been tainted by losing the knife. The party he had worked so hard on and had looked so forward to had left a bad taste in his mouth because of it. He had no choice but to wait until it resurfaced, which he hoped would be soon. What a serious thorn in his side the knife had turned out to be.

"The road to hell is paved with good intentions," Clint quoted irritably as he crossed the lawn.

When he thought about the grandchildren and their willingness to help, Clint intuitively glanced over his shoulder toward the forest. Stopping on a dime, he was stunned to see an animal at the edge of his property. An unidentified, motionless form was observing him.

Not sure why the figure was there, he watchfully moved to the porch, trying not to draw attention to himself. Curious if the animal was in the same place as before, Clint turned, but this time, instead of capturing the silhouette of an animal, he saw the figure of a man. Clint's heart felt like it was about to leap out of his chest. The lanky man with an extended hand beckoning to Clint was the identical man in the newspaper article.

Clint's legs buckled, forcing him to grab hold of the railing to the house. Otherwise, he would have fallen. Certain that he was

Chapter 33

not hallucinating, the deceased man he saw gesturing to him was proof-positive his property was haunted.

"God, help me," mumbled Clint as he took a hesitant step toward the forest and the apparition.

Clint's chest constricted, making it difficult to breathe. *This could be the dumbest thing I have ever done,* he counseled himself. *No one will know I am out here. At this hour, no one will come looking or even realize I'm gone.*

Clint stopped halfway. Questions darted around in his head. *Why is he here?* He contemplated the darkness of the forest. *Why back there?*

A fleeting memory of his father sparked to life. Gentle eyes and a loving embrace as he lay beside Clint, who was tucked into bed. Then, also shadowed from his past, a book face illustration of a treasure map, schooner, and a one-legged seaman carrying a parrot on his shoulder. Flashed into his recall, the ominous "Black Spot," signaling a crew of pirates had condemned one of their own. Frames of memories long forgotten streamed through his mind.

"What does the old man want?" Clint exclaimed, struggling to decode the voiceless message he was meant to interpret. Untranslated appeals from the grave summoned him closer. Burdened to follow the call, Clint inched further away from his house and safety.

Feeling powerless, he took a step backward, recalling his first conversation with Rod, Jr. The exact phrase Rod Jr. had spoken reeled like a news-ticker in his brain. "Only comes round when needed." The words, from their last face-to-face, quickly trailed. "Don't dismiss what you know to be true, Clint. Signs are everywhere. Pay close attention."

"Words of forewarning," Clint muttered as he crossed the boundary line into the woods.

A bluish glimmer emanated from deep in the forest. He tried to calculate the distance. *That light is coming from the shack location. Just as Lily described it.*

Every muscle in his body told him to get out of there, but his curiosity squelched his fear. He was past the point of running like a scared jack-rabbit.

"No, I'm staying the course," he stammered. "No matter what."

Once and for all, turning his back on the entity that had been attempting contact with Clint—as far back as Elise's funeral, he realized—was not an option. He was ready to look behind the curtain.

What about that shack lures people to it? pondered Clint as he made his way through the dense forest, heading that direction. He treaded the maze of undergrowth until he heard a rustling noise behind him. His steps were being mirrored. Then he remembered the animal he had seen before the man appeared. A large black cat.

He trudged on. At the opening into the grove of trees that cocooned the shack, Clint checked his surroundings, not sure if he possessed the nerve to finish what he had started. Although he was acting on an impulse, an inner voice whispered the shack held answers.

Clint walked inside. The space appeared illuminated as if an interior light had been turned on, except there was no light. He saw nothing out of the ordinary, other than the glaring fact the shack was self-illuminating. Bizarre yes, but not the most irregular thing Clint was yet to encounter.

To his left, judging by the thick dust and grime that revealed an impression, was where the book must have been laid. Clint walked over and touched the wooden slats with his fingers.

He heard a muffled sound, not outside the structure as he might have expected but from inside. Clint examined the tight surroundings. Nothing caught his eye. He turned toward the closet thinking maybe the noise must have originated from there. All he saw was an ordinary closet.

Clint moved toward it, looking for possible holes for an animal to squeeze through. He bent down to inspect a minor crack he noted on the inner wall. His fingers brushed across the rough

Chapter 33

interior. The wall was made of a reinforced wood material. A notch that felt unnatural to the touch drew his attention. The wood was uneven and misaligned. Not a huge difference but to a person looking for inconsistency, it was conspicuous.

Clint lowered himself to all fours. Crawling inside the closet to inspect what he had fingered, he saw a vertical crack. A glimmer of light shone through a crevice from the opposite side.

He ran his hand alongside the area, hoping it might give way, but it did not. Of sturdy construction, the wall was as it should be. Clint was curious. He studied it with great care. Something looked odd about its structure.

He squeezed his body inside the cramped space until his face was touching the wall. Again, he ran his fingers over the surface. This time the irregularity became clear. A panel had been constructed into the side wall of the closet. He was looking at a well-camouflaged trapped door.

This time he placed the palm of his hand squarely in the middle of the two-foot by three-foot section and indentation. The panel popped open. Clint was shocked to have discovered a secret panel.

What is this? he asked as he probed the wall. With a bit more force, he pushed the panel to the inside and slid it along an inner track. It buried itself into an adjoining section of the closet, leaving an open cavity in its place. Clint was surprised to be viewing a modest room on the opposite side of the wall.

No way was he going inside the small space with no means of light to guide his step. The room was strange in structure, with a round hole jutting out in the center. He sat on the ground with his legs folded wondering what to do. The answer came without a moment's thought. *I'll get the flashlight.* Designed for extremely dark spaces, the LD22 Fenix would be more than adequate to look down the hole. He needed something more than a standard flashlight.

Clint jumped to his feet, thinking he had finally uncovered the reason why he had been lured to the shack. What secrets lie on the other side of the wall were mere speculation, but he was about to find out. Hurriedly he rushed off through the wood back to the pole barn where he stored his tools.

Within five minutes, he found himself again peering through the open crack in the wall. He aimed the flashlight into the secret room. His adrenaline pumped wildly. The hour was late, and Clint was on guard. When he had gone to the barn, he had inserted new batteries into the flashlight, not wanting to take any chances. He crawled through the cavity to the other side of the wall where a circular landing had been built around a hole in the ground.

Why is this here? Clint asked, aware it was a manmade hole.

Clint's mind raced. Suddenly, he remembered his father had been in the shack the day he went missing. *What lies at the bottom of this deep hole could offer a clue to his disappearance*, Clint postulated. The question that sprung to mind was, did he dare risk descending into the bowels of the earth without backup?

Am I mad? he seriously pondered.

The devil was on one shoulder, saying, *Go ahead. You know you want to.* An angel sat on the other, putting her hand out, warning, *Don't Clint. It's a mistake!*

Clint chose the former, ignoring his better judgment. With the attitude of what doesn't kill you makes you stronger, Clint lowered himself into the crack in the earth. His father undoubtedly had been aware of the shack and the secret panel. The hole had been created for a reason, and he suspected his father knew why.

In pitch darkness Clint moved down a ladder—a ladder he believed safe enough to navigate. The flashlight was securely attached to his jeans, double latched through his belt loops. Carefully he negotiated one rung at a time.

From the smell and moisture in the air, Clint realized he was lowering himself into a cave system. The damp, clammy scent of earth evoked fond memories of childhood. He was surprised because the only cave he knew about in his area was Goss Cave. Though, he had no idea it ran this far back. Clearly, the chasm he was lowering himself into was not a natural entrance. He figured this entry had taken years to construct.

Clint pondered the thought, *why would my father have dug a hole in the earth to enter Goss Cave from this direction? There must be an easier way to get in.* Clint thought back to when he was a small boy. Not many memories from those days remained. Even so, he distinctly recalled conversations about searching for treasure. Probably what spurred Clint's lifelong fascination with staging treasure hunts for his kids.

As he lowered himself deeper below ground, his thoughts raced. *I remember stories about the Reno Gang treasure and how Dad was searching for it. There must be a connection between this and that. This shaft is connected to his quest somehow. I can feel it!*

Clint thought about his grandkids finding the book *Treasure Island. It was sitting on the bench in the shack, so we have established he was here. My money is on he entered the cave. The question is, why? What was Dad doing?*

At the bottom, standing on the earthen soil, Clint grabbed the flashlight. He turned it on. Searching in pitch blackness, he slowly and sure footedly progressed further into the depth of the cave having no idea where he was going. Water was dripping somewhere up ahead. The sweet smell of pungent earth instilled a sense of tranquility. *I always loved the smell of moist soil, remnants of the past, and walking through the forest with my dad.*

Clint stopped cold. He concentrated hard on a memory that was trying to break the barrier of yesteryear. *I remember being in the woods with my father. Could it have been the forest above? The forest he and I walked was the same as the one behind my house? My house is the one I lived in as a kid? Owned by my father in 1953?* Clint could hardly believe how the pieces were beginning to fit.

He thought about the many walks his father, and he had taken behind their place when he was a child. Hand in hand, they would turn over rocks, search the ground for signs of treasure, and keep an eye out for anything that was uncharacteristic.

Clint remembered as a young boy in the orphanage, pretending he was an archeologist, looking for ancient dinosaur bones or anything atavistic in nature. He amassed artifacts he believed valuable and stored them in a tin can under his bed. The very memory of those days warmed his heart.

Moving through indescribable darkness, along an unfamiliar trail, Clint sensed something was wrong. He aimed his flashlight ahead, checking the path for an obstruction but finding none. Instead, a tall, dark silhouette no more than thirty feet away took a step back, melting into the shadows. The man who had summoned him to the forest and shack had been waiting for Clint to catch up.

"Who are you?" asked Clint fearfully.

The figure, partially visible, spoke no words but pointed a finger in the direction he wanted Clint to turn.

"Are you Rod Radcliff, my father's friend?"

He received no response, only a directive. The dark figure continued up the path before fading from view.

Clint's rational mind pleaded with him to make a run for it, retrace his steps, and get to higher ground. He took a labored breath, thinking, *people die in situations like this.*

A few steps ahead, his foot caught. He tripped, falling face first. Clint's heart raced, not knowing where he would land. Fearful of plunging into a crevasse, he held tightly to the flashlight, his only means of survival. Geodes were everywhere, whole and broken, exposing colorful quartz-crystals all over the ground.

When the side of his head grazed a large golden quartz-crystal, pain ricocheted inside his skull in reverberating shockwaves. At that moment, his body detected a vibrational frequency penetrating through the ground beneath him.

For a moment, Clint thought he had dodged a bullet. He had not.

His head felt light, and an odd sensation overtook him mere seconds before he passed out. As his consciousness was fading, Clint

Chapter 33

saw the man he had followed into the cave standing above him, peering down. As Clint drifted into a space between dimensions—through expanded consciousness, he saw a different reality as a story never told unfolded.

Time moved in reverse, unveiling a profound story that began to take shape before his eyes—an emergence of clarity in a semiconscious state of converging worlds.

Clint was given the answers he had sought his entire life.

Chapter 34
A Tale of Betrayal
Christmas Eve, 1953

Eli double-checked the door. With his son asleep inside, he could not afford to make a mistake. He offered a whispered prayer of protection over his son and house until he returned.

"No more than three hours," he promised God. "Before the cock crows, I'll be home."

He stared out into the open field and down the highway where no cars traveled. The sun was hours away from clearing the ridge. The start of a new day and hope of a breakthrough fueled his ambition as he turned the corner of the house and proceeded through the yard.

A carpenter by trade and a treasure hunter by night, Eli felt in his bones that he and his partner, Luke, were on the verge of pinpointing a lost stockpile of riches they had been diligently seeking for years.

A legendary story in modern times, if his dream materialized, the discovery would change his day-to-day struggles into an unfettered life. At last, Eli could provide for his son without fear of tomorrow.

If I'm right, he entertained as he stepped into the woods behind his house, *at last, I'll be the father I hoped to be. Clint and I will never have to worry about money again, clothes, or if we can keep the house.*

Filled with expectations, Eli lit the cigarette he had pulled from behind his ear. Finding it difficult to quit, he had given up on the belief he could kick the habit. The first smoke of the day for him was always the most satisfying.

Old habits die hard, he chuckled. In a relaxed mood, Eli told himself what he was doing was worth the risk.

Chapter 34

He zigzagged through the forest on his way to the shack where he and his partner were expecting to hook up in three minutes at 3:30 a.m.

Eli had brought Luke McCauley on board four years prior. Considered a perfect partner, Luke assisted Eli in his endeavor to unearth the Reno Gang's fortune. As a trusted friend, his brawn had advantages. Together they scoured the land, which so far had yielded no results. Eli had reason to believe that was about to change.

Late nineteenth-century accounts alleged the bounty was hidden somewhere in Goss Cave. Where in Goss Cave was anybody's guess. Many had searched the large cave system, but none were successful.

A well-hidden secret, Eli's contention was that the stash must be in an extremely remote location, far from where other fortune hunters searched.

A place no one would ever expect treasure to be discovered.

The grave holds many a dead man's secrets. So it was that Eli and Luke were forced to follow a trail of deciphered clues from archived newspaper editorials and decoded messages that gang members had passed on to their relatives.

This much Eli understood. An arm of the intricate cave structure ran under his dad's and his property. To date, Luke and Eli's efforts had generated only minute indications they were on the right track, but Eli could feel them zeroing in.

Both men reasoned that when they discovered the hoard, they would be wealthy beyond their wildest dreams. From the onset, they had agreed when it was located, they would turn the fortune over to the authorities. They'd be content with their fair share of the spoils and take nothing more than what they were due.

Shaking hands on the promise that greed was not in either one's nature, they executed a blood brother's oath. At Eli's kitchen table, after midnight and a few too many beers, the two honorable men sealed the deal.

A Tale of Betrayal

Eli knew these many acres like the back of his hand. Every inch had been a playground when he was a kid. Combing over the same land, searching for signs of hidden treasure, he never dreamed the most vital clues would point him back to an earlier discovery his father had made after noting an irregular split in the earth on his property after stumbling upon it in a fluke chance. Later, he discovered the gap opened into Goss Cave. Shortly thereafter, Eli's father built a shack atop the location to conceal its location. At that point, the seed had been sown.

After Eli matured and married, he too constructed a house. On the far north end of his father's property, he built the house where he and Clint now lived.

Interested in the Reno Gang's fabled fortune, Luke and Eli collaborated, joining forces to uncover their unclaimed amassed fortune. Reno Gang stories were many. They were bandits who robbed trains and towns, harassing southern Indiana with their riotous lawlessness.

The brisk a.m. hour felt refreshing. The coffee Eli held tightly in his hand warmed his palms. Sleepy-eyed, he turned to the darkened house where his son slept. He'd placed a note on the counter instructing Clint not to go outside or answer the door until he returned. Wait for their father-and-son special knock: two raps, followed by a long silence, then one last knock.

Eli lumbered into the woods, still half asleep. At his feet, he noticed uneaten dinner scraps from the night before. He smiled, thinking, *I bet he had bigger fish to fry.*

He and his son did not have much, but what they did have, they shared with the green-eyed puma that roamed the forest. Regularly seen in the yard late at night, Eli had grown quite fond of the creature.

Treating the feral cat as a pet, each evening after dinner, Eli would walk morsels of food out and drop them at the mouth of the forest, knowing the cat would show up later to see what had

Chapter 34

been deposited. It seemed natural to feed the animal what leftovers they could spare since, for Eli, the payoff was a close-up view of the puma.

As unnatural as it was, after a few years of this, the cat started to appear at the same time as Eli. Standing back, he would approach without aggression, almost as though he enjoyed Eli's company.

Eli had nicknamed the puma Picasso because of his extraordinary grace and beauty. The cat reminded him of a living, walking portrait. The payoff of presenting treats to him was a glimpse of the most beautiful creature Eli had ever seen. Picasso's emerald green eyes, framed by a glossy ebony coat, were stunning. Not to be trifled with, Eli was under no illusion that if provoked, this cat could turn deadly.

Eli followed the trail that led to the shack. He was a bit early as he entered the tiny windowless structure containing one room and a closet. The cottage was so small Eli felt claustrophobic, so he finished his cigarette outdoors. Through the trees, darkness outlined only the nearest objects.

The evening newspaper mentioned a storm was brewing up north and would possibly hit the area by midday if conditions remained the same. A serious snowstorm with heavy accumulation in southern Indiana was unheard of, yet that is what was forecasted. The good news was the bulk of the storm was expected to land on Kentucky and miss Indiana, leaving only eight inches or more in their area, thank God.

Luke called from the path, "Mornin'."

"Good morning," Eli returned the greeting.

Luke lifted his thermos to eye level. "Strong coffee cures any ail. This'll rev our engines."

"I've already had two cups but, if you twist my arm, I'll be forced to give in," Eli joked.

They chatted about their last visit into the cave, confident they were in the right location. Eli mentioned, "You know it's no wonder the treasure was never found if it's where we think it is."

A Tale of Betrayal

They entered the shack and pulled open the closet to release the sidewall latch. The secret panel had been camouflaged by Eli's father, Phil, the first to pursue the Reno Gang's treasure. Eli had eagerly continued his father's legacy.

The two men lowered themselves down an unyielding hole of darkness. Carrying a lantern and pocketing a flashlight, Eli handed the lantern off when they reached the cave floor. The route in was arduous at best with its complex channels of cave passages.

They moved along corridors of weathered rock into a chiseled recess they had been working. Eli was convinced the hidden treasure lay merely a few feet away. It had been a long time coming, and the discovery would rock the world when announced. To have their names headlined on every newspaper across the US was a treasure hunter's dream.

"Take a look," Eli said, moving to the side to make space for Luke to have a gander. "I think this is significant." His voice had an excited ring to it.

On the other side of a cave wall, through a fissure that only one of them could negotiate, Eli—the smaller of the two men—squeezed. Luke had a half foot in height on Eli and over fifty pounds, which made it impossible for him to push through the narrow crack. Because of Luke's brute strength, they often joked that Eli was the brains of the operation and Luke the brawn.

"What are you going to do with your share of the treasure when we find it?" Eli asked Luke as they labored to enlarge the opening enough for Eli to wedge himself past.

"First thing I'll do is quit that dumbass job of mine," Luke chortled. "Coal mining is the devil's work."

"I'd have to agree, not an easy job," commiserated Eli. "I wonder how much we'll clear?"

"You still saying we should report it?" Luke grumbled. "That's crazy. We do all the work, and the authorities pocket our efforts."

"Luke, how many times do we need to go over this? These things

Chapter 34

are not ours to keep. They never were. We agreed," Eli reminded Luke. "They belong to the descendants of the people the gang stole them from. And the businesses they raided, including the railroads."

"I know," said Luke begrudgingly. "It's just those people don't ever expect to have their belongings returned. So, what's the harm?"

"But we would know," was Eli's quick response. "That's the harm! There'll be more than enough to share." He was tired of having this repetitive conversation with Luke. At the start, his partner had been on board with returning the goods. They would find the treasure, report it, and share in the wealth.

Although Luke seemed the obvious choice to partner with, lately, Eli was having doubts as a greedier side to Luke's personality had raised its ugly head. The closer they came to seeing their efforts pay off, the more Luke grumbled and whined.

Earlier, when they happened on an abnormal number of quartz-crystals at an entrance to a rockface that led to a cluster opening, that was the defining moment in their pursuit. The area had stopped them in their tracks. Because where the rest of the cave was made of limestone, this location had granite and quartz rock. But the weirdest thing about it was, the space felt as though it was magnetized with some bizarre energy. That had been at the end of last week.

In their downtime, Eli set out to read about what would have caused the anomaly of having crystal quartz in Goss Cave. He was surprised to learn quartz-crystals possessed powerful magnetism and was shown to generate measurable energy. Quartz conducted an electrical charge and vibrated at a specific frequency due to the electrons contained within. Even though Eli did not understand fully the scientific property of quartz-crystals, he knew they were unlike other rocks.

In the dim light, Eli could not believe his eyes. Gold and jewels lay inside the alcove where he had been laboring. He even saw a scattering of Spanish doubloons that had spilled from a leather pouch strewn over the ground in the vast shimmering treasure.

A Tale of Betrayal

In a guttural tone, he shouted, "Luke, we did it, buddy! We located the treasure!" Eli turned toward Luke. "Our lives have been blessed beyond measure. Wait until you see what is in here. We hit the jackpot, my friend!"

He swiveled in the opposite direction to face the treasure. Eli declared excitedly, "This stuff has to be worth millions. It's so much more than what we hoped to find."

Within the tiny space he'd chiseled, Eli dreamed of his new life. How their lives were about to be enriched by the crimes of a gang of ruthless, coldhearted robbers who plundered their way through southern Indiana. The reality of him and his child gaining from the wickedness of a lawless gang from the late 1860s was inconceivable.

He wrestled with the tight space until finally Eli broke through to the inner chamber where the Reno Gang's pillage was spread over the ground. He hefted a bag of coins.

When he wriggled out of the cleft, he was clutching two gold coins and a pearl necklace, ready to show Luke. The coins were amazingly heavy. He figured later they would cut into the rock, making it wider and easier to access.

Eagerly, he turned to Luke. "Can you believe this? You and me, partner, we're rich. We did it! The Reno Gang treasure—an astonishing feat!" He offered the pieces, taken from the pile inside, for Luke to inspect. The gold gleamed in his hand. What had always seemed theoretical was suddenly real.

Eli drew a sharp breath when he looked closely at his partner in the dimness of the cave, not anticipating what came next. He felt an odd cold feeling in the pit of his stomach. Paralyzed by a reality too unexpected to believe, he studied Luke's face.

A knife was aimed at Eli's chest. "What are you doing?"

"Sorry, bud. No can do," Luke apologized. "Can't let you turn it over. Give it to them that ain't earned it." His narrowed eyes showed contempt and were full of anger. "Are you crazy, man?" He grinned. "I'm not sharing with anyone, you included. Divvy up my spoils? Don't think so."

Chapter 34

For years Eli had faithfully carried a French Angel coin as a talisman of protection and good fortune. Luke knew Eli would have it on him.

Early on, Eli had explained to Luke that French captains refused to set sail without them and that he always carried his. For good luck. At Eli's kitchen table, Luke examined it closely. He listened while Eli pointed out the day before that at the Battle of Waterloo, Napoleon Bonaparte had lost his. US, Britain, and French World War I fighter pilots carried them into battle. When Luke asked where Eli had gotten his, Eli told him he found the coin in his father's cigar box.

Luke had admired the gold coin from the first time he'd laid eyes on it. Now he planned to take it! On one side, the image of the Guardian Angel, Genius, stood at a column, crafting an inscription on the French constitution. "I want the French coin," demanded Luke.

Eli was shocked. "What for."

"Just give it to me," Luke ordered.

"Okay, okay… just calm down. I'm sure we can come to an agreement." Eli reached inside his pocket and pulled out the coin. He handed it to Luke.

This was the first time Luke had noticed the rooster. He turned it over and saw a common wreath circle with twenty Francs in the center. Below that was the year 1898. Encircling the wreath were the words Liberte Egalite Fraternite.

Luke flipped it into the air. "Angel, I win, Rooster, you lose." When the coin landed in his hand, the twenty Francs side was showing. Luke tilted his head to the side and said, "You lose!"

A Bowie knife was the weapon of choice to do the deed. Luke thrust it hard and, without hesitation, aimed at Eli's heart. He then wiped the blade clean and returned it to the sheath.

Luke bent down to retrieve the gold coins and pearl necklace that lay on the ground at his feet, where Eli lay gasping for air.

A Tale of Betrayal

Bleeding from the stab wound Luke had inflicted, Eli struggled to remain conscious. The weapon had missed Eli's heart but proved fatal. Barely alive, he was aware of the double-crossed nature of what had happened. Eli's eyes filled with tears. Warm against his skin, they trickled down his cheeks and fell to the cold hard surface.

In anguish, he whispered, "I'm sorry."

At dawn, as Clint slept, Eli's plea was barely audible. With his dying breath, he cried, "Forgive me, son."

Chapter 35
The Devil's at the Door
Late Christmas Eve

As the storm intensified above ground, inside the cave, Luke feverishly worked on expanding the slope of rock that separated him from his historic discovery. He needed more breathing space before he could fit his large physique through the two barrier walls that kept him an outsider looking in. Hours ticked away when he finally sat down for a break.

Never expecting to follow through on what he had been mulling over for a month of Sundays, Luke circled to his right. Staring at Eli's dead body, aligned with the outer cave wall, a tincture of excitement rushed over him.

There's no honor among thieves, he mentally quoted with a weak smile, having heard the phrase and liking it.

Luke poured a cup of hot coffee from his thermos and sat down next to Eli. Scrutinizing the situation, he looked over and complained, justifying his actions. *Imbecile! I had to do it. You were going to turn it over to the state! Give our booty away! What choice did I have? You had to be stopped. Understand?*

Not wanting to look at Eli's face, he stood and got back to work. Pieces of stone lay on the ground. He sighed. With a shake of his head, he turned, "Not too bright, are ya? Should have known better!"

When he put the chisel to the wall, he cocked his head, *That monkey's off my back! No more wondering what to do. I made a good decision.*

His eyelids grew heavy. Tired from exhaustion, expectation, chiseling, and the *deed*, his head bobbed. He was drained from getting up at 2:45 a.m. and could no longer dodge slumber. Lying on the ground, sleep came without resistance. Fourteen hours passed while Luke slept.

When underground, one does not feel the passage of time as they would otherwise. So was the case with Luke when he awakened on the damp cavern floor in total darkness hours later. The lantern had grown dim, barely shedding enough light to recognize Eli's body, no more than five feet away. The degree of time that had elapsed was unclear, and Luke had no concept of the hour. Christmas Eve had faded into yesterday.

The crystal on Eli's watch had cracked, stopping when Luke rolled him vigorously against the stone wall. Luke thought timepieces were a bother and didn't own one but wished he had one now. He pulled Eli's flashlight from his back pocket. *Thank God he had the presence of mind to bring a backup. Good ole Eli! Always thinking on his feet.*

Luke's only option was to return topside. Concern over the predicted storm was on his mind, and a breath of fresh air was an invigorating notion after breathing in the musty, earthy smells of a cold, damp cave. He needed to think. With Eli out of the picture, the burden of transferring riches from its current location to a more secure site fell directly on Luke's shoulders.

Eli would warn him not to move anything too soon. To draw attention to himself would be stupid. He would pick wisely where to pawn and sell the assets, one piece at a time. He had the two coins—twenty dollars each—that he could use for pocket change for the time being. Later, after enlarging the area, he would come back for more.

I need to be extra cautious, Luke discussed with himself time and again as he ambled toward the opening. *Distribute things evenly. Ain't going nowhere, been there for a hundred years; won't grow legs now.*

He turned toward Eli. *Dumb sod. I'll need to move your body. Don't want those eyes staring at me while I'm working. That'd be creepy!*

When Luke arrived at the space Eli and he had descended earlier, he went up the ladder, negotiating the tight fit that connected his

Chapter 35

world to the one below. He hoisted his disproportionate hefty lower half from the ladder and into the narrow closet by the power of his massive arms.

The realization that pointed to the Reno Gang treasure buried on Reeves' property had come as a colossal surprise to Luke. Eli's relatives had constructed the tunnel. To access the cave from Phil Reeves' property, Eli and his father must have collaborated. The shack was their shared secret, until now. The shack, hole, and discovery were all in Luke's possession. No more debates over who would share the wealth.

The shack was excessively dark when Luke crawled out from behind the panel. With no windows to shed light on weather conditions, he moved to the door, expecting to leave but noticed a strange sound coming from the other side.

Luke pressed the latch, but the door didn't open. He didn't see any signs a blizzard of unparalleled proportions had wreaked havoc on Salzburg while he and Eli were beneath the earth in Goss Cave. A record weather phenomenon had dumped thirty-two inches of snow on their town. Not eight inches as forecast.

While Luke was sleeping, forty miles an hour winds wailed, blowing snow drifts across the land. At its strongest, the storm released an unprecedented four inches an hour. The bulk of the weather had been projected to hit south of Salzburg, into Kentucky. Forecasters had miscalculated and residents were blindsided. Everyone was caught off guard. Roads became impassable as snow continued to fall.

Luke did his best to jimmy the door but quickly realized the odds were nil. The door was blocked. A small crack revealed what had happened. A pile of snow was seen on the ground. Luke was trapped. His mind raced. With little to go on, he had to act fast. Confused by the time of day, he leaned on the door, clueless about how to react other than by brute force. No matter how much he pushed and shoved, the door would not budge.

The Devil's at the Door

He made light of the situation at first. *I'll settle for not being the smartest man in the room,* he joked, poking fun at himself, but then swallowed hard. *This ain't good. Wish Eli were here. He'd know what to do.*

A loud thud scared Luke to full attention. The unnatural noise repeated. *Footsteps?* he questioned listening to the movement outside. *How is that possible? All I see is snow, and you can't make a sound like that in snow.* His blood drained from his face.

A long minute passed in dead silence. Then a boom crashed into the door. This time louder and more insistent than before. His heart hammered inside his chest. Somebody was knocking at the door. Something wanted in.

Thump, thump, thump!

How could anyone know I'm here? he agonized. *Only Eli and I know about this place.* A thousand questions raced through Luke's mind, none of them settling.

I've got to get out of here, he fretted.

The sound was heavier and more disturbing the fourth time. Terror hijacked Luke's thoughts. He couldn't move his legs. A scruffy noise scratched at the door like something was trying to claw itself through. Luke could hear scraping at the top of the door, and after a brief second, a snarling hiss crisscrossed past the door. Then he heard the thing crawl onto the roof like it was trying to find another way in.

He jumped to his feet. The only way out was to return to the cave. He would have to find an alternate exit. *There might be water somewhere down there but no food. I've got to find a way out.* He looked at the door. *That's not an option.*

Like lightning, Luke vanished down the hole, determined to find an escape route. In the early days, he and Eli used another entrance when mapping the various fingers of the cave. *I'll take that if I can find it. Never done it without Eli.*

Chapter 35

Closing the secret panel behind him, Luke's hands were trembling when he grabbed ahold of the ladder. A feeling of panic charged through his body. As he lowered himself into the abyss, it occurred to Luke the flashlight should be used sparingly. The batteries would last only so long before he'd find himself in total blackness. If he didn't play his cards right, it would be lights out—not only for Eli but for him too.

He moved swiftly through the interior of the cave. With the flashlight projected ahead, Luke relaxed, glad to have escaped the danger above. His gait quickened until, at last, he arrived where Eli's body lay. Turning away, he beamed the light toward the fractured opening.

Flanked by rocks, Luke strained to see the hoard of riches deposited at the other end. It wasn't a mirage. They had indeed discovered the Reno Gang's lost treasure from 1868. Unable to fully view the entirety of his new wealth, Luke knew he'd have to work diligently before he could fondle his fortune. That would bring exuberance on a scale he could hardly imagine.

He made his way over to Eli with the intention of moving the body past the work site but decided it could wait until he returned. He felt pressured to find the original entrance they had used before completing the one beneath the shack. Luke considered the limited battery life in his flashlight. *I must stay focused.*

He slipped through the passageways. The air, balmy for winter, felt dank, tepid, and troubling. Out of curiosity, he switched the flashlight off. He wanted to experience the darkness. It was beyond any blackness he had ever encountered. And though he could not see any specific features, he could feel the surrounding limestone. Space could be deceptive. A vertical drop was not out of the question. Echoes were deceptive as well and not an indication of wall distance.

The quietness was mind-numbing. From what he knew of caves, his best bet was to follow the breeze. It would lead him to an exit. The weatherman's prediction regarding the storm had been a setback. A lot of snow had been dumped, preventing him from leaving through the shack. Something he hadn't planned for.

The flashlight had dimmed. He was under no illusion. Locating an escape route was a paramount mission. When finally, to his relief, an opening was spotted.

Holy Mother of Mary, Luke rejoiced.

Onto a mound, Luke crawled through a hole in the ground. Hours had passed since the day had faded into night. He resurfaced to a blanket of snow. Fortunately, the canopy kept the snow accumulation at a minimum, allowing Luke to dig his way out. The entrance was about a mile from the shack.

Sprawled in a tree overhead, a black cat observed Luke wriggle out from a crack in the earth. Draped over a branch, the puma was familiar with the opening, having used it often for shelter and to drag prey. At sunrise and sunset, the animal bedded down in Goss Cave.

In this spot, where it often perched, the puma remained silent, waiting for the human to leave. A cagey creature, legendary for its stealth, Picasso's nature was to be vigilant. And, watchful.

This evening Picasso found no food at the edge of the forest. No treats or leftovers were placed at the property line.

Eli's departure had not gone unnoticed.

Chapter 36
Degrees of Wickedness
December 25, 1953

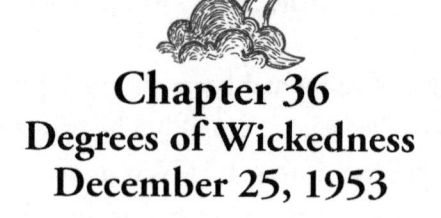

Greed had fanned the flames of foul play. Evil took root, sparked by the pursuit of riches. One man's heart had turned to stone. The calloused killer walked away.

Knee-deep snow had made Luke's return journey to where the day had begun, during the wee hours on Christmas Eve—a taxing trip.

As he approached the shack, he noted the rickety roof and the many layers of snow it struggled to support. He examined the scratch marks on the wooden door with keen interest. He ran his fingers over the deep grooves and wondered what had made them. Why he was unable to open the door from inside was apparent. Snow was piled high around it and blocked passage.

Luke shoveled a small area to allow him entrance into the shack. He noticed tracks beneath the snow. They were faint but discernible. The four-inch-wide prints, approximately three inches in length, clearly belonged to a large creature. Luke assumed it to be the same entity that had tried unsuccessfully to gain entrance. The unnatural sounds heard hours ago rang clearly in his mind. He visually scanned the area but saw nothing of concern.

Whatever that was, it sounded otherworldly, thought Luke.

The shack's secret passage into and out of Goss Cave was an ideal link to the Reno Gang's underground fortune. In the future, with this latest crisis behind him, he would cautiously access the shack only after dark—a picture-perfect camouflage to withdraw his loot, bit by bit, coin by coin, and bar by bar.

The plan was to relocate the bounty to his residence, at which time the goods would be converted into cash. All that kept him from the next stage of the operation was the wall of separation that prevented him from his treasure.

Luke collected his gear, leaving behind no trace of human activity. Unless someone was specifically searching for the secret panel, they would not easily spot it. However, Luke would not take any chances. As partners, he and Eli had prepared for this day, down to the letter. Eli, a careful man, left no stone unturned. His only flaw was gullibility.

He shoved a dirty oilcloth inside the closet wall along with a pail spotted with paint. Luke studied the small space with a skillful eye, looking for anything that would draw unwanted attention. Satisfied he had covered his bases, he turned toward the door, ready to leave.

The shack had a musky smell, one of yesteryear. Dampness could be felt in the walls. Eli had shared his memories of spending time at the shack with his grandfather, Earl Reeves. He was a gentle man who had taught Eli how to sculpt shapes out of wood. They played checkers and tossed horseshoes on Sunday afternoons.

When Eli described his stories about the good old days, Luke could hardly stomach them. Unrelatable to Luke, his childhood was anything but rosy. He had no fond memories of his parents or grandparents. In fact, he harbored bitter feelings about them. Curt, his father, skipped town when Luke was ten. Caught for stealing, and terrified of serving jail-time, he walked out on his family, leaving them to fend for themselves.

Shutting the door behind him, Luke wedged it securely. In the woods, through the opening that led to Eli's backyard, Luke dreamed about his new life. Piles of stolen property lay down in the cave. He saw the trunk and stash of jewelry and coins in his mind, scattered plentifully over the ground.

Eli and I thought big but not that big. Luke grinned. *That place is a sight for sore eyes. Beyond anything we could have hoped for.*

Sitting among the spoils was a large lidded container. Luke was excited at the prospects of its content. As soon as he'd chipped the rock wall away enough for him to enter, he planned to start hauling everything up.

Chapter 36

On his way back, he passed through the clearing. Caught off guard, he was catapulted to the ground by a tree stump jutting out from the forest floor. It was dark, and his mind had traveled elsewhere. When he got up, he cursed loudly, swearing at his carelessness.

"Stop being such a klutz," he demanded. "You can't make those kinds of mistakes when carrying cache from the cave." When he checked his pockets for the coins, he was relieved to feel them at his fingertips.

Passing by Eli's house, he noticed the lights were on. *Clint's up,* he thought with a pang of guilt. *Sorry, kid, your dad ain't coming home.* Luke wondered how Eli's boy was going to react when the totality of the situation surfaced.

The snow subsided, improving visibility. Luke made his way out into the street, determined to get home before midnight.

Devoid of any human activity, random tracks, mostly deer and rabbit, were scattered about in a picturesque winter-wonderland scene. The storm had produced both a spectacle and a serious snag. He couldn't see a single tire track anywhere. Quiet simplicity, a panorama of tranquility lay before him. *All was calm—all was bright...* everywhere except in Luke's head.

Snowflakes floated through the air. It was eerily quiet when Luke approached his truck under a mountain of snow. Parked to the side of the road, his vehicle was well camouflaged. No one would ever know that Eli and his treasure hunting efforts had paid off. As partners, they had vowed to keep their search between them in fear of other treasure hunters catching wind of their endeavors.

Driving home in less than favorable road conditions was not smart. Getting stuck somewhere, or worse yet, stopped by the police near Eli's place, would be downright foolish. Determination drove Luke forward on foot, heading into Christmas morning. His goal was to get out of the treacherous environment without freezing to death.

When he arrived home, snow was falling heavily. He tossed his gear onto the table and reached into his pocket for the gold coins. However, he was surprised not to find the pearl necklace. He checked the opposite pocket thinking maybe he had absentmindedly moved it over. To his dismay, the necklace was in neither one. Then, in a flashback, he remembered the tumble he had taken in the woods.

At first disappointed, Luke gestured with a sweep of his hand, "Oh well, there's more from where that came."

A hot shower was in order, and then a good night's sleep. As he stood in the steam, Luke schemed. He would build a fine log cabin with a pole barn to hold his toys, putting all others to shame, on three-hundred acres. Nothing less would do. His dream home was on the drawing board.

Everything was closed on Christmas Day. What little food he had in his cupboard would have to do until tomorrow. On Saturday, he would drive into town and buy a proper meal. Until then, he'd bide his time.

Luke slept long and hard. When he awoke Saturday morning, he sprang to life. The time was 8 a.m. His body ached from the brute force it had taken to follow through with what had been only contemplative days before. When he acted on his instincts, it had surprised even him. He thought about Eli's body lying in Goss Cave. His truck needed to be relocated before Eli was reported missing. Otherwise, his truck would implicate him if discovered. He figured by now, Clint might have notified the police. This was a problem that needed fixing.

Before closing time, Luke planned a trip to the General Store. The celebration he had in mind required provisions he could never afford, until now. Rod's dependability to keep the store well-stocked and open, no matter what, was commendable. The only day he closed was on Christmas.

Luke would make a quick jog to get his truck before heading that way. Full of knick-knacks, groceries, tools, and whatnots, Rod's had everything from A-Z—a real hodgepodge of merchandise.

Chapter 36

"No way will local restaurants serve up the kind of meal I have in mind." Luke boasted out loud with bolstered spirits, trying to forget about Eli. "This meal will be fit for a king!"

When Luke left his house, he was starving. The temperature had climbed to a balmy thirty-seven degrees. As he neared Eli's house, he noticed the lights were on. No cars were parked in the drive. He took that as a good sign. Although the roadway was hazardous, he managed through the snow-covered streets with relative ease.

On the way to the store, he pulled into the gas station. As he watched the attendant wash his windows and fill the tank, he thought about what being rich would feel like—to spend money hand over fist, without regard to cost. No more worrying about how to come up with the rent each month. No longer would he be at the mercy of the coal mining company where he worked ridiculous hours and was underpaid. He was going to build and buy his house outright.

Luke tipped his hat at Pearl Teague as he strutted through the door of Rod's General Store.

She, in turn, kept a watchful eye.

"Howdy," he gleefully addressed her on his way to the meat counter, anticipating a nice selection of steaks.

This was not Luke's typical greeting. Pearl was surprised at his pleasant demeanor, as she had never been treated with anything less than contempt by him. She frowned. Suspicious, she stepped to the side and observed him strolling down the aisle.

At the meat counter, she watched him shift packages around. From one side to the other, until finally, he grabbed two and tucked them under his armpit. On aisle three, with his free hand, he reached for a bottle of A-1 steak sauce. He looked around, certain he wanted to buy something more. He took a box of Cracker Jacks from the shelf, then off he went with pep to his step to the front. Tugging a cart from the coupled group, he tossed the steaks inside and urgently disappeared down aisle five, where he knew the alcohol was.

"Got clobbered this time. Didn't we? Buckets full!" Luke cheerfully volunteered as he approached the cash register. "I was afraid to drive the truck. Rear-wheel is an accident waiting to happen! But she did a fine job." Tapping a cigarette from the pack, his smile was a crooked one.

Flick, flick… flick, flick. The wick of the lighter finally caught hold, igniting a flame. Luke knew he wasn't supposed to smoke indoors. He even saw it posted at the entrance when he came in.

"I suppose so," Pearl replied disgustedly. "Pushed farther north than anyone expected. Took us all by surprise!" She pointed to Luke's cigarette. "Put that lighter away and cigarette out. You can't smoke in here. That stinky smell gets all over the food."

"That's my Pappy's lighter. Stole it from his things before he split town." Luke sneered. "Look, woman, I'll smoke wherever I damn well feel like." It occurred to him politeness was a better approach rather than to rile her up. "When did it start snowing?" Luke asked politely, unaware that his question might raise a brow.

"What do you mean?" Pearl quizzed, taken by surprise. "C'mon, Luke, have you been living under a rock? It's been snowing for two days! And clean your mouth up. I don't appreciate your language." She stared daggers through him, "I meant what I said, put that cigarette out this minute! Don't make me come over there and put it out for you." She wagged her finger in warning.

"I was just making small talk!" Luke protested. "Give me a break. Of course, I'll put it out." He snuffed the end of the cigarette out on the counter to irritate her. "I know when it started snowing. I just forgot." A smile crept onto his face. "I've been sleeping a lot." He thought back to the scene that greeted him when he emerged from Goss Cave after killing Eli on Christmas Eve."

"Too much merriment at your place? The kind of spirits that last two days?" Pearl mumbled sarcastically.

Luke, none too happy with being made fun of, replied, "Watch your mouth, Pearl! When you address me, use respect!"

Chapter 36

He reached into his pocket and withdrew one of the coins taken from Eli. Excited to hold a coin with a face value of $20, he slapped it down on the counter.

Pearl looked at the gold coin and then up at Luke. "What's that?"

"Don't you know real money when you see it?"

Pearl picked it up, shocked at its weight and date. "I don't know about this." She looked at the liquor in his cart. "Do you think you have enough beer?"

"Good grief, woman. You are getting on my nerves. That's a twenty-dollar gold piece. Same as bills! Twenty of them. Just take it and shut up. I'm tired of your lip!" Luke grabbed his goods, but Pearl yanked them back.

"Are you nuts? A twenty-dollar gold coin is worth a heck of a lot more money than a twenty-dollar bill."

"Just take it," demanded Luke.

"Hold on. I need to get Rod's approval. We don't take that sort of payment." With a suspicious glance, she inserted, "At least I don't believe we do." She dialed Rod. On the third ring, he answered. After Pearl explained the circumstances, Rod reluctantly gave his approval. Said he would settle things with Luke later.

As Luke exited the store, he spit in her direction. "Fat cow! I don't get mad, Pearl. I get even!"

"What did you say?" she called back, not certain she had heard him correctly.

"You heard me, bitch!"

"Someday, you're going to have to answer for your actions, Luke," snapped Pearl reluctantly, afraid of his tone. "The good Lord doesn't approve of that kind of talk."

"Get in line, Pearl!" Luke barked. Thinking he sensed fear in her voice, Luke smugly grinned.

"Everything is about to change." He warned. "I'm the big man in town!"

Chapter 37
Eyes Opened
Daybreak, September 23, 2003
Fifty Years Later

Hours had passed while Clint's body lay limply on the clammy cave floor. He heard a disembodied voice, awakening him to the power of purpose. A quiet calm filled his spirit, and he knew why the apparition had brought him to the shack and down the secret passage into the cave.

"The man in the hat wanted me to find my father," Clint told himself in a quivering voice. "He knew he was here."

The revelation of what he had seen in a lucid dream weighed heavily on his mind. Only bits and pieces spliced together but enough to expose the truth.

Sitting upright and gazing into utter blackness, an overwhelming feeling of gratefulness rushed over him. He was grateful to know what had unfolded but crushed with anguish that his father had been betrayed. Before becoming unconscious, Clint had seen his father's brutal murder and had heard his dying words. The only words Clint could clearly recall.

Clint buried his head in his hands and cried. "His last words were to me!" His soul ached as tears fell. "He didn't abandon me."

He swept the clay cave floor, searching for his only means of getting out. Not knowing where the flashlight had landed, his heart raced, afraid he might not find it. Then he felt the cold hard metal at his fingertips.

"*Thank you*," he whispered to whoever might be listening.

Having no idea if the flashlight was still operational since it wasn't putting out any light, he felt for the switch and quickly realized that when he'd dropped it, it had been jarred off. It wasn't out of juice or broken as he had feared.

Chapter 37

Standing upright, Clint closed his eyes, trying to steady his heart and soul. Somewhere in Goss Cave, his dad's body lay. He had seen it with incredible clarity. Eli had been deceived by a person he trusted.

In the vision-like dream, Clint had witnessed a man he remembered from his childhood. He had once sat at their kitchen table, sharing beers with his dad. The two men talked spiritedly long after Clint had gone to bed. He could still see the kitchen light shining onto the bedroom floor through the cracked door. He remembered how comforting it had felt.

That same person took my father's life. But why? Clint wondered. *They were partners.* The scene that appeared in his mind was sketchy at best as he only remembered parts of it. *From the look on my father's face, this man's deception was unexpected. He was blindsided!*

Clint didn't dare guess why the hostility had occurred or what may have provoked it.

Did a heated disagreement turn ugly? Why did they turn on each other like that? What would have spurred such hostility? The knot in Clint's stomach tightened. He had seen his father collapse on the cave floor. A heartache on a massive scale.

Clint hung his head, same as he had all those many years ago when caught stealing bread. His father's intention was not to leave him fatherless. In ripples, the realization rushed over him.

How could Dad have known the violence his partner was capable of? pondered Clint as minutes passed.

I believed something that wasn't true. I thought the responsibility of having a kid was too much for him. Clint wept, releasing years of anger and hatred for a man he now knew, for a fact, loved him. Then the book his father had intended to give him on Christmas morning came to mind. *It was a clue,* he said softly. *I wonder if Dad knew I read Treasure Island.* Clint's eyes grew sad, hoping that he did.

In the vastness of Goss Cave, with an immeasurable understanding of clarity, Clint knew what came next. Rod, Sr., his father's best friend, wanted Eli's remains put to rest.

Clint thought about the day he and his wife had driven past the property and how it had called to him. Everything was so clear. The house and land wanted him to come home and expose the truth behind his father's disappearance. At the age of five, he was taken from this house and property. Both wanted him back.

Somewhere in the cave, answers awaited. He aimed the flashlight in the direction his gut told him to head. Seeking the truth, Clint moved forward until he happened upon a large gap that drew his attention.

The inner wall jutted out more prominently than anywhere else he had been. He could see clusters of smaller, rounded rocks scattered about. He first assumed their unusual shapes and sizes were caused by streaming water and carbonic acid. Yet this area appeared unnatural in some way. Approximately two to six inches in diameter, the rocks at his feet reminded Clint of large marbles. Then, it dawned on him these rocks were geodes.

"Those are only found near lakes or riverbeds—never in caves," said Clint. "This doesn't make sense! Geodes are above ground rocks. What are they doing here?"

Moving along the cavern wall, hands firmly on its surface to maintain balance, he carefully inched forward. Clint had no idea which way to turn until a curved part of the cave became noticeably altered. To track his route, he had made notations every eight feet or so by scratching on the wall with a rock he carried.

I'd better make certain I can get myself out of here, thought Clint looking at the huge void that encircled him. *Mark my way, or I'll be trapped with no way out.* A sobering thought.

He wondered what might have been going through his father's mind as he walked these same passages fifty years earlier. Clint would have sworn he felt his father's presence. A long way from

Chapter 37

any natural entrance, he felt puzzled why they had dug a hole into the earth, under the shack to come down? Why create a manmade entrance? The mystery needed solving.

All Clint was certain of was something that prompted his father and partner to take drastic measures. To excavate the earth for an alternate route into the cave must have had its challenges but served a purpose. Tunneling by hand took a great deal of time and energy. But why?

After a short climb, Clint entered a narrow area even tighter than the place he had advanced through moments ago. Not resembling a natural geographical formation, it was clear the split quartz-crystal rocks that had been transported to this location were deliberate.

A fracture in the wall appeared chipped and broken, arousing Clint's curiosity. He moved closer. To his surprise, inside the opening, he saw a chisel lying on the ground, indicating human presence.

Could my father have been here? wondered Clint as he inspected the space even closer.

Clint held the flashlight above his head, aiming it into the cracked limestone. From within the darkened void, a new reality emerged. The inner crevice revealed spiky, uneven edges of stone that had been struck until a substantial pile of limestone lay on the ground between the opening leading to the other side.

"What is this place?" he asked, uncertain what he had stumbled upon. "Why would they want to enlarge this space?"

Clint forced his body further into the constricted slit between rockfaces that only allowed sideways movement. Unable to push forward any further, he retreated from the opening.

There must be something of interest on the other side of that fracture, Clint speculated.

Uncertain what his next move ought to be, he backpedaled out, expecting to lean against the cave wall for a moment until he could catch his breath and think through his dilemma. His time was limited, and taking risks was not an option. Nothing was worth losing his life.

What he had seen in his vision was real. He felt it in his bones. What had taken place down here, long ago, happened. The full truth could wait till another day. Until he was better prepared and with the authorities. Being in a cave alone could have major negative consequences that he wasn't willing to take.

Cliff stiffened as he felt a cold hand.

Then he heard a voice. "He's here."

The person who held the answers to what transpired those many years ago was near. Clint's voice cracked. "Rod? Is that you?"

Disquiet filled the chamber. Clint distinctly remembered hearing the same words in the forest last spring in the clearing area. The words had spooked him then but not now. In this moment, they held great significance—the answer to a fifty-year-old mystery.

On the far wall a transmission of light materialized into a human form. Without words, Clint's most pressing question was answered. The figure was, in fact, Rod Radcliff, Sr. The man in the straw hat.

Clint felt perplexed. *Why isn't my father the one to shed light on the mystery of what happened to him?* he contemplated. *Seems odd Rod Radcliff would be the one to lead me to the truth. Why him?*

When no words were spoken or action taken, Clint bravely turned to leave. But just as he did, an irregular shape in his peripheral vision caused alarm bells to clang. The blood drained from his face. Afraid to acknowledge the truth of what it was, he was looking at a mere foot away, Clint took a step backward to collect himself.

He easily identified the shape of human remains. Taking one step toward the lump, resting against the wall where only seconds ago he'd seen the spirit, Clint examined the body to a degree he could not imagine himself capable of. He touched the flannel shirt,

Chapter 37

bandana, and gloves that covered the bones. Heavy cloth trousers loosely fitted the bottom half of the corpse—a male figure.

My dad? he breathed, knowing the answer to the question.

"Is this what I'm supposed to find?" asked Clint to the powers to be. He closed his dampened eyes, confused as to how his dad ended up here, rolled alongside the wall like discarded trash.

What took place was witnessed in his vision.
Who this person was had been revealed.
When his father died, need not to be asked. That was December 24, 1953.
Where the killing took place was evident.
However, the most important question of all had no answer.
Why?

The man who killed his father visited their home often. Clint could testify to that. Thanks to the man in the straw hat, who had been relentlessly shadowing him for months, Clint now had answers to his questions. All but one!

That mystery will unravel in due time, he told himself. *When forensic investigators get involved.*

He put his hands over his eyes. *I can't leave now that I've found you?* he said to the body at his feet. *I've been looking for you my whole life.* Clint slid to the ground beside his father and placed a hand on the dead man's chest.

Clint retraced his movements in his mind. It wasn't wise to wager on the flashlight holding power. He was too old to make an error of that magnitude. The time had come to return topside. But, in Clint's case, emotions had replaced logic. He wrestled with his feelings. Without a doubt, he knew the body he had discovered was his father's. Rod Radcliff had shown him where to look, leaving crumbs of contact until the discovery was unearthed. Slowly he backtracked from the crime scene, easily finding his way to the ladder.

Eyes Opened

Hours had passed since Clint climbed out of the cavern. Sitting under the stars, his mind raced with whom he should make first contact. Assuming Scott, his friend on the police force to be the right choice, reporting it to the authorities was a no-brainer. He trusted Scott not to blab the news to anyone until the appropriate time.

Confusion churned from his core. *Jules will have something to say about this!* he grinned. *Especially when she hears of my encounter with the old man in the fedora and that a ghost directed me to my father's body. My questions about Dad were shown to me in a dream.* Tears trickled down Clint's cheeks as he gazed at the stars, his heart broken all over again, but this time for altogether different reasons. Eli's face was etched in his mind's eye, and the last words he uttered as he drew his final breath.

"I'm glad I followed my instincts," Clint whispered as he headed indoors. *Didn't let fear keep me from the truth.* He congratulated himself on his bravery. *Can't explain what I saw, but what I did see was real. That chapter in my life can now be closed. End of story.*

Or so he thought.

Chapter 38
A Story from the Shadows

In the east, daybreak scaled the horizon as Clint hastened toward the house. He noticed the landscape was swathed in signs of autumn. Fallen acorns and walnuts lay on the ground, and leaves had blown into the yard. The smells were aromatic and intoxicating.

Unthinkable insight, held close to his heart, had completely altered his perception of reality. The burden of truth that surrounded his father's disappearance had to be reported to the authorities.

Like *Alice in Wonderland*, his life had been turned upside down in a single moment. Tumbling—not through a rabbit hole, but into a cavern of clarity—every part of Clint's former belief had been exposed for what it was, a falsehood.

As the sun rose above the tree line, the songs of early morning birds elevated Clint's spirit. *First things first*, he told himself, *I'll ring Scott and ask him to drop by for a cup of coffee. Tell him I have some news I'd like to share.*

He opened the door and went inside. Emotionally stymied and somewhat dazed, he went around the house and opened every window. From the table, he lifted his cell phone, ready to make the call.

At the sink, he stared at the bare spot in the foyer where the antique mirror had once hung. Now stored in the pole barn, it no longer held Clint hostage to its mystical, spellbinding powers. *I'll go out and get it. Hang it back up where it belongs*, he smiled. *Enjoy it without worry.*

He dialed the number written on a folded piece of paper he had taken from his wallet. His call was answered on the fourth ring. "Salzburg Police Station, Drew Littleton speaking."

"Hi, Drew, this is Clint Reeves. May I speak with Scott Edwards?"

"Certainly, let me check to see if he's here. Hang on a minute."

A Story from the Shadows

With thoughts streaming through his mind, Clint pondered how to start the conversation.

"This is Captain Scott Edwards."

"Scott, this is Clint," he said tentatively. "I'm glad I caught you."

"Clint, good to hear your voice. What's up?" Scott energetically responded.

"Hey, do you think you'd have some time to stop by the house? I need to tell you something, and I'd rather not talk about it over the telephone."

"You all right?" Scott inquired with concern, detecting stress in Clint's tone.

"Yeah, I'm fine. I'd just prefer to discuss this face to face."

"I have a lunch break coming up," volunteered Scott. "Could drop by then if you don't mind David Andrews tagging along."

When an officer entered the room to ask a question, Scott covered the phone. After an extended delay, he offered an apology. "Sorry, Clint, I didn't mean to cut you off. When you come in at 6 a.m., noon cannot roll around quick enough. To answer your question, I'd be glad to stop by. I could use a break from this place. I assume you have no objections to David joining me."

"No, that's fine," Clint reluctantly agreed. "It's just that what I have to say is of a private matter. Plus, I have something you need to see." His eyes rolled. "A picture is worth a thousand words."

"Goodness, could you be more cryptic, Clint?" Scott chuckled heartily.

Clint realized how vague he must have sounded. "Sorry, pal. Don't mean to come off so secretive."

"That's fine. How about 1:15, give or take?" Scott said, sloughing off Clint's comment.

"Perfect. Thanks, Scott. See you then." Clint listened for the phone to disconnect on the other end before sitting it down.

Relieved to have placed the call, Clint looked forward to escorting Scott and David to the shack, showing them the entrance

Chapter 38

into the cave and having them follow his lead to the human remains he had uncovered. They would make an assessment, of course, and take it from there. Clint had the ball rolling on his end.

Next, he would leave a message with Jules. She had been called into work when the new girl failed to show. Jules would take it for granted that he would stop by the diner for breakfast and had said she would be watching for him. At this hour, she would be tied up with customers, and for that, he was grateful. When her shift ended, he would call again. Talking to her presently wasn't convenient; however, he felt letting her know she was on his mind was important.

She'll be wondering why I didn't show up this morning. He pictured his poured coffee sitting on the table growing cold.

After he washed the dishes, dried them, and stacked them in the cabinets, Clint headed for the bathroom. Being in the dank underground of the cave necessitated a hot shower. He figured twenty minutes of steaming water on his shoulders should relax his muscles, plus wash the foulness of his vision from his mind.

He withdrew a pad and pen from the drawer in the hall. He felt writing down the details of his experience would help him remember them precisely when relaying the information to Scott. The assurance that the man in the hat had accomplished what he had set out to do was concrete. He looked up at the ceiling. "Thank you, Rod. At last, the truth is out there, and we both are at peace."

Clint was dressed and ready for whatever the day had to offer. He polished off his second cup of coffee at the kitchen table while he contemplated what to do in the hours before Scott arrived. He had already straightened the house, making it presentable for company.

The cave came to mind and the fact his father lay on the cold hard ground—feet below the shack. The thought of Eli lying there for the past fifty years sickened him. Everything about it felt repulsive.

A Story from the Shadows

To think I've been living in this house for six years and never knew he was down there. Clint's eyes clouded over. The thought crossed his mind, *I'll never be this close to him again. After today everything will change. They'll come in, remove his corpse, and that will be that.* A progression of considerations led to the thought. *A proper burial will be in order. The funeral home will be next on my list once I talk to Scott.*

An overflow of emotions flowed through Clint. He took a seat. Queasy at the idea of what he was entertaining, he concluded that fear of revisiting the cave would not control his actions. He would make this trip with a fresh pair of eyes. He had seen the truth of his father's demise, and he had nothing left to dread or know. Rod had successfully completed his objective of exposing the murderous deed that had taken place.

Determined to get in and out before Scott and David showed up, Clint strolled back to the shack with gloves, Ziplock bags, a flashlight, and a fully charged phone. He brought the phone along not to make a call but to take pictures. He knew it would appear morbid to most people, but he yearned to record what he had seen in the cave—a freeze-frame in time.

When he entered the shack, his heart felt heavy. He and his father were to be reunited one final time. Part of him regressed back to being a child as though five years old was a permanent state of mind accompanied by the dreaded fear he was being followed or threatened by some invisible force had vanished.

He crouched to his knees, pushed on the secret panel, and crawled through to the other side before closing the door behind him. The hole in the earth appeared much smaller than the first time he lowered his body into the void of darkness. Carefully he placed his feet, one rung at a time, on the ladder of enlightenment.

Standing on the earthen floor, Clint's pursuit of knowledge was steadfast. The bend that led to the geode stones and the body came into focus. He felt confident he had time to inspect the area at his

Chapter 38

leisure without cutting it too close. Toting two flashlights provided him the freedom to explore, along with eliminating his anxiety over entrapment. All he really wanted to do was say goodbye before forensics appeared on the scene. They would painstakingly remove the body from where it had lain for half a century and subsequently close Eli's missing person case.

He studied the area with fascination and noted that of all the cracks and crevices surrounding him only one was heavily marked with geodes. Finding the anomaly curious, Clint used his flashlight to move along the path they pointed. The larger crystal quartz consolidated into smaller ones, all funneling into a remote section of the cave not sighted on his earlier visit.

Every five feet or so he marked the direction he had traveled with chalk. Before exploring further, Clint did his best to commit the layout to memory. His attention was diverted when he thought he heard an underground stream. Peering to his right, he turned the corner and was greeted by a strong current. As though a door had been opened, a whooshing breeze surprised him.

The pleasant smell of river water hung in the air. Clint remembered overhearing, although, at the time, the information held little interest, that the cave had three levels. Locals all referred to it as Little Goss Cave. Aware that the two main access points were located three miles from Greenville, off Highway 150 on route 335, Clint found it hard to believe the fingers would run this far from the only recognized entrances. But apparently, his father and the man who killed him knew the cave had other means of entry.

It dawned on Clint he had ventured further than intended. Even though he found the adventure tempting, it also made him nervous, so he made an about-face.

"All the flashlights in the world aren't going to help me if I get lost," he warned himself. He quickened his pace in the opposite direction. *Familiar territory is the only place I should be exploring when I have policemen coming to the house. I came here to be with my father!*

When he reversed course, an object on the ground grazed the cuff of his pants. He made a fast maneuver to dodge the potential hazard, except in doing so he lost his balance and stumbled into the rockface. Pins and needles raced up his spine at the near miss.

"Clint, for God's sake, you do not want a repeat performance," he spoke harshly, thinking back to the last time he fell.

As he stepped away, an unusual shape captured his attention. He turned his flashlight in the direction of a jagged split-rock formation. Tucked inside—partially in, partially out—he saw a body.

"Good grief, not another one!" gasped Clint. "Two dead bodies?"

A hideously grotesque corpse stared up toward the cave ceiling.

Putting his hand over his mouth, Clint felt his heart pound. Dumbfounded by what this latest development signified, he leaned in for a closer inspection. For the life of him, he would have sworn whoever this body was, the person had been dragged to this location. The size of the figure indicated an infinitely larger person than the one he found yesterday. This six-foot-tall man, by all accounts, had been tightly wedged into the wall.

Shredded clothing gave the impression of a struggle before death. Ribbons of cloth hung from the corpse's shoulders, waist, and upper thighs. In the dank chill, a humid redolent of decay drifted.

Then, just as Clint was ready to retreat, understanding this was a situation for the authorities, his leg was caught by the outstretched hand of the dead, and his balance was severely compromised. Both legs gave out from under him, and from buckled knees, he saw something that defied reason in the sepulchral tomb that he had been standing.

His eyes could not believe what he was seeing. What had been lost was now found. On the cold clay floor, at the fingertips of the deceased, a Bowie knife lay. Earmarks of a twin to the one that had gone missing, Clint suspected they were one and the same. All the

Chapter 38

inner strength in the world would not have kept him from doing what came next.

Unable to stop himself, he kicked the blade off to the side with his foot, away from the boney fingers that held it. He reached over to bring it to eye level.

Is the handle engraved? he wondered. Carved letters were on the grip: F.R. It was the identical knife Clint had bought at the bookstore for the treasure hunt and was, he thought, misplaced. Here it was in Goss Cave next to a dead body. The only difference between them was this knife had the appearance of age where his was relatively new.

Clint sat on the ground, his head and heart were both hurting. A million questions raced through his mind.

"How can this be?" he probed, hearing his own shaky voice question what he saw with his own two eyes.

How did it get down here? Who brought it here? The old guy? Questions mounted, one after another, but none of them had rational explanations.

As a drop of blood dripped from his finger, from cutting his own hand, Clint saw the light—the truth.

The man he had seen on numerous occasions, Rod Radcliff, Sr., and the young boy from his dream had redeposited the knife to where it had originally fallen. The boy had followed the older man, who had come through the antique mirror into the woods.

In his vision, Clint had watched the boy dig something up in the clearing and run off with it, responding to the old man who had disappeared into the shack. A coordinated effort to rewind an action that Rod, Sr. had previously staged when he placed the knife into the curio cabinet at Rod's New and Used Books had been reversed.

And there was a witness to the deed. Lily had seen Rod Radcliff Sr. twice that same day. Once during the treasure hunt and a second time when Clint experienced his so-called dream.

Simultaneously, they both watched the man in the fedora enter the shack. She thought he was beckoning her when it was the child he was communicating with.

For him, a clear connection was made. Both the child, his alternate self, and his father's best friend had a vested interest in Clint uncovering the dreadful truth of Christmas Eve, 1953.

Shakily, Clint stood to his feet. Tears flowed inside at a sight too impossible to fully absorb. The deceased person crammed between the cracks in the cave rock, Clint believed, was the man he saw in his vision the day before. Only this time, the man, his dad's partner, also had been killed. Dragged and killed—or killed and dragged—to this exact location.

Moving away from the large man's corpse, Clint slowly approached the area where Eli had perished. Wanting to understand what had gone down, Clint felt assured that at least some answers would be provided when forensics got involved. Professionals at untangling how events unfolded, Clint felt confident they would unravel the mystery.

Presently, a conversation with his dad was all that mattered. Clint sat on the ground next to him. He wanted to express his sorrow for the tragedy that had befallen Eli and to tell him how much he was loved and missed. Whatever reasons he had come into Goss Cave that fateful Christmas Eve, Clint knew Eli never intended to abandon him.

In the strange silence, a sense of enduring love prevailed. It was as though his father's devotion engulfed him. Then, through an astral plane between worlds, a spirit appeared. The man who stood above Clint—not his father, but the one in the straw fedora who had roamed in and out of his life for six long years and even entered his dreams—had not moved on.

"What do you want from me?" pleaded Clint in desperation.

Chapter 38

The spirit did not answer in words but did in a gesture of instruction. Moving to Eli's body, he indicated Clint should do the same.

Clint accepted Rod's command. "You've not led me wrong so far. Why should I doubt you now?"

Before taking another step, Clint stared intently at Rod. "You placed the knife in the curio cabinet at Rod's New and Used Books along with the other items that ultimately coaxed the grandchildren and me to the shack. You wanted us to follow the trail. The knife led to the truth about my father, and you validated your existence through Lily, Trey, and Dylan. The geode rock snow globe resembled a cave entrance. These were all clues."

Clint thought about the other items. He figured they must not have been part of Rod's larger plan. The chest and key, locomotive, bandit figurines, whip, etc., all followed the same theme but held no real significance that he could tell.

Suddenly, in a moment of lucidity, Clint's face paled. He remembered other manifestations. "You made yourself known to Jules and Patrick. You used the movie, *Somewhere in Time*, to draw my attention and assure me time travel did, in fact, exist. Not to doubt my instincts."

The man's face remained placid. With an unchanged expression, he pointed to the body, signaling Clint should look closer. Stepping into the shadows, Rod faded behind a curtain of darkness.

On closer observation of Eli, he noticed the most peculiar thing. An unfamiliar shape was entangled with Eli's body. He hadn't noticed it from the right side, and it dawned on Clint a separate figure was interwoven alongside his father's remains. There was no way to make sense of what might have happened, but one thing was obvious, a smaller something had lain down with Eli, and it too died.

Did they die together or separately? Clint measured, asking the void for an answer.

A Story from the Shadows

Confused as to why this fact had been brought to his attention, Clint frowned. *So, I'm to know my dad didn't die alone, that some creature kept him company at the end.*

He was bewildered. "Why would any animal do such a thing?" That was another tale waiting to be told.

He remained motionless, not able to bring himself to leave. He peered into the darkness and wondered if Rod was still around.

Chapter 39
A Hard Sell
September 23, 2:30 p.m.

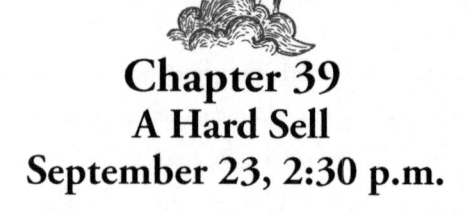

Greed and betrayal were the mindsets of an immoral man that blizzardy winter day a half-century ago. And even though Clint was unaware of the complete details of the incident that played out in Goss Cave, he knew enough. After a lifetime of faulty, judgmental thinking on his behalf, he had seen the deceitful act for what it was—murder.

Only the why remained.

Bringing closure to Eli's disappearance had been a long time coming. As bittersweet as it was, Clint was relieved to finally know what had truly taken place that kept his dad from coming home that Christmas Eve. In his heart, Clint believed Eli had also found peace. At last, he could be laid to rest, thanks to the fortitude of his friend, Rod Radcliff, Sr.

Before departing, towering over his father in the dankness of the cave, Clint humbly whispered a prayer. He sought reconnection for both Eli and him. He needed to put things right with God. Ask him to forgive the bitterness and anger he had carried in his heart throughout life, all the while blaming God for not answering his childhood prayers to bring his father home. His anger had been misdirected. It should have been aimed at the coldhearted wickedness of a stranger he barely remembered.

Committed to locating a proper burial site for his father and the loyal animal that had stayed with his father even in his own final moments, Clint would call Three Pines Park Cemetery to see if there were any plots available near or next to Elise. The bones at his feet would be laid to rest jointly. Aware the clock was ticking, Clint turned to head home. When Scott and David arrived, he had to be there.

A Hard Sell

He'd only taken a couple of steps when his movements were brought to a halt. The shadowy figure was back, standing between him and the stone wall to his right. Rod Radcliff, Sr. had not departed as Clint assumed. At the gap in the wall, the figure lingered, where the greatest number of geodes were piled. Clint knew from experience something of importance waited.

Clint moved to the spot where Rod had been standing a moment ago. Although he could no longer see Rod, he felt his presence strongly.

This part of the cave was different from anywhere else Clint had traveled. Noticing a divide in the rockface, he saw a double-sided fissure nearly wide enough for a person to squeeze through. It resembled the area where Clint had discovered the second body, minus the geodes.

The flashlight was tucked into his back pocket. To hold it and navigate the tight space would have been impossible. Clint had to apply pressure to crowd his middle-aged body into the crack. He inched sidelong through the split, taking abbreviated steps through to the intense blackness.

Blacker than any black he had ever seen, Clint wondered if Rod would be waiting at the opposite end. With his final step, Clint felt the space he had been working his way through, give way. He reached for the flashlight and turned it on.

Stupefied at what he saw, Clint staggered into the wall, unable to conceive of what lay before him. It soon registered that he was standing in a hideaway of gold and silver bars, along with jewelry and gems spewed everywhere as though tossed into the air and landed but never touched. Coins galore were scattered at random here and there with scores of purses, wallets, and sizeable diamonds. The limestone walls were lined in small black pouches. Certificates were stacked and bills piled. The contents of the lair covered the entire space. All too ludicrous to process.

Once Clint was able to control his emotions, he asked aloud, "So, this is what it was about! Why Dad was killed? Because they

Chapter 39

unearthed the Reno Gang's treasure? Then greed raised its ugly head!" Clint stared in disbelief at what surrounded him. "This is what the fight was over!"

The vision from yesterday resurfaced. It was the partner who had killed his father. Later the partner also died but in a different section of the cave. According to Clint's new knowledge, he supposed his father might have landed a lethal blow as well. Either way, both men lay dead beneath Hoosier State Forest in Goss Cave.

Clint could only imagine how the fight must have begun, but he was crystal clear on how it ended. The aftermath lay at his feet. Neither man ever saw their dream come to fruition. No one cashed in.

The realization that he was the lone person to know where the Reno Gang's plunder was hidden was mind-numbing.

So, is it, speculated Clint, *technically mine?* At such a preposterous thought, he laughed hysterically.

Eyeing every inch of the space, Clint questioned if Rod was still around. He didn't see the man, but Clint asked his question anyway. "Did you want me to have it because my dad found it first? Because it was his, you think it should be mine?"

Then Clint asked another question he doubted Rod would answer. "Why you, Rod? Why are you the one showing all this to me and not my father?"

Stillness followed with no response.

Memories of listening to his dad and partner talk lost treasure stories from the kitchen after Clint went to bed drifted through his mind. The maps on the kitchen table drifted plainly through in his mind's eye.

Connecting the dots between their world and his, Clint took in the vast fortune that encircled him. He alone knew where this treasure was hidden, and for the time being, it would stay that way. Until his brain sorted it out, he would sit on the discovery.

A Hard Sell

Squeezing through the marginal passage, Clint was convinced only one person could be trusted with such an enormous secret. *Just her,* he breathed.

As he rushed up the ladder, his mind was traveling a million miles a minute. *I sure as heck am not going to mention it to the boys over the telephone. This story will have to be delivered in person.* He thought, cracking a huge smile.

Just then, Clint saw Jules' pretty face in his mind. *I can't imagine how she will react when I explain how this all came about and the sequence of events that led me here.*

When he reached the top rung, reality greeted him. He had cut his time way too close. *Scott should be here any minute.* He crawled into the shack and the light of day. After being in the cave, his eyes slowly adjusted. Sitting in the closet, he put his hands over his face, allowing only a smidgeon of light to filter in.

With improved vision and at lightning speed, Clint sprinted through the forest and into the yard, where he observed a police car pulling into the drive. The engine was killed and two uniformed officers stepped out.

Not in the best physical condition, Clint barreled through the rear entrance, kicked his hiking boots to the side, and slipped his house shoes on. He made a mad dash to the kitchen when the doorbell rang, having just made it.

Sweaty, flushed, and panting for breath, Clint opened the door. "Hey, guys, thanks for stopping by," he greeted them. Turning sideways, he said, "Please, join me in the kitchen."

David immediately picked up on the fact Clint looked like he had just run a marathon. "Looks like you've been working out," he casually commented. David always watched for signs of things out of the ordinary. He was keen on the unobservable as cases were often solved on what was hidden in plain sight.

"No, not really," Clint grinned. "Exercise and me, we don't get along. Give me hard labor, and I'll be at it all day, but not treadmills

Chapter 39

and exercise bikes." Clint nonchalantly turned toward the counter, cognizant of David's discerning eye.

Scott took a hard look at Clint, trying to figure out what was different. Having no idea why he was adamant they speak in person rather than over the phone, Scott assumed it was something important.

"So, what's up?" he inquired curiously. "You must have something noteworthy to share, or you wouldn't have asked to see me." Scott crossed his ankles and leaned back in the chair, folding his arms behind his head.

He felt relaxed. This was not Scott's first visit to Clint's residence. They'd played more than a handful of poker games at this very table, not to mention lots of drinks. Clint enjoyed a good poker game now and again with a handful of guys: Joe, Scott, Patrick, and Ivan.

"Can I offer either of you gentlemen a cup of coffee?" asked Clint, turning to check the pot, knowing it had switched off.

Buying time to collect his thoughts, he added, "Only a few hours old. Should still be good."

Moving to the corner cabinet, Clint cracked a smile. He poured a smaller cup into his normal one and stuck it into the microwave. Intending to delay the conversation, he held up two additional mugs. "So, what'll it be? Coffee or Coke?"

Scott answered for David. "Neither. We just finished lunch. Why don't you just have a seat and fill us in on what's troubling you." Scott was puzzled by Clint's odd conduct and had detected a nervous vibe the moment he stepped through the door. Not wanting to beat around the bush, he stated, "You seem distracted."

Clint sat down, unsure how to layer his story. "Well, to start out with, I need to report an incident." His brows creased and his eyes grew dark. "A serious situation has arisen, and it's of a personal nature. That is why I asked you over." His face looked pained.

"What I'm about to say stays in this room. Or at least part of it must! Kept between us. Do you understand?" Clint lowered his head to avoid eye contact. "I am aware my story will get out eventually. It would be naive of me to think otherwise."

Scott looked at David then over at Clint. "I think you need to tell us what this is about." His eyes drifted back to David's. "I can't make promises, Clint. You know that. If it is sensitive material, I'll do my best to protect you and your information."

Clint turned to face the window, not sure if he could finish what he had started. "Okay," he said. "Here goes nothing." When he swiveled back around, he realized David was watching him intently.

"Please don't think I'm off my rocker," he said sheepishly, locking eyes with David and aware he was being scrutinized. "Last night, I was on my way back from the barn when something happened that defies explanation."

Shifting his weight, he turned to Scott and fanned his hands. "Scott, I'm not prone to exaggeration. I don't make stuff up! You know that."

"That's true." Scott chuckled, wondering what that had to do with anything. "What happened? Just spit it out and stop all this hem-hawing around."

Clint grimaced when he saw David's face. Regretting that he had agreed to allow David to accompany Scott in the first place, guardedly, Clint continued. "I've never believed in the paranormal." Turning away, he mumbled, "I do now. I saw a man on my property last evening after leaving the barn. I was on the way to the house like I said. He was standing at the property line of my yard, just inside the forest."

In a woeful voice, he stated, "Scott, it was a figure that I've seen multiple times over the last three or four months." He raised a brow. "At first, I told myself I was imagining things and simply ignore it. That was impossible to do last night."

Scott stood. "An intruder? Is that what you mean? Someone's been stalking you?" Scott's voice sounded alarmed. "Why didn't you call or say something?"

Chapter 39

"No, no!" Clint doggedly reacted, trying not to hit the panic button. "You aren't listening. It's nothing like that." Clint's face turned stormy. "God help me!" He joined Scott, leaving David as the only one still seated. "What I saw was an apparition. A ghost! Spirit... whatever you want to call it."

The air could have been cut with a knife. Neither officer knew exactly how to respond to such a cockamamie story. Silence fell over the room, the tension building until David patronizingly offered, "Look, we hear this sort of thing from time to time, and there's always an explanation for the unexplainable."

"I know what I saw," Clint replied in a raised voice. He turned to Scott. "You need to listen with an open mind. Can you do that?" His tone was angry.

All three men took their respective corners. After a few minutes, Scott broke the ice. "What time was this?" he asked.

David rolled his eyes when Scott took a pad from his pocket and started jotting down notes. "Tell me what happened after that."

Clint knew Scott wasn't going to pass judgment. They had known each other too long. He avoided eye contact with David when he answered, "I'd say around nine o'clock, but I can't be sure. What came next is the weird part. It felt like the entity wanted me to follow him, so I did."

When Scott sat down and leaned in, Clint did the same. It was time to tell the whole truth and nothing but the truth...

"There is a shack in the forest. I had been there once before, a few days earlier. After my treasure hunt last Saturday for the grandkids, one of them, Lily, wandered off and ended up there. But that's another story for another time." He closed his eyes, thinking how much had happened since then.

"After you got to the shack, then what?" David asked impatiently. He checked his watch and glanced at Scott.

Clint's hands were turned palm-side up. "I went inside. There was only one room and a closet. In the closet, though, I discovered a secret passage."

A Hard Sell

"Seriously? The place is small but big enough for a secret room?" David countered, for once acting like he was genuinely interested in what Clint had to say.

"Yeah, well, it wasn't a room. I said passage. Difficult to get in and out of, in fact." Clint looked away. "Anyhow, I noticed an irregularity in the wall and thought it odd, so I investigated. It turned out to be a panel door. When I applied a bit of pressure, it opened right up. I found a manmade hole on the other side." Clint's expression showed he still couldn't believe he happened upon the secret area. "It was an alternate entrance into Goss Cave."

Scott's eyes widened. "Somebody excavated a hole into Goss Cave, and it's hidden behind the closet in this shack?" A baffled look appeared on his face. "Wonder which came first, the shack or the cavity?" In his mind, Scott sieved through the information Clint had laid out. "I didn't realize the cave was that considerable." He shifted his gaze to David. "Did you?"

Annoyed, David shook his head. "Don't ask me. I know nothing about Goss Cave."

Scott smiled, easily interpreting what David hadn't said, that he also didn't care.

To Clint, Scott said, "From your expression, I assume you went down into the hole. I also presume there was a problem, or we wouldn't be here."

"You could say that." Clint glanced over at David. "The man I told you about was down inside the cave waiting for me, and he led me to a body. I believe it's my father. Eli Reeves."

Visible shock was seen on the two officers' faces. "*What?* How do you know?" Scott asked, knowing how important this moment would be to Clint if it were true.

Clint's body sagged, and his shoulders slumped. Clearly ill at ease, he admitted, "Because… I saw it in a dream!"

David abruptly moved forward. "You what?" he asked incredulously.

Chapter 39

"You heard me!" Clint replied in a flash, visibly tired of David's skeptical attitude.

"I tripped, and my head hit a boulder. I saw his murder while I was knocked out. My father and another man were arguing, and Dad's partner killed him. I understand how absurd that must all sound, but I'm telling you my father's body is lying in Goss Cave. He's almost directly below the shack. I can't prove it, but you can."

"Absurd? You bet it sounds absurd!" David said in an agitated voice.

Clint's stare bore a hole through Scott as if to say, *Come to my defense.*

"Look, we need to talk. It'll only be a minute," said Scott, signaling to David to step out into the hall.

The officers moved to the foyer. With their backs to Clint, he could tell the conversation was a lively one. When they returned, David took the lead.

"We follow strict procedures in law enforcement. What you've told us is incredible." He glanced over Clint's shoulder at the wall. "If a body does exist, we need to investigate. You'll need to show us where the body is located. A crime-scene investigator will be notified immediately. We'll check it out, and if a crime has been perpetrated, we will get to the bottom of it. That's a promise."

"With all due respect, David, a crime was perpetrated, and the person who was killed is my father. That, I promise you!"

"Clint, who you found is yet to be determined," Scott emphasized with authority. "I believe what you say, but you need to understand we can't use what someone saw in a dream as evidence. Finding a body would be traumatizing under any circumstances. The stress of it alone could have, and probably did, trigger your dream."

"You'll see," Clint said defiantly. "Do you want to see the body?" Clint stood and grabbed his cap. "Otherwise, I'll bid you good day."

"We need to see the body, not *want* to see it," exclaimed David.

A Hard Sell

Hot under the collar as well, Scott charged, "You're lucky you didn't kill yourself. Your head hit a rock? What were you thinking? Going into a cave after dark with no backup," he said as he watched Clint disappear down the hall and come back holding his boots.

Scott was visibly upset. He considered Clint a friend, someone he thought had more common sense than what he had demonstrated. "The worst part of this is no one knew you were down there. C'mon, Clint! You're too old to do something that stupid." Immediately Scott knew he had crossed a line—and worse, David had witnessed it.

Clint opened the door to let the officers out. "I'll see you in the morning, I suspect since dead bodies don't get up and walk away."

"We'll return tonight! Not tomorrow. We call the shots. We decide where and when," David stated matter-of-factly.

As they stepped through the door, Scott looked at his watch and said, "We'll be back in two hours."

He hesitated, turned around, and looked at Clint. *Did he say, "dead bodies?" As in plural?*

Chapter 40
An Unexpected Development

The first thing Clint did after Scott and David left was call Jules. He had several missed calls on his phone, plus two messages. When someone does not do what they always do, it's bound to strike a chord of concern. Clint was a creature of habit and Jules knew that. However, this time not only did Clint not show up, but he also failed to call, which he would have ordinarily done.

"Patrick, is Jules there?"

"Sure, but she's with a customer. Can you wait a sec?"

"Certainly."

"Didn't see you this morning," commented Patrick. Without letting Clint speak, he added, "It may be best if I have her call you back. We just had three people seat themselves."

"No problem," Clint politely replied. "Something out of the blue came up. I meant to call but got sidetracked. Just have her phone when it's convenient." He looked at the clock above the kitchen door. "I'm not going anywhere."

"Will do!" Patrick responded. "See you Thursday, I presume, since Wednesday is Jules' day off. Today too. Seems people love getting hired but don't want to show up for work anymore. Jules saved our bacon!"

"Just have her phone, whenever. I'll see you Thursday. Have a good one!" Clint laid his mobile on the counter, not sure what should be done about the information he had not divulged to the police. Prior to their return, he considered telling Scott, thinking the blanks needed to be filled in. Then he thought better of it. Especially after the reaction he had received. Telling them about the second body could wait.

He wouldn't disclose the Reno Gang discovery under any circumstance. *I'll have to mull that one over. Read up on state law, I suppose would be a good idea. Find out if finders keepers is in effect in Indiana. After all, I made the discovery on state property.*

He pondered the thought, *If finders keepers does apply, I can make a claim.*

Clint chuckled at the dilemma he was faced with. *This is a conundrum Jules and I will have to tackle before I say anything.*

He sat at the table waiting for Jules' call but didn't have to wait long. The cell sounded and, on the display, he saw her name. He quickly answered. "Hello!"

"Hello to you!" Jules' voice was upbeat. "Patrick said you called. Sorry for all the messages this morning. I was starting to worry. Usually, you call to say you won't be here."

"I know and apologize. I'll explain later. Sounds like a busy day at work. Short-handed again." He said in the way of a question.

"Certainly is. Don't know what's going on. Seems like everyone wants to eat at Josie's these days. Our customer base keeps increasing, which is a good thing. I'm not complaining."

"Truth is, I was planning on phoning anyway. Even before I saw that you had called." Clint took a breath, "Jules, the most remarkable thing you can imagine has occurred. Do you think you could stop by on your way home? We still have a pot roast to consume!"

"Sounds intriguing. On my end, nothing has changed, other than it could be 6 p.m. instead of 5:30."

"That works perfectly. Gives me time to unwind. Believe me, what I have to say is earthshattering. On all kinds of levels." He laughed. "Right up your alley, Jules!"

"I can't wait to hear. I'll see you after work then," she said cheerfully. "I'll send you a text when I leave." She hung up the phone. On the way to the front, she wondered what had Clint so wound up.

Chapter 40

On Clint's end of the conversation, with nothing to do but wait for the police to arrive, he decided to revisit the shack. What else did he have to do? He knew little about the place but recalled as a child running through a wooded area to where his granddad was always found. The memories were spotty at best.

One room plus a closet didn't seem like normal living quarters, but he was convinced—since his house was the same as the one he lived in as a child—the shack was the place he had run off to in search of his grandfather. The only other thing he remembered from back in those days was a rocking chair outside the door.

Standing inside the shack, Clint took a hard look at its structure, undoubtedly built untold years ago. Once he thought about it, the shack did seem vaguely familiar. Puzzled by its construction, he soon became bothered.

No kitchen to cook foods, no bathroom or bedroom? Clint weighed what that could mean. *How did he live here without conveniences? I suppose he could have slept in the open area on the floor. People did things like that back in the old days! Still, a place to make his meals or go to the bathroom would have been necessary.*

Ready to go outside to walk the grounds, he stopped when he saw a glint on the ground. It was the key that was inside the wooden box he had bought at Rod's New and Used Books. One of Lily's treasure hunt gifts. The key had been tucked inside a small ornate box until she removed it.

Clint remembered Lily saying that she had put the key on a chain around her neck the night they went out searching for the Bowie knife. She told him the next day she'd dropped it.

He dropped the key in his pocket. "No sign of an outhouse," Clint mumbled. *Outhouses were typically placed thirty feet or so from the dwelling.*

That brought another possibility to mind. *Maybe the shack was never a dwelling.*

He checked his watch. Forty-five minutes had passed. Enough time remained to investigate the bordering area. Moving into a denser part of the woods, thinking it might reveal more structures, a thought struck him. He remembered the outhouse he and Jules had run across when exploring the forest. When he took her to the clearing to show her where the treasure chests would be hidden.

Coming across no other features, he was ready to give up. Then he saw it. In the distance was an outside toilet. *Paydirt! Problem solved*, he congratulated himself. Keeping a close eye on the time, he advanced toward the outhouse. His intention was to strictly check the area out. But what he chanced upon was not what he would have ever expected.

Yes, an outside toilet had been erected. Yes, nothing was out of the ordinary about the structure. He opened the door. A pit latrine—as anticipated. When he ventured to the west side of the building, things turned strange. An irregular, thick layer of soil caught his eye.

Initially, he thought it was probably the way the sun was filtering through the trees. When he stooped to feel the ground, his brain registered something entirely different. What he was looking at was a concealment of some kind. Beneath the soil, something else lay. He used his hands to dig through the top layer. What he discovered was shocking. A trap door lay a foot below the forest floor.

Clint took a step back. A grin crept onto his face. "Seems my family had more hidden secrets than I realized."

Unsure if he should proceed, he opted to wait. After the authorities left, he would come back. This morning he would have thought he could tell Scott anything, but their visit had changed his opinion.

By all accounts, something sizeable lay well-disguised beneath the forest floor. Curiously, it was in rather close vicinity to the shack. Had he known from the start where to look, it would have been a stone's throw. The outhouse appeared perfectly natural in its location. No one would think anything unusual about where it

Chapter 40

was placed. The assumption would be it was built for privacy. But what seemed odd was two outhouses had been built in the woods.

Walking back to the house, he checked his phone. Nothing so far. Inside the house, he fiddled, finishing off the last of the coffee and contemplating his next moves. The treasure awaited retrieving. Out of sight in an obscure hideaway, he should do nothing until he'd fully mulled over the discovery.

From the desk in the bedroom, he withdrew a tablet. To use the notepad on his android would be careless. To err on the side of caution was prudent. No paper trail other than what he held in his hands.

He heard cars and then the knock on the door. Clint got up to answer it. When he opened the door, Clint noticed two police cars and a van parked in the driveway.

Scott tipped his hat and walked in. David and a stranger trailed.

"I'm sorry. We are a little later than expected," apologized Scott.

"No problem," Clint replied with an edge to his voice.

"I'd like to introduce you to Jonas Shumacher," David stated. "He's our crime scene investigator. He will do a thorough evaluation of the case. After that, the body will be removed and taken to the morgue. Physical evidence will be collected and analyzed by the lab. Do you understand why we included a CSI?"

"Yes," Clint said, feeling annoyed and patronized. "To uncover the identity and cause of death. To see if a crime was committed. I didn't come in on the noon balloon, you know," he said sarcastically.

"Really, Clint?" Scott said with a hint of a smile. "If you don't mind, please lead us to where the body was found," said Scott. He put his hand on Clint's shoulder. "I know this is hard. I don't want you to think for a minute that I don't understand how difficult it is."

Not sure how to respond, he pulled away. Scott's attitude was a complete turnaround from two hours ago, in Clint's opinion.

"Thank you. It's not!"

Through the yard and into the woods the four men moved until the shack was in view. Once inside, Jonas touched nothing but scanned every inch of space with a glance.

"The entrance to the cave is in there." Clint pointed to the closet.

"How did you get down there? I assume there must be a rope or ladder?" David asked.

"Yes, a ladder is affixed to the wall," replied Clint, noticing a concerned expression on David's face. In uniform, lowering themselves to the cave floor was going to be a challenge. "Don't worry, it's sturdy enough."

"All right, let's do this," instructed Scott, pointing to the closet. "You first, Clint."

Crawling through to the opposite side of the wall, Clint vanished downward into the darkness. The others did the same. In the interior of the earth, they heard Clint's voice beneath them.

"It's a tight fit, scarcely large enough for a full-grown man. Not too much wiggle room, so be careful."

They appreciated Clint's message when the officers examined the circumference of the hole. The gear they wore could pose a problem if not careful. Single file, the group descended into the cave.

"Not much farther," Clint said. He turned to Scott. "My father's clothes should help you identify him. Thank God for DNA and modern forensics."

"You're right about that," Scott concurred. "I know you are in hopes this person is your father. The mystery that has always surrounded him will be explained if it is."

"I'm not hoping it's my father, Scott. I know it's my father. I told you I saw what happened."

"Right." Scott smiled. "Well, don't get your hopes up too high. In my line of work, I see all kinds of things and grant you psychic phenomena isn't something I have much experience with. If you are

Chapter 40

right, it will be one for the record books. You will make a believer out of me."

There was no doubt whatsoever the person lying parallel to the limestone wall had died a long time ago. The decomposition of the body was apparent. Jonas immediately got to work. The other officers aimed flashlights at the area to provide enough light to take photographs. Even if the quality wasn't perfect, they would be acceptable. All essential evidence was bagged and tagged.

"We'll have a team come back to collect the deceased," David stated, not realizing how cold and uncaring his voice sounded. He looked at his watch. "More than likely, it'll be tomorrow."

Clint looked down at Eli, knowing this would be the last time his dad and he would be together.

"I'll let you know what develops," offered Scott, "as soon as I know." Feeling empathy for his friend, Scott realized a lot rested on the outcome of the investigation.

Clint's eyes lifted from Eli. He stared at Scott and said, "This isn't the only body!"

Chapter 41
Collaboration

When the police pulled out of the drive, Clint breathed a sigh of relief. Once inside the house he thought they would just pack up and leave, but that wasn't the case. The consequential red tape had to be completed and documented followed by more questions.

The hour was later than Clint realized. The two bodies, from the cave's protective atmosphere, had taken time to inspect. Especially since initially, Clint had only told Scott about one of them.

Because of him, the team had come ill prepared for the task of recovering bodies. David made it apparent he was not happy. To finish the job, they would have to return the following day to retrieve the second corpse.

Prior to going down in Goss Cave, Clint had asked Scott to keep the animal remains in reserve. After the laboratory analysis was complete, he would include the bones in his father's burial casket.

When quizzed about the second body, Clint had conveniently blamed the team for his lack of disclosure. "You cut me off. Didn't allow me to finish my story," he had stated with fervor and a shy grin.

Despite that fact, Scott felt put off. If he was amused, he didn't show it. He accepted the possibility that he had not handled the situation as well as he could have.

After everyone had filed out the door, Scott apologized. "Clint, I'm sorry about this morning. I know you believe what you told us, and I really hope you are right. For the record, I am not as closed off about things of a supernatural nature as you may think. Not by a long shot, but when it comes to dead bodies, I must play it by the book. I trust you understand."

"I do," Clint replied directly. "Chalk it up to a misunderstanding. Nevertheless, you'll see what I told you is factual. Besides, what

Chapter 41

kind of a person would make up a crazy story like that? I'm not into ridicule!"

"You're right. This isn't easy for any of us," Scott agreed.

With their parting words, Scott and the crew had headed back to the station. Scheduled for 10 a.m. Wednesday, the remains of the other corpse would be brought up from Goss Cave.

Tuesday, September 23, 4:45 p.m.

"We need to talk," Clint expressed when Jules answered the phone. "The sooner, the better. Dinner is off. I ran out of time and couldn't put the roast in the oven. I'm sorry to call it off so late, but things got complicated. If you want to wait until tomorrow, I'd understand."

"No way," she interrupted. "I'm curious as heck as to what's been going on." She chuckled, "Give me ten minutes, and I'll head out. We can eat pot roast tomorrow if that is still in the offering."

"Yes, yes, it is," responded Clint with relief. "I could use a listening ear and a friendly face around here!"

"Rescue is on its way," she excitedly affirmed. "Have a cup of Espresso. I'll be right there."

When Clint hung up the phone, he felt a thousand times lighter, like a weight had been lifted off his shoulders.

In less than thirty minutes, she was in the kitchen. No longer did she knock as she once had. "Man, it feels like forever since I've seen you. I know it hasn't been, but it feels that way." Dressed in jeans and a pale cashmere sweater, her smile brightened the room.

With a cat that swallowed the canary grin, Clint declared, "You are never going to believe what I have to say."

"Try me!" she challenged, taking a mug out of the cabinet. "Do you have any Oolong tea by chance?"

"Yep, sure do. In the cabinet left of the stove. I have all kinds of tea."

"I'll put the kettle on," she said as she rummaged through the cabinet for the Oolong. "You want a cup?"

"Come to think of it, I do. Thanks!" he replied comically, noticing how at home Jules made herself.

Waiting for the water in the kettle to boil, Clint brought Jules up to date. He started out with the presence that had led him to the body.

She didn't bat an eye.

When he explained how the other body, and the condition in which it was found, was chanced upon, she had a different reaction. Bowled over, Jules asserted that from the start she suspected Rod Radcliff, Sr. was somehow connected to the strange happenings in Clint's life. Every sign pointed to him. The bookstore, mirror, movie, missing Bowie knife, and so forth. She poured piping hot water into two mugs of loose-leaf Oolong tea, listening as Clint narrated the sequence of events.

Clint had elected to omit one important piece of the puzzle. The treasure! He was saving that for a boots-on-the-ground first-hand revelation. A picture is worth a thousand words kind of experience.

"It's possible I'm leaving out a thing or two." His eyes smiled thinking of the trap door near the outhouse. Clint grinned, knowing the Reno Gang's discovered treasure was going to knock her socks off. "But the second one will have to wait until later."

Jules squinched her face, then chuckled. "That sounds intriguing!"

Passing over her remark, Clint continued. "I had a two-hour window between the police officers' first and second visit. To make use of my time, I went out to inspect the shack. Thought maybe I could get a better understanding of what went on out there."

"You did?" Jules said excitedly, searching his face for telltale signs of where this was leading. "Why do I get the feeling you found something of value?"

Chapter 41

"Bingo!" Clint acknowledged. "I kept thinking, why isn't there a kitchen, bedroom or bathroom? It didn't make sense. At a minimum, you would think living quarters would have a kitchen area. If someone, indeed, lived there. You know, a sink, stove, or food preparation area for meals."

"That does seem weird now that you mention it." Jules frowned as though thinking about the rudimentary design. "And you concluded…"

Clint talked with his hands, exposing the palms. He said, "The missing bedroom could be explained. No big deal, people in the old days slept on living room floors. The missing kitchen, though, was a different matter. Eating is essential. Plus, there was nowhere to go to the bathroom. Then I remembered outhouses were common not all that long ago. But my instincts kept telling me it didn't add up. So, I set out to see if I could find an outhouse."

"Strange that the normal creature comforts were missing. If the shack were a living quarter, you would think there might be indications of it." Jules' confusion was written on her face.

"You betcha," Clint enthusiastically concurred. "I did find another outhouse. I would have expected it to be much closer, though. The appearance was perfectly normal. Then I observed a curious patch of ground. Under a heavy layer of soil, I unearthed an odd feature. If I had to describe it, I would say it felt like an entrance to somewhere. It was remarkably camouflaged."

"You've got to be kidding!" Jules' face lit up. Amazed at this latest development, she exclaimed, "With all the other things that have gone on, you'd think nothing more could happen." She reached out and took his hand. "So, what was under it?"

"Well, that's just it. I don't know. There wasn't enough time to investigate. I shelved it until you and I could go out there together. That is, if you want to join me." Clint raised a brow gave her a faint smile.

"You won't have to ask me twice." Jules agreed. "When?"

Collaboration

"After Scott and his group leave," Clint replied, thinking about the stone entrance to the treasure. "After that. I have one other thing I'd like you to see. How do you feel about going down in Goss Cave with me? Once they are gone?"

"Are you kidding? I'd love to. Are you going to show me where you found your father?"

Clint didn't answer. Instead, he asked a question. "Jules, can you keep a secret? What we are going to do has to be done under wraps, after the authorities are gone and on the sly." The sincerity reflected in his eyes was clear when he added, "You are the only one I trust."

Perplexed as to what would make him say such a thing, Jules replied, "I feel honored that you trust me with whatever you are referring to."

"By anybody's standards, what I'm about to show you is monumental."

She nodded. "Count me in. My lips are sealed. I guess this means we put the pot roast on hold until next Tuesday!" Jules laughed hard at how many plans had been rearranged.

"I guess it does." Clint also laughed. "Excellent then... until tomorrow," he said in an upbeat tone.

At the door. they embraced in a longer than normal hug. When exactly Clint had crossed the line between friendship and caring deeply for Jules he could not say, but he was aware his feelings had changed.

"If all goes well," she had mentioned, "expect me around 1 p.m. By that time, the police and forensics should have finished their work."

Gazing into the fire he had built while waiting on Jules to arrive, Clint contemplated his predicament. Too wired to read, his head was spinning with speculations. How would he ever find sleep when he knew he was sitting on the historic Reno Gang's lost treasure? A treasure trove so vast there was no way to calculate its value.

Chapter 41

History was about to be made. When the press got hold of the news, they were going to have a field day. There was a fifty-fifty chance the spoils would be turned over to Indiana since they were discovered on state property. Clint had no idea how something like this might play out—other than with extreme theater.

Will I receive a finder's fee? he considered, thinking he should research the question. *It would be nice!*

To show the ill-gotten gains to Jules was going to be exciting. *Can't imagine her face. It'll be a real shocker.*

Random images of Goss Cave floated through his recall. Images of the two decomposed bodies distastefully flashed in his brain. He knew it was subjective, but it was impossible to stop thinking about how the scene must have gone down.

How did the second body get to where it ended up? Quizzically he considered, *An argument or disagreement erupted? A likely fight over the treasure? If Dad's partner killed him, how did his partner die? Unless Dad injured him so badly, he bled to death.*

Clint's eyelids grew heavy while he sifted through various theories. *The Bowie knife was on the second body, still in his hand. It looked like the man crawled or was dragged into the gap where I stumbled upon him.* Clint thought about that scenario but became confused. *But then again, if he was dragged there, who dragged him? Could a third person be involved in the murders?*

Oscillating speculations made his head hurt. Of the mountains of questions that presented themselves, one stood out from the rest. Why would an animal succumb at his father's side?

Unless somehow, Clint reasoned, *the animal was involved! After the second body is taken to the morgue for an autopsy, answers will find the light of day.* Clint comforted himself. *I'll have my answers.*

He took his cup to the kitchen, laid it in the sink, and returned to the bedroom.

In the morning, feeling like he was standing on the edge of a precipice, a whole new set of problems waited in the wings.

Chapter 42
The Family Secret
September 24, 2003
Wednesday, 8:50 a.m.

Rap, rap, rap was the sound heard from the foyer. From down the hall, Clint could see silhouettes behind the glass pane.

"Be right there," he shouted. On his way to the door, he dragged a comb through his unruly black hair and tucked his shirt into his trousers.

Boy, the difference a day makes, he mumbled.

"Hey, Scott," Clint said, wearing a smile while observing the people standing behind his friend. He opened the door to let in the four men standing on the porch.

"Good morning," Scott answered as he walked through to the foyer.

"Come on in," Clint said chipperly to the remaining three who had followed Scott's lead into the house. "Coffee, anyone?"

"Yes, please," accepted Scott without hesitation. "Been up since five! Today promises to be a long one." He glanced over at the other three men, gesturing for them to take a seat in the kitchen.

Clint's brow knitted. "Yeah, me too. This situation has been a tad bit exhausting, I'm afraid. Nothing like a good mystery to drain the brain."

Scott's face showed no reaction to Clint's joke. His comment had been directed at the extra work Clint had created for the team, not the heaviness of the subject to which Clint was referring.

"We'll be in and out of your hair in no time," volunteered Scott. "Brought extra hands along this time. I know we agreed on ten. I hope you got my message. Today should go quicker than yesterday." He took a sip of hot coffee after pouring a small amount of half-and-half and two teaspoons of sugar into it. He sat the cup down.

Chapter 42

"Nothing easy about extracting two bodies through a hole as tight as that one. Doable, but not easy."

"When do you think you'll know something concrete about my father?" Clint inquired as he poured coffee into two of the three remaining cups. One of the men had put a hand over his cup just as Clint started to pour.

"I assume you'll share what you know as soon as it becomes available. That goes without saying. Right? Mine is a vested interest," he said, wearing an expression of expectancy.

"Of course. You'll know as soon as I know," Scott agreed. "I figure a week or two. It could be sooner, but don't hold your breath."

Scott pointed across the table to a man in a dark gray lab jacket with the name Jonas Shumacher stitched on the right chest pocket. "Jonas will have a tooth ground, or femur bone scraped for DNA sampling. Millions of cells will be analyzed. Hopefully, we will achieve definitive results without delay."

As soon as he saw Clint's distraught face, Scott quickly apologized. "I'm sorry, that was insensitive of me."

"Don't worry about it." Clint reacted with a wave of his hand. "Common verbiage in your line of work, I suspect. No way around it if the decomposing remains are expected to supply answers."

Clint wore a puzzled expression as he lifted his cup to his lips. "What about the second body? I told you who I think it is. I'd be hard-pressed to cough up a name, but I believe he lived nearby." His eyes locked with Scott's. Like I mentioned, he was at our house a lot, and I think he and my dad were partners."

"That should help narrow the search, especially if he did live in these parts." Scott's tone was one of caution, and then he changed the subject. "Nothing worse than waiting. But don't worry. I suspect we'll have our answers within the week. On the outside… two." He gave a half-smile. "Don't hold me to that."

Clint's eyes narrowed in on the group. "For the first time since 1953, I have hopes of getting some answers. To wait a few more days is no big deal. Don't want mistakes made because we hurried things."

"Exactly," agreed Scott. "When things wrap up, I'll stop back by. Contamination is an issue. The fewer people in the cave, the better."

"You know where to find me," Clint stated nonchalantly. "I've got plenty to do." Scott's subliminal message had come through loud and clear. The team going in did not include him.

Stepping into the yard, Clint watched the men vanish into the dark forest as he headed to the barn. When he mentioned he had plenty to do, he had lied. The truth was he felt like a cat on a hot tin roof. Patience was never his strong suit. The second he went into the barn, his phone rang. He hit the answer icon after seeing Jules' name on the screen.

He heard her cheery voice on the other end. "Good morning," she said with a snicker. "You sure answered fast."

"Yeah, I was carrying it with me. Didn't want to miss your call. Scott and his team went to the shack. They are headed to the cave." Clint grunted. "Scott said he didn't think it would take too long to remove the bodies. Thank God for small favors."

"I know you'll be glad when they're out of there."

"Truer words could not be spoken," he admitted. "After all these years, to find my dad and then have his body treated like an object is disconcerting in the least."

"I can only imagine what you are feeling right now, Clint. I'm sorry you have to go through this, but I also know you are relieved to uncover the truth, no matter how distasteful." There was silence for a moment, then Jules inserted, "I'll wait for a text from you before I leave here."

"That sounds good. The second I see them return, I'll text you."

Clint felt relieved to have Jules help him explore the area he had stumbled upon the day before. He had no idea what was below the disguised entrance, but his gut told him it was noteworthy. Plus, he had the bigger surprise yet to divulge.

Chapter 42

"My guess is they will be out of here by noon, providing everything comes off without a hitch." Clint sighed. "If anything changes, I'll give you a call. Otherwise, I'll see you in a few hours."

Clint hung up the phone. Looking through the window, he was anxious about his irrefutable claim and that a murder had been committed. The idea he could be mistaken made him nervous. He would feel like such a fool if he were wrong.

He thought about his conversation yesterday with the police. As he described what he had seen in Goss Cave, Clint remembered watching Scott politely take notes while Jonas looked on dispassionately. He vividly recalled the way David looked at him when he referred to his lucid dream.

Scott had respectfully listened to what Clint had to say, but not David. In response to Clint's insistence that the body belonged to Eli Reeves and that a murder had been committed, the expression on David's face telegraphed discord. Although not expressed, Clint could see in David's eyes that the police would be the ones to determine the identity of the body. They thought assumptions were amateurish.

Clint confessed in his head, the story was beginning to sound a little wacko, even to him. He hated to admit it, but he supposed he could have misconstrued things. The blow to the head, when he fell against the rock, could have affected the way he interpreted what he later discovered. Possibly conjecture and nothing more caused him to jump to conclusions because he wanted to believe his father had been found and assumed the body to be his.

As predicted, by noon, Scott and the crew had left the premises. Watching them carry their cargo to the van and unload it was a gruesome reality. The second body in two days had been carried across his yard and taken away.

Clint went to the freezer and withdrew two ribeye steaks. Comfort food. Not a pot roast but a close second. Grilling could take place whenever they felt like it since they were not limited by Jules' work schedule. After everything settled down, he would stoke up the grill and put foiled potatoes on while she tossed a salad. They needed to take advantage of the weather while they could.

He threw sliced ham on two slices of bread. Mustard and pickles covered the meat. Clint took a bite. He had skipped breakfast and felt starved. He piddled around burning time until finally, he heard the knock on the door.

"Clint, I'm here," Jules called out.

"In the living room," he replied.

Jules sat down across from Clint, watching him eat his sandwich. She could not help but notice his face and how fatigued he looked. "You all right?" she asked.

"Yeah, sure," he answered. "Want to join me?" he asked, pointing to his ham sandwich. "I left everything out on the counter just in case. You know where the condiments are."

"I do," Jules quickly accepted. "I forgot to eat breakfast."

Clint chuckled, thinking, *Two peas in a pod*. "It's just been a little stressful with the police in and out of the house for two days. You can imagine! Scott is trying to make it as painless as possible but that is a tall order considering what we are dealing with. Says we'll know the results of the DNA testing in a week. It could be a little longer, but I hope not."

"I'm glad for your sake that's all the longer it will take. And… the other body? You say you remember him from when you were a kid?"

"I think so."

Jules smiled. "Don't fret. Whatever happens, happens. If it *is* him—your dad's partner—maybe forensics will get to the bottom of what happened in Goss Cave. Strange to have two people and an

Chapter 42

animal all die in virtually the same location. Especially since one of them had the Bowie knife clutched in his hand. I wish I had been with you. I can't imagine what you thought when you saw it. Here you were looking for the knife, worried you had misplaced it. This is the craziest thing I've ever heard."

Jules went to the kitchen to fix herself a sandwich. When she returned, Clint said, "You are a breath of fresh air. You know that?"

"What a nice thing to say," she replied with a happy smile.

When they were finished inspecting the trapped entrance that Clint had stumbled upon the day before, he would take Jules down into Goss Cave so she could get a more hands-on feel for what he had been talking about. That was his plan. The best part was he would be able to show her where he'd discovered the treasure.

Clint stood, "Ready to do some exploring?"

"Sure am," she replied without reservation.

"All right then, let's go do some investigating." Clint grinned handsomely. "A mystery awaits us, Dr. Watson."

Into the forest, carrying high expectations, Jules and Clint marched.

"Why would somebody construct a concealed area so far out in the woods? Away from everything except an outhouse?" he asked Jules over his shoulder.

"That is a good question," she called ahead to where Clint was walking. "The only thing I can think of is it's a shelter?"

"One thing is for sure. We are about to find out," he assured her. He had stopped off at the barn to pick up a few supplies and felt prepared for whatever issues they might encounter.

Jules trailed behind Clint until he came to a full stop. "This is it," he said. "Tell me if you can find what I described?"

She searched the area and had no idea where the feature was. "Got me," she said after a few minutes.

Clint aimed her focus to the right. Then he removed the top level of soil, partially exposing the underneath side.

"Clint... that looks like a storm cellar!" Jules squealed. "You know during prohibition these things weren't so uncommon. Maybe they stored liquor down there."

"Only one way to find out." He laughed, feeling tingles of excitement wash over him. "Lots of daylight left. No worries there!"

Together they toiled to unearth the top of the hatch. Packed heavy dirt between planks made it difficult to excavate. The structure was approximately three to four feet below surface level and wider than Clint had calculated.

They continued to move soil from the wooden slats until eventually enough dirt was cleared away to allow entry. A musky odor of stale air waylaid them when the door was first lifted. It had taken both hands to fully raise the door. He noticed there were pull-down dowels on each side. He spotted two precision depressions in the wood that framed the opening. Clint pulled the rods down and placed them into the notches, rotated them clockwise, and secured them into position.

The darkness beneath the sod was daunting. When their eyes adjusted, they saw steps leading down into what looked like a trench.

"I'll go first," suggested Clint. "Don't want you coming along until I know it's safe."

Jules grinned, believing him protective.

Down the steps, he went into a space no more than three feet high. He could see the entrance was not designed for full exposure but constructed with camouflage in mind. He lowered his body into the inky blackness.

Jules kept her flashlight trained on the steps and Clint's progress until he reached the clay bottom. Shockingly, he saw it was solid wood once past the initial base. He was bowled over when his flashlight revealed a room much larger than anything he could have imagined. Clint stopped and stared into the spacious area.

"We're good," he called up. "It's safe." With a quick chuckle, he added, "Wait till you see this!"

Chapter 42

One careful step at a time, Jules descended the ladder until, at last, she stood at Clint's side. Inside what appeared to be living quarters, she queried, "What is this place?" Astounded by the sheer size of it, she yelped, "My God, it's enormous!"

"Check this out," he said, pointing well past where they were standing. "There's a bedroom with a small rolltop desk. Do you see it?" He swiveled his flashlight in a different direction. "And a place to make meals! Plus, a lean-to structure attached to another wing at the back."

"Who do you think lived here? I guess this explains why the shack lacked ordinary necessities." Jules and Clint locked eyes when she suggested, "The shack is a ruse."

"I think you're right," he concurred before answering her question. "If I had to guess, I'd say my grandfather. His name was Phil Reeves. I remember him but not very well. Just bits and pieces of sitting on his lap in the shack. I do remember his smile."

In Clint's eyes, Jules could see the pages of his past. "But why live down here?" she asked.

"I have no idea. Seems really bizarre. It's almost like he might have been hiding."

When they examined the lean-to area, they realized no back wall existed. Using their flashlights, they continued deeper into the void until it became obvious that they had entered a tunnel.

"I don't know about this," Clint said cautiously. "What do you think? Should we continue?"

"We've come this far," she replied in a heartbeat. "Let's see where it leads."

"Man, you must have nerves of iron." Clint turned to face her. "Are you sure about this?"

"I am. Don't you want to see where it leads? There has to be a reason for it."

"Okay then," Clint warned. "Be extra careful and, for heaven's sake, watch your step!"

"I will. You do the same! I haven't had this much fun in years." She laughed.

They took several steps that ended at another ladder, where halfway up, a door appeared. That opened into yet an additional length of tunnel that stretched in darkness and converged into a pinpoint of dim light.

"Lord have mercy!" Jules snickered. "I feel like I'm in a labyrinth of burrows."

"Hold the door, please," Clint requested as he passed through the second doorway. "I'll go in and see what's what."

The words were never uttered, but Clint felt nervous about the two of them getting shut in this artery of nothingness without a means of escape.

"I understand," she agreed. "We should take it slowly."

When the second tunnel connected with a third, hints of dripping water ricocheted up from the cave below. Rustling with sound, their questions were answered.

"Son of a gun," Clint bellowed. "Jules, you are not going to believe this!" he roared.

"What," she asked.

"This tunnel connects with the one that runs from the closet. A well-designed access, coming from behind the shack tunnel. The junction is totally masked. That means the shack, Goss Cave, and that place we were just in," he shockingly declared, "are all joined, linked together. This also means my dad and his partner did not dig the tunnel from the shack. My grandfather, Phil Reeves, must have. But how could one man do this? Unless… my dad knew about these tunnels and assisted my grandfather."

Chapter 43
Triple Tunnel
September 24

The two adventurers wriggled themselves through the most recent tunnel until it eventually steered them back into the original opening used to get into Goss Cave. When they arrived at the rounded-out passage, they climbed back up the ladder. Shortly they were lifting themselves through the opening into the shack closet. They'd made a complete circle of goings-on.

Jules giggled. "Well, that was a joy ride!"

Clint joined in the laughter, "A real adventure, I'd say! Never in a million years would I have expected to be doing this today."

He thought about the construction of the tunnels. "It's evident how my grandfather navigated from place to place. If indeed he was the one living in those quarters. Moving about without detection would have been easy as pie."

Clint thought about Jules' earlier words and was convinced he knew the answer to the riddle. "I keep wondering why anyone would want to go to all the trouble to create elaborate channels like these for no apparent reason. Other than what you suggested for an escape route."

Clint was sitting beside Jules in the closet, trying to make sense of what they had chanced upon. Instincts were signaling a link.

"Jules, I have some information that I haven't shared with you yet," whispered Clint. His eyes brightened as a grin crept onto his face. Clint had a gargantuan revelation to share. He'd held the finale of the exploration to the last, but that was about to change.

"You must be joking!" hooted Jules in disbelief that anything of significance could be left to tell. "This is a strange situation, Clint. Your granddad was ingenious. I'll give him that. The amount of work it must have taken to construct those underground passes was enormous. It would have taken years, literally, to tunnel through.

A continual work in progress, I suspect. I'm having a hard time believing all that work was done by just one man."

"True." Clint beamed. "My belief is he was motivated for a good cause." Clint turned to Jules with a look that spoke volumes.

"You prepared for the biggest surprise of all? Now seems like the right time to show you what I happened across. Unfortunately, that means, if you will join me one last time, we need to go back down the opening into the cavern. Before nightfall, though, because I don't like being out here after dark."

Clint got up and walked to the door to see how much daylight they were working with. "Ready for one more adventure?" he asked with a grin.

"This is beginning to feel like *Raiders of the Lost Ark*." Jules replied agreeably, having no idea what she was getting herself into.

Moving down the ladder, they went through the hole until they reached the cave floor.

Clint reached for Jules' hand. "Look, I need you to stay close. We do not want to take any chances. Not in a cave."

Jules was curious. Whatever Clint had in store, she figured it must be epic by the way he was behaving. When he stopped abruptly, she asked, "Are we there yet?" Her smile gave her humor away.

"You could say that." During this visit, Clint had no trouble retracing his steps. When they passed the place where he had discovered the first body, he said, "That's where I found him. Right there," he pointed to the wall. "The other body was about thirty feet that way." They both looked in the direction Clint indicated. "However, what I'd like you to see is this!"

When he stepped to the side, his face brightened. "Take a look!"

Jules gathered she was about to see something extraordinary. She walked over to where Clint was standing. "Why do I get the feeling this is big?"

"Because it is." He smiled. "Really big!"

Chapter 43

He led her to the fissure. "Turn sideways and move forward. There is an alcove on the other end." He waited for her reaction. When she squealed in shock, it made Clint laugh out loud. "Thought you would like that!"

"Holy Toledo! Clint!" she shrieked with excitement. "No way, Jose!" Jules put both hands over her mouth. Her eyes were huge when she swiveled around. "It's the Reno Gang treasure. Isn't it?"

"Yes, I believe it is! If I was a betting man…" Still in disbelief of the vast amount of riches in the concealed area, he added, "If I had to take a wild guess, I'd say this is the reason my dad and the other person were killed. It must have been an argument or a disagreement of some kind. Conjecture, I know, but it's what my gut is telling me."

"I agree. I think you are exactly right." Jules moved about in the small space taking in what surrounded her. "People kill for a lot less. This is unfathomable! The Reno Gang sure amassed an amazing stockpile of stolen property. Look at all that gold. Can you imagine the value?" Then she saw the silver bars. "Geez Louise, where would they have gotten all this stuff?" She pointed to the stack. "It must be worth millions!"

"I researched the internet after I found the treasure. Did you know the Reno Brothers were the first gang to raid a moving train, even attempted to rob government ones?" He raised a brow, showing his surprise.

"Honestly, I know next to nothing about them," injected Jules, "other than hearsay at the diner. I'm not from these parts."

"They caused havoc in their day." Clint thought about what he had read, "After the Civil War, they gained notoriety. During the same period as Frank and Jesse James. Although their legacy isn't talked about much nowadays, back then everyone in southern Indiana knew their names and were petrified by them. They took no prisoners when it came to robbing people, banks, and trains. Stealing cash, silver and gold bars, and government bonds. They were a ruthless bunch."

Jules shook her head. "That is a lot more than I ever knew." Her face scrunched. "So what now?"

"Don't know to be honest," he answered. "It's not every day you find lost treasure. I suppose the first thing I should do is notify the State of Indiana. This is their land. It'd be nice to receive a finder's fee." He laughed. "Even that, I bet, would be sizeable."

"Worth a pretty penny or two!" Jules agreed. Her expression turned serious. "Do you suppose the pearl necklace and diamonds I found came from here? Remember how unique they were?"

"You could be right," Clint answered. "I'll tell you what... if I do receive a reward, we'll celebrate with a steak dinner. At a fine restaurant. Maybe over at West Baden. I bet we can find a good meal in French Lick! Never been over there, but I'm willing to make an exception." Clint grinned. "Compliments of the Reno Gang!"

Jules snickered. "You're on! Money bags!"

Clint laughed raucously at Jules' wisecrack. "We'd better go. I don't want Scott to come looking for me. The last thing I need is for him to find us down here."

They made their way up the ladder, but instead of going through the shack, they headed to the living quarters they uncovered when they started the day. Clint wanted to secure the opening they had used to get inside. No stone should be left unturned at this juncture.

Clint disguised the closet panel before leaving the shack. He knew they would not return. It was important the appearance remains exactly as it had been when Scott and his team were there last.

The space where his grandfather stayed was to be thoroughly examined in detail. From the looks of it, the greater part of his life had been spent underground. Clues about what transpired in those days hopefully would shed light on Clint's dad's involvement, if there was any.

With the clock ticking, they wanted to get a feel for the place before sunset.

Chapter 43

"Jules, look at this," Clint called from the backroom to the kitchen where Jules was pulling out drawers.

"What did you find?"

"It's a map, and if I didn't know better, I'd say it was of Goss Cave. Check it out!" Clint spread the map out on the desktop, placing a weight on each corner.

Both heads came together. Eyeing the drawing closely, Clint's assumption was confirmed when Jules noted the space where they had come from was indicated on the map.

"Doesn't that look like the alcove we were just in?" she pointed out.

"Certainly does. The map shows several possible directions to follow and no notation of where the treasure was, other than that small red dot." He looked at Jules. "I bet that was on purpose. Maybe granddad didn't want to draw attention to that area. Played it safe."

"This looks like it took years to map out," she added. "If the map is accurate, Goss cave is more massive than I realized. And to think, it runs right below the shack." Jules' deep concentration showed on her face. "Do you suppose he built the shack where it is because he knew the cave was under it?"

"What I think is my granddad was looking for the treasure before my father. And when he died, my dad and his partner took up from where granddad left off. This map proves my theory."

"We should get back to the house," warned Jules. "The last thing on earth we want is to expose this place. I think we should give it a once-over. Later when there is more time."

Clint checked his watch: 5:10 p.m. "You're right. I'm taking the map with me, though. We can examine it more thoroughly at the kitchen table."

With that, they headed topside. The lid was lowered carefully into place, then they walked back to the house. They had a lot to discuss and decide.

"Okay, it won't be West Baden, but I do have two steaks in the refrigerator thawing out. We have a lot to consider. Are you on board with grilling out?"

"Sounds wonderful. I've worked up an appetite." She teased, "A big fat juicy steak might fit the bill."

"If you peel the potatoes, I'll put them in foil with some onions and set them on the grill before I start the steaks."

"I can do that." She laughed. "Anything else, boss?"

"Set the table, and toss the salad." Clint chuckled. "We are beginning to sound like an old married couple."

Jules almost laughed out loud. She rushed ahead to open the back door and let Clint go in front of her. "Brains before beauty!" she joshed.

When they got inside, there was one message on Clint's phone. Not from Scott, but Lily.

The message said, "Hi, Grandpa, I hope you're doing good. Could you give me a call tomorrow, please? I forgot to tell you something when I was at your place. Thought it could be important. I get home from school around 4:30. I have soccer practice this evening, but I'm free after dinner tomorrow. Could you call after 6 p.m.? That would be best. Love yah!"

Chapter 44
Truth Doesn't Die
December 27, 1953

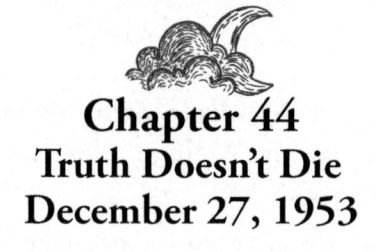

The sun rose on a day stained by the violence of a soulless man. Having stayed up half the night from the sounds of sirens, Luke's foggy brain cleared around 11 a.m.

Groggy, he put his feet to the floor and stood slowly. He'd downed one too many beers the night before. Red-eyed, he scratched his butt as he made his way to the bathroom. Arching his back, he aimed in the general direction of the commode, not caring if he hit or missed. In his mind, he had already moved into nicer digs.

"Today is the first day of the rest of my life," he said flippantly, repeating a phrase Eli often recited. "Don't need to worry about money no more or going to work to earn it. Do I? I'm a rich son of a bitch," he boasted in a braggart's voice. "And, if you play your cards right," he slurred. "You'll stay that way. No more using gold shit to pay for your groceries, lame-brain." He laughed boisterously. "I'm a pig that can fly straight."

Luke continued to lecture himself, hellbent on getting his act together. "Next time, I'll cash a couple of diamonds at a pawn shop," he mumbled on his way to the kitchen. "Take up 'em north to Paoli."

He stepped into the shower to wash away yesterday's filth. Although some regrets lingered, Luke reminded himself, what had been done he did out of preservation.

"Silencing Rod ain't no big deal! The man was old enough. His days were numbered anyhoo," He reasoned.

But Eli was a different matter. Luke grumbled, "That gringo was wet behind the ears. He just wasn't a smart cookie."

Luke figured he wasn't to blame for what had gone down. *A simple disagreement gone awry. Cold hard facts,* Luke reassured himself. *I had to stand up for myself, or Eli may have done to me what I did to him. Money does that to people,* he grinned slyly. *I read about it all the time in the papers!*

From the porch, he stared at the snow-covered streets. He went to the side porch and picked up the newspaper. He laid it beside him in his chair. He hoped to have something to revel in. The account of the fire, written from the night before, but figured it may have come in too late for the morning news. Would the fire at the general store in Salzburg be chronicled on the front page? He doubted it since the paper was published in Vincennes, over seventy miles away.

Life is anything but dull, he thought, cracking a smile. *Who'd ever think I'd be this rich?*

Cupping a hot mug of coffee in his hands, Luke pondered what he would do for the rest of the day. In the bitter December air, coffee tasted good. He decided to visit his treasure. He'd gloat over his recent fortune.

I could organize it, he weighed. *Put it in piles. That way, when I bring everything up, it'll already be separated.* He set the paper aside. A decision was made. *After lunch, I'll set out for the shack. The roads were close to impassible yesterday. They would have plowed more of them last night.*

Twice Luke had gotten stuck in the snow on the way back from Eli's, and once his truck slid off the road. Grateful for the sand he kept in the bed for emergencies, plus the loose boards he didn't even know were there, he had finagled himself out of two potential catastrophes.

"The plows will have cleared the main arteries by now," he stated confidently, which was instantly followed by a snicker. "Not having any friends sure comes in handy. No one will care where I am or come looking for me."

Gulping the last of his coffee, Luke set the cup on the porch and closed the door behind him. In his other hand, he held the

Chapter 44

last cold beer from his frig. It was never going to be too early to celebrate, not in his new world.

His resignation from Stuart Mining would go into effect first thing tomorrow morning. As far as he was concerned, calling in wasn't necessary—today or ever. They'd figure it out soon enough that he'd quit.

Luke remembered a nursery rhyme that made him belly laugh. "The king was in the counting house, counting out his money. The queen was in the parlor eating bread and honey." When he got into the truck, he decreed, "King McCauley!"

On the way to the shack, Luke decided to drive by the General Store to see if any of it remained. He was disappointed not to find gawkers standing near the rubble or the yellow police tape that had been strung up. Luke parked next to the curb on the side street.

Keep Out signs were posted at the perimeter of what used to be a building, warning—No Trespassing. Luke approached from the south and found a squad car idling on the far northeast corner. He crept to the opposite end, where the back entrance of what was once Rod's General Store used to be. He felt compelled to take one last look at his handiwork. He couldn't help himself. In a place where no one would see, Luke patted his own back on a job-well-done.

He stopped on a dime, glancing over his shoulder on his way out. There was something out of place. He hesitated for a moment and took a step backward. The charred cash register came into focus. The door was ajar. The paper bills had been reduced to ash. The drawer appeared empty, but then he saw it.

Is that my coin? he gasped, shocked to see his twenty-dollar gold coin in the drawer.

He crept over, stepping atop smoldering cinders. He carefully chose spots that would not singe the soles of his shoes. The door was jimmied with his Bowie knife until it finally gave way. To his astonishment, he saw his gold coin partway under the case compartment where bigger bills had been deposited.

Truth Doesn't Die

Stroking its smooth surface, Luke regarded the coin with more respect than the last time he handled it. When he dropped it into his pocket, he made certain no one was watching. *No one else is going to enjoy the fruits of my labor,* he grumbled as he rounded the corner with the coin securely tucked in his trouser. He hopped back into the truck and drove away.

When he strolled past Eli's house on his way to the forest, he noticed the windows were exceptionally dark. It appeared no one was home. *Wonder where Eli's kid is?* he pondered. He pushed the thought aside. Luke knew Eli was a devoted father. Not wanting to ruminate over what might happen to Clint, Luke took it for granted that someone would fill in Eli's shoes and take care of the kid.

"Poor kid," muttered Luke, shrugging his shoulders, like, what could *he* do. "He'll adjust. Kids don't feel things like grown-ups."

As Luke neared the shack, he hastened his pace, turning one last time to make positive no one was shadowing him. *Never can be too careful,* he counseled himself.

The shack had an eeriness to it. Unlike the last time, he was there when Eli was with him. That day they were excited about an unexplored section of the cave. In the end, Eli's hunch had been exact, as it usually was. Eli took after his father. *A chip off the old block,* he once told Luke. Thorough in his work ethic, Eli's hunch was intuitive.

Luke descended into the hole behind the paneled closet, this time, going into the cave with the knowledge he was the sole owner of the Reno Gang's treasure. It was hard to contain his exuberance and his dreams of grandeur.

Taking his foot from the final rung, Luke pulled a flashlight from his back pocket and switched it on. This time he carried a standby in his thermal jacket just in case something unexpected occurred. Moving toward his destination, he decided only a few handfuls of silver coins would be taken.

Chapter 44

Silver coins won't draw unwelcomed attention like the gold one did, he told himself.

When Luke reached the recessed area, where the treasure was hidden, it occurred to him on his next trip he would have to bring a lantern along. The opening had to be enlarged to fit his large body through. It was a narrow space to work. A flashlight alone wasn't going to cut it. Eli had been half the man he was. That was why he had slid through the small space so easily. Not the case with Luke.

An Eye for an Eye

There is a fundamental law in nature. Balance. Good versus evil, right versus wrong. And… there are two sides to a coin. Time is transitory, and so are we. The only thing that matters in life is did we treat others as we ourselves would have wanted to be treated. It is a fact, when a pendulum swings to the far right, it will eventually swing back to the left at the opposite equal distance.

What goes around comes around.

Luke had taken only a few steps toward the opening that led to the treasure trove when he sensed he wasn't alone. Eli's collapsed body was over against the wall. The presence he felt was not that of a dead body. It was something other than that. Luke sloughed the feeling off, thinking he was being oversensitive, and got to work, chipping away at the stone.

The crevice that disguised the entrance was slight. Luke squeezed his substantial body as best he could through a slit no larger than two feet wide. Eli mastered it, but Luke quickly understood he needed another eight inches or more if he expected to reach the goods. On the off chance that someone in the future entered this section of the cave, he decided the crack in the stone should not be widened much more.

To draw unnecessary attention was not Luke's objective. This was his find, and he planned to keep it that way. No matter if he had to shoehorn himself through a space a child would have difficulty getting in and out of, it would be done.

Between the stone Luke was chiseling, he peered into the void that lay at the far end of the opening, giddy with excitement at what his flashlight would reveal. Disappointed with the restriction he felt, he conceded that the space still needed work. He would have to chip away even more stone if he expected to get through to the other side where the treasure was deposited.

When he shifted his weight, ready to back out of the split, he was caught off guard. Luke stopped dead in his tracks when a pair of piercing green eyes was seen blocking the exit that led back into the open space.

The puma moved backward, not once taking his eyes off his target. Picasso's intentions could not have been misunderstood. Large cats of prey did not make social calls.

Side to side, the puma restlessly paced. After a few minutes, it retreated into the dark recesses beyond Luke's vision. Moments later, the cat circled back to where Luke stood frozen in place, out of reach, trapped in a fissure where he would not be able to remain.

The puma went over to where Eli's body rested on the dirt floor. He stopped. The cat nudged the carcass with his forehead. When the body wobbled but otherwise did not respond, the cat became visibly agitated, making an ungodly sound Luke had never heard before. It turned. A merciless glare locked on Luke.

Luke withdrew his Bowie knife from its sheath, his only means of defense. Wiped clean of Eli's blood, he was prepared to bloody it again. "Scat," he hollered from the safety of his hideaway.

The cat did not flinch nor falter.

Luke stepped out of the gap, flailing his hands in the air. He would take out his lighter, figuring the flame would intimidate or scare the animal into retreat.

Chapter 44

He slid his hand deep into his front pocket, but it was empty. To his horror, nowhere in any of his pockets was the cigarette lighter that he always carried. The one he never left home without.

Luke's face grimaced with fear. He felt perplexed. Did he put on the wrong pair of pants? Never without his lighter, he dug into the right pocket a second time. He pulled out Eli's Guardian Angel coin. This made no sense. Both items had been on his person, in that pocket, the night before.

"Damn it!" he yelled. "It must have fallen out somewhere."

Then it dawned on him, the last place he remembered having it was at Rod's General Store. He made a point of flipping it open and closed simply to irritate Pearl Teague, the cashier. He tried to recall any other circumstance where he might have used it but drew a blank.

The only place I used it was there. He cringed, thinking of the ramifications. He thought hard. *I used a match at home to light my cigarette! Crap... it could tie me to the scene of the crime.*

In Luke's panic, he let his guard down.

The puma leaped forward, and as if by magic, halted his attack midair. He had contorted his plunge into a half-twist and landed back on all fours precisely two feet from where he had sprung. Picasso, unfazed by Luke's attempt to frighten him, stared straight ahead with cold, menacing eyes.

Luke had been told cats toyed with their prey. Determined, he stepped forward. He wasn't planning on being anybody's dinner. His only choice was to kill—or be killed.

With the Bowie knife clutched tightly in his fist, Luke prepared for battle. He held his ground, mirroring the puma's stance. The puma was no more than twelve feet away. Luke pondered the likelihood of a wild cat wandering this deeply into Goss Cave. It didn't add up nor seem natural.

Luke rationalized, *unless... he came in from another entrance. Not the one I used yesterday to get out but a different one. There must be an opening somewhere closer than that one,* Luke reasoned. *How else could the puma have gotten this far back?*

Pumas are powerfully fast creatures and judging their strength by size would be a mistake, a deception. With strong shoulders, legs, and jaws, a puma, with its sharp canine teeth, could drag food to unimaginably difficult feeding locations.

Luke entertained the possibility that he was in the wrong place at the wrong time. *Did I happen on a puma guarding its kill?*

Was Luke in the wrong place at the wrong time? Not a chance. Their encounter wasn't by happenchance. Taking Luke by surprise, the puma spun around, and with the grace and swiftness of stride that only a cat can perform, he slowly strolled away.

Luke got the impression the puma was no longer interested in him. The thought crossed his mind that maybe he was finished. *So it's over? He's done horsing around?* Luke pondered humorously.

Quick as lightning, the cat leaped from the darkness a second time. With a screech that put chills up Luke's spine, the animal extended the length of two men and sprang directly at him. He stopped inches from landing a blow.

Luke shouted, flapping his arms, "Get out of here!"

The two opposing forces sized one another up. Luke's brain scrambled on how not to let the puma get the upper hand, believing he was superior because of his size.

"I'm smarter than you," he yelled at the puma. "Don't' mess with me." He glanced around for an object to throw. "You worthless sack of shit, I told you to get lost."

When the cat charged for the third time, it propelled itself forward without warning. Picasso wasn't backing down, nor was he deterred by Luke's rants. Its swift reactions were vehemently underestimated as it pounced on Luke's head and tossed him to the side like a featherweight. His claws dug deep into Luke's skull.

Pinned under the animal's weight, Luke reacted immediately. He thrust the knife deep into the animal's neck.

Chapter 44

Picasso shrieked with pain but held firm, wrapping even tighter around Luke's head.

A big man, Luke possessed a fighter's instinct for survival. Although he was convinced he could outlast any adversary, Luke's will was no match for the fury of a 180-pound puma with a bone to pick.

A devoted bond had abruptly come to an end because of Luke. At his hand, a nefarious deed had been perpetrated. The puma had witnessed the betrayal and intended to settle the score. Neither would walk away from the match. Neither would claim victory.

A bloodcurdling cry thundered through Goss Cave as Picasso retreated from their entangled embrace. The infamous cry, of which pumas are well-known, reverberated in all directions.

Luke was terrified by the awful wailing sound the cat had made. Not certain his blow was fatal, Luke stepped back and waited.

The animal recoiled. The gash impaled into Picasso's neck, and side were deep and deadly. Undeterred, he managed to project an impression of defeat.

Luke professed his triumph. "You dumb, stupid animal! What made you think you could outsmart me?" he warned, blasting his rage. He went in for the kill to finish the job.

Taken off guard, the puma did not withdraw as Luke expected. Instead, the full force of Picasso's fury stormed out from behind the shadows. With claws fully extended, an ear-shattering, ghastly cry rang out as he swiped, three times, at Luke's head. Digging deep into his skull, the animal pushed his full weight into Luke's torso. A third laceration pierced Luke's chest. A gash that sliced through his ribcage and into his lungs. He dropped to his knees.

Luke had made a grave error, and for one agonizing moment, identified what his fatal mistake had been. Recalling Eli's account of a feral cat he fed each evening, a puma Eli called Picasso, Luke had underestimated the power of devotion.

Truth Doesn't Die

Crouched on the tips of his calloused fingers, Luke cried out in agony. His breath labored as a profound reality was faced. The treasure he sought so hard to acquire would never be his. It would sit in this undisclosed location, unclaimed, as it had since 1868, undetected.

Luke needn't pray to the man upstairs for help because he wasn't listening.

Darkness bled into his vile soul. But there will be no rest for the wicked when the devil hasn't been paid his due.

Chapter 45
Blood on the Blade
September 25, 2003

At 8:22 a.m., the phone rang. The Salzburg Police Station was requesting Clint's presence at 10 a.m. that morning. From what Clint was told, Scott had definitive information to disclose. Excited to be kept in the loop, Clint quickly shaved, got dressed, and filled his mug. He left the house early. Thursday promised to be a busier day than normal.

Clint parked the F-100 behind the diner. He hopped from the cab, snuffed his cigarette out, and dropped the butt into his pocket. Lighting up was proving to be a more difficult habit to kick than anticipated, especially these days when even a good night's sleep was hard to come by. He walked to the newspaper stand.

When Clint entered Josie's, the place was packed. Business was booming. Jules waved as he made his way to his booth. He looked forward to a short chat with her before his meeting.

"Be right there," she mouthed.

"Take your time. I'm not going anywhere," he said with a wink.

Soon she was at his table, a generous smile hidden by the carafe of coffee she was holding. Simultaneously she scanned the diner and then took a seat. "How are you doing today?" she inquired.

"A little shellshocked! How about you?"

She responded in kind, "Yeah, me too. Sensory overload on my end. Any ideas on what to do about *you know what*?"

Relieved to see her sitting across from him, he answered, "Call the state, I reckon. They will come out to assess the situation. But before I do that, I want to read up on Indiana law. Don't want to come off like a yahoo, totally unknowledgeable. Maybe talk to a lawyer."

"Are you certain we can't slip a few of those small shiny, round thingies into our pockets beforehand?" Jules teased. She put her hand up, "Don't bother answering. I would be extremely disappointed if you said yes!"

Clint's eyes brightened, "All kidding aside, it's easy to recognize why someone would turn to drastic measures in pursuit of such things. Resort to violence. Especially if they were short on scruples."

Jules agreed, "You hear about that all the time. Crime mysteries routinely focus on that type of person and situation. Money and greed are said to be the root of all evil." She eyed a couple as they walked through the door.

Patrick seated the pair and then glanced at Jules—his message clear.

Clint noted the subliminal message. "FYI," he spoke in a voice louder than their earlier ones. "At 10 a.m., I've been asked to stop by the station. Scott has something he wants to run past me. Too early for DNA results for either one of them, so I'm clueless about what he wants to discuss."

"Is that right? I guess you'll know soon enough," she replied curiously. Eyeing the clock, she tried to reassure him. "You have ample time to eat a leisurely breakfast. Try to relax, Clint. Everything will come out in the wash," she said, patting the table before walking away.

Jules extended a pleasant smile to the new customers. "Good morning," she greeted them, "welcome to Josie's Diner."

Clint observed Jules pouring coffee into one of two empty cups three tables away. Patrick had set on the table. She immediately went into her spiel of reciting today's special highlighted on the display board. With a grin, she slyly glanced over at him. Later, on one of her trips to the kitchen, she laid a reassuring hand on his shoulder as she passed by.

When Clint thought about Jules, he felt relieved to be able to unburden his secret. He could feel a heavy weight lifted from his shoulders. No longer would he have to tiptoe around or hold anything in reserve from her. Unfazed by the fortune sitting in Goss Cave, she seemed more interested in finding out about the

Chapter 45

second body than the treasure. On a napkin he wrote her a message, stating he would call her after his meeting to bring her up to date on any developments.

Clint left the diner and crossed the street. No point in taking the truck when the station was only a few blocks away. The closer he got, the more nervous he became. The receptionist looked up from her desk when Clint opened the door.

"I'm here to see Scott Edwards," Clint announced.

"I'll let him know you're here," she politely replied before dialing his number. When she put the receiver back in its cradle, she said, "Scott will be with you shortly. Please have a seat."

Not more than five minutes had passed when Scott walked out of the elevator. When he saw Clint, he extended a hand. "Thanks for coming in."

"No problem. I come in most days anyway to have breakfast at Josie's."

"You seem chipper," Scott noted.

"Life is starting to look up, at last! It's been a long time coming." Clint's eyes narrowed. "Why am I here? Did the results of the test come in?"

"No, no, that's not why I asked you to stop by. I have a bit of news but don't want to discuss it out here."

Clint followed Scott up the stairs rather than taking the elevator to his second-floor corner office. He could tell by the tone in Scott's voice something noteworthy was up.

"Please have a seat," Scott said, offering a chair on the opposite side of his desk. Scott closed the door. On his side of the desk, he leaned in. "You know that knife we took from the crime scene?"

"Yeah," Clint replied hesitantly.

"Well, it appears to have a history—a notorious one, in fact."

Clint did his best not to change his expression other than to appear curious. "Is that right?"

"Did you notice it had initials carved into the handle?"

At this juncture, Clint had to either play dumb or tell the truth. Remembering how things went the last time they were together, and how he was ridiculed after spilling the beans, honesty wasn't his preferred state of mind.

He glared at Scott. "No, should I have?"

"Didn't know how close you had gotten to the body." Scott stared hard at Clint as if he wasn't divulging a piece of knowledge. "Had you... the initials would have been hard to miss."

Guarded and realizing Scott was driving a point, Clint inquired, "Is the knife special?"

"You might say that!" Scott's eyes watched Clint's closely. "Do you recall ever hearing about the Reno Gang's treasure being hidden in these parts?"

Clint locked his gaze on Scott. "That's an odd question. You and I have talked about it multiple times. Why are you asking?"

"That's right. You moved here from Seymour, where the Reno clan were raised. Five brothers and one sister, if I recall." He cocked his head and rubbed the back of his neck. "Those kids were a bunch of hellraisers! Products of extremely strict parents, I'm afraid. Isn't that what you told me?"

"From what I remember, the whole family was legendary," Clint stoically replied.

"Well, here's the thing, that Bowie knife we bagged looks like it belonged to the older brother and leader of what was referred to in those days as the Band of Brothers. It was Frank Reno's from every indication. Thus, the initials F.R.! It was crossed-matched with an old photograph retrieved in the archives. Sure enough, it's an exact match."

"No way?!" Clint was shocked, having never made the connection until this moment.

"It's true. Forensics thoroughly examined it—authentic, sure enough. They were able to identify trace elements on the blade, blood samples. That should help with the investigation and provide

Chapter 45

clues as to what truly took place down there. We will never know for sure, but hopefully, it will point us in the right direction."

Scott shook his head. "Modern science can decipher DNA from a weapon over a hundred years old. Can you believe that? Fortunately, the only DNA we need is fifty years into the past, according to you. Frank Reno's knife should be layered in blood and easy to pull samples from." Scott looked over his glasses. "A mere fifty years shouldn't be too difficult!" He had a contagious laugh, but Clint wasn't laughing. "What's wrong? Cat got your tongue?"

"You said over one hundred years? I don't understand. Are you saying that knife the dead guy had in his hand has been around for more than a century?"

"Correct. Think about it. If it was Frank Reno's, to begin with—and let's say he had it by the time he was sixteen—it has to be at least 150 years old. Who knows where it ended up after they hanged him."

Clint tried to reconcile the fact that he was in possession of the knife less than a week ago. Purchased from Rod's New and Used Books last spring. *How can this be?* he asked himself.

"Looks like we are close to identifying the second body," Scott tossed in, cutting into Clint's concentration. "The deceased made it easy on us. Inside his trousers was a set of keys. Turned out the keys belonged to a Studebaker. Shouldn't be long until the bureau chases the owner down."

"So is that what you wanted to see me about. You're getting close to identifying the body?"

"No, not really. However, that is part of it. I wanted to know if you were aware of the knife prior to finding it in the cave?

"Why would I be?" Clint tentatively answered, knowing full well that he was.

"Because your fingerprints are on it! Odd, don't you think?" Scott cocked his head as if to say, *Is there anything you're not telling me?*

Clint was quick on his feet with an answer. "Maybe I picked it up. Don't really recall." He fanned his hands. "Can't think of any other explanation." He debated on leveling with Scott. The story of how he came into possession of the knife was as bizarre as the one about his dad. An unwise move. Clint decided to keep tight-lipped.

Scott studied Clint's facial tells, certain he was holding something back. "Clint, your fingerprints were all over it. Not just the handle, but I suspect your blood was on the blade too." Scott pursed his lips. "So far, the only fingerprints we could identify were yours."

A scowl appeared on Scott's face. "Clint, I didn't know you had a police record." He peered across the desk. "When we ran the prints through the database, your thumb and fingerprint popped up as an exact match. Can you imagine my surprise? After that, out of curiosity, I checked your medical records for blood type. We made a DNA comparison and the fresh blood on the knife matches your blood type." His eyes narrowed.

Clint looked away, remembering an arrest in Seymour thirty-three years prior. A disagreement had gotten out of hand. A fist fight broke out, and he and his coworker were both hauled off to jail to cool down. That was after one of the officers was assaulted, not by him, but by the other person involved in the quarrel.

Although Clint knew Scott expected an explanation, none was offered. The thought crossed his mind, *I'm not here to discuss my past.* Over Scott's shoulder, Clint stared out the window at the clear blue sky. "Like I said, I must have forgotten that I picked it up. It makes sense I might have forgotten, considering it's not every day you run into a corpse."

"Okay, we'll leave it at that. For now." Scott said as he shuffled through the paperwork in front of him. "We found something else of interest. Overall, we extracted a total of four different blood samples. That includes new blood and one that is nonhuman. Doc says it's a feline—a cougar, perhaps. Forensics will dig a little deeper and report back to us on the two other samples when they become available."

Chapter 45

That Afternoon

Clint considered the feline blood found on the blade. *Could that be how the second person died? He had a confrontation with a cat, and it killed him? The body did appear to be dragged to where I found it. Deposited there.*

Different scenarios churned in his mind. Two sets of human prints were found on the weapon, besides his. He found it impossible to believe the same knife that had been put into Trey's treasure chest only days earlier could be the same one forensics had in their possession now. No blood was on the blade last April when he purchased it. In fact, it looked relatively new.

Clint realized how his blood got on the blade. When he saw the initials F.R., after kicking it out of the dead man's hand, he picked it up to examine it. Carelessly he let it slip from his grip, and it cut him.

Clint's cell phone began to ring, breaking his concentration. He looked to see who was calling. "Hello, Lily," answered Clint.

"Hi, Grandpa," she replied. "How are you doing?"

"Doing good! I was just getting ready to call you. Walked in the door two seconds ago. You were the first thing on my list."

"I needed to start my homework. Figured it was better for me to call you. Glad you answered. I know I told you six o'clock, but I got done with dishes sooner than expected."

"That worked out well for both of us. You said you had something you wanted to speak with me about."

"Yes, I do," replied Lily. "When the boys and I went out to look for the knife, something strange happened that I forgot to mention."

Clint's stomach tightened. "What about it? I thought you told me everything."

"Not exactly. A couple of things slipped my mind. One has to do with the key. It had been hanging on my necklace. Remember I dropped it?"

"Yeah, I remember," Clint said, wondering where this was leading. "Just so you know, I found it."

"Oh, that's great," she said happily. "The reason I dropped it was because something weird happened. The thing started to move. We all saw it. I keep getting the feeling that I should have told you. Like it's important somehow."

"What are you talking about. It moved?" Clint could feel his pulse quicken. For him, everything about that night seemed to be tied.

"It's just like I said. It began to shimmy," said Lily with a bit of an embarrassed giggle. "It's nothing, just me being silly. But I thought you should know."

"Believe it or not, what you've said makes a difference. It holds meaning to me. I found the key outside the shack, where you said you dropped it. I have it on my nightstand. I'd like to keep it for a bit if you don't mind. I'll explain later."

There was silence on the other end of the line. Then Lily said, "Sure. That brings me to the second thing I wanted to talk to you about. This will sound corny, but the snow globe acted just as strangely that night. I thought it was battery operated at first because the crystal quartz inside it began to glow. But it didn't have any." Lily hesitantly said, "Probably some reasonable explanation because it hasn't happened since. I think we told you, but I wanted to be certain."

Clint took a sharp breath, not sure how he should react. He suspected the snow globe's strange behavior was meant for him as it related to the cave and the place where he uncovered the treasure. A place where quartz rocks were plentiful. A covert message, same as with the key. Except the key had not figured into anything… that he knew of.

Chapter 45

"I'm getting too old for this kind of stuff, aren't I, Grandpa?" Lily laughed jokingly.

"Don't be silly. I'm glad you told me, honey. On both accounts. The bottom line is, do you feel comfortable with the snow globe now?"

"Oh, I do. It is beautiful and incredibly unique. It glistens in the sunlight. I have it by the window."

"Been meaning to ask," Clint said, "would you like to come for another visit? Maybe on fall break? Along with Dylan and Trey?"

"You bet I would," she instantly responded. "Fall break is October 30 and 31, I believe. I'll have to check. I could stay Thursday through Sunday."

"Perfect, I'd love to have you. I'll call your parents to make sure there aren't any conflicts," Clint volunteered.

"Super! It'll be nice to see Jules again, too. I really liked her."

"I'm sure she'll be glad to see you also. You have a good evening, Lil."

"Love you, Grandpa!" Lily said as she hung up the phone.

Clint immediately went to the bedroom to examine the key, more confident than ever it was somehow tied to the story that had begun to unravel. Rod Radcliff, Sr., though long deceased, had given Clint extraordinary insight into the past. Of which, Clint now believed the key was part.

His instincts indicated there was more to this story.

Chapter 46
Treasure of a Different Sort
Tuesday, September 30

Over the weekend, Clint and Jules had agreed not to return to the hidden shelter until Tuesday when they could utilize both of her days off. The plan was to do a more thorough investigation.

Clint's feet hit the floor earlier than usual Tuesday morning. More than ready to get the day going, he headed for the kitchen.

The night before, Jules had informed him that she would be at his place bright and early. Somewhere around 8 a.m. Clint had showered and shaved and was sitting at the table enjoying a second cup of coffee, waiting for her knock. Fried ham sat in the iron skillet, and scrambled eggs were kept warm in the oven.

To tide them over for the next three hours, they would need a good breakfast. The plan was to revisit the treasure as well as search the space his grandfather called home.

"Good morning, I'm almost there," Jules said when Clint answered the phone. "Do you need anything?"

"No, thanks. I have breakfast fixed and coffee on. I thought we could pick up dinner at the grocery later today." He looked outdoors at the seasonal shades of autumn. "We should take advantage of this weather while we can. Nothing like autumn to make you want to be outdoors."

"I'm on board with that," Jules agreed.

A few minutes before eight, Jules walked in the front door. "Hey!" she said, announcing her arrival.

Clint went over and gave her a hug. "Good to see you. We've got a big day ahead of us."

"Yes, we do. I can't wait to get a better look at the treasure. To think it has been down there all this time just waiting for you to find it," she said. "It certainly is well-hidden. When do you plan to tell Scott?"

Chapter 46

"Don't know. There hasn't been a good time. Soon, though. Sitting on information like that for too long isn't a good idea. A headline story for sure. At least around these parts!"

During breakfast he relayed his conversation from the night before with Lily and her revelation about the key.

"I wasn't planning on taking the key with us, but I am now. Sounds like it could be significant. Lily was asking to come visit at the end of the month, during fall break. Probably a good time to fill the family in on what has been going on. This is going to be a shocker!"

"Where is the key?" Jules asked.

"It's in the bedroom. I'll go get it." Clint pushed his chair back from the table. "I'll be right back."

As Jules waited, she thought about the phantom figure who had shown Clint where his father's body lay, the treasure, and, she believed, led him to the secret area. The question that remained was why Eli wasn't the one to direct his son to the truth. Rod, Sr. was a contradiction.

Clint revealed from the first day he and Elise had moved into the house strange things had occurred. Convinced there were explanations for everything, Clint had ignored what now seemed obvious. Rod Radcliff haunted the property. As Eli's friend, he wanted Eli's child to know his dad had not walked out on him.

"Here, I'll give you the key," laughed Clint. "Women are better at things like that. If I keep it, I'll probably misplace it."

They stacked the dishes into the sink with the promise of washing them when they returned, and off to the forest they went. The cool autumn breeze promised to reach comfortable temperatures by midafternoon, but the morning air still held a bite.

As they removed the concealed grass covering from the entrance into the earth, they speculated on what more they could learn in the hideaway. Anything to lend credence to the mystery that was developing would be helpful. After talking to Lily, Clint's intuition told him to keep his antenna up. The key from the bookstore was significant.

Moss covered the dark walls moving beneath the ground. Limestone encircled the living space. In Clint's memory, a recollection arose. Maybe the smell of the place, worn like a cologne, triggered a memory of his granddad's essence. Snippets of senses overlapped in his mind like a book being read. Distinct, as if only yesterday. Clint was sitting on Phil's lap in the shack. He unmistakably recalled words from his granddad suggesting a field trip.

The air felt dank and reeked of mustiness. Papers were stacked in every available corner. Clint realized the quaint rolltop they'd observed the last time they were in the room appeared much smaller than modern-day versions. The writing surface was abnormally low as if constructed for a child or short person.

An ink well and pen sat beside a piece of paper where notes had been jotted. A half-smoked rolled cigarette sat in a square amber ashtray, holding down the corner of a map. It was as though his granddad had been in the middle of writing and would return shortly to finish his musings. A Smith-Premier typewriter on the table beside the desk was identical to the typewriter on the far left side of the rolltop.

Jules and Clint decided to separate, picking different rooms to delve into the backstory of Phil Reeves' life.

In the tiny room where Clint had gone, a mirror of poor reflection hung above a sink. Toiletries were arranged on a wooden shelf: a block of Lifebuoy soap, an alabaster mug with shaving cream and a horsehair brush, a box of Arm & Hammer baking soda, and a yellowed rough cloth. Basic hygiene necessities. Beside the sink, on a three-legged pedestal, sat a pitcher and bowl. A feeling of melancholy came over Clint with the insights to the man he called granddad.

"Clint!" called Jules, "Come here!"

Chapter 46

He turned with a start. From the inflection in Jules' voice, Clint was afraid something bad had happened.

"Good God!" she hollered.

"What?" he called out.

"You are not going to believe what I just found. This will knock your socks off!" she proclaimed excitedly.

"What is it?" he asked, feeling bewildered at what would get her so wound up.

Jules was sitting on the floor with a box in her lap when he entered the room. She was holding the key high, so he would see it.

"What's that on your lap?" he asked, full of anticipation. "I take it Lily's key fits that box."

"Yeah, I think you'll find these papers particularly interesting." Her arched eyebrows lifted. "Several documents are in here, but one I think you are going to find especially noteworthy."

Clint's eyes narrowed. He sat on the floor beside her. "Okay, you have my attention. I can tell by your face this is something big."

"Clint, this paper," she cried, raising a legal document in her hand, "says Earl Reeves owned thirty-acres of land. A map is attached. Shows all the land around here, including yours, belonged to him. See?" Enthusiastically she pointed to the document. "It's notarized by the state, dated June 23, 1907. A legal land grant. A deeded certificate showing him as the owner."

She took a much-needed breath. "So, wouldn't that mean it legally would belong to you, as Earl Reeves' heir?"

Clint's eyes grew huge. Thoughts raced through his mind. "I guess!" he stuttered. "Holy cow! Earl Reeves was my great-grandfather. I thought my granddad, Phil Reeves lived here, not my great-grandfather."

"I think our next move is to check into Indiana state law," Jules said with the cutest expression Clint had ever seen on her face.

"My inclination is to call an attorney. Like right away," he said, putting a hand to his mouth in disbelief of what Jules had uncovered. "Find out how the law would construe a case like this. Good Lord, can you imagine telling a lawyer we've located the legendary Reno Brother's treasure and the land it is on belonged to my great-grandfather?"

"What do you mean, Kemosabe?" she giggled. "I didn't find anything. You did!"

Tears pooled in Clint's eyes. "No, no, I didn't, it was him—Rod Radcliff, Sr. He was the one. He wanted me to find it the same way he wanted me to find my father. Jules, this is astonishing. I'm blown away! Think about it… the box I bought at Rod's New and Used Books held a key that unlocked my great-grandfather's lockbox showing he owned the land where the treasure is hidden."

Clint buried his head in his hands, too shaken to say anything more.

"A little mind-boggling, isn't it?" she responded in kind.

"Do you recall me telling you the state escheated twenty-acres and divided it into ten-acre tracts? Finalized in 1996. In 1997 ten-acres were sold at public auction and ten were annexed into the Hoosier National Forest? The state claimed the ten-acres we are on, so technically, it belongs to them. Or, I guess I should say, *did*." Clint's grin was broad. "I don't know about the other ten acres referenced in the document."

Jules held it up, "This proves the land belonged to Earl Reeves." She laughed but then frowned. "What the heck does escheat mean?"

"Sorry!" he said apologetically. "I had no idea either. Until I bought my house. Which I now know belonged to my father, which in turn means I purchased land I already owned!" Clint laughed with dismay at the craziness of how that sounded.

Jules laughed. "That's nuts!"

"Yeah, it is, but since dad never came back and I was carted off to a children's home, no one was around to claim legal rights to the property. Nothing was located because the paperwork went too far back. Basically, the state repossessed the land because no papers

Chapter 46

were found that showed ownership. Indiana listed it as unclaimed property for a set period, and when no heirs came forward, they divided it up. Half to the state, half went up for public sale."

"Were there a lot of people bidding on your property?"

"No. That's the strange thing. A couple of people initially put a bid in but withdrew, leaving only Elise and me. We literally got it for a song and a dance. Which is a good thing because we hardly had two nickels to rub together. Always living paycheck to paycheck when we lived in Seymour. The proceeds I received from the early retirement settlement from the sawmill was what we used for earnest money."

A peculiar look appeared on Jules' face. "Seems like you've been on a real-life treasure hunt. With the help of an unseen player."

Clint howled, "Good one, Jules."

"I try," she grinned, flashing a dimple. "I wish I could see Scott and David's face when you lay this one on them."

"Our next conversation should be a doozy!"

With the steel lockbox in tow, Clint and Jules returned to the house. On the kitchen table, they sorted through Earl Reeves' legal papers: marriage license, birth certificate, 5 Union Pacific Railway stock certificates—purchased in 1902, and correspondence between him and Clint's great-grandmother during the first World War. Centered like a paperweight was a WWI Silver Star Medal sitting on top of the letters.

Also, atop his great-grandfather's things, they found Phil and Marcy Reeves' marriage contract and a silver wedding band attached to the document.

On the bottom, a sepia hand-drawn map was folded. Circles and arrows placed randomly onto the page dotted the brownish-gray frayed paper in red, deep blue, and black.

Clipped to the back of the map was a penciled sketch. Clint was startled when he realized it was a drawing of the tunnel system that connected all the underground hidden spaces. It showed the hollowed-out entrance inside the shack that led to Goss Cave along with the adjoining secret area he had uncovered by the outhouse. Obviously, clandestine behavior was in mind when the passageways were constructed.

Looks like this is what my family used to pursue the treasure. They were closing in on its general locale. My father must have picked up the thread and taken it from there."

"But, if that was the case, and he had access to this map," Jules pointed at the paper on the table, "that means he knew about the underground quarters all along."

Clint grew introspective. "Did I tell you my grandfather was killed in a hunting accident a month or two before my dad disappeared?"

Jules' face showed her surprise. "No, you did not. That must have been devastating."

"It was. My dad was terribly upset. Cried a lot, but other than that, I don't remember much."

"Clint," added Jules, "if Earl or Phil Reeves had an inkling about the general location of the treasure, that knowledge must have died with them. Right? Because otherwise, Eli would not have been still searching for it. I don't think he saw this map." She pointed to the drawing, "If your dad was aware of the extra passages, he must have kept that to himself because the place was clearly undisturbed."

"I agree on both counts. I figure my dad and his partner had enough information to zero in on an approximate location, figuring it was just a matter of time before the treasure was located. My dad must have shown this map to the man who came to our house, and they partnered up. Meaning he knew about the secret area because they had a map to guide them. If not this one," he put his finger on the original map, "a version of it."

Jules felt dazed, inserting, "But how do you really know who killed who?" The minute the words slipped from Jules' lips, she regretted them. "I'm sorry, I didn't mean to… " She lowered her head, ashamed of speaking so bluntly.

Chapter 46

"It's all right, Jules," Clint assured her. "You aren't suggesting anything I haven't already thought. The truth is, I didn't really know my dad. I was only five at the time. All I have is an essence of who he was." Clint's face clouded over. "I remember him as a great guy, but that doesn't mean he was. And, of course, what my dream revealed. That his partner killed him."

On Tuesday morning, October 7, Clint finally got the call he had been anxiously awaiting. The twelve days since his meeting with Scott had gone by at a snail's pace.

DNA results were in. The two bodies discovered in Goss Cave had been identified. A voicemail left on his cell phone said the Salzburg Police Department would like to speak with him. Clint had been preparing himself for bad news but hoping for the best.

If locating a deceased father could be considered good news.

Chapter 47
A Mystery Surfaces

When the group walked into the office, Clint was sipping lukewarm coffee from a Styrofoam cup. Staring out the window with his back to the door, he was nervously awaiting the forensic report on the bodies found in Goss Cave.

Captain Edwards pointed to the three empty chairs next to Clint, suggesting to Sergeant David Andrews, CSI Jonas Shumacher, and Sean Ferrer, a reporter with the *Salzburg Times*, "Have a seat."

On the other side of the mahogany desk, Scott pulled out a chair. The group sat in a semicircle, waiting for the dialogue to begin. Atop a small stack of papers, an evidence report was opened.

"Clint, I requested your presence here today because the evidence we collected has a direct correlation to you. From the blood samples we gathered, we built a profile. I'll address that in more detail later."

Scott turned to the reporter, "Accurate interpretation of DNA is crucial in this type of investigation, as you know. Two bodies have been discovered in Salzburg. Matching victim DNA with living relatives can assist in our efforts to identify a body, but that hinges on the relationship between individuals. Close blood relatives, as in this case, provided conclusive findings."

Swiveling around to face Sean, Scott offered, "The reason I invited you to sit in on this meeting is that a fifty-year-old local mystery has been unraveled. It's rather sensational." Scott's eyes widened. "I've selected you to summarize a narrative about it to the media. I've heard nothing but good remarks about your professionalism."

"Thank you for your confidence. Whatever it is, it sounds newsworthy," Sean admitted in a deep, husky voice. His curiosity piqued when he peered round at the other faces in the room and saw a tincture of excitement.

Chapter 47

Scott's eyes settled on David. "Because Clint shared information with us that had an impact on the case," Scott looked down at the report, "on Tuesday, September 23, I requested a blood sample from him as standard procedure. Considering the evidence that was presented, analyses did, in fact, authenticate that Eli Elton Reeves, Clint's father, is one of the two victims."

David, having not been told about Clint's DNA blood sample, looked startled at the development. "Is that right? What about the other body?"

"We'll get to that. I promise," Scott said. "Let's take a minute. I'm going to refill my cup. When I get back, Jonas will fill in the blanks."

Turning to Clint, David expressed his remorse, "I guess I owe you an apology. This is one for the record books. At least mine." His faced turned troubled. "I am sorry for your loss, Clint. I can't imagine how you must be feeling right now."

Clint, too shocked to speak, felt his body start to quiver. He had been vindicated. Tears pooled. His emotions could not be held in check. He broke down and sobbed, lowering his head in embarrassment. Minutes passed before the exchange continued.

"Thank you," Clint said sorrowfully, cognizant that the anguish he had carried his entire life, aimed at this dad, had been baseless. Clint had underestimated the amount of tension he had been holding in anticipation of this moment. He confessed, "I knew it was him, but to hear it validated, I can't say I was fully prepared for that. I thought I was." Clint's agony showed on his face.

"I'm sorry, Clint. This is major. I realize that." Scott said when he returned, also voicing his regret. He immediately noticed Clint was shaken. "It does bring closure to a lifelong question I've always carried. What happened to your father was a true mystery."

Clint gave a quick nod in recognition of Scott's remarks without reply.

"Some extraordinary circumstances surround this case," Scott informed everyone. "It turns out the second body belonged to a

A Mystery Surfaces

man named Luke McCauley." Scott concentrated on Clint when he stated, "This man was a lowlife! I won't go into it right now but suffice it to say, the man did some prison time at the penitentiary over in Terre Haute before he moved to Salzburg. Assault with the intent to do bodily harm showed up along with a list of other offenses."

"Is that right?" Clint remarked, realizing his dad was vulnerable and more than likely naive as to who he had partnered with.

"Yes, and no matter how you cut it, Clint, it was murder, so if you would rather bypass this part, I'd understand. The details will not be easy to hear."

"I did not come this far to pull back now," Clint quickly replied. "I want to hear it all."

"Okay," Scott agreed reluctantly. "From what we can ascertain, evidence suggests Luke used the Bowie knife we recovered from the scene to kill Eli." Scott turned to the investigator. "Jonas, would you like to elaborate on that point?"

Jonas faced the group. "The animal bones were a real puzzle in all this until we were able to piece together a sequence of events. Initially, it looked like the second victim either was attacked directly after killing Eli or came back and was killed later when he encountered the puma. But that changed with a more detailed report." Jonas leaned in, closer to Clint. "This is the same animal we discovered alongside your father."

He opened the report to another section. "This is what we ascertained. The second conflict, the best we can tell, occurred days after the first event. Deeper in the cave from the original incident. We located blood splatters on the walls and puncture wounds in the puma's throat and ribs. Luke McCauley was badly battered by the animal as well. Multiple claw marks were located on his head and torso, plus his clothes were shredded. Signs of an attack were evident when we examined the body in more detail. Even before removing the clothes, we could tell he had been mauled."

Chapter 47

"So, you're saying a cat killed Luke McCauley. After this man killed my dad? And then the injured animal made its way over to dad and died?" Clint looked baffled. "Why would he do that? We are talking about a cougar, aren't we? Not exactly man's best friend. I doubt he would have attacked a human without provocation."

"The evidence indicates that is what happened. To be precise, it was a black puma. Those have not been spotted in Indiana since the 1930s, so I have no idea how one ended up in Goss Cave. It is a forest area, though, with plenty of prey around. They are supposed to be extinct, but that is inconclusive." Jonas looked at Clint, "To answer your question, if they did attack a human, it would be a small child or someone who could not defend themselves, like an invalid."

"The team uncovered one other thing." Jonas turned to Scott. With a surprised expression, he added, "It looks like the animal dragged his victim into that small space where he was crammed. The body was forced in there like it was being covered up. A deliberate act."

Everyone looked astonished.

Knowing he was about to tell a partial lie, Clint commented. "That seems extremely out of character. What would a puma be doing in Goss Cave in the first place? Not a typical habitat for them. And why were they all down there?

"Yeah, that's the million-dollar question, and your guess is as good as mine," responded Jonas immediately. "That's one mystery I suppose we will never have an answer to." Then he made a scoffing sound, injecting, "We did uncover a French Angel Guardian coin in McCauley's pocket. Some protection that was."

"I'd say not," Scott answered with a smile. He shuffled the loose papers on his desk, putting them back inside the folder. Pushing his chair back, he said, "Clint, I'm having a summarized copy of the report prepared for you. It will be ready before you leave. Just stop by the front desk on your way out." He shook his head, "I'm glad we got to the bottom of this."

"Me too," agreed Clint. "I'm grateful to know the truth why dad never came home, no matter the circumstances."

"I'll give you a call when his remains are ready for collection," stated Scott.

"What about the puma?" asked Clint. "I want him to be included, please. I get the feeling there is a lot more behind that story."

"I'll pass along your instructions." Scott nodded in agreement. They shook hands. "Hopefully, now you can file any unanswered questions about that chapter of your life away. Although it's not pleasant information, the truth should help you sleep better."

"Thanks, Scott," Clint replied, thinking nothing could ever put the memory of that petrifying Christmas Eve to rest. But there was peace in his soul that his dad didn't intentionally leave him.

After the other three men left the office, Scott sat down in the chair Jonas had vacated. "Have a seat, Clint. If you don't mind."

"Sure," Clint replied, taking the seat across from Scott.

"To tell you the truth, in this specific case, I have no idea how to reconcile your dream. What to do with that piece of information is beyond me. Do I make a note of it? I think not. The fact you knew the outcome of our investigation before we knew it defies logic. Psychic powers, in my line of work, aren't exactly looked upon favorably. I wouldn't feel comfortable putting your statement into the files–for your sake. I hope you understand. Along with drawing any attention to the fact your prints were on the knife.

Clint waved his hand in dismissal. "Don't worry about it. I'm not keen on it either. Trust me. I have a hard enough time explaining it to myself, let alone others." His face became thoughtful. "You wouldn't happen to have some spare time, would you? For a drink, maybe. I have a couple of things I'd like to run by you."

At Scott's core, he felt he was about to learn more. "I have time right now if you'd like. We can talk right here. I'll close the door."

Chapter 47

"No, that's all right. It's nothing that can't wait." Clint looked away, not ready to share what was on his mind. At some point he would have to tell Scott about the treasure, but not at this exact moment. Over drinks yes, but not here in his office.

"That's fine," Scott responded, not wanting Clint to leave without scheduling a meeting. "How about, In a Pig's Eye, say about 5:15?"

Clint stared at Scott. "Not today. What about Thursday? Same place and time? I have a couple of things to do before we speak."

Clint needed to meet with a lawyer before spilling the beans to Scott. Nonetheless, Scott needed to be advised about the treasure before the newspapers got ahold of the information.

"Sure," he answered, curious about Clint's odd behavior. "Is everything okay?"

"Yeah, I'm just busy the next couple of days. Though, I'd like to get together."

Scott patted Clint on the shoulder. "See you at 5:15 Thursday, pal!"

"Great." Clint smiled. "I look forward to it."

Walking out into the sunshine and cool breeze with a copy of the forensic report in his hand, Clint pondered how Scott was going to react to his explosive news. He grinned, knowing his friend's reaction in advance.

Tuesday Afternoon, October 7

If a puma killing a human—and a human killing the puma—could be considered homicide, then a triple murder had taken place in Goss Cave in 1953 while a wintery blizzard raged above ground. Death had come calling in a most gruesome way.

A Mystery Surfaces

Clint wondered what Jules would say about the forensic report. A motion picture could be made from the details laid out to him at the police station.

It was hard for Clint to digest the details of his dad's murder. Killed by his partner, and then, sometime later, an altercation took place between his partner and the puma, who then killed the partner. Though the animal endured repeated stab wounds, according to the pathologist, he maintained enough strength to drag Luke's body and crawl back to Eli before he too died. An unusual act of devotion for a wild animal.

On his porch, Clint searched Google for lawyers around the Salzburg area. He was going to need a good one considering the bombshell he was about to unleash. Hesitant to use a local attorney, especially for something as momentous as this, Clint planned to do an extensive background check before settling on any one law firm.

He glanced up when he heard Jules' car pull into the drive. When she approached the porch, she greeted him. "You look involved."

"Yeah, it's been an interesting day. I'm still trying to wrap my head around it."

"Oh my," Jules replied. Sitting next to Clint on the porch swing, she put her hand on his. "Want to share?"

Clint responded, "I plan to at dinner. Looks like Patrick let you off early. I'm glad."

"Yeah, it was slow for a change. He knew I was coming over here, so he told me to scat!" Jules laughed. "Didn't have to ask me twice. It has been a long week, and I'm glad to have a break. The next two days should help."

They went inside. Something simple had been made in advance for dinner. Old-fashioned chicken and noodles sat on the stove. While Jules waited at the table, giving her feet a rest, Clint dished dinner into their bowls. He took crescent rolls from the oven, placed them on a plate, and covered them.

Chapter 47

During their meal, Clint recapped the day's activities, telling her everything that had been said in Scott's office that morning.

"I'm sorry to hear about your dad," Jules said sadly. "Although you already knew how he died, it must have been hard to hear. To think… the one person he put his faith in was so untrustworthy."

"I'm sure the betrayal came as a horrible shock." Clint's face turned woeful. "Jules, my dad's last words were to me," he looked at her with a wistful expression. "I still have trouble believing Rod Radcliff revealed to me my dad's last moments. In the dream."

"I'm pleased you witnessed it. And, you know it was you he was thinking about at the end. It's heartbreaking but important for you to understand."

"I'd rather know, than not," acknowledged Clint. "I will say the puma was my biggest surprise."

"What happens from here?" Jules inquired.

"Find a good lawyer, I guess. We need to start asking around."

"I'll ask Patrick if he knows of anyone," she suggested. "I won't tell him why, only that I may need an attorney. Being a businessman, he should have some reliable contacts. A good place to start."

"Good idea. I'd feel more comfortable with a referral from him."

After dinner, on lawn chairs under the stars, they discussed a variety of subjects before settling in to watch the fire. The one question that remained was why the man in the straw hat had been the one to intervene on his father's behalf. It was the most important unanswerable question Clint had and one he would have to make peace with.

Staring up at the heavens, he said, "I suppose it makes no difference how I learned the truth, only that I did. Rod Radcliff, Sr. was my father's best friend, according to Rod, Jr. Apparently, he and my dad must have been like brothers for him to have cared so much." Clint took Jules' hand, "I can't begin to tell you how much I appreciate your support. I'm glad I didn't have to go through this alone."

A Mystery Surfaces

"I care about your well-being, too," she expressed. An hour later, Jules got ready to leave. She put her arms around his neck. "I'm glad I could be of help. What are friends for, if not to lend support when times get tough?"

They walked to her car and said goodnight. At the end of the drive Clint watched Jules' taillights fade into the night. He moved up the gravel driveway and onto the leaf-covered yard. He decided to sit on the back step and listen to the sounds of the night before retiring.

As he passed the side of the house, he could see the dim light of the table lamp through the picture window. The three-quarters moon shown down, casting moonlight over the trees in the forest.

Clint sat down. From the edge of the woods Rod Radcliff Sr., watched.

Chapter 48
Strange Encounter
Wednesday, October 8

The day had started out on an upbeat note. Clint and Jules had a short trip planned. Country drives always cleared Clint's head, and their destination was breakfast in Paoli. Something enjoyable to do on Jules' day off—a day trip to lighten their mood.

Puffy white clouds floated lazily across a powdery blue sky. Warmer than usual temperatures were forecasted, already having reached forty-nine degrees, the windows of the Camaro were cracked, letting in the fresh autumn air. On his way to Jules' place, Clint sang along to an Eagles' song he knew by heart. *Taking it Easy.*

On the internet Clint had researched a lawyer he found in Paoli. The law firm, in general, had received excellent reviews. Clint wanted to get a feel for where the office was located before making an appointment. The plan was, on their return trip from Paoli, they would stop by Rod's New and Used Books. Clint had questions only Rod, Jr. could answer. He should know more about Rod Radcliff's death than anyone.

Getting ready to leave, Clint lowered the ragtop on the Camaro. He switched the heater blower fan to high. "You okay with the top down?" he asked with a sheepish grin after already having started the process.

"Sure," she answered, not in the least put off. "I'm adventurous! Hang on, though, while I grab a warmer jacket."

Only four and a half miles northwest of Salzburg, the place Clint had in mind to take Jules to for a meal was nearby. He ejected the eight-track tape from the player so they could talk on their way without distractions. Putting the Eagles tape back into the sleeve where he had originally found it, in Gary's things, Clint handled it with kid gloves. Gary Walden's spirit lived on each time Clint got behind the wheel of the 1967 Yenko.

After an enjoyable breakfast at the Whistle Stop, a restaurant converted train depot parallel to a set of nonfunctional railroad tracks, Jules and Clint drove into Paoli. Cruising around the courthouse circle, he scouted for landmarks of the attorney's office he had seen online. Satisfied it looked reputable, they jumped back on the highway and headed home.

Clint's visit to the bookstore was a top priority. His purpose was two-fold, to introduce Jules to the owner and ask Rod some questions. An unconventional sort of fellow, Rod, Jr. was wildly unpredictable and highly entertaining. Clint planned to bring him up to date on the latest developments he had learned at the police station. In turn, he hoped Rod would have additional information concerning Rod Radcliff, Sr.'s death.

In a dream he had last night, Clint briefly remembered a lanky man in the hat walking back and forth inside a building, stacking things on shelves. When he awoke, nothing came to mind other than a desire to dig deeper into Rod, Sr.'s past.

Since Jules hadn't been able to locate the storefront, she was thrilled Clint was taking her there. Settling on the theory its location must be elsewhere from where she had been searching, she reckoned she'd made a mistake. Particularly since Clint had been in the bookstore after she couldn't find it. On their way into Salzburg, they mapped out the remainder of the day. The idea of returning to the cave came up but was not decided on.

"How do you suppose the Reno Gang moved all those objects through that fissure and into the alcove where the treasure was stashed?" asked Jules. She was holding her hand against the wind, snaking it in and out of the air as they drove along Highway 150. "That must have been a challenge. It couldn't have been easy considering that tight space."

Chapter 48

"Beats me. Probably took it in by the handfuls. No way could they fit much through the constriction of those walls. People back then were much thinner than they are today," Clint chuckled. "I suppose one of the skinnier gang members was tasked with the job. I figure once things died down, they must have planned to redistribute the goods. Turn everything into spendable currency."

"I hadn't considered that. What got me is all the crystal quartz lying around. An unnatural amount of them. Besides, geodes are river rocks, found near limestone quarries, always above ground, never in caves." Jules grinned, "When I was a kid, my dad had geodes running alongside our driveway. I remember my older sister and brother breaking them open. All of ours were purple."

"That sounds like a fun memory," Clint commented, picturing the driveway in his mind. "I envy you." Then he remembered something Lily had said. "Did you notice there was one inside Lily's snow globe?" He turned to face Jules, "Lily said when they entered the shack, the quartz-crystal reacted and became illuminated. Like it had an energy source of some kind. But there wasn't any, and it hasn't happened since."

"Oh my gosh! How weird is that?"

"Yeah, I'd say." Clint thought back to his first venture into Goss Cave. "Did I tell you when I had that remarkable dream about my dad, and the circumstances behind his death, I fell and hit my head on one of those rocks prior to my vision? There was this energy vibrating all around me and I heard and felt a low droning sound."

"You mentioned the incident but not to that detail. That must have felt strange."

"Not something I will ever forget!" Clint laughed, switching gears and thinking about where they were headed. "Before we get to the bookstore, I want to warn you the clerk is not an ordinary guy—far from it. He's an oddball, in fact. Talks in riddles all the time." Clint smiled knowing firsthand how hard it was to get a straight answer from the man.

"I figured that, by the way you describe him."

Strange Encounter

"I actually like the guy. With all the things that have happened over these last several months, the one that never leaves me is when I saw Rod, Sr. for the first time in the antique mirror. The one that is now hanging back in my foyer." Clint smiled. "Can you believe that was last April? He was standing behind me, wearing that crazy straw hat." Clint shook his head. "Well, he wasn't actually there because I never could find him. Now I know why!"

"That's right!" Jules said enthusiastically.

"The part that was confusing was when I asked to speak to the owner, Rod said, his dad only came around when he was needed. I still don't know what that was supposed to mean since we now know his dad is deceased and would not have been coming into the bookstore under any circumstance."

"I guess he meant metaphorically. Sort of like pretending a loved one is guiding or watching over you." She shrugged, not knowing what else to say.

"I suppose," Clint agreed. "But that still sounds like a weird thing to say. Unless…" He turned to face her. "Sometimes I wonder, since Rod, Sr. was the guiding hand that led me to solve the mystery behind my father's disappearance and ultimately leading me to the treasure, if Rod, Jr. wasn't aware somehow of what was to come. Because, the truth is, his dad did show up when he was needed."

Arriving in Salzburg, Clint turned onto Grandview and parked the car. As before, they had to travel the distance from where the sidewalk ended to the storefront via a footpath.

He walked around to Jules' side of the car to open the door. Looking down the street, waiting for her to get out, he was disturbed not to see the shop. He felt a moment of trepidation. The street looked vacant from his vantage point, and that would mean she had been right all along. He pushed the thought from his mind.

Taking his hand, Jules grinned. "Thank you! How gentlemanly of you!"

"My pleasure, M'lady."

Chapter 48

They hadn't gone far when Clint let out the breath he was holding. He pointed ahead. "There it is!" he said with relief. "Every time I come down here, it looks different. I can't explain how. It just does."

Jules' eyes widened. Clint was right. Rod's New and Used Books was exactly where he said it was. A queer feeling washed over her. The street had an unusual aura. It felt wider than she recalled, and she could see remnants of red bricks beneath the top layer, indicating at one point, it must have been a brick road.

Stately trees stood tall on the north side of the street. She could see an open meadow. Woodlands graced the beautiful expanse of land. A peaceful feeling that was hard to define swept over her. A dense fog covered the fields. Built in a faraway section of town, Jules was convinced she had given up too soon the day she drove the street looking for the bookstore nearly two weeks ago.

"Don't you love the look of this place?" Clint asked, pointing to the display window and awning. "Like a mom-and-pop store when we were kids." Teasingly, he said, "More mine than yours." He walked over to the entrance. "The awning gives it a nice flare. Don't you think?"

Jules gave it a once over. "I'd have to agree. They built a store with an old-fashioned flare. It is unique." She stood in front of the bay window examining the odds and ends scattered on the other side of the pane. "Not very tidy," she observed, turning to Clint. "If you want to attract customers, I'm not sure that is the way to go about it."

He was wearing a look that telegraphed, *What can I say?*

"I honestly don't know how I missed this," she said. "Didn't drive far enough, I guess."

They walked inside. The bell above the door jingled, announcing their arrival, but no one showed up to greet them. For Clint, this came as no surprise.

"You practically have to go to the backroom and get him," Clint laughed. "I've been trying to figure out how he stays in business."

He waved his hand at an empty store. "Not once have I seen a customer in here."

Jules moseyed through the store, taking her time examining the unusual pieces for sale. She disappeared down one aisle while Clint walked over to the curio cabinet room where the items for his treasure hunt were found.

She poked her head around the corner. "Clint, have you checked out the books on these shelves? They are old titles that look brand new."

"Yeah, I know. Many are first editions. I noticed that the first time I was here. This is where I picked up an original copy of *Moby Dick*. Rod also gave me a hardback of *Bid Time Return*. Remember, that was the book the movie, *Somewhere in Time* was based on. He keeps many rare works of art on the shelves."

"May I help you," came a voice from the front of the store.

"Yes, thank you," Clint replied quickly. They walked to the register, but the person behind the counter was not someone Clint recognized. "Is Rod here?" Clint politely asked, a little bewildered at seeing a new face.

"Rod?" the man repeated, a puzzled expression on his face.

"Yes, Rod Radcliff, the owner! Is he here?"

For an embarrassing moment, the clerk studied Clint's face as if he didn't understand the question. Then he exclaimed, "Are you, Clint Reeves, by any chance?"

"Yes, yes I am," Clint responded in a surprised tone. Curious how the stranger knew his name, he quizzically inquired, "Why do you ask?"

"I have something for you," the man called over his shoulder as he scurried to the other side of the curtain.

Jules and Clint exchanged glances that spoke volumes. *What's this about.*

"Here you are," said the clerk handing two sealed manila envelopes over to Clint.

Chapter 48

Clint was taken aback when he saw his name written on them. "Thank you," he said, taking the envelopes. "Who are these from? Rod, I presume."

The man looked vacant, like he wasn't listening. "Sorry, I've got to go! My assignment is complete. Not trying to be impolite or anything, but I only came in as a favor. Rod is preoccupied. He asked me to hand these to you."

Clint looked at his watch—2:45 p.m. "A little early to be closing up shop. Isn't it?"

"Oh, not really. I was told it's time to go."

Jules had to stop herself from snickering. Clint had told her the place was a little wacky, but this guy's behavior had taken even her by surprise. The man was on the brink of being discourteous.

"Will Rod be here tomorrow?" asked Clint hurriedly, afraid the guy would leave before he could get his question in.

"I'll let Rod know you stopped by," the clerk replied quickly. "Now, if you don't mind."

"You can't be in that much of a hurry?" Clint said impatiently, feeling put off. "Just answer the question."

"Be assured, your message is being delivered," he said persuasively before he vanished into the back room.

"What the heck was that all about? Sounds like he sent my message via email," chortled Clint. A chain reaction of laughter exploded between them. "Am I missing something here? Aren't we paying customers? And… he still didn't answer my question."

Jules had a hard time containing herself. Doubled over, she squealed, "That guy did everything but show you to the door. I won't say you didn't warn me!"

Clint roared. "Well, that was plain and simple Nutsville! At least he proved my point!"

Outside, Clint noted the Rod's New and Used Books' wooden plaque above the door was gently swaying. It creaked as it rocked, as if it had been nudged.

392

Strange Encounter

"I'll come back tomorrow after breakfast," Clint stated firmly. "I'm disappointed because I wanted to introduce you to Rod." He scowled at the entrance. "That fellow should be let go. Grant you, Rod might be a tad bit odd, but he is never rude. It's the middle of the afternoon, and this bozo is charging out of there like he has an emergency!"

"He certainly appeared to be in a big hurry. Didn't he?" agreed Jules with a giggle.

"You could say that." Clint reached for Jules' hand. "Come on. I owe you a hot fudge sundae."

She cracked up laughing. "You do?"

"Yep, I do. For putting you through such rejection!" With laughing eyes, Clint claimed, "Follow me! I know a perfect place to get one."

They returned to the car in silence. Clint put the envelopes between them on the console. The engine roared to life. Their destination was Josie's Diner.

"Maybe you could ask Patrick if he knows of a descent lawyer. I'd rather have a lawyer someone recommended," Clint suggested.

Inside the diner, Jules led Clint to the booth closest to the kitchen. "You didn't bring the envelopes? Aren't you curious?" she asked when they sat down.

"Stuck them in my jacket when we got out of the car." He grinned, acknowledging they were on the bench beside him.

"Oh good," Jules said. She jumped up and scurried behind the counter to grab two cups. She put them on the table and said, "I'll make the sundaes." It was understood desserts and coffee were *on the house*. Dishing ice cream into the bowls, she kept one eye on Clint while he opened the envelopes. She watched as he examined the contents. He seemed engrossed, but then he stopped reading.

Clint's expression had turned grave.

Chapter 49
Multiple Truths
Wednesday, 2:30

"What's going on?" Jules asked with concern when she sat down and placed only one ice cream sundae between them: butter pecan ice cream, hot fudge, whipped cream, pecans, cherries, and two spoons. When she saw Clint eye the sundae, Jules said, "I decided it was too close to dinnertime for me. Besides, I'm not all that hungry. Hope you don't mind sharing."

"No, that's fine. You aren't going to believe this," remarked Clint in astonishment. He slid a stack of papers across the table. "Two separate police reports from 1953. They cover the fire at the general store."

Jules' eyes brightened. "What?"

"Just look." Clint waited for Jules to absorb the report. "As I said, there are two of them."

"Why would he give these to you?" she asked, holding one of the reports up to examine.

"Why is anybody's guess, but I suspect they were given to me for a specific reason. My feeling is Rod, Jr. wanted me to have the reports without delay."

On the table sat an official police report dated Sunday, December 27, 1953. Signed by Lieutenant Alex Freeman. The edges were frayed, and the paper yellowed. A stain, which Clint thought could have possibly come from a coffee spill, had soaked into the top left-hand corner of the page. The report was dated the morning after the Rod's General Store was destroyed.

"Hey, what are you two doing in here? On your day off!" Patrick said comically to Jules but instantly realized he had interrupted something.

Jules had observed Patrick moving toward their table, but Clint had his head buried in a report and didn't hear his approach. "We helped ourselves to a hot fudge sundae," she replied sweetly, sitting her purse beside the papers so they couldn't be seen. "Josie's is like my second home!"

Patrick patted her on the shoulder. "Good answer!" he enthusiastically responded.

Clint's eyes lifted from the pages he was holding with deep concern written on his face. "Hi, Patrick! How's it going?"

"Busy as always. Not that I'm complaining. Keeps groceries on the table."

Clint combined the documents from the two envelopes into one and set it below the table on the bench. It didn't escape him that Patrick had strained to see what he was looking at before he swept everything out of sight. "Excuse me a minute. I need to use the restroom," Clint said. "I'll be right back."

They had agreed before coming inside that if Patrick came to the table, Clint would say he needed to use the restroom. That way, Jules could ask Patrick if he knew of a reputable attorney. One he felt comfortable recommending. Jules was to get a name and number if possible.

Once Clint was out of earshot, Patrick sat down. The diner was pretty much empty, with only one couple on the far side of the building. "Clint looked startled when I walked up. Is everything okay?"

"Yeah, he's just got a lot on his mind," Jules offered in defense of Clint's strange behavior. "I'm glad he went to the restroom because I wanted to ask you a question. I was going to call, but since you're here…" she grinned.

"Sure, shoot, but you may want to make it quick. The one table I do have should be up soon."

"It's a private matter," she said in a soft voice. "Would you happen to know a good lawyer?"

Patrick's eyes narrowed to slits. "Is there a problem? What kind of lawyer you lookin' for?"

Chapter 49

"A general run-of-the-mill type. Someone who can handle normal, everyday stuff."

Patrick picked up on Jules' vague reply but decided not to pry. "Well, the best attorney I know and use, is Jeremy Sullivan. He's reasonably priced and has a good head on his shoulders. A no-nonsense kind of guy. Doesn't try to gouge people." Patrick watched as Clint headed back to the table. "Call me if you need some help with that, Jules. You know I'm here for you. No matter what."

Jules' eyes lit up. "I know, Patrick. You are like family to me. You are a real pal."

"I'll get his number. It's written down in the office somewhere."

Jules smiled. "Thanks."

"I'm back. You can stop talking about me now!" joked Clint.

"That's tough to do when you give us so much ammunition." Patrick punched Clint on the arm as he walked away.

"Did you get it?" Clint asked as soon as Patrick was out of earshot.

"Yeah, he gave me the name of a Jeremy Sullivan. He's getting the number. Says that's who he uses. Sounds like someone you can trust. Fair-priced, according to Patrick."

Jules stared hard at Clint. "I don't understand that envelope." Her eyes glanced down at the bench. "What are you supposed to do with old police reports? Why would Rod give them to you?"

"You aren't asking anything that I'm not already thinking," confessed Clint. "I'd like to look over them after dinner. If you don't mind."

"No problem. I'm as curious as you are."

Clint sighed. "I thought this situation with Rod, Sr. was over with, but now I'm wondering if my assumption was premature. I can't think of a logical reason Rod would want me to have copies of police reports about the day his dad's general store burned."

Jules put out a challenge. "Unless something was fishy about it. Have you thought of that?"

"But if Rod, Jr. had a question about that night, why wouldn't he have looked into it himself?" countered Clint.

"If he's there when you stop in tomorrow, you can ask," Jules suggested.

"Oh, I will. Other than today, he's always at the store," Clint replied, concerned about the reason Rod, Jr. was off. He got to his feet, ready to leave.

On the way out, Jules saw Patrick wave, motioning her to come to the kitchen.

"You go on," she directed Clint. "I'll meet you at the car."

Clint saw Patrick and understood. He held tightly to the envelope as he walked through the glass door into a crisp autumn air.

A different story, other than the one described on paper, was about to be revealed.

"I got it," said Jules brimming from ear to ear.

"Excellent. I'll look him up online tomorrow. See if I can get an appointment set." Clint reached over and took the paper Jules held in her hand. He folded it and put it into his billfold.

"I'll take a couple of pork chops out of the freezer when we get home. Do you like pork?" he asked, unsure if she did.

"Sure do. I prefer pork over everything, except a fat filet." She grinned before her face turned solemn. "Clint, that report is driving me nuts. Talking about piquing a person's interest, I can't come up with a reasonable explanation why Rod, Jr., if that is who is behind it, would want you to have the actual police reports of something that took place fifty years ago? What does he think you'll do with it? Why would you even want them?"

Chapter 49

Her face turned animated. "It doesn't seem to have a connection. You haven't told him about your dad or the treasure."

"True," Clint agreed. "Rod, Sr. was my father's best friend. That we know. Back then, no one would have known anything about the information given to me yesterday. Back in 1953, all they were concerned with was the fire and closing the case. Certainly, no one was aware of the events that had taken place down in Goss Cave or why my dad never returned home. So why would I need to know about the misfortune that surrounded the general store?"

Clint's eyes grew dark. "Unless…"

"Unless what?" asked Jules.

"Unless somehow they *are* connected." He turned toward Jules with a mystified look on his face. "How could the fire be related to Dad's death? It couldn't be. They are totally separate situations. Right?"

"Wait a minute," Jules said in an excited tone. "I think you might be onto something. Your dad was killed on Thursday, December 24, and Rod's General Store burned late Saturday night, December 26. Two days later."

"The incidents were days apart." Clint's wheels were turning. "So, they can't be connected." His face gave him away. He didn't believe what he had said. "I'll not know until I speak with Rod, Jr. Maybe all he wanted to do is to share some of his own family history. We did talk about the fire once. That could be all there is to it."

Neither one of them was buying into Clint's philosophy. When they entered the house, he flipped the foyer lights on and walked into the kitchen. The sun was close to setting, going down earlier with each passing day. In another month, it would be dark by six o'clock. He went to the living room to start a fire. When it was without worry of going out, he returned to the kitchen.

Clint removed the meat from the freezer and the potatoes from the bin. Jules poured water into the brewer for an evening pot of decaf. The fresh air flowing into the house from a partially open

Multiple Truths

window in the living room felt cozy against the warmth of the fireplace. They unloaded the dishes from the dishwasher and set the table before pouring ice water into glasses. Not a word was spoken, but the dialogue in their heads looped from incoming messages.

Clint put the frozen pork chops in the microwave to thaw. Ten minutes passed, the bell dinged, they were ready to broil. Jules peeled the potatoes. An hour later, they were sitting on opposite sides of the table, blessing the food.

We need to examine those reports with a fine-tooth comb." Clint proposed expectantly. "I can't say why but it feels like we are overlooking something. A vital clue we failed to pick up on."

"I feel it too," concurred Jules. "Something is off. I agree. We have a lot of material to go through. We only scanned the highlights." She pointed to the papers sitting on the counter and turned her palms outward. "Why don't you just call him?"

Wrinkling his forehead, Clint responded, "Why didn't I think of that? You're brilliant, Jules. I could call the bookstore and request Rod to return my call if he is not there."

He took a quick glance at the clock on the coffee machine and frowned. "The store will be closed at this hour." Reconsidering, he stated, "But I could call in the morning to let him know I plan to stop by. Tell him I received both reports and would like to discuss them."

"Doesn't keep us from diving into the reports this evening. That is if you are up to it. I've heard two heads are better than one," she teased. "Especially in our case!"

Clint chuckled.

After dinner, they washed the dishes and put them away before heading to the living room with the files and coffee in hand. In front of the fireplace, they drank coffee in silence by the warmth of a crackling fire.

"Okay, here's how I see it. I'll give you the second report, and I'll go over the first. Then we switch. If either one of us finds an inconsistency, we'll bring it to the other's attention."

Chapter 49

"I agree," she confirmed with a nod.

With the reports on their laps, Clint glanced over at Jules, "Put your thinking cap on! And keep a sharp eye."

"You can count on it," she answered with a salute.

The sound of wood crackling in the fireplace was a relaxing backdrop as they flipped through the pages, searching for anything out of the ordinary. Clint read the first of five pages but turned up nothing.

Jules, on the other hand, made a comment at the start. "Boy, things certainly were done differently back then."

"Why do you say that?"

"Because they gave their opinions freely without regard to being labeled judgmental. Today they'd be reprimanded or sued for some of these remarks."

"I'm not sure what you are referring to. Did I miss something?"

"The officer who wrote this report seems biased," Jules spoke matter-of-factly.

"Is that right? Mine isn't that way," interjected Clint.

"Subtle, but it's there," she stated. She went on to the next page. Nothing of interest on that page. Page three was the same. But on page four, that's when things got interesting.

Chapter 50
The Rest of the Story
Wednesday Night, October 8

Lying in bed in the stillness of the night, Clint stared wide-eyed into the darkness trying to piece together a mountain of information too impossible to reconcile.

Combining fragments of the incident report from the night the general store burned, coupled with the knowledge Clint had of what took place days before in Goss Cave, was a complicated feat to stitch together. Even though they did not seem to have a connection, Clint felt in his bones they did.

I have those reports for a reason, Clint avowed. Although he was unable to put his finger on it, his gut told him something was askew. *I need to look closer.* He started a check list in his mind:

- Weather on the night of the blaze was nothing of consequence.
- It had snowed heavily three days prior, but that night the skies were clear.
- High winds were not a factor.
- The excessive blaze was unexplained.
- Firefighters arrived shortly after the fire started but were unable to contain it.
- By the time they got to the location, the building was already engulfed.
- The casualty report was straightforward. One person perished.
- The report had been redacted, which was suspect.

Clint thought about his last point. Before the press release, Lieutenant Alex Freeman had gone back and changed what the reporting officer, Detective Edward Joseph, had written, rephrasing it from the original version.

Chapter 50

Earlier that evening, Jules and Clint had been reading two different versions of what took place the night of the fire. Clint had Lieutenant Freeman's version and Jules read Detective Joseph's account taken at the scene. Until they reached page four, they had no idea how off course the accounts would veer. Then the full story emerged.

Apparently, a quarrel had taken place earlier in the day. One eyewitness report says Rod Radcliff and another man were engaged in a heated exchange in the alley beside the general store. Rod had thrown his hands in the air and walked away. Then he went indoors. Clint found it odd that the incident was omitted in Lieutenant Freeman's account—the first discrepancy.

Another more curious statement came from a woman named Pearl Teague. Jules pointed out to Clint his version did not have notes of the conversation between Detective Joseph and this lady—the second discrepancy.

Jules pointed out, "Clint, she told the police that Rod, Sr. was in the store around 5 p.m. He wasn't feeling well and thought he might have caught the flu. He insisted she go home, stating... if he was contagious, he preferred not to share his germs. She had already worked well past her shift and didn't argue. Pearl said Rod, Sr. was going to call it a day."

Jules read Pearl's statement. Clint listened. "Apparently, she had spoken to Rod, Sr. during the afternoon and thought he was coming in sooner than he did. Someone named Carl was expected to arrive to stock shelves."

Clint didn't find any of that so unusual or important, for that matter. He could not understand why it had been omitted from the official report unless the lieutenant thought it immaterial and wanted a shorter version for the files.

However, another discrepancy stood out. Lieutenant Freeman had made a point of mentioning Rod's smoking habits. Said he was a chain smoker and concluded the accident was caused by a dropped cigarette. On the contrary, Detective Joseph did not mention anything of that nature in his report. He made a notation that Pearl stated Rod planned to take a sleep aid. However, both men agreed the cause of death was asphyxiation.

Clint determined that Freeman's sole intent was to condense the incident report and simplify the findings by suggesting Rod most likely fell asleep holding a lit cigarette, which got dropped on the carpet or floor and ignited the blaze. Concluding that Rod had caused the fire through negligence made perfect sense in the light of how the case was being framed. Seemed pretty cut and dried in Freeman's report.

It would not be the first time a fire had been set by a burning cigarette, he thought, as he mulled over one more discrepancy.

Clint's eyelids grew heavy as slumber fell on his unsettled mind.

October 9
Thursday, 4 a.m.

Early Thursday morning a nagging thought awoke Jules from a sound sleep. She, too, could not get the police discrepancy out of her head. At 4:12 a.m. her mind searched for answers as to why Clint was given two conflicting police reports. Her intuition signaled Pearl Teague's statement held the key.

The bed felt comfortably inviting, and although Jules resisted getting up, she knew it was a waste of time to linger. No way would sleep find her a second time. Lying on her side, facing the window, Jules' mind churned with unanswerable questions. Such as, could Pearl still be alive?

Jules swung to the side of the bed, groggy and uninterested in starting the day at such an insane hour. She turned the tub water on in the bathroom and walked away, letting the tub fill and the coffee pot perk to life.

Chapter 50

Up a full forty-seven minutes ahead of her normal workday routine, Jules had the pot set for 5 a.m. Rarely did her circadian cycle let her sleep much past that. The prospects of a leisurely soak and a hot cup of coffee infused with amaretto creamer energized Jules' lethargic brain.

Time slipped away. She'd braided her long auburn hair and tied it into a bun. Slipping her uniform over her head, she headed for the door. For a change, today, she would arrive early. At lunch, she planned to stop by the library. She had never done a paid people search before, but that was about to change.

Patrick will be beside himself, she thought, tickled at the prospect of his surprised face when she walked through the door at a quarter till.

She was not disappointed. Patrick was delighted to see her. The morning hours whizzed by attending to the first patrons of the day—the regulars who lined up outside the door waiting for the sign to be flipped over from CLOSED to OPEN.

Two hours later, Clint was sitting in his usual booth. His coffee awaited him when he strolled through the door. He lowered the paper when Jules sat down in the booth across from him.

"Look, I know there isn't a reason to investigate this line of thinking, but maybe we could speak with Pearl Teague if she is alive. We could ask her about that day. In person, she may recall a bit of information that could help us. I woke up this morning and she was on my mind. I couldn't shake it. In my world, that's a sign!"

Clint wore a curious expression. "We could do that, I suppose. How do you expect to find her after all these years? If Pearl was, let's say, thirty-five back then, she'd be at least eighty-five now. She could be anywhere. Besides, we might not need to after I speak to Rod at the bookstore today. I plan to go over there right after I'm done here."

The Rest of the Story

"That makes sense. I'm sure he has an explanation for what he did. Giving you those two reports. Clearly, he had his reasons."

"No doubt about it," agreed Clint. "I'll find out soon enough."

"If you don't mind, give me a call after your talk," Jules requested.

"I will. It was a late night," Clint's face looked cautious. "I can see why it was on your mind this morning. It has been on mine too."

Jules stood, "If I don't answer when you phone, I'll call you back. It's been a busy morning so far. For some people, Thursday is payday!"

At 8:50, Clint left Josie's on his way to Rod's New and Used Books. He parked the car in its usual spot and got out. When the sidewalk ended, he stepped onto the path he had taken numerous times before.

The usual scene greeted him. The smell of fall filled his senses. The twittering birds made him smile. Clint loved autumn. Only a few more weeks before the winter season would usher in restrictions and colder temperatures.

This winter, he reminded himself, *Jules will be around.*

Clint put pressure on the latch, expecting to walk right in. He was shocked to find the door was locked. This had never happened before. Even in the early morning hours, the bookstore was open for business. Cupping his hands on the glass, Clint could tell no one was inside. The store was dark.

Something of a serious nature must have arisen for both Rod and the clerk not to be at the bookstore today, Clint decided with concern. *Maybe there really was an emergency yesterday!* Disappointed, he returned to his car.

"Hey, you aren't going to believe this. The bookstore is closed," Clint told Jules on voicemail. "I guess I'll go home. I have some phone calls to make anyway. When you get time, give me a buzz. Talk to you soon."

Clint had several chores awaiting him. The first on his list was to telephone Jeremy Sullivan, Patrick's attorney, to set up a

Chapter 50

consultation. The property deed Jules had found was in his safe in the cellar. Clint intended to take it with him to the initial meeting in the event he elected to have Mr. Sullivan represent him. One thing was certain if that did occur, Sullivan was going to have a lot to mull over.

He also wanted to phone Scott to confirm their meeting later that afternoon. Knowing Scott to be a stand-up guy and a friend, Clint was ready to spill the beans.

When Clint finished reading the unredacted version of the police report for a second time, he felt bothered. Lieutenant Alex Freeman had not mentioned any odors or burn patterns in his report. Yet on page five of Detective Edward Joseph's, a notation, suggesting the likelihood of gasoline as a probable cause was completely ignored. Joseph had inserted a bullet point at the bottom of his report indicating possible foul play.

So, why did Lieutenant Freeman, Detective Joseph's superior, not find that worth noting? Clint pondered quizzically. *It feels like the guy just wanted to wrap the report up. Blame the old man for it and be done.*

Clint wondered if these were the only two reports on record that referenced the tragedy. *Surely, the fire department would have filed an incident report,* he deliberated. *And what about first responders? They would be required to file paperwork as well, I reckon.* He rested his hand on the report. *I'll ask Scott when we get together.*

Filling his mug with fresh brew, Clint made a call to Jeremy Sullivan. They spoke for about fifteen minutes. At the end of the conversation, they'd penciled in an appointment. Though Clint hadn't divulged much information, he had shared enough to warrant an earlier meeting than he had anticipated. Monday morning at 9:30 a.m.

Clint fired up the truck, destination—Jules' house.

"Dinner is my treat," she had boasted when she returned his call. "We overestimated the beef and noodles thing today, and in my opinion, they do not heat up well. Turns to mush easily. Patrick told me to help myself. Besides, I have some interesting news."

When Clint pulled into the drive, Jules was raking leaves. When he neared, she put the rake down and gave him a hug. "Sounds like we both had a busy day. Mine flew by."

"Ditto on that. Except you got off early."

"Yeah, a little. The new girl wanted some extra hours. Patrick gave the green light for her to come in and for me to take off."

"I have an appointment set up with Jeremy Sullivan on Monday," Clint said, raising a brow. "He sounds like a person I can relate to. Pretty down to earth. It is easy to see why Patrick likes him."

"Super! I wish I could join you Monday. You know how that goes, though, specials out the wazoo. Need to get rid of weekend leftovers," she grinned, putting a finger to her lips. "Don't tell anyone. It's a restaurant secret!"

"I wish you could too," confessed Clint thinking it would be nice to have her accompany him.

"Do me a favor. Make sure you stop by the diner on the way home. It'll be killing me until I find out what he had to say. Are you taking the deed?"

"Yes, I am. It's a general land deed, a squatters-right type of thing. I don't know what to make of that. The type they issued back in the old days. I was reading about them online today. I hope it stands up in court. Sullivan will find out how legit it is."

"I wish I were a fly on the wall when you tell him about the treasure." She remarked as she walked inside, holding the screen door for Clint to join her.

At the steps, Clint apologized. "I heard your message about the beef and noodles. I am starving, but I can't stay. I'm meeting Scott at In a Pig's Eye at 5:15. But I can come around after that if you don't mind saving me some. Would you want me to text you when I leave? I'm not going to eat, and I don't plan to stay long. I do want to level with him before the media learns about everything going on."

Chapter 50

"That's right," Jules reacted in a flash, "you told me you were going to hook up with him on Thursday. No problem, I'll work on the yard until you get back. That way, we can eat together." She glanced at the piles of leaves scattered around the yard. "I have plenty of raking to do."

"Are you sure? It could be seven o'clock or later."

"That's fine. I don't mind."

"You said you had something to tell me?" Clint said.

"Oh yes! You will be pleased to know that Pearl is living in the Crestview Adult Living facility in Chambersburg. Can you believe that? She lives a stone's throw from Salzburg."

"Are you kidding me? How did you find that out?"

"I didn't. Bonnie dug it up. I was going to use one of those people search programs. But didn't have to. Bonnie has a backdoor one she uses at the library. She called around, and apparently Pearl has a daughter. The daughter filled us in. Bonnie made up a story about the research she was doing on Salzburg for the library."

Clint laughed at Jules' ingenuity. "That's great. When can we have a chat?"

"I called the daughter, Georgeann, when I got home. Bonnie told her I would be in touch. Georgeann's only stipulation was that she was present for the interview."

"So, how does this work? We can't interrogate the woman in a nursing home." Clint chortled at the idea.

"We won't have to. Georgeann invited us over to her place. She'll pick Pearl up and bring her to the house. She says Pearl is sharp as tacks. She does a crossword puzzle every morning. Plus, according to Georgeann, Pearl has a memory like an elephant. That should work in our favor."

"I don't like doing this under pretense, though." Clint frowned, not comfortable with being dishonest.

"Relax, Bonnie told me, to be on the up-and-up, she would gather information and write an article about the blizzard of 1953,

The Rest of the Story

which would include recollections from residents, including Pearl and possibly a few other people. Georgeann said if we would like to come by on Tuesday at noon, that would give Pearl time to get settled in before we arrive."

Clint looked at his watch. "I'd better scoot."

From the truck, Clint called out, "See you around seven."

Chapter 51
In a Pig's Eye

"I'm glad you're sitting down," Clint expressed with humor as he slid into the booth across from Scott. "Because I have a humdinger to hand you!"

Scott, baffled by Clint's animated remark, fired back, "Nice lead-in." He smiled in the way of a greeting. "Sorry, bud, but I don't think anything could top that last bombshell of yours." He took a generous pull from the beer he'd ordered prior to Clint's arrival. An extra Bud Light sat on Clint's side of the table. Scott pushed it toward him.

Clint laughed vigorously, also taking a swig. With a grin plastered to his face, he answered, "You just wait! This'll put you on your heels!"

Scott's eyes flashed with humor, waiting to hear Clint's earth-shattering news. "Better than solving a murder through paranormal assistance? Nah, I doubt it!"

Checking in all directions so as not to be overheard, Clint spoke in a low voice that faded to a whisper. "Here goes nothing!" He looked both ways and, with a big grin, said, "I know where the Reno Gang's lost treasure is hidden."

Scott's eyes grew enormous. "*What?*" he yelped.

"Shhh… keep it down!" Clint waved his hand, to lower his voice .

Not believing his ears, but in a more subdued tone, Scott reacted, "Clint, what are you saying?"

"Just what I said," he chortled. "No joke, I know where the Reno brothers and their gang hid their treasure." His eyes scanned the room to make certain there were no eavesdroppers and then slowly mouthed. "It's in Goss Cave."

"You've got to be joshing me?" Scott bantered, unable to wipe the grin from his face. A puzzled expression replaced his smile.

"How did you find it?" He became contemplative. "Clint, why didn't you mention you've been treasure hunting? You know I would have volunteered my services."

Before asking his next question, Scott scanned the bar thoroughly. "Is that why you were down in Goss Cave and happened upon both dead bodies?"

Scott immediately realized how insensitive his words must have sounded. Shamefully, he lowered his eyes, diverting them from Clint's. "Good grief, man, I'm sorry. That was callus of me. This job can take the humanness out of us." He turned his palm over with a look of apology. "I did hear, and believe, what you told me about how you found your father and Luke McCauley down in the cave. A spirit guided you there."

Clint nodded, affirming Scott's admission. "Don't give it a second thought," said Clint graciously. "I understand how hard your line of work must be. You see the side of life all of us try to avoid."

"Thanks, Clint, I appreciate that. To be a policeman, you must take the good with the bad. A thankless job on occasion, and at times, a soul-searching commitment."

Clint's face brightened. "Remember the day I told you how I knew my father was killed?"

"Yeah," replied Scott, wondering what that had to do with the Reno Gang's lost treasure.

"I left out a bunch of the story that day," he confessed. "The response I received was a bit jolting, so I decided to wait until we could meet one on one, away from the house. Didn't want to take any risks."

Clint thought back to the apology he received from David, grateful for his candor. "The fewer people who know at this point, the better. I did tell Jules. She is the only one who knows, other than you, now."

"A wise decision," stated Scott. "I feel honored."

Chapter 51

"I trust you," Clint reached out to shake Scott's hand. "I'll keep you in the loop. On Monday I have an appointment set up with a lawyer to figure out what comes next. Something else interesting surfaced. I unearthed underground living quarters, by happenstance. My grandfather apparently lived in this hollowed out area by design. Initially, I assumed he lived in the shack I showed you, but it turned out that was a ruse. Not only for him but my great-grandfather as well." Clint smirked. "That land around there was full of surprises."

Scott appeared perplexed. "Could you fill in the blanks? This isn't making any sense."

"I suppose it wouldn't. A picture is worth a thousand words, my friend." Clint lifted his drink. "Here's to the Reno Brothers and their gang of thieves! A rotten bunch."

Scott tipped his glass, "I'll drink to that! Now finish what you were saying. Please go on."

"I'll go one step further. I'll show you." Clint's eyes sparkled with excitement, and then he said, "You do understand I found none of these things on my own. Inconceivable the way it materialized. It truly is. And, a note of caution, my story, for the time being, stays between us. Promise?"

"Yes, you have my solemn promise."

"From the first day I drove past the land where I now live, back in 1997, I had a strange feeling about the place. It was as if I was lured to it. Then, after I purchased the property, I became convinced it was haunted."

Clint took a drink and watched Scott's face closely before continuing. Convinced Scott was fully on board, he stated, "It turns out I was right. There is a guy named Rod Radcliff. He once lived in Salzburg, back in 1953, and owned a business here in Salzburg. Rod's General Store. He was my father's closest friend, it turns out."

"Really?" Scott replied, surprised by what Clint had revealed. "You thought your place was haunted? All those fishing trips we took, and you never brought this up?"

"Yeah, didn't want to sound like I was off my rocker," Clint winced at how insane it sounded to admit he believed in ghosts. "At the beginning, I tied it to Elise's passing and the stress I was under about losing her. You know what it was like for me in the days that followed her funeral." He took a moment to regroup after uttering a phrase that never came easy.

"Those were tough days," Scott empathized. "I can't imagine. I don't know what I'd do under the same circumstance. Prob'ly crawl into my shell and never come out. Like you did."

"As time went by, I became convinced a presence haunted the property. Not Elise, as I hoped, but an older gentleman. I would get glimpses of him—or thought I did. It wasn't until I saw him in a mirror at the bookstore that things changed. He was wearing a straw fedora."

Scott's face twisted comically. "He was in a mirror and wearing a straw hat?"

"Remember that mirror in my foyer? He was in that one." Clint grinned sheepishly. "A real lanky guy. Skinny as a rail. I saw him several times before the dots actually started to connect." Clint shook his head. "That is a much longer story that I'll share with you some other time."

He scanned the room before picking up where he had left off. "I will say Rod Radcliff is the reason I went into the cave that night. Like I told you. He is behind everything, in fact, including my discovery of the treasure. If it weren't for him, we wouldn't be having this conversation."

Clint's expression turned mindful. "My guess is he wanted the scales balanced. Wanted the truth about Dad's disappearance known. It does seem weird that his spirit remained behind and not my dad's. They must have been incredibly close for the murder to have kept Rod tethered to this place."

"I'd have to agree. A strong bond indeed. That is wild, the sort of stuff they make movies of," said Scott, agreeing. "I take it you

Chapter 51

are free of his spirit now that the crime has been solved and the case closed. All the facts are known. You haven't seen or felt his presence since, right?" Scott turned a splayed hand, assuming he was right.

A scowl appeared on Clint's face. "Well, not exactly. I had a dream the other night that was bothersome. Not the first one with Rod Radcliff in it. Like the one I initially told you about, he was trying to communicate. I could not make out what it was, though. I get this feeling there is more to this story."

"Is that right?"

"A nagging feeling is all I've got, nothing specific." Clint seemed lost in thought. "Can I ask a favor?"

"Maybe. It depends…" Scott replied with a grin. "Don't forget. I am a cop!"

Clint laughed freely, along with Scott. "Nothing illegal! All I'd like to know is if an archived police report exists of a fire that occurred on December 26, 1953, at Rod's General Store. Rod Radcliff died in that fire."

Scott's tone turned somber. "I thought I recognized that name. Didn't make the connection until this very minute. I remember hearing about that fire. The store was on Grandview if my memory serves me correctly."

"That's right. Just east of Rod's New and Used Books. That is Rod Radcliff's grandkid, I believe!"

Clint revisited a bizarre conversation he had with Rod, Jr. about his relationship to Rod Radcliff, Sr. He remembered feeling confused about three Rod Radcliffs. Clint was given the impression Rod Radcliff, Jr.'s father had also been involved in a fire but survived. Which made Rod Radcliff, Jr., who owned the bookstore, the grandson of the first Rod Radcliff. It was a complicated conversation that put his head in a daze.

"I'm in possession of two police reports. Given to me, I presume, from the bookstore owner. I need to verify that yet, but I think he is the one who is behind it. A Lieutenant Alex Freeman signed off on one. However, the original report was filed by Detective Edward

In a Pig's Eye

Joseph. I want to validate what I have with your files. And… see if other versions exist."

"Whoa, wait a minute!" Scott responded on impulse with a hand in the air, realizing he was unaware of such a place. "Salzburg has a bookstore? How did I miss that? And this guy acquired copies of police reports and gave them to you? How odd is that? That would be outside the normal protocol. I wonder who supplied them to him?"

"Yes, we have a bookstore, and don't feel bad. I didn't realize it either." Clint smiled, knowing how Scott felt. "Rod, Jr. must know someone at the police station. I will say, the heartburn I'm having has to do with the final report being altered. Freeman redacted it. Left out some vitally important stuff. I think you will agree when you read it." Clint reached into his jacket, withdrew an envelope, and slid it across the table.

"That's interesting. I wouldn't think any official statement to be missing vital information once it was reported," Scott commented as he glanced over Clint's shoulder into the bar. "So, what exactly do you want me to do?"

"You can keep those. I made you a copy," Clint said, pointing to the envelope. "I'd like to see the fire department's account, if possible. I suspect there is a file somewhere in the archives. Don't you think?"

"Probably," Scott acknowledged with a nod. "But that's been a minute, and who knows where it might have wandered or been stored if it exists. Why do you want it?"

"Because, honestly Scott, I believe the old man is still around, and I can't figure out why. In my head, things were put to bed. It turns out that the land where the shack is belongs to my ancestors. We found a land deed in the underground area I told you about. Part of the reason why I'm seeing a lawyer. That ten-acres behind my property," commented Clint, "was deeded to my great-grandfather, Earl Reeves, back in 1907. Dated, stamped, and notarized by the State of Indiana. Can you believe that? Imagine my surprise."

Chapter 51

"That is incredible. Tell me again, where did you find the deed?"

"Found it in a lockbox down there in the place my great-grandfather called home. The weird thing is the entrance was well-camouflaged. Not far from an outhouse. Maybe forty feet from the shack. Inside this bunker area, we found all kinds of maps, legal papers, and the signed, recorded land deed. Only later did I remember the shack from when I was a little kid. I used to visit my grandfather there."

"Clint, I'm a little befuddled. It's a lot to take in, even for me. I've seen and heard a lot of things in my time, but this one takes the cake. Don't get me wrong. I believe you, Clint. I do, but holy cow," he said with laughing eyes, "that's some heavy stuff!"

Scott drained the last of his beer and held up two fingers, indicating to the waitress to bring another round. "I'll see what I can dig up in the archives. Give me a couple of days." He saluted Clint. "I'm on the case!"

Clint found Scott's reaction humorous. They were having a good time, just two friends in a bar drinking beer, a repeat performance of other such occasions at In a Pig's Eye.

The waitress came over and sat two Bud Lights on the table. She walked away without a word, holding three more drinks on her platter for another table.

Clint said to Scott. "Tuesday, Jules and I are going to speak with a lady who lived here in 1953. My understanding is she worked at Rod's General Store. Knew Rod Radcliff personally, I'm told. Maybe she can shed some light on the situation."

Scott cocked his head and grinned. "We have our work cut out for us. Are you positive about revealing the location of the treasure? Maybe you should keep that a secret, even from me. Until the lawyer can advise you."

"I trust you, Scott. Plus, I suspect a formal report needs to be filed anyway. That should be done by you."

"All right. After you speak with the lawyer, give me a ring. Until then, my lips are sealed."

"Thanks. It was hard keeping it from you. You can't imagine how much is down there. Tons. Gold and silver bars, money, coins, jewelry, precious gems, you name it."

"I can't wait to see," Scott confessed. "If anyone deserves a break, it's you. After everything you've been through. Like I said, keep me posted."

Clint grabbed the bill. "Let me get this. For prosperity's sake." He laughed, shaking Scott's hand.

"Help yourself," Scott joked. "I hope it becomes a habit."

When they got outside in the bright light, Clint said, "I will call you Monday after I see the lawyer to decide on a day and time for us to hook up."

"Absolutely. I look forward to it." Scott wagged his head in disbelief at the information Clint had laid on him. When they got to their vehicles, Scott leaned over the top of his. "Please… keep me informed."

By the time Clint and Scott had concluded their meeting, the hour had turned late. The sky had darkened behind Scott's car as he backed out of the parking lot, wearing a broad grin. Although Clint was not told as much, he suspected Scott was headed back to the station to do some digging into an old case file.

Clint dialed Jules, asking for a raincheck on the meal she had promised to keep warm. He explained, and she understood, that after going over the details of his latest discoveries, he felt drained and wanted to call it a night. Maybe one too many beers had caused his fatigue, but either way, he would go home, relax, and read.

Friday, October 10

Over the weekend, Clint organized his thoughts, committing them to paper. While Jules worked, he returned to the secret space. A strange sensation came over him as he moved in silence through

Chapter 51

the rooms where his relatives had once roamed, plotting tunnels and treasure hunting escapades that would eventually culminate with Clint discovering the treasure.

Combing through the contents of boxes containing notes and correspondence from ancestors, Clint felt overwhelmed with gratitude for the many artifacts he now possessed. Large envelopes containing letters—some as far back as World War I—lay atop correspondence bound in cheesecloth and tied in twine.

Peering into the personalities of long-deceased relatives, Clint read through their private communications with extreme interest, yet at times, he felt guilty for prying. Hours ticked away as the inner thoughts of script revealed events his kinfolk had endured. People Clint never knew existed came to life on the pages of time, making his heart swell with pride.

He discovered that his great-grandfather was the first to search for the treasure. Having been alive during the misdeeds and hangings of the Reno Gang, Earl Reeves was hellbent, according to the writings, on finding the cache of stolen goods off Highway 150, near Goss Cave. The place where the plunder was reported to have been stashed.

When Clint crawled out from the underground bunker, the sun had gone down. He and Jules had decided to wait to see one another until Saturday evening. Sunday was up for grabs. Both were exhausted, agreeing additional rest sounded appealing.

Monday, October 13

When Clint arrived in Paoli, he was pleasantly surprised to see Sullivan's office was in the same Feldman Law Office building Jules and he had driven by the week before. On the main thoroughfare, Clint pulled into McDonald's to refresh his coffee and buy an Egg McMuffin.

At 9:25, Clint walked into the lawyer's office. Soon he would have the answers he sought.

Two hours later, on his return trip to Salzburg, Clint was joyous. No other words could describe his emotions. Jeremy Sullivan had looked up Indiana law and determined the Finders Keepers law applied in his case.

"Basically," Sullivan stated, referring to a law book open on his desk, "the rule dictates if a person finds treasure on his property or anywhere else in the State of Indiana, it belongs to the finder."

He peered over his glasses at Clint. "Treasure trove," Sullivan paraphrased, "is most often gold and silver, or paper money, hidden or deliberately concealed. Typically found underground but not always. Sometimes treasure can be happened upon in planes, under mattresses, inside unclaimed safes, and/or in the ground or yard," he translated to Clint. "Indiana law states if a person doesn't trespass, they get to keep whatever they find."

At that juncture, Clint shared his larger-than-life revelation. He told Sullivan about the treasure and the property deed. Sullivan's reaction was one of astonishment.

Clint chuckled when he recollected how Jeremy Sullivan had choked on a sip of water, taken just before Clint's colossal announcement. He had jumped up to pat his newly hired lawyer on the back, finding the whole episode quite amusing.

During their meeting, Mr. Sullivan advised Clint to make a Last Will and Testament as soon as possible. Sullivan also requested that Clint return Friday morning, same time, so they could discuss the matter in more depth, particularly the subject of removal and relocation of the valuables. The treasure needed to be addressed in greater detail. In the end, Clint gave his attorney permission to move forward.

Later, when Sullivan phoned, he informed Clint that he had moved quickly in acquiring an excavation team, hand selected for the project. He was pleased to have secured the company and specific people he had in mind. The aspects of the contract would

Chapter 51

be shared with Clint for his approval once Sullivan received final compliance and terms.

Feeling relieved with how their meeting had progressed, Clint's concerns had been directed at how, when, and where to excavate the treasure. He was keenly aware it needed to be moved to a more secure location, soon. According to his lawyer, there was one caveat. If any of the items, cash, gold, or silver, could be definitively traced back to the government, state, or personal property, it could mean the original owners had limited rights. Clint wasn't concerned, considering there were more than enough riches to go around.

"A team will be out to start the extraction process soon," Sullivan had told him. "Are you on board with taking your assets to Evansville? I will act on your behalf today to lock in a vault if you wish. Be assured you can change the location if you prefer a different location. If Evansville doesn't meet with your approval, a backup choice might be Louisville. We need to do this without fanfare and before word gets out, which might be a challenge. Either way, my advice is to deposit it somewhere near."

"Evansville is fine. I don't care as long as it's someplace safe. Hopefully not more than an hour away," Clint suggested.

Clint walked away from his meeting, holding a folder filled with forms to read and/or have completed by the next visit. Homework.

His attention shifted to the arrangement he and Scott had in the hopper. He'd placed a call and left a message, asking Scott if Friday afternoon would work for their upcoming meeting.

In his mind's eye, he saw them lowering themselves into the man-made hole that led into Goss Cave. He saw them moving along the corridors of time back to the place that Clint knew Frank Reno and his gang of brothers and bandits had gathered to deposit stolen treasure. The wheels on the truck hummed to the tune of the highway while Clint visualized the past and how it must have all happened.

Tomorrow, a new day would dawn on a whole different reality.

Chapter 52
Golden Memory

Into October's brisk morning air Jules stepped, her senses awakened by the sight of dawn dancing through the tawny trees and the scent of an awakening earth.

From her front steps she waited for Clint's arrival. Clothed in an ankle-length kelly-green dress, Jules' shoulder-length auburn hair glistened in the sun like red wine. Dressed for a special occasion, the day promised insight into Clint's quest for the truth.

Georgeann, Pearl Teague's daughter, had them penciled in at noon for an interview. Beforehand, they'd chosen an early brunch in Chambersburg—at a Gristmill eatery—because of its small-town charm. The place conjured images of yesteryear with its turn-of-the-century ambiance.

"You should initiate the conversation," suggested Clint, thinking Pearl might be wary of strangers. "I suspect Pearl will feel more comfortable talking to a woman at the start."

"Considering she's up in years, you're probably right," Jules agreed. "We need to walk her through that December Saturday step-by-step to see if she recalls anything that might affect the case."

"So far, with Jeremy Sullivan, things are falling into place quite nicely. He is filing a new deed. That turned out not to be as complicated as I had imagined. According to Sullivan, though, the treasure will be a bit trickier, it must take priority. He is looking into the legal framework surrounding relocating it but says he doesn't anticipate any issues. I hadn't considered how long I would leave it down there, but he says we shouldn't delay. We need to move fast.

"Sullivan says the discovery falls under the Finders Keepers law in Indiana. Says, barring no unforeseen complications, the treasure is mine." Clint grinned big, not believing what he had just said. "Crazy to think about. Isn't it?"

Chapter 52

Jules laughed with amusement. "That's an understatement!"

"If I had to be honest with myself, Jules, it feels wrong to keep the things the Gang robbed. That stuff is stolen property, taken from innocent citizens and transport trains belonging to the government.

Can you imagine how heartbroken and violated those people must have felt at the time? I read the government turned to outside law enforcement to hunt the Reno Gang down and apprehend them. They never located the pilfered goods."

Clint's thoughts were churning when he inserted, "I proposed to the attorney that the banks may still have serial numbers they could crosscheck to file a claim."

Jules focused on what Clint had suggested. "I agree with you," she said, of the same mind. "Banks or descendants could file a claim for lost property. What about posting a notice in the newspaper? It could be a great way of giving back." A reassuring smile graced her face. Even though, she cautiously added, "Proof should be required, or every Tom, Dick, and Harry will be knocking on your door and crawling out of the woodwork."

"Exactly," Clint agreed, thinking how miserable that scenario sounded. "On the other hand, Sullivan says he doubts they kept that good of records in the late 1800s. He believes I could be opening Pandora's box—a fool's errand—if I'm not careful."

"Didn't think about that! Knowing how people behave these days, it could turn into a fiasco." Jules changed the subject to ask a question Clint wasn't expecting. "I meant to ask, is Scott coming over?"

"Yes, he is," replied Clint. "I called him on the way home yesterday and asked him if he could stop by Friday afternoon after I meet with the lawyer. The timing should be ideal."

Scott had left a message on Clint's mobile. "All systems go," he said eagerly. "Be at your place mid to late afternoon Friday. Looking forward to it!"

Golden Memory

"So, you are seeing Sullivan again?" inquired Jules. "That soon?"

"Yeah, I forgot to tell you. He recommended I make a will out immediately." Clint laughed anxiously. "Makes my head spin! I understand there is a lot at stake."

Jules' expression turned serious. "Your life is never going to be the same, Clint. Especially once the media gets a hold of this. Your place will turn into an absolute circus, crawling with reporters wanting to hear the backstory of how you found the *notorious* treasure. Better be prepared for the tsunami that's coming."

"I've been thinking about that. I really don't know how to approach it. The only people who know are Scott, Sullivan, and of course, you."

She giggled. "If I can't find you, I'll know where to look. Your great-grandfather's hideout!"

Clint burst out laughing. "At least I have a place to escape to. It could turn into my underground palace."

Jules didn't hear the word she had hoped for—*we*. She was under no illusion. Their lives would never return to normal after this. Notoriety on this scale, coupled with enormous wealth, had the ability to change people, and not always for the good.

How could it not? she internalized in angst. *Clint is going to be, to some extent, famous.*

"What are you thinking about?" he asked, noticing she appeared far away. "You look deep in thought."

Unaware he had been studying her, she replied with a lie. "I was wishing I could see the expression on Scott's face when you show him the treasure!"

Clint grinned big. "Yeah, that'll set him on his heels!"

Chapter 52

The Interview

When Jules and Clint walked through the door, a gracious smile greeted them. Georgeann's home was lovely. Light from the windows in the back part of the house shown through the hallway to the front entry.

The foyer showcased soft LED pin-lighting inserted under the ceiling trim, accentuating a small domed, blue crystal chandelier.

On the opposite wall a winter scene depicted a farmhouse and falling snow. A barn set in the distance further romanticized the wide-open spaces of rural America. Jules was in awe by the grandeur of Jon Vaughn's painting prowess.

"Hello, I'm Georgeann," said the smartly dressed middle-aged woman. "Glad to finally meet you."

"Good to make your acquaintance," responded Clint. "This is Jules Jenkins. I believe you two have spoken over the telephone. I'm Clint Reeves."

"Mom is waiting in the sunroom," Georgeann aimed their attention to the end of the hallway. I'll show you the way. We were just pouring some hot tea. May I offer you a cup?"

"That would be lovely," Jules replied without hesitation. She looked at Clint with a raised brow.

Getting the unspoken message, he answered, "Yes, thank you."

When they entered the glass-enclosed sunroom, Clint spotted an aged lady, hands folded neatly in her lap, seated on the couch. Wearing a black dress, she was the picture of elegance. At the neck of her pleated, pale blouse, a stunning antique brooch was pinned. With the face of an angel, her alert eyes studied Clint closely.

"Mother, these are the people I told you about. They'd like to ask you a few questions," stated Georgeann as she poured tea in a bone China cup. She added two lumps of sugar and handed it to her mother.

Pearl nodded, pointing to the chairs opposite her. "Have a seat. Please."

"Thank you," they said in unison.

"How may I be of help?"

Clint looked to Jules, indicating she should take the lead.

"Salzburg is doing a piece on the blizzard of 1953, and we thought perhaps you might be able to fill in some of the details. My understanding is you lived in Salzburg at the time. Is that right?"

"Yes, I did. Don't know that there is much to say though," Pearl quickly replied. "Other than it was one heck of a storm. Came on Christmas Eve out of nowhere. I wasn't supposed to hit us. I didn't think it would ever stop snowing. If I'm not mistaken, thirty-plus inches fell before it was all said and done. That is not something easily forgotten." She grunted. "Put a damper on Christmas that year."

Jules leaned forward. "Mrs. Teague, I understand you worked at the general store in town."

"Please, call me Pearl, dear." Pearl patted Jules' hand. "Yes, yes, I worked there." Her face had a far-away look. "It was one of my favorite places to have worked."

"I heard it burned down right after Christmas. Terrible timing for something so tragic," injected Jules.

Pearl's eyes shifted to her daughter. A sadness filled her eyes. "Yes, it did. Poor Rod, he was such a good man. A terrible way to end one's life."

Clint glanced at Georgeann, who was observing the conversation with interest. He turned to Pearl. "I read a statement you gave the police. Everything was lost, according to the report." Remembering the interview was supposed to be about the blizzard, he asked, "Was it snowing at the time of the fire?"

Chapter 52

"No, it had stopped by then. We could hardly move around. The entire town was closed. Not Rod's General Store, though. His place was always open, come hell or high water." Pearl smiled as though she had said a bad word. "It was a travesty how they tried to blame the fire on Rod," she stated, looking as though she might cry. "The newspaper insinuated he fell asleep smoking a cigarette, and that's how the fire started. I say bull hockey!" Pearl's eyes turned fiery. "I didn't believe it then, and I don't believe it now. Rod Radcliff was way too responsible to do something that foolish. Besides he wasn't feeling well and planned to take something to help sleep."

"If not that, what do you think happened?" Asked Jules. "Could it have been electrical?"

"Don't have a clue. None of it made a lick of sense," Pearl muttered in frustration. "Rod had a bad cold that night. I remember that. Said he was afraid he might have caught the flu and was going to turn in early. No way would he have been smoking in bed when he felt that sick."

She leaned in toward Georgeann as though telling a secret. "I told them that was hogwash. But no one cared what I had to say. Seemed all they wanted to do was be done with it." She wagged her head. "Carelessness was not the cause of that fire."

Jules wasn't certain how to proceed. It was apparent Pearl was riled up. They were supposed to be writing a story on the blizzard, not the fire. "Are you okay to go on?" Jules asked Pearl gently and then glanced over at Georgeann, who was signaling it might be time to wrap things up.

"Of course, I am," Pearl replied, putting her daughter on notice that she was perfectly capable of continuing the interview.

Georgeann bobbed her head in approval, knowing when her mother set her mind to something there was no changing it.

Jules let her instincts guide her. "With the blizzard causing so much havoc, that is to say—making it difficult for people to get around—provisions must have been collected on foot." She smiled sweetly, "In my experience, some of the worse times in life often produce the fondest memories."

Pearl's eyes softened, "Yeah, it was beautiful. Like a winter dreamland. It was so quiet and peaceful!"

"Was it just you and Rod working that day?" asked Jules.

"Yeah, and the kid who stocked shelves." Pearl stared dreamily ahead. "I think his name was Carl. My children were young'uns, so I worked only when Rod needed me. I was the last resort." She laughed. "He paid me well, though, for being a fill-in."

"Did anything about that day seem unusual? There must have been a lot of snow still on the ground. Not many customers, I bet. But, again, if Rod's General Store was the only real market to buy food, that is where everyone would go. Right?" Jules was letting her imagination put her into the moment.

"Not really. Most people stayed home because of the harsh conditions. Just a straggler here and there. I'd never seen anything like it. The storm was supposed to pass right over us. Instead, we got a direct hit!" She laughed at her own joke.

"I wish more pictures had been taken," Jules expressed with regret. "It must have been something. Especially this far south in the state. Bonnie, the librarian, showed me a few of the newspaper accounts from back then."

"I have a few in a shoebox at the center if you are interested," Pearl quickly piped up. "Taken with my Brownie." She beamed, "The investigators didn't like me taking pictures, but I didn't care. Told them it was my right as a citizen. Must have been one o'clock in the morning and colder than a grave digger's shovel. *Or a witch's…*" Pearl glanced over at Georgeann and grinned, not finishing her sentence.

Georgeann returned Pearl's mischievous smile, knowing her mother had a million and one vintage sayings hidden up her sleeves. A strong woman who knew her mind, Pearl would not have warmed up to someone telling her what she could or couldn't do.

Chapter 52

"The ones taken inside the building after the fire aren't much to look at, but you're welcome to them. Couldn't bring myself to toss pictures out from those days."

"I'd love to see them." Then Clint hesitantly mentioned. "There is no way you would know this, Mrs. Teague, but my understanding is your boss and my father were good friends."

A glint appeared in Pearl's eyes. Her face showed her shock. "Who was your father?"

"Eli Reeves. I doubt you'd remember." Since his father went missing, Clint assumed Eli's name would not sound familiar.

"Eli Reeves?" she wailed, "I do… I do indeed!" Animated in her expression, Pearl exclaimed, "You're Eli's boy?" Her face lit up. Not giving Clint a chance to answer, she excitedly declared. "Oh, my Lord and Savior, I am beside myself!" She turned to Georgeann, "Eli and Rod were great friends. Rod was like an older brother to Eli." She put her hands on her knees, slapping them vigorously. "I can't believe my ears and eyes!" Pearl squealed with delight, "Yes, I remember him, and you too laddie!"

Clint sheepishly looked around, not sure how to respond, "Me?"

"Clint Reeves!" Pearl went on. "I caught you stealing bread. Around the same time the store burned. You were so little and cute as a button! And scared." Pearl's face looked pained. "Your father disappeared on Christmas Eve. Rod was worried sick about him and you. He fretted endlessly over it."

Clint was tongue-tied. The air was electric. He hadn't expected the conversation to turn the direction it had just gone. "I remember that day. Oh my gosh," he chortled. His face showed his surprise. "Now that you bring it up, I remember you too. You were the lady behind the counter. I didn't have enough money. You made me take the bread back, and when you turned your back, I ran out with it." He looked to the side, struggling to remember what he had spent his whole life trying to forget. "Didn't I stay with you?"

Pearl reached out and took his hand. "I'm so sorry, Clint. I had you put the bread back so I could call the police. I knew something was dreadfully wrong. You stayed at my place that evening. Until we could decide what to do. All the while hoping Eli would show up. Those were tragic days. First your father, then the fire."

Clint was on the verge of tears. Almost cried at the touch of her hand, remembering the scene like it was yesterday. "They took me to the orphanage in Vincennes. I lived there until I was sixteen." Melancholy blanketed his face in a gravely shade of pale.

Pearl knew not to ask why he had left the children's home. That was a private matter. Between Clint and God. "Well, from all accounts, it appears you turned out a fine young man."

She turned to Georgeann. With fatigue written on her face, Pearl suggested, "I suspect I can't help these good folks any more than I have. Best to be getting back." She glanced over at the mantel clock. "Lawrence Welk starts in two hours. Don't want to miss that!" She turned to Clint. "Dinner is at six sharp. It's spaghetti and meatball night."

Jules stood, having translated the hidden message.

Clint did the same. "Thank you so much, Mrs. Teague. You've been a huge help. It's better to have someone who was living at the time when telling the story. I've learned more than I could have ever hoped for." Clint bent down and gave Pearl a heartfelt hug.

"You're a good boy." She sighed, grateful for his embrace. "Always was."

Memories flooded back of Clint sitting on Pearl's lap while she read to him. A little guy, only five, it was the weekend before the orphanage came to collect him. She could still see his little fingers lifting the loaf of bread to the counter that morning at the general store. He had dug deep into his pocket to pull out nineteen cents. Her instincts had warned her, if Eli wasn't with Clint, something was wrong, and she called the police. Her whole life, Pearl had regretted not adopting Clint. She thought about him often, wondering where he might be. She felt like crying because here he was right in front of her.

Chapter 52

"Doesn't feel like I added much, honey. Same old stuff everyone talked about back in those days."

"Your pictures will be a great addition to the story. They will shed light on the actual event with more clarity than words alone. A picture is worth a thousand words, they say," Jules winked.

"That's true," nodded Pearl. Pivoting toward Clint, she said, "Your father was a wonderful man. I didn't make the connection at first, but you favor him. If I remember correctly, your mother died when you were just a baby. Eli took good care of you." She could tell by the look on Clint's face she had touched on a tender spot. She patted his arm, "You take care, young man. Please stay in touch."

"Thank you, ma'am," said Clint. "You do the same. I will stay in touch. You can count on it."

Georgeann followed Pearl, Jules, and Clint to the front of the house. "I will bring the pictures to you. Just tell me when and where to drop them off."

Georgeann pulled Jules off to the side as Clint and Pearl talked on the steps. "Mother has a memory like a steel-trap. Whatever she says, I'm certain, it's accurate. I'm very happy she got to do this. I can tell it has lifted her spirits."

Jules smiled tenderly, "I noticed she's sharp. You are lucky to have her. I lost my mother when I was thirteen. Not a day goes by that I don't think of her."

"I'm sorry to hear that. Mom is a true inspiration in my life," Georgeann replied, touching Jules' arm.

Turning to Pearl, Jules said, "You can deliver whatever Pearl finds to the Salzburg library. Once the article is finished, we'll return everything." They stepped outside to join the others.

Suddenly, Pearl started to chuckle. She had recaptured a moment from the past that had struck her funny bone. Gazing up at Clint, who towered over her, she said, "I remembered your dad was always talking about treasure. Rod would let him go through our change to see if we had taken in any unique coins. Eli collected pennies, nickels, and dimes. Probably what you tried to buy your bread with," she laughed.

"Really? That's fun to know. I am too!" He glanced over at Jules, who was looking everywhere but at him, trying not to make eye contact. Jules was smiling, looking down at her feet, thinking, *How ironic is that?*

Pearl put a hand to her chin. "You know the day of the fire I recall taking in a gold piece Eli would have flipped over. It was a beauty." Her brows creased as if remembering. "Rod told me to save it for Eli. To put it under the cash register drawer. Rod was going to give it to your father when he returned. As a Christmas gift." Pearl's face turned grief-stricken. "Rod was so worried about Eli."

Jules turned to Clint in shock. Their faces conveying the same message, *This might be the clue we've been hoping for.*

"How did you come into possession of that?" asked Clint with heightened fascination.

"Oh, one of the locals brought it in. A real numbskull." Pearl made a *crazy* sign with her finger at the side of her head. "A twenty-dollar gold coin dated in the late 1800s he thought was only worth twenty dollars. Wanted to pay for his groceries with it. I called Rod. He didn't know what to do, so he told me to accept it, and later he would talk to the guy."

Inside Clint's head, lightbulbs were flashing. "You wouldn't happen to remember the guy's name. Would you?" Then he added, as nonchalantly as possible, "Did Rod take the coin?"

Pearl frowned, trying to recall. "Oh yes, Rod said to. It was in the cash register the last I saw." She closed her eyes. "I'll never forget his face or name. Luke McCauley, it was—one nasty piece of work! Drove me nuts flipping that stupid Ace of Spade's cigarette lighter of his off and on repeatedly. Can you believe he blew smoke in my face?" She pursed her lips. "Always in an upheaval, causing trouble. Nothing but a smart-mouthed blowfish!"

Chapter 53
Missing Evidence

During the evening, Pearl's words echoed in Clint's mind. *It was in the cash register, the last I saw. I'll never forget his face or name, Luke McCauley. One nasty piece of work.*

Clint and Jules discussed at great length how Pearl's information had shed a whole new light on their inquiry. Confusion roiled as their attention shifted from the fire to the gold coin Luke McCauley had used to pay for groceries.

Luke McCauley was the second victim found in Goss Cave. Clint could not get it out of his head that he just happened to be in the store the same day it burned. *Always in an upheaval, causing trouble,* was how Pearl described him.

A restless night followed.

9 a.m., Wednesday, October 15

Georgeann called first thing Wednesday morning to say she would be dropping her mother's photos off at the library at 11 a.m. Pearl had located six in all.

As soon as Clint hung up the phone, he called Jules. "How soon could you be ready?" he asked when she answered.

"When would you like for me to be ready?" She laughed. "At the moment, I'm in my nightgown but can be out the door in forty-five."

"I don't mean to rush you, but I thought we could stop by Josie's for breakfast before going to the library. Georgeann called and said she would have the photos to Bonnie by 11 a.m."

"That's perfect."

"There's another development you'll be interested in. Scott left a message on my phone last night saying he had found the original file describing the fire. Plus, he has additional photographs."

"Whoa… sounds like things are falling into place."

"Hope so because I had another one of my weird dreams last night."

"Tell me," Jules coaxed, curious about the dream.

"Nothing much really, other than I saw Rod standing outside the display window at Rod's New and Used Books. It was like he was waiting for me. There was a long silence, then he said, "That was it."

"Clint, has it ever occurred to you the bookstore is less than thirty feet from where Rod's General Store was? And, the two places where Rod's energy seems to be concentrated are at the bookstore and your place. We know why he was on your property—to help you find your father's remains. But why do I get the impression the proximity of the bookstore is important?"

"Jules, you're right," Clint readily agreed. "There must be a correlation between my father's death and the fire. The problem, for me, is how do they tie together? This whole affair seems more complicated than I first thought."

"It's an enigma. That's for sure," she said, ready to hang up. "I'll be ready by ten til."

Clint turned the Camaro engine over, never getting tired of its throaty sound. Gary's memory traveled along with him. Clint loved everything about the car. His only regret was it had taken him so long to start driving it.

Over breakfast, they charted out their next moves. Clint mentioned he had thoughts pertaining to his new will but didn't mention what they were. They had additional 1953 reports to review. One was submitted by Lieutenant Alex Freeman, dated the afternoon of the fire. The other, a report Scott had uncovered at the fire department. His message indicated Clint could stop by the station at his convenience to pick up the extra copies.

Chapter 53

Bonnie came outdoors to deliver Pearl's folder containing remarks and photographs of the 1953 incident. Georgeann shared with Bonnie, when she dropped the folder off, that her mother had gone home the night of Clint and Jules' visit and made detailed observations and comments about the blizzard and fire.

When they pulled away, Clint texted Scott to let him know they were on their way. Five minutes later, Clint and Jules were standing outside his open office door.

"Hey, Clint. Jules…" said Scott when he heard the knock on the doorframe. He jumped up and walked to the opposite side of his desk. "Please, have a seat." He gestured at the two vacant chairs.

At the file cabinet, he withdrew a large, sealed envelope. "Here you go," he said handing the envelope over to Clint. "All you need to do is sign for it. Didn't see much there, but maybe something will surface. Even though I made copies, I prefer to have the original back."

Clint nodded. "If nothing else, a different viewpoint might hold value. How closely did you examine them?"

"Like I would any document." Scott glanced over at Jules. "Pretty routine stuff."

"One thing did catch my eye. An officer reported that Rod Radcliff had requested to see him on the day of the fire." Scott looked at Clint over his glasses. "Said he had information concerning Eli Reeves' disappearance. When Detective Edward Joseph pressed the issue, Radcliff said he preferred to speak face to face. Didn't want to discuss it over the telephone. Joseph made a side note stating Rod seemed agitated."

"Is that right?" Clint's ears perked up. "Are you okay if I review the report while I'm here in your office? The photographs you have are remarkably clear."

"Sure, help yourself. I've not studied them. You never know about cold cases. What one officer doesn't see, another one does."

"In your line of work, it helps to have a trained eye." Clint sifted through the photographs. Nothing unusual stood out. The burned inner structure of the building was charred beyond recognition, except for the cash register that sat in the middle of the rubble with the door open. The photograph was as expected—a total loss. The paper money had been reduced to ashes. Only the coins remained."

"Thanks, Scott," said Clint

"Excuse me a minute," said Scott stepping into the hallway to speak to a colleague.

When he returned, Clint asked, "Still planning to stop by this Friday?"

"Wouldn't miss it for the world." He grinned. "What time?"

"When I leave the lawyer's office, I'll give you a buzz. If I had to guess, I'd say around two-thirty or three. That'll give me time to get settled in."

"Good timing. Fridays around here are typically laid back. Can't promise but that time should work."

"Can I keep these for the time being?" asked Clint pointing to the files.

"You'll need to sign it out," Scott said, pointing only to the top file. "Later, I'll make copies for you to keep if you'd like."

"Thanks, that would be great. I'll give them back on Friday."

With a heavy burden hanging over his head, Clint turned to Jules with a request. "Would you be all right if we went over this stuff at your place? I feel like there is more here to study but to be honest, I don't want to do it at my house." Clint's expression revealed his inner turmoil. "Too close to the source."

"Of course," answered Jules. "I was going to suggest it anyway. Stop by the store. I'll pick up a pound of hamburger and some buns. Hamburger sandwiches and seasoned fries make a fine, healthy meal," she joked.

"Just what the doctor ordered," laughed Clint. "We'll spread all of it out on the table and go through it with a fine-tooth comb. If you want, we could just pick hamburgers up at Josie's to save you the work."

Chapter 53

Jules recoiled. "I'd rather make them. I haven't had an old-fashioned hamburger and French fries since I can't remember when."

After stopping by the grocery, they headed home. Pulling into the drive, Clint leaned over. "Thanks, Jules, for making everything easier. I can't imagine going through this without you."

She squeezed his hand. "Things do seem to flow between us. Don't they?" She was afraid to say much more. Other than, "We are great pals. Good for each other."

"I guess that is one way to describe us." He laughed, lessening his tension. In his head, he was thinking, *She's a lot more than that. I don't know what I would have done without her over these last couple of months. She's my rock!*

Inside, Jules went straight to work at frying hamburgers, one for her and two for Clint, along with seasoned wedged potatoes. After dinner, they sat at the table scouring through the evidence and photographs that dealt with the blizzard of 1953 and the fire and ultimate destruction of Rod's General Store.

They would examine the fire department's account of the incident, the official police report with photos, Alex Freeman's statement, Detective Joseph's two reports, and Pearl's comments and photos before the night was done.

Clint felt let down that nothing in the stack clearly stood out as significant. *Somewhere in these papers and pictures, the rest of the story is written*, he told himself feeling convinced a piece of the puzzle was missing.

With a full pot of coffee, the two amateur sleuths got to work. They took separate stacks of papers from the folder Scott had loaned Clint and dug in. As the hours flew by, Jules and Clint grew weary. High expectations waned when nothing substantial leaped from the pages to set them in a new direction. With the last of the pot drained, the insight they had been hoping to find, evaporated.

Same as Scott, the only thing that snagged his attention was a handwritten notation on the top left-hand corner of Detective

Joseph's report. Worthy of mention, Joseph had written a curious remark that was found nowhere else in the files. It read: *"Rod has vital information regarding Eli Reeves' disappearance."* The entry suggested that Joseph had intended to drop by the general store the evening the fire broke out. Joseph's next words were haunting: *"I might have prevented this senseless tragedy, and saved Radcliff's life, had we kept our appointment."*

Clint read every word of the lengthy note closely. Detective Joseph had gotten tied up at work and couldn't break away as planned. When he called Rod to say he was running late, Radcliff told Joseph what he had to report could wait until Monday. Moreover, Rod thought he might be coming down with the flu. If he felt better the next day, they could possibly meet at the café for coffee and a chat. Otherwise, it would be Monday.

Clint pondered what he had read. *Sadly, the next day was too late*, he muttered.

Pearl's photos drew significant interest. The cash register, in one photo, stood open with no visible contents other than coin currency.

Clint was surprised to find, in yet another report, mention of salvaged items collected from the debris site. Although referenced, the itemized account was not attached. The list was missing from the report. He wondered where the articles had been stored. Clint made a mental note to ask Scott about it on Friday.

Chapter 54
The Devil in the Details
Thursday, October 16

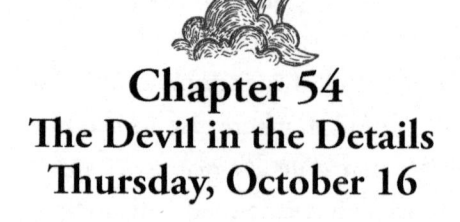

"I located one extra report in a file cabinet down in the basement," Scott informed Clint over the phone. "Sorry, I didn't think to check the evidence room before we met the last time. We archive hardcopy recovery logs down there. Could be a few additional photographs, never know."

Scott took a sip of cold coffee and opened the folder to peer at the first page. "I haven't taken a thorough look at the file yet. The cause of the fire might be addressed in more depth. In terms of the fire being accidental or not, I mean. Ignitable liquids detected at the scene would be cited if found.

"I'd like to check one other location. It's on Manchester."

"Great! When could I have a look at this file?"

Scott squinted at the clock on the wall. "You available at 9 a.m.?"

"Yes!"

"Then how about you meet me at 789 Manchester Avenue. That's where we keep offsite records. Physical paper trails aren't as reliable as computer files. When information is kept in boxes or bags, evidence often gets lost or misplaced. Can be intentional."

"It'll only be me. Jules is at the diner today."

"Okay, I'll see you at 9 a.m."

At 10:30 a.m., Clint walked into Josie's Diner carrying a second file Scott had loaned him. The contents were signed out for twenty-four hours. Sitting at a table, as far from customers as possible, Clint took extra care not to expose the pages he planned to inspect.

The Devil in the Details

After his coffee was poured, he began to scan through the stack of materials for important clues. The folder Pearl had contributed to their endeavor sat on the table off to the side, separate from the police and fire department reports.

In Scott's latest report, Clint found a photo of the cash register sitting in charred remains, nearly identical to the one Pearl had taken. The rubble and fragments in the second photo were sickening to see. He observed the photo. Something wasn't right. He slipped Pearl's photo out from her file to compare the two. After concentrating closely, Clint concluded it was nothing more than the angle from which the shot had been taken.

When Jules sat down, the focus changed. "Good morning," she greeted him. "What are we looking at?"

"Oh." He smiled, "I'm just comparing a police photo of the cash register to Pearl's. Scott gave me two extra folders, one from the Evidence Room at the police station and one from an offsite location over on Manchester where physical evidence from cold cases is kept."

"May I see?" she inquired.

"Sure," he replied by sliding the photos to her side of the booth. "At first, I thought the cash register in this picture appeared different from Pearl's." He tapped on the police photo. "The paper bills have been scorched beyond recognition. Even so, the coins are still in the till. Just a different angle, I suppose."

Jules frowned, cocking her head. She looked up, making eye contact, and pointed to the drawer from the police report. "What's this?"

Not sure to what she was referring, Clint said, "What do you mean?"

"Look at Pearl's picture. Now look at this one," Jules replied, directing his attention to the police photo. "Is that the twenty-dollar gold piece Pearl told us about?"

Clint lifted the police photo close to his face. His eyes widened. "What an eye. I think it is!"

Chapter 54

"Looks like it to me." She grinned, delighted for having made the discovery. "I'll go get Patrick's magnifying glass. He keeps one in his desk to check for phony bills."

Clint watched Jules rush into the kitchen behind the swinging door. In a shake, she was back at the table. Under the magnifying glass, the coin in the police photo stood out. The Liberty Head gold coin in the drawer was distinguishable. Remarkably different from the other coinage.

"That is no ordinary coin. No wonder Pearl took exception to it," Clint commented, amazed by its brilliance.

Big as life, the coin Pearl described that Luke McCauley had used to pay for his groceries was in one photo but not the other.

Jules studied the police photo. "I'd say, even from my vantage point, the coin is like nothing I've ever seen before."

"I guess," exclaimed Clint, taking the photos back from Jules to examine them more closely. Setting the two pictures side by side, he said, "The drawer is open a bit wider in Pearl's photo, and the coin definitely isn't in the register."

"That's because I don't believe it is," proclaimed Jules. "I have a hunch!"

"Okay," He held up his hand. *"Don't tell me!"* said Clint excitedly. "If the coin was there when the police first arrived on the scene but was not there when Pearl took her picture in the morning, it was removed from the cash register sometime between those hours."

"Exactly." Jules' face beamed, certain they were on the right track.

"Do you suppose one of the firemen or police officers could have taken it?" suggested Clint. "I mean like stole it?"

"It's possible," Jules answered. She put a hand to her chin. "People steal all the time, Clint. Just ask Patrick. So, I suppose it's possible."

She examined the café to see if any of the customers needed a fill-up on their drinks. Convinced they were content, she swiveled back around. "Since it was an extremely valuable item, do you

The Devil in the Details

think it was taken out of the drawer and put into evidence? Possibly placed there for safekeeping. In a different location than you and Scott looked?"

Clint considered what she had said. "No, I don't think so. This morning Scott and I went through those things. Truthfully, the physical evidence looked more like trash. Anything of importance is right here. This is what we have to go on."

He put his hand on the file. "This report specifically states the fire was ruled an accident, resulting from Rod's smoking." Clint fanned his hands. "That's what they concluded. Rod was at fault. An easy assumption to leap to, considering he was a chain smoker. It was as if the case was being pushed in that direction. Nothing else was contemplated."

"Well, if that is true, it's a shame. Because from every indication, he sounded like a nice fella. He deserved to have his death investigated," Jules scowled. "My guess is the coin was pocketed. Considering its value, I'm not surprised. Especially in those days. Not as many checks and balances back then."

"Yeah, that's my feeling too. I can understand the temptation."

Jules gave the diner a quick once-over. Several people were looking around, probably needing their waitress, she imagined. "Better get back to work. Duty calls!"

"Thanks for walking through this with me," Clint said, noticing the patrons were stirring. "Can we hook up later?"

"Absolutely!" Jules answered, waving goodbye from behind her back.

Clint switched to iced tea and settled in. Thumbing through the statements one final time, he glanced over at Pearl's photo. Something caught his eye. A crystalline moment materialized when an object Clint had not noticed before was seen. Near the edge, barely in the photo, an object triggered clarity. A pivotal mistake had been made, coming full circle. The presence of this one simple item would alter history.

Chapter 54

Clint dialed Scott. On the third ring, he answered. Clint said, "Hey, you got a minute?"

"Yeah, what's up?"

"I uncovered a couple of things you might want to check out."

"Is that right? Lay 'em on me." Scott chuckled, knowing it had to do with the files he had signed out to Clint. "You're just full of surprises these days."

"I surprise even myself," chuckled Clint. "If you don't mind, I'd rather speak in person. I need to show you, rather than tell you. It could be an important turning point in the case. I'm over at Josie's. Could you join me? If not, I'll be glad to come over there?"

"No, I'll come to you. I need a break anyway."

Clint couldn't believe he hadn't made the connection before. The object he had identified in one of the photos gave credence to the theory the fire wasn't an accident but, in fact, arson.

When Scott entered the diner, customers immediately stopped what they were doing and looked up. A uniformed officer never failed to stop people in their tracks.

"I'm so glad to get out of that place," stated Scott as he slid into the booth. "It's been a ridiculous day." He waved at Jules when he noticed her looking at him.

Knowing her customers like the back of her hand, Jules carried a large cherry coke and a plate of fries to the table. "How's it going?" she asked, extending a gracious smile.

"Exhausted," Scott offered in a one-word reply. "It's one of those days." He shook his head in frustration. "Domestic squabbles and fights that require intervention seem to be every other call. On payday Friday, varmints—like we are playing Whac-A-Mole—raise their annoying heads."

Scott grinned at his analogy. Sitting across from Clint, he raised a brow. "What's on your mind?"

Clint answered in a flash. "Plenty." He looked over at Jules. "Can you stick around for a second?"

The Devil in the Details

Jules scanned the room. "Sure."

Clint locked eyes with Scott. "You will have to be the judge, but I think I might have found the game changer. I was looking at these photos." He pushed all three across the table. "The one you gave me this morning and the other two Pearl's daughter, Georgeann, dropped off yesterday."

He searched Scott's face and saw he was, without question, intrigued. "I shared earlier that we conducted an interview with Pearl. In 1953 she was a cashier at Rod's General Store. She now resides in Chambersburg. "Well, between her photos and yours, there is a telling discrepancy."

He gazed up at Jules, who was standing behind Scott. "Pearl told Jules and me Luke McCauley had come into the store the day of the fire. He had tried to pay for his groceries with a twenty-dollar Liberty Head gold coin, believing it to be worth twenty dollars."

Scott had zoned into Clint's every word. "Yeah, I remember," he said. "Pearl said she didn't know if Rod would accept it or not, so she called to get his permission."

"Exactly." Clint glanced at the photos. "If you look hard, you'll notice the gold coin is in the cash register drawer in the police photo, but not in Pearl's. This means either a policeman or fireman took it from the drawer after the photo was taken or someone else did later. Pearl told us the next morning the place was taped off. She stepped over the tape to take photos."

Scott lifted the photographs. Before he could comment, Clint extended his hand as if to say, "*Wait.*"

"I considered the fact someone might have stolen it," Clint said. "I'm certain now that wasn't the case."

"Why are you so convinced?" asked Jules.

"Well, according to Pearl, she took both photos that morning. From different angles." Clint pushed Pearl's second photo toward Scott's side of the table. "This one is from a slightly different angle. It shows something that's not in the other two."

Scott examined all three photos with an expert eye. "What am

Chapter 54

I looking for? They all look pretty much the same."

"Jules," Clint exclaimed, "you're going to love this! I can't believe we both missed it. Check out the photo. Tell me what you see?"

She leaned over Scott's shoulder for a better view and concentrated deeply.

"On the left side of that one," Clint pointed. "Do you see it?"

Scott lifted the image to a foot of their faces.

Clint grinned when the look on Scott's face didn't change, but Jules' did.

She wailed, "Oh my God, Clint. It's the lighter! The one with the Ace of Spades engraved on it! The lighter Pearl told us about."

Scott appeared baffled as if to say, *What am I missing here*? "Fill me in, please," he requested.

"I was expecting that." Clint chortled. "When we interviewed Pearl, she told us Luke had a cigarette lighter he kept opening and closing, like a nervous habit. Drove her nuts with it. Walking up and down the aisles, then to the counter. He played with it constantly.

"Why is that so important," Scott questioned.

"Bear with me," Clint politely said. "Pearl stated Luke had gotten extremely irritated with her when she informed him she couldn't accept his gold coin for payment without checking with Rod first. She needed Rod's permission. Then to make matters worse, she told him he couldn't smoke indoors, and he'd have to put his cigarette out!"

Scott looked confused. "So what does that have to do with the fire? I don't get it."

"The point is… Luke got livid with her, went outdoors with his groceries, sat them down by the entrance, and lit up. Pearl recalled, clear as day, the insignia on Luke's lighter. It was the Ace of Spades."

Clint's features grew dark. He studied Scott's watchful eyes, then said, "So, the question is, why would Luke's lighter be found in the ashes, among the fire debris? Unless… he was in the store after hours. My suspicion is exactly that. He was in the general store after Rod had locked up for the night and had gone to bed. In there while Rod was asleep. Pearl said Rod told her he was going to retire early that evening."

Eyes shifted. "That's a good question," Scott said in agreement. "But dead men don't tell tales. Do they? Luke is the second body you discovered in the cave. Remember? It's not like he's alive, and we can ask him. Not like Pearl."

"Yeah," stated Clint. "Here's another hypothesis," he conjectured. "We've established Luke didn't die the same day as my father. What I think happened was this, he murdered my dad and then crawled out of the cave and went home. He must have gone back sometime later. That's when he encountered the puma." Clint raised a brow, "I know it sounds ludicrous, but I propose the puma was waiting for him to return." He glanced over at Jules, "What a puma was doing that deep inside the cave system has only one answer, in my mind. He was there for a purpose. Revenge. Plain and simple, an eye-for-an-eye."

Scott shook his head, trying to absorb what Clint had suggested. "You do realize that is a totally unnatural behavior for a puma. I could see one dragging its prey into an opening, but not that far from an entrance." He turned contemplative, "However, your theory fits the violent claw marks we found on McCauley's body."

"Sorry guys, but I need to get back to work," Jules regretfully interrupted. Her eyes met Clint's, "You and I need to talk about this after I get off."

Scott chimed in with identical sentiments. "Let me do some checking. See what else I can turn up on Luke McCauley. That dude was one bad ombre. Someone should have taken him out behind the woodshed. Or maybe they did, and that was the problem."

"Thanks," offered Clint, reaching out to shake Scott's hand. "I was hoping you would say that."

"I'll keep you posted," Scott replied as he slid out from the booth. "Like Jules, I've got to get back to the job." He glanced over at Jules, who was taking an order four tables away. He motioned

Chapter 54

for his ticket, but she shook her head, *no*.

"Thank you," he mouthed.

"My pleasure," she countered.

Later that evening, Clint phoned Jules to discuss their meeting with Scott. He also wanted to share his Friday schedule with her. Tied up until after she got off work, his appointment with the attorney was in the morning, and Scott was coming over in the afternoon. He didn't know how long he'd be with Scott but would reach out when he could.

"Okay," she said. "Just call me whenever you have a chance. Sounds like a full day. I wish I could be there to see Scott's face when you show him the alcove full of treasure."

"Yeah, that ought to be fun," chuckled Clint heartily. "I wish you could be there too."

"There's no rest for the wicked." She teased. "Would you like me to fix dinner tomorrow?"

"Depends on what time Scott can break free. I'll text you with an update. We can decide after that."

When Jules disconnected the call, a twinge of uneasiness trickled through her. She suddenly felt vulnerable and could not understand why. With respect to Clint, keeping her feelings in check hadn't been easy. After thinking about their conversation in more depth, she settled on her hesitation concerning his tone of voice baseless and had more to do with her own insecurities.

What Jules could not have predicted was both of their lives were about to take a dramatic turn.

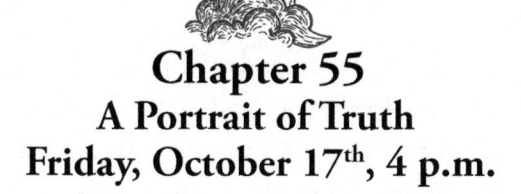

Chapter 55
A Portrait of Truth
Friday, October 17th, 4 p.m.

Counsel had given Clint the answers he sought. Although their meeting lasted longer than anticipated, his time had been well-spent. He climbed into the cab of the F-100 with a spring to his step. They were tying up loose ends, and he could now move on to phase two. If anything were to happen to him, his fortune would fall into the right hands.

He thanked the powers that be that Indiana law supported his claim. It was legitimate. The property and treasure were both his. Sullivan had traced the original deed back to repository records that were overlooked when the state processed seizure of the land back in 1996.

Clint had given his permission for the treasure to be relocated to Evansville on Saturday. Sullivan had hand-selected a crew. He had referred to the company at their last meeting. A security team would be on hand to closely monitor the treasure's removal and transport.

On the drive back to Salzburg, Clint phoned Scott. When his call went to the answering machine, he left a message. "Hey, Scott, thought I'd let you know I'll be home in about thirty minutes. You can stop by at your convenience. I'll be waiting."

His second call was to Jules. She answered on the second ring. "Are we still on for dinner?" he asked in an upbeat tone.

"We are! How did the meeting go?" Jules inquired.

"It went well," he answered quickly. "I'll fill you in once Scott leaves. I'm thinking it could be six or seven. Is that okay?"

"Absolutely," she replied. Anxious to hear what Jeremy Sullivan had to say, Jules joked. "I'll leave the light on!"

"Great." Clint chuckled. "I'll text you when I'm headed your way."

Chapter 55

On the way home from Paoli, Clint had intended to pay a visit to Rod's New and Used Books. Nevertheless, he was pressed for time and forced to postpone the trip until Saturday. Clint felt an obligation to convey the truth of what he knew to Rod. It didn't matter if Rod Radcliff, Jr. was the old man's son or grandson. He was owed the details of the events that masked Rod Radcliff, Sr's tragic demise a half-century ago.

On his porch at home, he gazed out into the open field. Scott was expected to arrive any minute. It was getting harder to contain the excitement that was building. Grand plans lay ahead. A daydream visualized in his youth but considered an unrealistic fantasy as an adult was coming true. In his bones, he knew he'd made the right choice.

The shack in the woods will stay right where it is as a reminder of this extraordinary chapter in my life. Preserved for all time. He laughed aloud at his predicament. Still feeling stunned at his good fortune, he contemplated a different future than the one he would have experienced. *Now I can afford to fix this place up properly. Elise would be so pleased with the changes I've got in store.* Amid his daydream, huge changes waited in the wings.

Clint's concentration was broken when he spotted Scott's police car rounding the corner. He watched as Scott pulled into the drive and got out of the squad car wearing a copious grin.

"I've been waiting all day for this!" Scott exclaimed. "Not every day do I get to witness real booty," he howled. Grinning, he said, "Thought it was safer to avoid the *official* word. Just in case."

"Yeah, because most people would think that word meant something else," Clint kidded. "Can't wait to show you. I'll tell you what, it never gets old!" Clint snickered. "I'm not going to make it easy on you, though. I found an easier way in and out, but I'm not telling. We'll use the shack opening going down, and then, on the way out, I'll show you another exit."

"You're on," said Scott displaying his excitement. "I brought a change of clothes." Scott felt like he had reverted to his youth—a nice switch from his day-to-day routine.

The two friends walked shoulder to shoulder across the lawn until they reached the trail at the mouth of the woods. Along the path, they advanced through the denseness of the forest. Since he had been to the shack twice before, Scott didn't need to be shown the way.

The shack's presence loomed large when Clint and Scott turned the bend. Built in the clearing, surrounded by the forest, the shack represented a complicated, entangled story.

Clint passed through the open door, trailed closely by Scott. The closet area had been enlarged by the team who had come in to remove the two human remains. The wall had been knocked out to make the excavation more accessible. They lowered themselves into the hole. Down the ladder they descended until, at last, they were standing in the dank environment of Goss Cave.

Scott switched on his tactical flashlight he carried, which emitted considerably more illumination than Clint's cheaper version. They passed through the corridors of the cave until they reached their intended target.

"You ready for this?" Clint chortled and then added, "I don't think that's possible because I wasn't. I still can't wrap my head around it."

"I'm as prepared as I can be, I suppose," Scott answered in anticipation of what was about to be revealed.

Clint moved to the side. "It's right through there." He pointed to the fissure. "Be warned. It's a tight fit. Good thing you removed all that gear you were wearing."

"Whoa," replied Scott after seeing the space they had to squeeze through to reach the treasure. This time he went first. Soon they were on the other side of the wall standing in an open space surrounded by the Reno Gang's hoard.

Chapter 55

Scott was tongue-tied. His jaw dropped as he stared at what laid before him. Gawking, his eyes could not reconcile what he was looking at. "Are you kidding me?" he shrieked. "This is insane!"

"I know," responded Clint. "Think what it must have been like trying to get all that stuff through that slender opening. Piece by piece is the only way they could have managed it. They couldn't have brought the goods in any other way. It appears to have been enlarged."

"You've got to give it to the gang," Scott sniggered, "they chose an excellent spot to hide their plunder. No wonder it was never found. Those geode stones they used to mark the location was a brilliant choice. A person would have to know what they were looking for. Otherwise, you'd walk right by and never notice a thing. Aligning a few exposed crystal quartzes in strategic places along the path was downright ingenious. A great idea! X—or should I say, crystal quartz—marks the spot," he said with a grin.

Scott turned to Clint, "So now what?" His eyes scanned the piled-up treasure lying at his feet. "I can't imagine how much this stuff is worth."

"I know," Clint said as he picked up one of the heavy gold bars. It had taken two hands to lift it from the ground and hand it to Scott.

"Can you imagine, according to my attorney, it's all mine unless it can be traced back, by serial number or some other means, to the government or person it originally belonged. If we are fortunate enough to find where some of the pieces originated, I'll, of course, return whatever is here to the rightful owner. I should say families because no way would any of the previous owners still be alive today. From what I read, the Reno Gang members were hanged in 1868."

Scott laid the gold bar on the ground. "Holy cow! That thing weighs a ton," he groaned. "At least twenty-five or thirty pounds." He rolled his eyes. "How they transported all this down here and through that opening is inconceivable."

"They had plenty of incentive," Clint jested. He took a handful of coins from the pile. "If I were a betting man, I'd say this is where Luke's gold coin came from. Look at the dates." He handed over a black, tie-string pouch. "Take a look. You won't believe your eyes."

The expression on Scott's face was priceless when he opened the small velvet bag. "Good grief!" he cried in laughter. "How many do you think are here?" he said, looking to the side wall where more bags were heaped.

"I figure at least twenty. I haven't counted them," Clint stated. "That's a lot of diamonds! Makes you wonder how they got their hands on them. You might think a shady acquisition was afoot, ransacked from a shipment possibly."

Scott laughed vigorously. "Yah think?" He sifted his fingers through the loose diamonds and then glanced over at the gold coins. "By the way, did you notice that entire stack of twenty-dollar Liberty Head gold coins is dated 1861? Pretty suspicious, don't you think? The one in the photograph is identical." Scott's forehead creased, thinking through how the Reno Gang could have come into possession of so many coins with the same date. "Train robbery, you reckon? Taken from a transport shipment of uncirculated 1861 Liberty Heads?"

"Who knows," Clint responded, clueless how so many items had found their way to the hideaway. "The coins were minted a few years prior to the hangings, and the band of brothers were famous for train robberies." He examined one of the coins. "This one was minted in Philadelphia. Could be the railroad was moving them from state to state for circulation purposes."

Scott suddenly remembered something he had meant to say when he first arrived. "Hey, I got a call on my way over. David dropped a report off. It's on my desk." His countenance changed. "Guess what? No one reported Luke missing for nearly a month."

Mocking the irony of the situation, Scott added, "What a *gem* he must have been for no one to have noticed he was gone. Pun intended, in case you were wondering," he joked, and then his

Chapter 55

face turned somber. "Rather sad when you think about it. David said articles were retrieved from his residence and later sold at auction. The report didn't list what they were, just that they were transported to a safe location. Apparently, they were kept for years, not knowing if he was alive or dead, before eventually being sold."

"Might provide some insight," remarked Clint, wondering if the coin would be listed among Luke's possessions.

"Just a hunch, but I have this feeling we are going to see a reference to the gold coin," Scott predicted, as though he had read Clint's mind. The dates on a separate cluster of coins were noted. "Every coin in this group is dated 1864," he said handing one over to Clint. "They too appear to be uncirculated." He eyed the collection of separate coins. "The same robbery, you suppose?"

"Who knows," answered Clint. "One thing can be said about those guys, without refute. They were expert thieves and impartial who they stole from."

As they got ready to leave, Scott brought up the process Clint would use for extracting the goods. "I assume you have a secure place to store everything once it's brought up from the cave. It'd better be high security."

"We are talking about a huge sum of valuables," replied Clint, looking at the mounds of objects sitting about. "It's hard to wrap my head around this, to be honest. Not just the cache and hoards of items they stole, but a lifelong riddle has been solved. Clint's face beamed when he said, "Question: Where did the Reno Gang hide their stash of treasure? Answer: Behind a stack of geode rocks in Goss Cave!"

"I know. Crazy, isn't it?" Clint commented. "That I would have discovered the treasure, I mean? I have the old man to thank for that."

Clint glanced at Scott to check his reaction to what he had said. Satisfied that he was on board with the credit given, he added, "My attorney has consulted a retrieval company on my behalf, Bellwether Excavation Services. It would be great if you would help supervise the operation. I'd like to have your opinion on the team Sullivan has selected. Plus, I have a complication I can't avoid. I'm stuck between a rock and a hard place and could use a friend."

"You want me to assist in the retrieval endeavor?" Scott asked with a glimmer of excitement as he rephrased Clint's request. "When are they expected to come out?"

Clint laughed heartily and a little apologetically when he said. "Well therein lies the problem."

Scott pulled a face, "Okay…"

"Sullivan says they will be out tomorrow morning at 8 a.m." Clint grimaced, thinking it would be too short of a notice for Scott. "It turns out that everything worked out better than Sullivan had anticipated. He asked if they could start tomorrow. He wants to move forward as quickly as possible. According to him Bellwether Excavation had a cancelation, and he jumped on it. The next available opening wasn't until a week from next Wednesday. I told him that was fine, but after I hung up remembered I had a conflict. I spaced it. Worst case scenario, I can cancel my plans. It's my fault for speaking too soon."

Scott grinned big. "Doesn't really matter to me. I have tomorrow off, and as far as I know, we don't have anything scheduled. Don't cancel. I'm pleased to assist any way I can." Scott relished the prospect of participating in the operation, and it showed on his face.

"Thanks, Scott. You're a real pal. If it doesn't wrap up within six hours as Sullivan promised, I may have to ask one more favor."

"So, what's the problem?" questioned Scott.

"I had made plans to visit Rusty tomorrow. He needs to know what has been going on before everything hits the fan," stated Clint with concern.

"He doesn't know?"

"No, I haven't told the boys yet," Clint confessed, thinking maybe he should have spoken to them sooner. "It will be great to have a second pair of eyes as they bring the items up and pack them

Chapter 55

into the transport vehicle. My plan is to drive up north to visit the family in the late afternoon. Sullivan told me he didn't expect the operation to take more than six hours. I figure you could be up on ground level while I am in the cave supervising."

"Where is cargo being taken?" asked Scott.

"Oh, I forgot to say. They are moving it to a vault in Evansville."

"Well, if that's the case, I'll go one step further and offer my services with the transport of the cargo. If you like, I'll give them a police escort."

"I swear you must have been reading my mind. My problem is if I'm to be at Rusty's in the late afternoon, I can't follow them to Evansville as I had planned. Sullivan says they are licensed and bonded and have security, but I didn't feel comfortable with not following them and overseeing the treasure being placed into the vault. It's a boots-on-the-ground sort of thing, ya know? Sullivan has the keys and will be there when they arrive."

"Hey, I'll be happy to be your second in command. Don't fret. I'll keep a close eye on things," Scott assured Clint with assurance.

"I can't thank you enough for your kindness, Scott. Maybe I'll take you and the missus out to a steak restaurant when this is all said and done. It will be Jules' and my treat."

"That sounds fantastic. I'll hold you to it," agreed Scott with smiling eyes, thinking Jules was being included in most everything Clint did these days.

"You've taken a load off my shoulders. I've had so much going on lately that I feel like I'm meeting myself coming and going. I know I can trust you, which is a huge relief."

Together they retraced their steps back to the ladder. Clint took the lead. When they came to the junction that led to his grandfather's living quarters, he crawled through the tunnel in that direction.

Scott was caught off guard with the switch, not sure what to think. When they arrived at their destination, he was taken aback, shocked at what he was looking at. The place had a strong earthy smell. "This is where your grandfather lived?" he asked in astonishment. "The place you told me about?"

"Yep. Surreal, isn't it? I figure it was constructed between seventy-five and one hundred years ago. I don't know who occupied it first, my great-grandfather, Earl Reeves or Phil Reeves, my dad's dad. My guess is Phil Reeves lived here. We found remnants of his presence everywhere."

"This is unreal!" Scott said. "How could anyone construct something like this on their own? Must have taken years to complete," he speculated.

"Over there is where Jules found the property deed," Clint said, pointing to the box in the corner. "I took a metal case to the house. It held all sorts of historical documents." He looked around. Waving his hand, he said, "Maps were spread everywhere. Still are. I took two of them."

Scott moved through the rooms, eyeing the papers strewn about. "It's almost as if he, or they, stepped out for a moment and expected to return any minute." The desk chair was pulled out, a pen lying on the map and a half-smoked rolled cigarette in the ashtray. "Creepy to think someone actually lived here, and now they are gone. Weird to be looking into the distant past like this."

"Like Jules said, it looks like a scene right out of *Indiana Jones*," Clint said. "Everything is as we found it, *in situ*... other than the safe box I removed." They made eye contact. "The more I think about it, Scott, the more convinced I am that my father knew this place existed. The maps served in pinpointing the treasure's location. How would he not have known? Considering, Phil Reeves undoubtedly spent time here too. My hunch is Luke McCauley didn't know and wasn't told about it."

"Your life certainly is an adventure nowadays," Scott teased, patting Clint on the back.

"No shit, Sherlock!" he roared with laughter. Then something popped into Clint's head he had yet to address. "By chance, were you able to locate the list of items salvaged from the fire?"

Chapter 55

"We did. Well, let me restate that, David Andrews did," Scott teased knowing David was as curious and knee-deep in uncovering the truth as they were. "It's on my desk. If you get a chance to stop by the station on Monday, we can take a look."

"I certainly can and will," Clint quickly reacted, anxious to have a gander. "I'll buzz you when I'm on my way. On Mondays, I usually eat breakfast at the diner. I'll stop by after that." Clint glanced at his watch, "I should be getting back. A dinner invite awaits."

A faintly upturned smile appeared at the edges of Scott's mouth. Reading between the lines, he said, "Me too. Got to get home. Friday is game night. The kids have us penciled in for Mille Bornes and pizza. Wende makes homemade pizzas. There is nothing like it. She makes one for the kids and one for us. She loads my side up with pepperoni and extra cheese." Scott bragged, "When I get home on Fridays, the place smells like a pizza parlor."

When Scott pulled out of the drive, Clint dialed Jules. "Hey girl," he said in an upbeat tone. "You still my date for this evening?"

"If you'd like to call it that," she replied, enjoying his choice of words. "I made chili and blueberry muffins. I'm all about comfort food on Fridays."

"Perfect, I'll be there in two shakes," he responded, thinking it funny Scott alluded to the same thing.

Later, sitting at the dining room table, they discussed Scott's visit and reaction to the treasure. It was a fun conversation, full of amusement and high spirits. He told her about the missing person's report, filed on Luke a month after the incident in Goss Cave. He also highlighted Luke's possessions were put under lock and key until eventually they were auctioned off. In addition to that, there was a Salvaged Item Report from the fire Clint would have a chance to view on Monday.

"We should ask Pearl what she remembers about any of this," suggested Jules excitedly. "What about Tuesday? We could call and see if she's available."

"Excellent idea," Clint concurred. "When we take her photos back, we'll ask."

Jules patiently awaited the rest of the conversation to resume, hoping Clint would share the details of his morning meeting with his lawyer. To her disappointment, the subject was never broached. Considering the nature of the business he'd conducted, she didn't feel comfortable pressing him on the subject. Especially when it dealt with advice over his newly acquired fortune and Will.

When he left for home, Jules felt confused and somewhat upset. Clint had implied over the phone they'd discuss his attorney's advice at dinner. Still, the part that bothered her most was the feeling he had deliberately withheld the information from her.

At 6:25 a.m., Saturday morning, Clint was already seated at the diner sipping coffee, forking a readymade breakfast, and paging through the newspaper.

When Jules came and sat down across from him, she broke into his reverie. "So, what do you have cooked up for us this weekend?"

A pang of guilt riffled through him. "Sorry, I was going to talk to you about that."

"Oh," she said, not sure what he could mean.

Since Jules worked the weekends, Clint figured this was a good time to make the trip up north. He thought some space would do them both good. "I need to talk to Rusty and Molly to fill them in on what has been going on. I think I'll run up there later on today and stay overnight. Probably won't be back until late tomorrow." Clint thought he saw a flash of disappointment in Jules' eyes.

"That will be nice," she replied sweetly. "It's a gorgeous day for a drive."

"I haven't seen the children for a while, and with all that's been going on, they need to be filled in. They should hear the entire

Chapter 55

story and what Sullivan had to say before the news conference takes place." He chuckled as though he had said something funny.

"Yeah, I agree," Jules said. "Don't want them hearing it on a news broadcast. That would be dreadful!" She grinned awkwardly because Clint hadn't told her the full story either.

"If you are okay with it, I thought I'd stop by on my way home Sunday, say early evening? I could bring a dessert from Cracker Barrel to share. Coffee and cobbler."

Jules looked hesitant. "Sure. Do you have any idea what time?"

"Not really. I'll only stay for an hour at the most."

In Jules' mind, it sounded like Clint was forcing a visit so he wouldn't hurt her feelings.

"Are you sure you want to do that? I'm off Tuesday. We could just get together on Monday night after work or Tuesday, whichever works best. I'll see you at the diner on Monday morning anyways."

When Clint didn't immediately respond, Jules felt she was right. Uncertain what to say next, she added, "It would only be one or two days later." A long silence followed. "Next week, for you, must be busy. With so much going on, I'm sure you have a few irons in the fire."

"Yeah, you could say that." Clint looked preoccupied. "By the time I leave up north, and who knows how long the conversation will take, it might be best." He nodded, "Okay, let's get together Monday, or Tuesday." His handsome face radiated the excitement bubbling below the surface. "Deal?"

"Deal," she said, extending her hand out to shake.

"Initially, I was planning on stopping by the bookstore this morning," he casually mentioned. "But when I called, no one answered. The message said they've changed their hours of operation. Before, they were open all hours. Now it's only open from eleven to two. I'm beginning to wonder if the place is going out of business. It wouldn't surprise me if it did, the way Rod runs it."

A Portrait of Truth

"I have an order up," Jules interrupted abruptly. "Gotta go! Call later if you have time."

She rushed away to address a man with a small child at the opposite end of the diner.

Clint thought about her last comment. *Was there an edge to her voice?* he pondered. *Why wouldn't I have time to call?* He wondered if there was more to her words. He instantly countered the negative thought. *You're overreacting, Clint. Give the woman a break! She's busy!*

He had to admit, there were a lot of moving parts in his life recently, and time was at a premium. *She has a lot on her mind, too. Don't start reading between the lines, you idiot!* he scolded his logical, mature side. *We'll see each other on Monday after work, if not before.*

Clint scooted out from the booth, destined for home. Then it dawned on him that he hadn't had a chance to tell Jules about the treasure being extracted and moved to Evansville. He made a mental note to bring it up when they talked next.

After his meal, he intended to phone Lily. He hoped her desire to visit over fall break remained. He'd run the same question by Trey and Dylan once he was assured of her visit. Clint knew the boys' fall break didn't always coincide with Lily's. When that bit of information was known, Clint would finalize plans.

Scott was expected at his house by 7:45 a.m., and Bellwether Excavation Services was due at 8 a.m. Excitement was building. Soon he'd see the treasure brought up and placed into the transport vehicle. After that it would be relocated to its destination in Evansville. He also felt good about his friend Scott being part of the entourage to make sure it got there safely. He could relax on his way to see his family in Crothersville without worry.

When he arrived home, Scott was already parked out front. He greeted his friend, and they walked inside. While they waited for the retrieval company to show, they chatted. Their faces revealed their eagerness to get started.

Chapter 55

At 8 a.m. sharp, a Bellwether Excavation Services truck pulled into the drive. Two men jumped out. Behind the first truck, another flatbed pulled in. Two additional contractors got out. The project was underway.

Straightaway, Clint greeted the team. He immediately led them to the shack and to the hole that would eventually take them to the treasure. Once the project had begun, Clint and Scott took their respective posts to maintain a close eye on the undertakings. At 3 p.m., seven hours later, Clint's precious cargo had been loaded into the truck and was on its way to Evansville, with Scott leading the procession.

Clint headed north. The time had come to have a conversation with Rusty and Molly in person before things got more involved than they already were. He would call Wade and Clara after that. For his children to hear the incredible news third hand would be shameful on his part. Jeremy Sullivan was taking care of the specifics on where and when the news release would take place. When the treasure was safely housed, the information would be made public.

Since Crothersville was a considerable distance from Salzburg, it made sense to ask Rusty if he could spend the night. During his stay, he would bring them up to speed. Everything had happened so quickly Clint's head was still in a freefall. He had become a very wealthy man—thanks to a gang of thieves.

Chapter 56
Day of Reckoning

On the way to Rusty's, Clint phoned Wade and told him he had something of great importance to share. Life-altering news, to be precise.

"I don't know if you can swing it or not, but when Lily comes over for fall break, could you and Clara join her? Take a couple of days off?" he asked. "I talked to Lily. She said you approved her visit. I'd gladly pay for an airline chaperon to assist her if you can't make it. At fifteen, they tell me she no longer needs one, but I'd feel better if she had supervision."

"Yes, we were happy about her visit. It's possible, I suppose, but I'd have to check with the wife," Wade responded, a man of few words. "Thanks for the offer. I'll have to get back with you about the flight."

"Truth is some events have transpired that you need to be made aware of," Clint said with some urgency to his voice. "In other words, we need to talk. Sooner than later and in person. That's why I asked for the extra time." He nervously chuckled. "And, before you start trying to figure out what I am referring to… no, I did not get married. I'll nip that one in the bud."

Together they laughed in unison because they both knew that was exactly what Wade was thinking. "Thank you for clearing that up, Dad," Wade chuckled. After a short hesitation, Wade added, "Not that I'd object, mind you. Just to make things clear."

"I know, son. You have always supported me. But what I have to say is momentous, and on a scale I can't even absorb. You could guess for the rest of your life and not figure this one out."

"Okay, now you've got my attention!" Wade reacted with a snort, noticeably stumped with the conversation. "I'll see what I can do. I'll give you a call tomorrow to let you know what I've worked out. How long will you be at Rusty's?"

Chapter 56

"Until midafternoon tomorrow," answered Clint.

"Okay, Dad, I'll give you a ring in the morning," Wade said. "Love you, Dad!"

Wade's sentiments were mirrored. When the call ended, Clint grinned because he knew when he had claimed, *You could guess for the rest of your life and not figure this one out*, it was accurate to the nth degree. Finding the Reno Gang treasure would never be on anyone's radar.

Rusty, Molly, Trey, and Dylan met Clint outside as he was exiting the Camaro. The boys hugged him so hard he thought they might break a rib.

"I'm glad to be here," Clint said cheerfully, moving toward his son.

"Us too, Grandpa," said Dylan, with Trey chiming in behind him.

"Mom says you might stay overnight with us," whooped Trey. "Can we play Spoons? I love that game!"

The group laughed robustly, aware of how violent the game of Spoons could get when people started pulling spoons from the center of the table after one of them had been removed. The indication was someone was out of cards. Which, in turn, started a chain reaction of anxiously grabbing for the remaining spoons. With more people than spoons, someone was going to be eliminated.

"You're on, young man! That is if mom and dad aren't too scared to accept our challenge." Clint winked at Molly.

The family went inside. Trey carried Clint's bags to the guest room before joining everyone in the kitchen. After a short while, the boys drifted down the hall to the family room to finish the video game they had put on pause.

Hot from the oven, Molly withdrew a pan of cinnamon rolls and set them on the stovetop to cool. She poured a round of coffee and placed the carafe, along with a pitcher of fresh cream and a bowl of sugar, on the table between them. Grown-up talk was at hand. Molly sat down on Rusty's side of the table and folded her hands.

Across from Clint two expectant faces stared. His children's lives were about to experience a serious course-correction. "Of late," Clint opened the conversation, "life has been like a roller coaster ride. Since all of you were at the house in September, much has transpired." He giddily qualified, "The treasure hunt seems to have started an avalanche of shocking events." He shook his head in disbelief that it had not even been a month.

Clint had a difficult time keeping his jubilation under wraps, especially since he knew the treasure was en route to Evansville. He jumped right in, filling in the blanks of his prefaced remarks. When he was finished, he asked them if they had any questions or comments.

Rusty's and Molly's faces were amusingly animated. Rusty's jaw had dropped, and Molly's eyes had grown huge.

Clint explained the situation and where he stood momentarily, in terms of the treasure's extraction and arranging a proper funeral for Eli—and the puma, who had died alongside him.

When asked about the spirit that haunted his property, Clint told a partial truth. *No need to worry the kids*, decided Clint. *Besides, now that the mystery and treasure have been solved, the old man has surely been released from what had kept him tied to Salzburg.*

Unable to pin his suspicions down and without proof to back them up, Clint carried an uneasiness that Rod Radcliff, Sr.'s spirit, remained in Salzburg. He sensed Rod waiting in the wings and watching from the shadows. Clint realized his feelings were unfounded because he hadn't seen any sign of Rod for a long while. The problem was he could feel him.

The night had been a pleasurable one. Molly served baked hen with mashed potatoes and gravy, corn-on-the-cob, green beans, and yeast rolls. The conversation at the table turned lively, with the grandsons acting up and showing off. Afterward, while Molly and

Chapter 56

the boys tidied up, Clint and Rusty took a stroll through the field behind the house.

"I have no clue how this thing is going to shake down, but I do know this. The press will be on it lickety-split." He turned to face his son. "When they ask me how I stumbled onto the treasure… what will I say?" He joked, "A ghost led me to it?"

"That would be a story in and of itself!" Rusty stated, his voice laced with humor. "You have a lot of decisions to make, Dad. The treasure alone should keep you busy. Until the novelty has died down, you'd better be on your toes. Find a place to lay low is my suggestion. Like that hideaway, you told us about."

"It's funny you say that." Clint cracked a smile. "Because that is exactly what Jules advised."

After his grandsons had gone to bed, Clint, Molly, and Rusty talked a short while before they too turned out the nights.

The next morning Clint was up early. He had slept well and woke up refreshed. When he entered the kitchen, the coffee was already brewing, but no none was around. The pot, he figured, must have been set to activate at 6:45 a.m. He poured a cup and sat down. Shortly thereafter, the family began to file in one by one, sleepy-eyed and ready to eat.

Rusty hugged his father. "Good morning. I hope you slept well."

"Very well. Thank you. Didn't wake up once. That's unusual for me." Clint moved to where Molly was standing at the sink. "So, how are you this morning?" he asked, offering her a hug as well. "I'd like to make the eggs if that's all right by you."

Molly grinned at Rusty. "I love it when a man insists on being a chef in *my* kitchen." She hugged her father-in-law and said, "That would be great, Dad," she said to Clint. "While you do that, I'll put some ham in the skillet and biscuits in the oven."

Breakfast was leisurely served. Once again, the family conversation turned animated, with Trey and Dylan acting excited to have their grandfather at the table. When the boys excused themselves, the discussion swung from normal life activities to the treasure in Goss Cave.

Then, just as Clint was grabbing the coffee pot to refill their cups, his cell phone rang. He grinned when he saw the caller ID. "It's Wade. Do you mind if I take the call in the bedroom? I'd like to tell him what I told you yesterday."

"Sure, no problem," replied Rusty. "Boy is he in for a big surprise." He put his hand to his head. "He's not going to believe this one."

Molly and Rusty returned to the kitchen with plenty to mull over. They stared across the table at each other without speaking. No words were necessary; what they were thinking was evident.

When Clint emerged from the bedroom, he was wearing a grin. He strolled into the kitchen and announced, "That was a fun conversation." He chuckled and pointed at Rusty, "Wade wants you to call him."

"I bet he does." Rusty sniggered.

When they walked outdoors, Rusty gave Clint a promise to let the boys visit during fall break. The hope was Wade and Clara would be able to share some quality time with Rusty and Molly while Clint had the grandkids.

On the drive home, Clint's mind journeyed back to the night of the fire and what it must have been like. The tragedy played out in his mind. A visceral reaction arose–Rod had suffocated. Ultimately, he suffered a horrible death. Worse yet, in Clint's opinion, he was unjustifiably blamed for setting the fire. It made Clint angry because, in his heart, he believed Luke McCauley was behind the devastation that took place. By killing Rod, Luke had silenced him. The unfairness of that, if it were true, cut deep.

Clint said sorrowfully, "Poor Rod. No one should suffer what he went through." Wiping a tear from his cheek, Clint had to blink to see the road.

Chapter 56

Thinking he needed a diversion, he dialed Jules. On the third ring, she answered. Pleased to hear her voice, Clint softly said, "Glad you answered. Do you have a minute to talk?"

"Sure," she replied in an upbeat tone.

Clint recapped the highlights of his trip and how he had been battered in a game of Spoons with his family.

Jules found his description of the game hilarious. "I'm glad you went to see the family. You needed to spend time with them," Jules commented when Clint had finished highlighting his visit. "The kids ought to be prepared for the tsunami that could be headed their way." She thought about the news media and how they swarm the people they focus on. "Things might not settle down for a while."

"You're not kidding. I have no idea what to expect when the news is released. Could get crazy!" Clint confessed.

They had only talked a short while when Jules interrupted Clint, stating she needed to get back to work. When she said goodbye, she reminded Clint his table would be ready at Josie's the next morning at his usual time. Unless she heard otherwise.

Clint assured Jules he'd be there. The moment they hung up, a disturbing thought crossed his mind. *I forgot to tell Jules about the treasure! That it was moved today.* He felt disappointment. *I meant to bring it up but forgot again.* He made himself a promise. *I'll tell her tomorrow.* He pulled to the side of the road and jotted down a reminder on a yellow sticky-note, and attached it to his dash.

As soon as Clint had hung up with Jules, he phoned Scott. Curious how things had gone that afternoon, Scott assured him everything had moved along smoothly without a hitch. Jeremy Sullivan had been in Evansville when they arrived and had made certain protocol was followed, down to the letter. Clint was relieved by Scott's assessment of the operation.

Sullivan had Clint's Power of Attorney. He could not have been more grateful that he had signed it over to him.

Day of Reckoning

By the time Clint had reached his residence, he was past ready to get out of the car. He walked into the house and immediately plopped down on a kitchen chair. He had only been in the car for an hour and a half and shouldn't haven't felt so exhausted. Nevertheless, he was.

After a few minutes, he got up and strolled to the back of the house to the mudroom. He walked outside and stood in the cool autumn breeze, gazing at the forest, aware… no longer did the Reno Gang treasure lay hidden in Goss Cave. Clint's fortune had been relocated to Evansville. He mused, *I bet Dad would be beside himself if he knew I located the treasure he had searched for so long.* A triumphant grin appeared on his face.

A decision was made, midday, start of the week, he would stop by the bookstore to disclose what he knew about Rod Radcliff, Sr.'s death and Luke McCauley's involvement in the general store fire. Rod Radcliff, Jr. was owed the truth.

What he had uncovered wasn't 100 percent provable; not yet, but he trusted his instincts would soon be validated. The files that sat on Scott's desk were expected to reveal the real story behind what happened the night of December 26, 1953, and, as a result, confirm Clint's theory. In his opinion, the common denominator between the incident and the actions that led up to it was the perpetrator, Luke McCauley. Rod, Jr. was the only person fully capable of appreciating the gravity of Clint's knowledge.

The only question that remained was why Rod would speak of Rod Radcliff, Sr. as if he were still alive. The man died in 1953! The truth was when it came to Rod Radcliff, Jr., little made sense.

Monday Morning, October 20

The next morning at 5:45, Clint was out of bed and dressed. The night before his mind just wouldn't turn off. Drinking coffee in

Chapter 56

the kitchen, he thought about the busy week ahead. With less than five hours under his belt, coffee was a need, not a want.

Sullivan had left a message on Clint's voicemail to say that he had penciled in a luncheon for Tuesday at 1 p.m. to address the proposal Clint had brought up in an earlier conversation. "Please call to confirm," he requested. "Your possessions are securely housed in Evansville. I'll bring you up to speed at our meeting."

Clint was nervous and excited simultaneously. Whether or not his idea took wings was yet to be determined. Various moving parts were involved in the outcome. Aware the stars would have to be aligned perfectly to pull off his proposition, Clint held his breath in anticipation.

For the umpteenth time, his attention circled back to Rod, Radcliff, Jr. The bookstore wasn't open last Saturday when he dropped by, which forced Clint to postpone his conversation until today. He'd hoped to catch Rod in. If not today, he'd do it Tuesday. Clint desperately wanted to run a proposal by Rod regarding a project he had in mind. Since the store appeared to be struggling anyhow, hopefully, Rod would be receptive to his brainstorm.

He also planned to drive to Chambersburg to return Pearl's photographs and notes. Speaking to her one on one was paramount because what they had to talk about was of a private nature. The latest information about the case would be shared, plus he'd explain how valuable her photographs had been in arriving at the truth. Clint felt confident that once Pearl was briefed on the police reports if anything more came to mind, she would say.

Exuberant they had reconnected after all these years, Clint was excited to pay her a visit. Clint could tell the feeling was mutual. He could hear it in her voice. It was as if the past had just melted away. Her generosity and loving embrace all those years ago were commendable. He vividly recalled the first night he spent at her home and how frightened he had been. The memory lingered. He could never forget, nor ever repay her kindness.

Day of Reckoning

After his chat with Pearl, a short, unexpected visit to Jeremy Sullivan's office would be planned. Clint hoped he was in. Although they had a meeting scheduled for the next day, he preferred not to wait. He wanted to hear in more detail about how things had gone on Saturday.

The police station was his first stop of the day after breakfast. He was highly anticipating getting a collective peek at the Salvaged Item Report from Rod's General Store and the other information that had not been available at their last meeting.

When Clint entered Josie's Diner, Jules' face lit up. Her smile brightened the room. Later an excuse would be made to explain why she had not been invited to participate in today's visit with Pearl. He knew if he'd asked, she might have taken time off. He could share the rest of today's agenda with her but not that. He'd disclose it after the fact.

When Jules approached his booth, Clint cheerfully asked, "Hey, how does pizza sound for tonight? On Friday, Scott talked about having pizza. I haven't been able to stop thinking about it. While I'm in Paoli. I could stop by Capozzi's."

"That sounds wonderful," she answered. "My place or yours?"

"Your place. Will six o'clock work?"

"It does," she replied. With the diner packed, business was booming. Steadily picking up clientele with the change in weather, a packed house gave her less time to chat.

"I'll be back around in a bit." Without thinking, she blew him a kiss. She immediately blushed, feeling foolish for the gesture. Glad she was walking in the opposite direction, Jules felt like a schoolgirl, silly for doing such a thing.

Clint finished reading his newspaper and was waiting for Jules to return to his table, but she had not found the time. She had been stormed by three new tables. He had planned to tell her about the treasure being moved, but that clearly wasn't going to happen—not this morning at least.

Chapter 56

Maybe tonight. On the way out, he laid the newspaper on the bench by the door. High expectations surrounded the additional reports David had dredged up. Clint hoped they would shed definitive light on the inquiry surrounding Rod Radcliff, Sr.'s death.

When Clint pulled up to the police station, he found Scott leaning on his patrol car, talking on the phone. Scott motioned for Clint to go on in, indicating he would soon follow.

Clint entered Scott's office and sat down in the seat across from the desk. Seconds later, Scott came round the corner. "Good to see you," he greeted Clint. "Your timing is impeccable. How was your weekend?"

"Excellent! Yours?" Clint laughed at the formality. He got right to the point. "So, what did David turn up? Anything useful?"

"You could say that." Scott smirked with insider's knowledge. "Hang on a sec. I'll buzz him. It's best you hear it from him."

Clint shifted in his chair. Whatever David had to say, it appeared to hold value.

When David entered the room, he leaned in to shake Clint's hand before taking a seat. "Good to see you, sir," he said cordially.

"You too, man," replied Clint, genuinely pleased to see David.

Scott requested David to proceed with the update of their newly acquired information.

David turned to Clint. "Can I offer you anything to drink first? A cup of coffee? Soda?"

"No, I'm good. Thanks," he answered, anxious to get into the nuts and bolts of things. "I just came from Josie's."

"Okay," David said, shuffling through the papers inside the folder on his lap. "It appears Lieutenant Alex Freeman did have a motive for amending the case report. One week prior to the fire he had announced his candidacy to run for Sheriff. I came across a news clipping. My guess is he didn't want any loose ends, like an unsolved murder weighing him down. Running for office can be a very time-consuming proposition."

Day of Reckoning

David pulled a thin stapled report from the stack and faced Clint. "You're not going to believe this, or maybe you will," he teased. "Do you remember that coin Pearl said she accepted from Luke for his groceries?" David watched Clint's face closely, knowing he, of course, did.

"Well, it looks like there were two of them," David declared, "both dated 1861 and minted in Philadelphia. Uncirculated as suspected," he glanced over at Scott. "They were retrieved from Luke's sock drawer—according to the investigator who signed off on the belonging's report." David lifted the paper closer to read a jotted note. "Says here the coins were stunning!"

"Is that right? No wonder Pearl Teague hedged." Clint reacted nonchalantly, trying not to show his prior knowledge of the coins. "I guess that's as good a place to hide valuable gold coins as any," he joked sarcastically. Clint knew David's information was vital, including, and most importantly, that Luke had stolen his own coin back from the cash register. "So, what happened to them?"

"After seven years, they were sold at auction. Gold was only worth about thirty-six fifty per ounce back then, but relatively speaking, that was a lot of money. Since they were uncirculated coins, they received a handsome return. Greater than what was forecast, according to these notes." David turned to the third page of the abbreviated report he was holding. "It says here the coins attracted a lot of attention from collectors."

Scott could see Clint's wheels turning and almost laughed out loud. "Having said that, can you imagine what those two coins would be worth in today's market?" he interjected, aware that Clint's brain was in the middle of calculating the same question.

Clint cracked a smile, "Yeah, a fortune!" Adding two and two together from Scott's remark wasn't a stretch. To get what he was driving at, all Clint had to do was to think back to last Friday and the fist-full of coins they both held.

While Scott and Clint exchanged a veiled glance, David searched through the second file. "Here's how I see it," he said,

Chapter 56

lifting his eyes from the paperwork, "Luke went back to the general store and took the coin before Pearl Teague showed up at the site that morning." He raised a brow. "Because the coin wasn't there when she took her photos."

"I agree," Scott concurred, "how else would he be back in possession of it? I believe Luke went back to the store sometime after the firemen extinguished the flames and the police cordoned off the area. But, before Pearl Teague arrived. Possibly he went back to gloat over his achievement and noticed the coin in the cash register, or he specifically went back for it. Who knows?" His eyes shifted to Clint. "Not unusual for an offender to revisit the scene of the crime."

Clint's brow furrowed. "How does the lighter fit in?"

David's face brightened. He put the folder on the chair after withdrawing a paperclipped report. He handed it to Scott. "I found this categorized list, stamped December 27, 1953. The day after the fire. Not much there. Everything was pretty much incinerated. Just a bunch of charred ashes. The cash register was listed, no paper money—that would have burned—only coins were retrieved. Kitchen equipment and all metal objects were severely scorched but still intact. Other than that, nothing of value. "However, there is one notation I think you'll find of interest."

Being nearsighted, Scott removed his glasses so that he could see the small handwritten print more clearly. With a keen eye, he read every line and bordering notation word for word. A minute or so passed while David and Clint waited in silence. Then, Scott raised his head, made direct eye contact, and said, "We got him, Clint!"

The elation on Clint's face was indisputable. He exclaimed, "We do?"

"You betcha, we do!" Scott answered promptly, proud to have caught the small notation mid-page. "It says here, and I quote: 'Plus one, flip-top pewter Ace of Spades logo lighter. Victim's lighter was found in his sleeping quarters!'

Day of Reckoning

"Looks like you nailed it, Clint," praised Scott. "You have a sharp eye to have picked that small of an object out from that photo—partially covered in rubble. That moron, Luke, must have dropped it after setting the fire."

"Thank you, Scott. I was just fortunate, is all. Pearl's statement, validating who the lighter actually belonged to, was the real watershed moment," claimed Clint. "The fact Luke lit up just to aggravate her, right outside the door, was the game changer because that proved he had it with him when he left with his groceries. The only logical explanation was that he was in the general store after hours, set the fire, and dropped it without realizing it."

"All I can say is I'm glad you didn't give up. Your quest for the truth proved invaluable. We need to set the record straight! Rod Radcliff was not responsible for the fire. Nor did he cause his own death. It wasn't Rod's lighter they found, it was Luke McCauley's."

"The investigator's notes, insinuating Rod had lit his cigarette using that lighter, makes my skin crawl," inserted Clint, visibly angry. "It wasn't factual. They assumed it was his lighter without investigating, when, in fact, Luke's lighter had been dropped when he set the fire. The poor man, Rod Radcliff was defenseless."

Chiming in, David shared his thoughts, "And to think this guy, Luke McCauley, had the gall to return the next morning before the cinders had even cooled and took his gold coin from the cash register. Good grief, what a cold-hearted bastard he must have been!"

Scott's face turned serious, "Boy the news media is going to have a field day with this one," he moaned. "It's the stuff movies are made of, except this story is real."

Clint nodded. "Pretty wild, I have to admit. The movie credits will read, 'based on true events.'"

"Time to wrap this up. I believe we're done here," Scott suggested. He rose to his feet.

David gathered his things, understanding the unspoken message. He walked over to Clint. "I just want to say how pleased

Chapter 56

I am that you have gained closure in this matter. It's been a long time coming, I hear."

"Thanks, David, that means a lot." Clint smiled, thinking how skeptical David had been at the beginning.

Once David was out of earshot, Scott walked back to his desk and sat down. "Looks like Luke killed your Dad for the treasure and then gutted the general store to silence Rod Radcliff, Sr." Scott's face turned ashen. "He was a man without a soul."

"I figure Luke couldn't afford for Rod to expose him—plain and simple. Therefore, Rod had to be silenced," Clint deduced, after connecting the dots.

"My nose tells me Rod Radcliff made a fatal mistake. He told Luke that he planned to alert the authorities." Scott walked through how it might have gone down. "Even hinting that he suspected Luke was involved in Eli's disappearance would have been ill-advised. Fatal, to be exact. If you believe a crime has been committed, you don't threaten the murderer! When Luke grasped the gravity of his situation, the decision came easy. The deed would come in the form of an accidental fire, which conveniently did away with his nemesis."

Scott cocked his head. "Then, sometime that next day, Luke went back to ground zero, took the coin from the register, and continued on to Goss Cave to bask in his good fortune. What Luke couldn't have seen coming was a puma lying in wait for his sorry ass."

Scott speculated what came next, "I know this sounds absurd, but I propose the puma killed Luke out of revenge. An eye for an eye sort of thing. Luke's life for Eli's. How's that for a supposition and possible chain of events?"

Clint's jaw dropped, never having put all the pieces together so succinctly as Scott had just done.

"It makes no sense that a cat would do something so inexplicable, but I believe that is exactly what happened." Scott looked as though he were imagining how the killings occurred. "Then the puma crawled to your dad's side and died. From wounds inflicted by Luke."

Clint's thoughtful eyes stared into the distance. Finally, he said, "I fully agree. And I also think the injustice of it is why Rod Radcliff's soul couldn't move on. He wasn't at peace. He'd been accused of setting the fire. And they closed the case without really investigating. It was arson, and Luke McCauley ignited the flames that led to Rod Radcliff's demise."

Scott sat quietly, thinking about what Clint had said. His eyes turned sad. "Exactly. Luke walked away from the burning building, knowing full well Rod would be burned alive. That's an evil beyond abhorrent."

Chapter 57
A Clandestine Affair
Monday Mid-Morning

The information garnered at Scott's office clouded Clint's mind. As he drove to Chambersburg, half-dazed, he analytically processed the random remarks noted on the reports David had unearthed—all three game changers. Scott's final summation of how the events could have befallen was compelling and fit Clint's interpretation to the letter.

Clint visualized the ghastly affair of Christmastime 1953 from start to finish—a dark, gruesome tale not easily forgotten. When he arrived in Chambersburg, he sipped on a McDonald's iced tea in the parking lot before driving to the Crestview Adult Living facility.

He parked at the rear of the property. *Reserve the space up front for those more needy,* Clint thought. Sitting in the car, he speculated, *How does a person become that immoral?*

A periwinkle sky greeted Clint when he stepped out of the truck into the nippy autumn air. He tossed his Indiana Pacers ballcap onto the bench and shut the door. He believed to wear a hat in Pearl's presence would show disrespect. His boots clacked against the pavement as he strolled up to the building.

He opened the door and entered the lobby that secured the main entrance from visitors. Clint pressed the button that corresponded to Pearl's apartment. Only a few seconds had passed before the buzzer that allowed access into the building was heard. Inside, he took the elevator to where Pearl lived on the third floor in a spacious corner apartment.

Clint decided not to divulge everything he knew about Rod Radcliff, Sr.'s death to Pearl. Just enough to satisfy her curiosity and let her blow off steam about what a scoundrel Luke McCauley was. Clint figured when the details of the actual story broke, Georgeann could fill her in. Everything she contended would be verified.

One thing he did know was Pearl's opinion of McCauley would soon be validated—in spades.

The elderly woman showed Clint into the sitting room. With the light streaming through the arched windows behind him, Clint saw wisdom in Pearl's eyes.

"Mrs. Teague," he said softly, "you'll never know how grateful I am for the information you gave us. It was a huge help, in more ways than you can imagine." He deliberately omitted that it had blown the case wide open and tied Luke to the crime.

"My pleasure, young man," Pearl replied. "I hope we can stay in touch." She glanced at the window, wearing a smile often seen on old ladies. "And to think, you've been living over yonder in Salzburg all this time. We're practically neighbors!"

"Fate had a hand in it," he said confidently. His eyes became misty when he thought about how he mysteriously was drawn to Salzburg. He cradled Pearl's hand in his. "We were meant to find each other, and now that we have, we'll stay in touch."

The joy on her face was unmistakable. "I put the kettle on. Would you like a *cuppa* breakfast morning tea?" she kidded, using a British term she'd heard on PBS. "Came from London. Fortum & Mason. It's the best I've ever had."

Clint apologized, "Sorry, I can't stay. I have an appointment in Paoli. I promise I'll be back soon. Maybe next time."

At the door, Clint reached down and gave Pearl a hug, as a son might extend to a mother. "God has blessed me beyond all measure," he said. "To have you back in my life after all these years means the world to me. It was part of God's larger plan for us."

Pearl kissed Clint's hand. With teary blue eyes, she said, "Call me any time. We're family!"

"That thing I mentioned," Clint said with a secretive glance, "don't forget it's only between you and me. No one else. Not even Georgeann." His face turned serious, "Pearl, you are the only one who knows about that, other than my lawyer. Next week I'll pay a visit so we can discuss it in more."

Chapter 57

"You have my word. Pearl never breaks promises," she said in the third person. "We are in cahoots!"

Moving down the hallway toward the elevator, Clint whispered a prayer, giving thanks for the gift of Pearl Teague back in his life. He would never have expected to find her in the mix of consequences surrounding this episode. It was a serendipitous turn of events, for sure.

Thirty minutes later, Clint was sitting in the law office of Jeremy Sullivan going over future objectives. His Living Will among them, along with a conversation covering Saturday's operation. Clint briefly outlined projects he wanted to tackle. A concern of a different nature was also broached. Sullivan was pleased to oblige.

"Our meeting for tomorrow still stands," Sullivan confirmed at the conclusion of the impromptu discussion. "I'll see you at the Purple Dragon.

The substance of his day caused Clint to reconsider his trip to the bookstore. Rod deserved to know the truth, just like he had. But Clint also understood the urgency of telling Rod prior to the newsbreak. He figured one more day wouldn't matter.

Presently, all Clint wanted to do was sit with Jules and talk about anything other than Luke McCauley, the Reno Gang treasure, or the details of Rod Radcliff, Sr.'s death, and Eli's murder. Clint was up to his eyeballs with the story. He hated feeling powerless over an event he had no control to reverse.

The aroma of pizza wafting through the cab of his truck was driving him crazy. He had picked up a Capozzi's deep dish in Paoli on his way through town. He didn't dare roll the window down. He wanted it to stay hot as possible. He eyed it sitting on the seat. Did he dare sneak a piece?

On his way to Jules', Clint decided to stop in at his house for a long, hot shower. He felt compelled to wash the stench of Luke McCauley off and relax his mind before showing up at her place. He placed the pizza in the oven on warm and undressed.

Clint thought about Rod Radcliff, Sr. and the injustice of being accused of doing something he had no hand in. To be blamed for the destruction of his own general store was unfair. And, worse yet, to be judged so harshly, even pointing the finger at Rod for his own demise.

That was a tough pill to swallow when, in fact, the fire was not the result of smoking in bed, as predetermined. Clint contended those misconceptions must have been what entangled Rod's spirit to Salzburg. Why Rod had not moved on as Clint supposed. He could not rest until the record was set straight.

When Clint walked into Jules' kitchen an hour later, she was bent over with her head near the oven door. She was wearing oven mitts, reaching in for something that suggested a pastry. The house smelled of cinnamon and spice.

"Okay," he said, "I have no idea what you have in there, but I'm willing to skip dinner and go straight to dessert!"

Jules laughed out loud. "Over my dead body!"

She saw the pizza box on the table and opened it to sneak a peek. "Cheater!" she balked, "there's a piece missing." She slapped Clint's hand in protest. Then greeted him with a hug.

A variety of emotions moved through him. "You wouldn't say that if you'd had my day. I needed a picker-upper!" He'd decided earlier not to discuss any details of his day with Jules but soon broke his promise when he charged, "I'll tell you what… that Luke McCauley was a real lowlife!" He shook his head in disgust. "A man without scruples."

Although she was curious as to his meaning, she was not about to press the issue. Instead, she replied, "From what little I know, I'd have to agree. It was a shame your father trusted him like he did."

"Yeah, he made a colossal error in judgment with that guy." Clint closed his eyes. "Let's talk about something more uplifting, like what you have in that oven of yours," he teased.

"Cinnamon strudel coffee cake!" she gleefully replied. "From my experience, brown sugar and cinnamon form an elixir that

Chapter 57

cures all ails."

"Well, I can always use that kind of an elixir."

"You know," said Jules somberly, "if you ever want to talk, I have a listening ear."

"I know, Jules. I appreciate your sentiments. We'll talk about it, just not right now. I've had enough of death and dying for one day. Mr. Radcliff suffered terribly and for no good reason." Clint lowered his eyes. "Greed is such an ugly word. Rod's death is too upsetting to think about."

"From how it sounds, I take it you were able to tie the fire to arson."

"Yes, the report Scott and I read definitely put Luke at the scene of the crime. Between the cigarette lighter and the coin, no doubt remains."

"All right, we'll save that conversation for another day. But for now, let's eat. I have Pepsi in the fridge and a fresh pot of decaf brewed—your choice. We can have our dessert outside on the porch. Haven't sat under the stars for some time! Tonight might be the perfect occasion. If I had a telescope, like some people I know, we could scan the cosmos and get lost in the bigger picture."

"That's true," countered Clint. "I've missed that. Next time I'll fix dinner. Then afterward, we'll set up the telescope."

The rest of the evening went by pleasantly, with mostly small talk. When Clint departed at 10 p.m., he felt much more relaxed than when he had arrived. Since Jules was off the following day, neither one much cared about the lateness of the hour.

Although Clint said he might call, he knew it would be evening before seeing her again. Tuesday promised to be a huge day, something he had to do alone. A lunch meeting at 1 p.m. would make clear what the future held. His inquiries would be up for discussion. Although he wished Jules could accompany him, he would not ask.

A Clandestine Affair

Tuesday, October 21

Clint had changed his mind about trying to stop by the bookstore. His talk with Rod would have to wait. When he got out of bed, he felt tired to the bone. He had lost his desire to push himself any harder than he had already been doing. Rod's New and Used Books would be put down the list of priorities once again.

"I'll do it Thursday," he decided.

Clint knew his upcoming meeting would not be conducted in Salzburg. Prudence was advisable with something as important as what he had to address. He did not want anyone to see him with this group of strangers. Their discussion needed to remain behind the scenes.

Jeremy Sullivan arranged Clint's business luncheon to be carried out in Paoli. Sullivan would sit in and represent his client. He'd chosen the Purple Dragon restaurant for two reasons: first, Clint figured he'd be less likely to run into acquaintances and second Chinese food was a favorite.

Wearing khakis and a navy-blue long sleeve shirt, Clint had taken extra care getting ready, a key component in presenting himself properly. When Clint entered the restaurant, he felt nervous. This meeting was big, and he desperately wanted it to end with a good outcome. It would be a dream come true if it did. A lot rested on the verdict of the luncheon. If things worked out well, it could be the first of many.

The reception desk greeted him as if they knew him personally, which they did not. It was obvious that Sullivan had flagged them of his arrival. He followed the hostess to the back of the building, where few people were seated. Even fewer were in the private room he was escorted to. He suspected his attorney had arranged that as well.

Chapter 57

A middle-aged man in a dark blue suit stood to shake Clint's hand when he approached the half-filled table. "Hello, Clint, my name is Bradley Abers, of Kinsley, Abers & Sons. Glad to make your acquaintance. Heard a lot about you. All good, of course." He grinned across the table at Sullivan.

"Likewise," Clint replied with the same tone of formality.

The rest of the attendees arrived at the scheduled time, and the business meeting lasted well over two hours—much longer than Clint had projected. At the conclusion, he watched Bradley Abers and his colleagues leave the room, chatting excitedly as they exited. The meeting had gone well. Better than Clint had hoped.

Sullivan stayed behind. They had more to discuss. When the waitress came to the table to deliver the bill, Sullivan grabbed the check. "We'd like two Jack and Cokes please, unless you serve champagne!" It was obvious how Sullivan believed the meeting had gone.

The waitress frowned. "Sorry, sir, the only alcoholic beverages we serve is beer and wine. Our liquor license doesn't include hard liquor."

Jeremy smiled. "Okay, then, we'll take the King of Beers. Two, please, if you have it." He saw the deer-in-the-headlight look of his Asian server and laughed, "That's Budweiser."

She trotted off, pleased to be able to accommodate her patrons.

Sullivan congratulated Clint on his part of a successful meeting. He had presented himself well, resulting in a contingency pledge to move forward.

"Hey, by the way, I'm sorry I didn't forewarn you about Scott Edwards before Saturday. I meant to apologize for the oversight when we met at your office yesterday. Other than you and the crew that moved the treasure, he is the only other person who knows about it." Clint hesitated. He had told a partial truth. "Oh, and one other person."

Sullivan displayed a quizzical, uncomfortable glance. "Who else besides Edwards and Bellwether Excavation Services?" Sullivan asked with apparent concern.

Clint realized beforehand Sullivan would wonder why he had told anyone, for obvious reasons. "Look, Scott can be trusted," he responded quickly. "Guaranteed. He's a Captain on the Salzburg police force and up to his eyeballs in this whole affair." Clint chuckled, thinking how accurate his description really was. "You met him on Saturday. You could probably tell he's trustworthy."

"I don't need to tell you how high-security the situation was on Saturday. My job is to protect your interests, Clint. To be honest, I felt edgy having Bellwether Excavation Services or anyone else involved in this whole affair, but we had no choice. A service needed to be hired, and they were my first choice. Everyone who was involved signed a nondisclosure agreement."

Clint tried to soothe Sullivan's uneasiness. "Scott and I have been working on a separate case that happens to be indirectly tied to the discovery. The other person I referred to is Julie Jenkins." Clint gave his attorney a knowing glance. "You've met her."

"Yes, I remember her." Sullivan nodded. "She was at our first meeting. I understand she would be someone you might confide in, but as far as Scott goes, I'll have to take your word on him. I'm certain you are a good judge of character. Plus, he is a policeman, so there should be no reason to doubt his integrity."

"Yes, I can vouch for both," Clint stated with confidence.

"The gold bars will be cross-checked with any existing documents that might identify them," explained Sullivan. "I expect we will find something somewhere to identify them unless they are unnumbered and without markings. That will take time. The FBI has assigned an agent to the case. We want to be as thorough as possible, leaving no rock unturned."

"You would think we'd be able to trace them to a railroad, government, or bank." Clint disclosed an earlier experience. "I held one. Checked everywhere and saw nothing. No serial number,

Chapter 57

hallmark, stamp, manufacturer mark… nothing. Who knows where that one originated? The shape was odd, with no identification whatsoever. Amateurish at best."

"Must have belonged to a private individual. That's where the Finders Keepers law will work in your favor." Sullivan smiled. "I checked, and in today's currency, with as many bars as you said you thought could be down there, we are talking millions, Clint. To think those bars are only part of your cache. They will have a complete count later this month."

Clint thought about that. It sounded beyond belief. "Scott told me the excavation crew said those bars weighed a ton." Clint chuckled. "I bet they were glad when the job was finished." He wasn't about to tell Sullivan he had taken Scott down into Goss Cave prior to Saturday. That Scott could personally attest to the weight of a gold bar.

"Staggering, isn't it?" Clint chortled. "I'm still in shock and suspect I'll be that way for the rest of my life."

Taking the last swig of his Budweiser, Clint politely stood. "Guess we'll see each other tomorrow at the courthouse." He flashed a smile. "Should be exciting. It's not every day I'm involved in a press conference." Feeling dizzy with excitement, Clint tipped his hat, ready to leave.

"I'm pretty keyed up myself," admitted Sullivan. "Who would have ever thought?" Sullivan walked Clint to the door. "I plan to arrive early. After this is all said and done, I'm taking you to a fancy, five-star restaurant to celebrate properly. Champagne and T-bones! You can bring your girlfriend if you like."

Clint reddened. "Oh, she's not my girlfriend. But I'm sure she'd love to join us." The conversation suddenly felt awkward, so he quickly changed the subject. "You should know, I ran into the reporter I'm going to give exclusive rights to. Seems appropriate since the guy showed up at our initial police station meeting wearing a cowboy hat, spurs, and boots. Fits right in with our motif. Wouldn't you say? His Val Kilmer-deep voice cracked me up."

"Are you joshing me?" Sullivan chortled, "that's hilarious."

"Yeah, said he just got into town." Clint broke up laughing. "Up from Tombstone, Arizona, he claimed. Apparently, he's written several articles for *The Tombstone Eulogy*. Even participated in a reenactment of the Gunfight at OK Corral. Said something about playing the part of the sheriff."

Clint's brow creased. "Interesting, did you realize that shoot-out took place in 1881? Not long before the Reno Gang came into fame. That rowdy group would have loved this guy! He would have fit right in. I figured he'd be perfect for writing the article."

Sullivan couldn't stop laughing. "I'd say a good choice then. At least on stage he'll add character! Can't wait to meet this guy!" Sullivan checked Clint's face to see if he had caught the pun. He was pleased to hear Clint's snicker.

"Captain Scott Edwards, the reporter Sean Ferrer, and I have a conference set up before the announcement at nine o'clock at Scott's office. Would you like to sit in?"

"I'll let you know," answered Sullivan. "I probably will. I need to clear my calendar."

On the way home, Clint fantasized about an unforeseeable future. Bradley Abers had left a message while Clint was with Sullivan. He wanted to know if Clint could make time after the press conference for a short meeting. He had good news.

Clint immediately phoned Jeremy Sullivan. The answering machine picked up. "Hey, it sounds like we might be celebrating sooner than later," informed Clint. "Abers left a voicemail requesting a meeting after the press conference if I could swing it. I'd feel more comfortable if you were there. If you can't, I'll see about rescheduling it. Sounded encouraging, though." Humorously, he joked, "Sean Ferrer could be getting another exclusive!"

Tomorrow, Wednesday morning at 11 a.m., a large assembly of diverse individuals from all walks of life were predicted to gather for the scheduled press conference at the north entrance to Tobias Park, named after the town's founder, Tobias Salzburg. Sullivan

Chapter 57

had notified all the major television stations and public networks in advance of the announcement. He'd alerted newspapers and other sources of media as well.

Clint's amazing story was about to make headlines. Not the complete story, only a brief overview of events. His childhood ties to Salzburg would be mentioned, plus how he and Elise coincidentally came across his family homestead. Trailed by how he purchased the land, only to later discover the shack that eventually led to his extraordinary find. Some might say, "The find of a century!"

A Q&A segment would trail Clint's talk. After that, he would step aside to allow Salzburg's Chief of Police, Peter Carlisle, an opportunity to describe how the town's police department got involved. Eli Reeves, Luke McCauley, and Rod Radcliff, Sr. would all play their respective parts in a riveting tale of murder and mayhem. Onto a stage, set back in 1953, they would imperceptibly step. Their cold case file finally finding the light of day. A narrative of sensational description, ready for print and broadcast.

Tuesday Evening

"So… how was your day?" Clint asked Jules when she entered the house.

"Peachy," she chuckled. "How about yours?" Jules watched Clint's eyes careen away from her.

"Same!" he replied, avoiding eye contact.

"I've been looking forward to watching this movie all day," she volunteered, quick to change the subject.

Clint's shoulders slumped, unhappy with the wall building between them. Unfortunately, it was a necessary evil that could not be avoided. A personal issue held in reserve, Clint had not breathed a word to anyone of his dealings and wasn't about to make Jules the exception.

A Clandestine Affair

The evening passed pleasantly enough. Still, tension hung in the air. Irrespective of Clint's invitation for Jules to accompany him on stage the next day, little seemed to break down the barrier that had started to build between them. While *The Matrix* played, he asked, and she accepted his invitation.

When the movie ended, they retired to the backyard. Stars dotted the night sky while a ribbon of clouds drifted past the harvest moon hanging large overhead. It was an idyllic evening for operating the telescope.

Clint disappeared into the pole barn. Shortly he returned, wheeling the telescope across the yard. Two folding stools were positioned side by side. While Jules waited, Clint hand-plotted coordinates that would bring Mars closer.

Jules leaned into the eyepiece and squealed. "I think I see Angelo Secchi's Canale Atlantico!"

Clint burst out laughing, surprised she was able to roll the 1858 priest and astronomer's name off her tongue so fluently. "The *Canale* is better known as Syrtis Major Planum today. But I have a feeling you already know that!" He cracked up. "You know your stuff, woman!"

"I'm not as dumb as I look, buster!" she jabbed.

Clint laughed so hard his side hurt. "That calls for a glass of wine!" He darted to the house and was back lickety-split, carrying an open bottle of chilled Castello Del Poggio Sweet Rose.

"Here, smarty pants!" he teased. "Produced in Italy, my dear! This vineyard was established in 1706!" Acting silly, he handed her a glass and pretended to be a fancy restaurant waiter, putting a towel over one arm and pouring wine with the other.

For a split-second Jules was taken aback. She was unable to respond because her thoughts had been sidetracked. His joke was easily interpreted as Clint being silly, but what she found odd was him having an expensive bottle of wine at the house when he didn't drink wine. As far as she knew, he only kept wine around for her, and her taste in wine was of the low-end variety.

Chapter 57

Wonder if he has already come into some money? she wondered. *Maybe converted a portion of his fortune? Something must have happened because he would normally pay big bucks for a luxurious bottle of wine.* She couldn't help but notice how beautiful the bottle was when he poured her a glass.

"What a treat," she said sweetly.

Clint immediately realized he had made a mistake. To break the bottle open had been foolish. It all seemed so perfectly scripted at the time; but it had been earmarked for a special occasion. A gift to be delivered to Jeremy Sullivan as a thank you for his hard work. The plan was to present it to him at the steak dinner he had proposed.

Observing Jules' thoughtful expression, Clint moved toward the telescope. He bent down and looked through the observation glass. A diversion. "Hey, come take a view of the red planet," he suggested.

Jules set her glass down and walked over to the telescope to view Mars. Viewing the cosmos was a hobby they both enjoyed. Clint and Jules mapped the heavens, along with other points of interest until the bewitching hour arrived, and she realized she should leave.

At her car, Clint gave her a hug before opening the door and helping her in. "I'll see you tomorrow, then?" he asked. "Should be an interesting day."

"Yes, tomorrow," Jules replied, her voice trailing.

Driving away from Clint's, Jules was aware of how letdown she felt. Although curious, she had resisted the temptation to ask Clint what he had been up to for the last few days. She wasn't used to him being so closed mouthed. Her assumption was he didn't want her to know. Otherwise, he would have shared his latest developments with her.

Questions dangled unanswered on her way home. She was convinced his attitude toward her had shifted somehow. Nearly imperceptible, but there, nonetheless. All the little things were beginning to add up.

A Clandestine Affair

Wednesday, October 22

At 9 a.m., sharp Clint was standing in Scott's office accompanied by Jeremy Sullivan, David Andrews, and Sean Ferrer. They were waiting for the press conference to commence, going over the dos and don'ts of what to say and not say. Clint's words had been strategically crafted by Jeremy Sullivan.

Ferrer was ready to hit the press release button on his computer the moment Clint started to speak. His version of the story contained exclusive highlights, photos, and information not made available to the other news reporters.

No one in the room had an inkling of the next breaking news that was waiting around the corner. Only Sullivan and Clint knew what was going on. At his speech, he was to tell a partial truth of the activities that had eclipsed the treasure hunt he had hosted for his grandchildren back on September 20, leaving a lot of speculation as to the rest of the story.

"Keep it simple. Think in terms, *less is more*," Jeremy instructed his client in a serious tone.

Sullivan took a seat across the aisle from Captain Edwards and Chief of Police Carlisle. Sean Ferrer sat nearest to the podium. With the crowd noise growing louder, almost boisterous, Sullivan worked at turning a deaf ear. He tried to concentrate on the papers he held. He clutched the tip of his glasses, slipped them on, and began to read the fine print of a legal document that had been forwarded over from Bradley Abers. As Clint's representative, Sullivan was required to be conscientious with his responsibility.

Clint scanned the park for Jules' presence. The plan had been to meet at the Pavilion twenty minutes earlier, but she never showed. Clint was forced to leave without her. Considering he was the main

Chapter 57

attraction, he had no choice. He'd expected them to sit together, so she could bear witness to his story and lend moral support. He supposed he would have to do it alone.

Moments later, from the podium, Clint watched Jules carve through the heavy crowd, making her way to the platform. She scurried up the steps and plopped down on the seat beside him.

Clint turned with a grin, "Glad you could make it!"

"Almost didn't," she stated, trying to catch her breath. "Have you seen the streets? They are packed! Not a parking spot anywhere. I had to leave my car in Josie's backlot and walk over."

The announcement wasn't expected to take more than two hours in total. They would render a brief explanation of the story about the Reno Gang and how they acquired their trove of stolen goods along with Clint's discovery of it. He turned to the crowd and saw many familiar faces among them. When Captain Edwards signaled for the crowd to quiet down, all eyes focused on Clint.

A man of few words, Peter Carlisle, stepped to the podium alongside Clint. "The legendary Reno Gang's lost treasure, after 135 years," he announced into the microphone, "has, at last, been unearthed!" Carlisle's booming voice could be heard throughout the park. "The gentlemen standing here at my side," he turned to face Clint, "is Mr. Clint Reeves, responsible for the discovery. The location of the find remains undisclosed."

A spectacle of exuberance filtered through the crowd, followed by loud chattering. So loud it was heard around the park and out into the streets.

When Clint finished his part of the speech, an immediate Q&A segment began. It lasted about forty-five minutes with a promise of a follow-up press conference when more information was available.

Clint listened as Captain Edwards recapped the backstory of the cold case file. He made an official public statement that placed Eli Reeves and Rod Radcliff's murders, plus the general store fire, directly at Luke McCauley's feet. Best of all, Rod Radcliff's name was cleared of any wrongdoing.

A large dark hole, named notoriety, was about to swallow Clint's previous life and spit out a distinctively different one. Marketeers, trying to attach themselves to a fraction of his massive fortune, were already crawling out of the woodwork.

Jules scurried at breakneck speed back to her car. Clint was fast on her heels, trying to beat the crowds that pursued him. Reporters were not finished asking questions, but Clint was done answering.

Jules was apprised of Clint's one final meeting of the day. After that, he would join her at her house. "I figured dinner at your place perhaps is best," Clint piped up when the silence between them grew heavy inside the car. Jules' lack of response to the event and irritation with the crowd noise was apparent as they drove out of town. "I may need to hide at your place for a day or two if things get any crazier," he said, half-serious.

"My door is always open," she said sweetly. "We can keep you incognito. Wait until the coast is clear. That might take a while!"

"I agree. After my meeting, I'll come your way. Drop me off at the house so I can get the Camaro if you don't mind." Clint avoided her gaze into his lying eyes. "I'll come over after that. Maybe we can take a walk or just sit under the stars. He touched her hand, "I could bring dinner home if you like."

"How long do you think it'll take? Your meeting is in Paoli, I assume?"

"Not more than an hour to an hour and a half, I suspect." Clint looked into her green eyes, aware her question remained unanswered. Doubt was written on her face. He hated lying to her, but it was a necessary evil.

"Wonderful," she said calmly. Then a thought occurred to her that made her happy, *He called my place home!*

Chapter 58
A Spirit Set Free
October 22, 4:30 p.m.

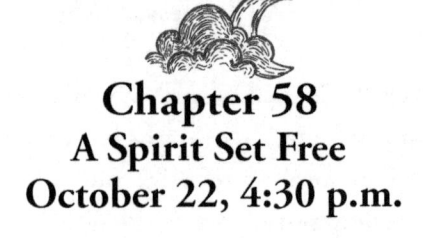

Knowing Jules would not venture into town, Clint had arranged for Abers' meeting to be conducted at the local bar. Not the likeliest of places to conduct business. Nevertheless, In a Pig's Eye, would suffice.

Clint called Dustin Corbet, the owner of the bar, in advanced, asking to be granted a table as far from the main seating area as possible. In compliance, Dustin took his friend's request one step further and cleared his office. Clint's dilemma was easy to spot, considering Dustin's staff had been juggling the demands of a jammed-packed, reporter-filled establishment since 10 a.m., as soon as the doors opened. Dustin instructed Clint to use his private entrance at the rear of the establishment. He would buzz Clint and his associates in when they arrived.

Into an eight-by-eight cramped office, Clint, Abers, and his associates stepped, shutting the door behind them. The group took seats in a less-than-ideal situation to conduct business. Smoke curls filled the air—blowing through the ventilation system and hovering at the ceiling. The smoke created a hazy atmosphere to work. From the opposite side of the room, a raucous commotion could be heard through the walls.

On the desktop, Abers opened his computer. He waited for the system to finish booting and then turned the screen toward the other two men. His objectives were in a simple-to-read format. Clint had laid a high-class challenge in Abers' lap, and he had delivered. Phase Two was ready—a lofty endeavor, but when everything was said and done, their effort would be well-spent.

"I ordered a pitcher of beer." Clint smiled. "I figured we could all use a cold one after the day we've had." He glanced at the door, "It's a jungle out there."

"Amen to that," chortled Abers, who was supporting a broad grin. "Not a typical day for any of us. Certainly not for Salzburg!" He turned to Sullivan, whose eyes showed his amusement. "This place won't see normal for a long time. Right?"

"You could say! Nothing short of craziness going on out there," agreed Sullivan.

"Hope you both like Dos Equis?" Clint commented. "If not, I can order something else."

"No, that's fine. Haven't had one of those in years," confessed Sullivan.

"I also took the liberty of ordering nachos," Clint said sheepishly. "I'm starved, and what goes better with Dos Equis than nachos?"

"Yep, those guys are bosom buddies!" Abers joked.

Clint liked this guy already. The vibes Abers gave off were friendly, and Clint liked his unassuming demeanor.

"First, I want you to see the tract topography I referenced. You'll have a better perspective of how suited it is when you view it. Seems perfect for the project." Abers opened a PDF file. "This entire section is available." Using his pen, he pointed to the screen. "Plus, this small section over here. I've talked to the owner, Terence Jordan, and he says he's willing to sell. For the right price." Abers lips curled. "I have no doubt you are willing to negotiate terms."

Clint stared at the screen, unable to believe his eyes. "Is that where I think it is?"

Abers answered, "Yes," and closed his computer. "You'll need to walk it, obviously. The parcel encompasses a large area. If you want, we can go there right now. Terence Jordan said to give him a call, and he'd try to make himself available."

Clint was stunned. "No, no," he shook his head. "Can't do it today. What about Friday morning? Would that work?"

Bradley Abers checked his phone calendar. "For me, it does. I'll give Mr. Jordan a quick call." Abers turned to Clint's attorney, "What about you, Jeremy? Are you available then?"

Chapter 58

"Absolutely. I'll make myself available." Sullivan readily agreed.

Clint's tiredness could be heard in his voice when he said, "I have someone waiting on me. And, truthfully, I can use some downtime. I've been hyped over this announcement thing for days and I'm exhausted. Glad it's behind me."

"I understand," Abers said. "What time Friday?"

"Does 10 a.m. work?" asked Clint.

"I'll find out and give you a buzz later." Abers looped his computer satchel over his shoulder, opened the door, and stepped out into the hallway. He looked at his two colleagues. "Do you want to meet back here, in the parking lot? We can drive over together. Or separately if you like."

"No, thank you, Brad. I appreciate the offer but would rather meet you there. I know the location well." He pivoted around to Sullivan. "My days start at Josie's Diner. Best breakfast in town! Don't want to change my routine too much. I kind of like that place."

He looked at Abers. "You should try it sometime. Can't beat their southern-style food." Clint thought about Jules and her bright smile each time he walked through the door. "Big changes coming down the pike. I don't plan on that being one of them."

"I understand," replied Abers. "Just to make certain we are on the same page, you did see Terence Jordan's initial asking price? Correct?"

"I did!" replied Clint. "Not that I'm an expert on the matter, but it looked reasonable to me. Maybe a little on the high side, but I'm sure we can reach an agreement."

"He did say he was willing to negotiate," Abers stated. "I suspect he'll bend a little if necessary. Don't want to insult him, though. Dropping the price a few thousand won't set off any alarms."

The three men shook hands. "See you at 10 a.m. unless I hear otherwise," Clint said to Bradley Abers and then turned to Sullivan. "Thanks, Jeremy, for sitting in. I appreciate your support and expertise. I'd be lost without you. I'll see you in the morning too, I presume."

"You betcha," Sullivan acknowledged. "I have to admit, I'm enjoying this as much as you are." He grinned, "Well, almost."

When Clint pulled into Jules' drive, he was surprised to find her lying in a hammock in the side yard. An iced tea sat on the stand beside her, and a book lay open. She smiled generously when he approached.

"You look comfortable. Is that new?"

"It is, and I am." Jules giggled. Her forehead creased. "I thought your meeting was in Paoli. Didn't take long." Surprised at the early hour, the smell of liquor on his breath, and smoke on his clothing, Jules wondered what sort of meeting Sullivan and he would have had that entailed drinking.

Clint brushed her forehead with his fingertips as he passed. "Yeah, we changed the location. Didn't have to drive his way after all. Stayed here in town." He sat down on the porch.

Jules rolled off the edge of the hammock, detecting something odd. *Good grief, he smells like a Mexican Restaurant!* Baffled by a whiff of Mexican spices, she weighed a vexing thought. *We don't have a Mexican restaurant in town! Where was he?* Jules hated to admit how much Clint's strange behavior was beginning to bother her. She could only imagine where he had been because it appeared he wasn't saying.

Clint volunteered an elaborate explanation, which added more fuel to the fire. "We met in town. Sullivan hadn't started back to Paoli yet, so we stopped in at Josie's for a cup of coffee. Honestly, I don't know why he thought it was so important to meet today. Wasn't that much to cover, just a few T's to cross and I's to dot. No big deal, really."

Chapter 58

He watched Jules' body language, seeing no tells that concerned him. Fanning his hands, he claimed, "Nothing that couldn't have waited. Should have rescheduled considering the place was packed with reporters." His laugh sounded nervous as if he had told a joke when, to the contrary, it rang of untruth. He said, "We're meeting again tomorrow at 10 a.m. It was just too loud in there to talk. That's why I'm back early."

Jules' eyes flashed, recognizing a lie when she heard one.

Convinced he had sold his story—hook, line, and sinker—Clint cheerfully inserted, "After breakfast, Sullivan and I'll hook up again. Of course, that means I'll have to drive to Paoli."

He gazed into Jules' distant eyes. *Is she even listening to me?* he questioned. She looked like she was miles away. "Sullivan wanted to meet earlier, but I said I couldn't. Made it clear I intended to keep my normal routine intact."

"Well, good!" she replied pleasantly. "Then I'll see you in the morning at the diner? Usual time?" Jules moved toward the house, ready to go indoors. She showed no other reaction to Clint's comments.

Clint trailed behind her to the house. "Yes, I wouldn't miss breakfast at Josie's or a chance to see my favorite waitress."

"It'll be nice when things get back to some sort of normalcy. This morning's circus was unsettling. Way too many people for my taste." She scoffed. "Not the kind of life I could ever imagine living."

As soon as the words slipped off her tongue, she wanted to reel them back in. To insert her will into his life was not her intention. Jules followed up the comment with something more palatable. "Attention on this level will not be easy to adjust to. The press conference this morning was energetic. I'll give you that. At the same time, it felt maddening. Life has certainly taken a hard-right turn for us. Hasn't it? I suppose commotion comes with the territory."

A Spirit Set Free

"It'll get better. Just a temporary inconvenience," Clint tried to reassure her. "My world did flip on its head. Didn't it?" He laughed vigorously. "Going in a good direction now, I'd say!"

Seeing Jules' shocked expression, Clint immediately corrected his mistake. "Not that it wasn't always good. You know what I mean."

Jules turned her back. Facing the window above the sink, she said, "Yeah, I think I so."

"I realize this whole thing has affected you as well. It won't last." He claimed. "The diner will be back to normal in no time. People lose interest quickly these days."

Taking the subject elsewhere, Clint inserted, "I appreciate your support this morning. I was nervous as hell." He cringed at his choice of words—not big on cussing around Jules but did not apologize. Considering he had a thousand eyes boring into him, a cuss word fit his mood. "I was terrified! Can you believe... my knees were actually knocking!" He looked embarrassed. "Never was much good at public speaking."

Jules took two large pork chops tucked into a bed of gravy-covered noodles from the oven. She had prepared dinner, thinking Clint would be hungry when he arrived. She placed the hot dish on the table. "I hope you saved some space!"

"Good Lord, that looks good. Haven't eaten since this morning," he said as he pulled out a chair and sat down.

Jules thought about the scent of Mexican food and beer she detected on his breath when he first arrived but said nothing.

During dinner, they covered a variety of topics but none of major importance. One stood out, though. Clint informed Jules of another media event in the making. "I'm more excited about this next one than this morning's," he confessed.

She waited for an explanation but was disappointed when he didn't elaborate. Instead, he said they'd talk about it later when he had more information.

Chapter 58

Clint did mention the extraction of riches that had taken place the Saturday before. The process had taken many hours to complete. He told her Scott had accompanied the excavation company to Evansville, and that is where the treasure was now housed.

After that, the conversation reverted to small talk. Mostly about the gardening and how large the German Johnson tomato plants had grown, his fall harvest yields, repairs on the house and vehicles, family, grandkids, and so forth. Their mutual interests were brought up, but no mention was made of Clint's meeting with Sullivan or what it entailed.

Deliberately keeping her out of the loop—not sharing the most pressing issues on his mind—was the impression Jules was beginning to form. Whatever was going on with Clint, behind the scenes, he was not making that known.

Where she had believed they could talk about anything, she was now certain some subjects were off the table. And, although he tried to explain, underneath she questioned why he hadn't told her about the treasure being transported to Evansville. She suspected the omission was deliberate. It was next to impossible to believe Clint could have kept that kind of information under wraps for so long unless it was intentional.

Thursday, October 23
10:30 a.m.

When Clint stepped outdoors, a cool breeze greeted him. Fall permeated the air. Pumpkins, field mazes, bales of hay, corn stalks, hay wagons, apple cider, smores, and pies were all part of the season. Everything he enjoyed about autumn. His favorite time of the year had just gotten better.

Clint climbed into the truck. He withdrew a cigarette from the pack, and for the third time that week, lit up. He rolled down the passenger window to let in the fresh air. His smoking habit was proving more difficult to give up than anticipated. On his way into town, he visualized what the days ahead were going to look like.

Clint was on top of the world. One week from today, his grandchildren would be playing Spoons at *his* kitchen table rather than Rusty's. They would be spending fall break in Salzburg and making memories. The weekend was still in the planning stages, with several projects slated. Clint couldn't wait for the fun to begin. He hadn't felt this excited in a month of Sundays.

He parked his truck on a side street, two blocks away from its usual spot. To his disappointment, he noticed the newspaper bin was empty. Clint frowned, thinking it was an inconvenience but knew he was the reason why no papers remained. The crowd indoors made it evident. His normal booth had four people seated in it. To escape notice, he pulled down his cap and proceeded to the left of the door. As far back in the diner as he could manage.

"Hey, how's it going?" Patrick asked Clint while filling his coffee cup. "I bet you slept in today." He glanced at the wall clock in the kitchen. "There was a lot of activity going on in town yesterday. As a matter of fact, we hit record sales, thanks to you!"

"I've never seen Salzburg that crowded," noted Clint. "I can hear the merchants saying, *chink-chink!* Glad to be of service," he teased as he took a sip of coffee. "I'm stopping by the bookstore. That's why I'm in later than usual. The store's hours have been cut back. I get the feeling they may be closing permanently. Only open from eleven to two Monday, Thursday, and Saturday. That's it." Clint casually searched the diner for Jules' whereabouts.

Patrick pointed in Jules' direction. "This place has been like a Mexican jumping bean, people popping in and out so fast we can hardly keep up. Serving food hot and fresh in a timely manner isn't as easy as you might think." Patrick pointed in Jules' direction. "That girl is a Godsend! Always has a smile for everyone. Customers are crazy about her! She's my greatest asset."

Chapter 58

Clint glanced at Jules as she scurried about. Her long auburn hair was wrapped tightly under a red-and-white cap. Josie's was a 50's diner and Jules was pretending to be a classic 50's waitress.

She emerged from the kitchen carrying three stacked and balanced plates on her forearm. She set them on a table and then pivoted to the counter and grabbed the coffee pot and one last plate. Moving to the table adjacent to the family she had just served, she took out her order pad and jotted down their requests.

The gentleman Jules was taking an order from, Clint guessed to be mid-forties and a reporter. The younger lady sitting across from him gave off the same vibes. They stood out in their fine attire from the people who lived in Salzburg—or southern Indiana for that matter.

Jules looked up and saw Clint watching her. An instant connection was made. Her face broke into a half-smile as his did the same.

"All I can say is you're welcome," joked Clint. "I even forfeited my booth for the cause."

Patrick chuckled. "Hey, I'm lovin' it. Keeps me on my toes." He tossed a newspaper on the tabletop. "Thought you might want to see this." From the front page, Clint's face stared up. "We have a celebrity in our midst," he teased. "Who would have ever thought?"

"I wish I could have done this thing some other way. Reporting the treasure without making it public would have been my preference." Clint looked down at the headline: "1953 Blizzard Blankets Double Homicide."

"Take a deep breath," Patrick advised, "everything will die down eventually. The attention span of a reporter is like that of a squirrel... about one second. Unless they are looking at an acorn, and then it's closer to four seconds!"

Clint exploded in laughter, "Let's hope you're right, ye old wise wizard! I'm counting on it." Clint glanced behind Patrick and saw heads turned, all aimed at him. "I think it's time to make a break for it," he kidded. Scooting out of the booth, he shook Patrick's hand. "See you in the morning, my friend."

Jules watched Clint's movement toward the door. On the way out, catching her eye, he held up five fingers, indicating he'd call at five o'clock. She nodded in response.

The next stop was Rod's New and Used Books. Clint sat inside the F-100 trying to muster up enough courage to face Rod, Jr. He felt terrible his trip had not been carried out prior to the news conference. It was insensitive of him not to have made Rod a priority, irrespective of the store's new restricted business hours. The astounding announcement that Rod Radcliff, Sr. had been cleared of any negligent behavior connected to the fire should have been delivered by Clint, not read in the newspaper as though Rod, Jr. was an ordinary citizen.

Surprised more cars weren't parked nearby, like they had been at Josie's, Clint pulled into his usual spot, close to where the sidewalk ended. A huge part of him dreaded the conversation he was about to have while the other half felt relieved to shed the burden he had been carrying. The rumbling engine stilled. He slid from the cab of his truck.

Gazing northwest toward the bookstore, he noticed dense clouds had replaced the sunny, cloudless sky of only an hour ago. An unusual formation caught his eye, and he spotted a grayish saucer-like cloud hovering at the far end of the street in the direction he was aimed.

Clint lamely joked, *Nice for the weather to accommodate my mood.* The sound of his clacking boots was heard from the uneven sidewalk underfoot. The path leading to the bookstore was a few feet ahead.

The story he was about to deliver had been scrolled with a poison pen by Luke McCauley. Any hesitation Clint harbored about revealing the truth regarding Rod, Sr.'s demise would die a quick death. The truth was obligatory, no matter how unpleasant.

Chapter 58

Rod, Jr., unlike the journalist from yesterday's news brief, would hear the true narrative behind his fortuitous find of the famous Reno Gang's lost treasure. And specifically, Rod, Sr.'s contribution in uncovering it. Most importantly, Clint wanted Rod, Jr. to know he considered Rod Radcliff, Sr. his personal guardian.

Despite the fact Rod, Jr. had referred to his grandfather—or dad, whichever the true relationship between them was, as still alive—his musings had to be pure fantasy. There was no doubt in Clint's mind that Rod, Jr. was speaking figuratively about Rod, Sr. and nothing more. Even though Clint hated putting a damper on Rod Jr.'s indulgence in wishful thinking, it was high time he disclosed the truth about the night of the fire in 1953 and that Rod Sr. was murdered.

Down the worn path, Clint trekked, moving closer to his destination. Unexpectedly, a shift in frigid air assaulted him, and a powerful current forced his body sideways off the path. He hastened his step with intensity. A storm was moving in.

He abruptly stopped. *This isn't right*, he said under his breath. An irregularity struck him as odd. The landscape ahead had changed–dramatically. He cocked his head, thinking, *It's different from the last time.*

The trees were bare! He couldn't see any autumn foliage anywhere. In contrast to the trees back at his place that still held their leaves, this scene almost appeared like a movie prop with no color on or through the branches. Full of gray and brown tones, the entire area had taken on a winterlike appearance. And, more shockingly, in the fields, Clint would have sworn snow was falling.

That's impossible, he scoffed, dispelling the thought. *How absurd! It's not that cold!*

No trace remained of the countryside. A completely different topography had replaced the meadows and fields he was used to. He started to take a step, but an invisible barrier stopped him. He saw nothing but felt the divide. Where a meadow had been on previous visits, a cornfield now appeared. In all directions, all he saw were unharvested cornfields. His mind couldn't process what was happening. That what had been meadowland was now something entirely different.

His mind screamed. *How can this be? Cornfields don't grow overnight!* A cold chill ran up his spine. Clint's attention was drawn upward to where three crows peered down. They were observing him, perched several feet above on snow-covered branches.

Clint started to move but was stopped by an invisible force. He had no way of knowing it, but Clint had taken a quantum leap back in time to 1953. Electromagnetic waves of energy were oscillated wildly. Observable matter faded in and out, drifting away from modern time, back to decades earlier. The scene was unrecognizable. The environment continued to change until, at last, it stabilized.

He withdrew his phone from his pocket and on the screen, instead of the galaxy wallpaper he had installed, a dark silhouette—surrounded by multiple swirling orb layers—each revealing hints of turquoise, coral, or purple at their fringes—appeared. A thin blue line ran down the curvature length of the profile image in the center.

He studied his phone curiously as a vibrational frequency radiated from it.

Clint cried out to no one, "What is happening to me?"

Well, almost to no one.

He refocused his attention on where the bookstore should have been. No longer did he see what he expected to find. His thoughts triggered a conversation he had engaged in with Jules a few weeks back at the diner. She had insisted no bookstore existed where Clint had told her one did.

In a microburst of clarity, Clint's understanding transformed.

Before his eyes, filtered through a shadowy ether of formless shapes, a scene of ruin emerged. No more than twenty feet ahead

Chapter 58

was the shell of a burned-out structure. Smoke curls rose into the air from the smoldering destruction below.

The scorched ground was cinder-charred, but through it all, Clint saw something his brain was unable to grip. There, in the middle of the burn site, a cash register rested, centered among the seared rubble. Clint's heart pounded rapidly. His breath caught, and tears streamed as he viewed a truth too impossible to accept.

A buildup of heavy snow bordered the perimeter of the smoldering building where Clint stood. He instantly identified what he was looking at—the burnt remains of what had once been Rod's General Store. No longer did Rod's New and Used Books occupy the illusory space Clint had been paying visits to. The phenomena he was experiencing was outside his ability to grasp, yet it existed.

Around the burn site, an electrostatic pulse was felt. When it stopped, a crystal quartz materialized at Clint's feet. Where the store's entrance had once been, a golden stone now lay.

Two multipart worlds had fused into one dimensional portal of space-time. The snowy fields of December 1953 were clearly defined along with the burned building, which oddly enough was still sweltering. Layered alongside the scene was the cornfield and empty street that existed in the current year of 2003—which Clint never knew existed or had even seen until today. Two epochs had merged into one unimaginable reality.

Clairvoyance turned crystal-clear in a flash. From the first day Clint had stepped onto the path, he walked through a corridor in time to a place where Rod's New and Used Books occupied. Rod, Sr. had sourced an in-between space to reach Clint and to manifest his will. To make solid items available to be intermingled with Clint's treasure hunt pieces.

Through the mysterious presence of the Bowie knife—and the other objects Clint had purchased at the bookstore—Rod, Sr. was able to lure Clint to the shack, where Clint would, at last, discover his father's remains. The items Clint had purchased that he found so reasonably priced were because Rod, Sr. had valued them at 1953 prices.

Standing in a transient gateway, amidst thousands of radiant orbs, the man in the straw hat appeared. Simultaneously, the crystal quartz on the ground began to emit, from its core, fractal designs wrapped in brilliant, patterned rues, creating a wall that encircled the orbs. Inexplicably the rock had interlinked with a shaft of light streaming through the dark gray clouds.

Clint was surrounded by circular patterns of mysterious geometry. The electromagnetic energy field narrowed in around Rod Radcliff, Sr., gravity pulling him into a curtain of spatial divide. The tall, slender man Clint knew to be Rod, Sr., walked through to the other side. Slowly the space began to close around him, reverting to its natural state.

"There is power in magic!" Rod Radcliff, Sr. declared with an all-knowing smile. "The crystal I leave you symbolizes divine energy. I've had time without end to consider what I wanted to do with the gift of tomorrow. Always remember, transformation of being is internal, Clint, not external. I encourage you to pursue your study of the heavens. Answers await your questions there. They will be scripted in the stars." Rod extended his hands toward the heavens. A golden light shown down.

Clint watched as his benefactor transcended into a realm. Clint was unable to merge with his version of reality.

"You make your father and mother proud!" Rod Radcliff stated. "Elise, Eli, and I are always near, around the corner in the… Silence of the All. I will miss you."

As his figure melded into the ultraviolet frequency that separates humankind from the divinity of the universe, Clint's guardian expressed his gratitude. "You have cleared my name and set the record straight. My death was at another's hand. I was not to blame for the fire that destroyed my general store. At last, peace has found me."

Chapter 58

Clint fell to his knees, facing the cornfield. The open space of 1953 had vaporized into nothingness, along with Rod Radcliff, Sr. A lump formed in his throat. Grateful for the wisdom of a man he never knew, the meaning of Rod's words was tucked safely into Clint's beholden heart of gratitude.

The quartz-crystal that lay on the ground, where a door had once been erected, shimmered like stardust in a lingering otherworldly light.

Clint moved to where the stone lay. Reaching down, he picked up the cherished gem and dropped it into the top pocket of his denim jacket. He turned one last time to absorb the incredible residual power that remained in the atmosphere. He breathed deeply. Tears pooled in his enlightened eyes, trickling down his face.

"Thank you for everything," he breathed humbly.

Clint took the first step back toward the truck and his new life.

Chapter 59
Secrets Kept
10 a.m. Friday

A restless night awaited. Clint had tossed and turned, watching the minutes and hours slip away until finally, at 4:30 a.m., he got out of bed. He was too excited to sleep.

In the kitchen, he flipped the switch on the coffee maker and walked down the hall to the bathroom to take a long, hot shower. After getting dressed, he filled his thermos. Predawn, Clint drove toward town ahead of his agreed scheduled meeting time with Bradley Abers.

The sun had barely cleared the horizon when Clint parked his truck in Salzburg on a side street close to Grandview. Their rendezvous location was just around the corner. Electing to take the footpath back to where he had been the afternoon before, he noticed nothing was as it had been. Hours slipped by while he thought, schemed, and planned.

"You're here early," Abers commented as he approached Clint from behind. Standing a comfortable distance away, he inserted, "I didn't expect you for another half hour. And I thought I was early!"

Confused as to why Clint was sitting on the ground, Abers stated, "It looks like you didn't have any trouble finding the location."

The remains of yesteryear and Rod's General Store had entangled Clint's thoughts with the present. So much so that when Bradley Abers walked up, Clint was thrown off guard. "What are you doing here?" he asked, a little dazed.

Chapter 59

Shocked as to why Clint would ask such an odd question, he replied, "Because this is our agreed time to meet. Remember? Well, actually up there," he pointed up the street to Grandview. Watching Clint get to his feet, looking as though he had no idea where he was, Abers inquired, in a concerned tone, "Are you all right?"

Clint turned to look at the cornfield. "Yeah, I'm fine."

"I don't mean to be rude, but is this a bad time?" queried Abers. "Look, we could reschedule if you'd like."

"No, I'm sorry, you caught me by surprise, is all," Clint said, turning away from the cornfield, knowing the secrets it held. "Weren't we supposed to meet up there?" he politely pointed to where the sidewalk ended at the intersection of Grandview and Ridge Crest. "I didn't expect you to come looking for me. I'm ready if you are. We can walk back so you can show me where the property begins."

"You're looking at it," exclaimed Abers. "This is it! A total of three hundred fifty-five acres, which includes the land we are standing on." Abers waved his hand toward the cornfield and the surrounding space.

"I intend to drive you around the entire parcel. The reason I suggested starting at Grandview is so I could show you the access point from Salzburg, which is right here. You saved me the time of bringing you down here. That's why I was shocked to see you. As you can imagine, more than one entrance exists. Actually, there are several."

"Including this land?" Clint pointed to where the Rod's General Store had once stood.

"That's correct," answered Abers. "This location is included in the contract as well."

Clint was astounded. "You do realize this is where Rod's General Store was once located? I addressed the subject of the general store in the news conference yesterday?"

Secrets Kept

"I hadn't put two and two together. Not until on the way over," Abers admitted. "That's quite a coincidence. Isn't it? Since I was working from a topographical map, I didn't make the connection. Three hundred fifty-five acres covers a lot of territory. Back then, the town was more spread out. Didn't connect the dots that Terence Jordan's property extended this far up. The paperwork I viewed says he's owned it for twenty-odd years." He glanced up the street. "Shall we get started? We can take my car."

As Clint ambled alongside his realtor, he thought about the timeframe in which Terence Jordan must have purchased the property. In the early 1980s, the property belonged to this landowner. When they reached Bradley Abers' Lincoln Continental, Clint said, "I'd like to see that original paperwork if you don't mind."

"Sure, I'll bring it along to our next meeting. I really think this is the perfect property for your needs," Abers stated confidently as he drove down Main Street on his way out of town.

"I have no doubt it is." Clint grinned, possessing an insider's knowledge that the deal had been set in motion long before Abers got involved.

After hours of driving, walking, and trekking through some difficult terrain, Clint Reeves and Bradley Abers put in what they felt was a generous offer. Clint trailed Abers to Paoli, and they waited at Starbucks. They had given Terence Jordan only two hours to respond.

Clint was not surprised when the proposal email response came back earlier than anticipated. Before Abers purchased their second drinks, Clint's offer was accepted. Bradley Abers was shocked a counteroffer hadn't been submitted. Clint was not.

Had Bradley Abers not been with him, Clint would have danced an Irish jig. As it was, they shook hands and congratulated themselves on a successful negotiation.

Chapter 59

Friday Evening, October 24

"Hello," Jules answered.

"Hey, it's me," said Clint. There was a long pause before he reluctantly stated, "I hope you don't mind, but I'd like to have another rain check for this evening."

"Of course," Jules replied quickly, disappointed for the second night in a row they wouldn't see one another. Clint had indicated he would call her at five o'clock the day before. When he did phone, it was to say he wasn't feeling well and wouldn't be coming over. He'd asked to see her on Friday, and now he was canceling Friday.

"Is everything okay?" she asked.

"Yes, everything's fine. I'm just tired, is all. I think the activities of the last few days have finally caught up with me. I'm not as young as I once was, and my energy level wanes easily. Takes longer to recharge my batteries these days!"

Jules heard a muffled chuckle on the other end of the phone and realized Clint was half-joking about being old. "I bet it does, you old fogey you. You've been burning the candle at both ends for a couple of months now. What would you expect? Maybe it's time to start taking Geritol!" She giggled.

"Thanks. That makes me feel tons better," roared Clint. "All kidding aside, I'm afraid my age is creeping up on me. The body doesn't work like it used to. Don't know if I'll make it to the diner in the morning either. I'm thinking about sleeping in and fixing a leisurely breakfast at home. I haven't done that in a long while. Sit on the porch and enjoy the smells of autumn. From where I sit right now, that sounds delightful."

Jules had to digest what she had just heard. She had always flattered herself into believing Clint drove into town nearly every day to Josie's Diner primarily to see her. Now she realized her thinking was flawed.

"Well, then," she coaxed, "that's exactly what you should do." Jules didn't ask about dinner the next evening. Something told her not to.

"Thanks for being so understanding," Clint responded. "Feels like the air has been sucked out of me. I guess that twelve years age difference between us is starting to make a difference."

To make matters worse, Clint just threw more fuel on the fire. Jules wanted to curl into a ball. What Clint suggested didn't sound very promising. Clint had been dropping subtle hints for the last couple of weeks, or longer, but bringing up their age difference was the mother of all bombshells.

"Hope you aren't coming down with something," she commiserated.

"Nah, nothing like that. I'll call you tomorrow," promised Clint. "Sorry I bailed out on you again."

"I look forward to it. Sleep tight," Jules said softly. When she hung up the phone, a sadness washed over her. She sat on the couch and blankly stared at the wall. The future wasn't looking too rosy, at least in respect to her and Clint. It didn't take a rocket scientist to figure out he was constructing a wall between them. In her mind, the reason was clear as day. And she had a name—treasure.

Jules' chin started to quiver, and her eyes filled with tears. "I suppose I can't blame him."

Clint had done his best not to behave suspiciously. His business dealings had to be kept under wraps at all costs. That's why dinner plans were out of the question. He'd give himself away otherwise. Never good at lying, Jules would see right through him. She'd known him too well. Besides, phone calls and arrangements had to be made and received, of which none could be done at her house. His elation over the land deal would have been impossible to hide.

Chapter 59

"It isn't every day a man buys three hundred fifty-five acres of land." He chuckled, thinking how crazy that sounded.

The first thing Clint did when he walked through the door was to slip on his Notre Dame lounge pants, shirt, and matching slippers. Gifts from Wade and the family from last Christmas.

I'm an old man, in a younger man's clothes. He laughed. Prepared for a long night, Clint made an espresso, picked up the cell phone, and began to dial.

Clint considered the house and property. An endearing thought to know it was originally owned by Phil Reeves. The wooded space behind it also belonged to his ancestors. Squatters' rights were common back in those days. Earl, his great-grandfather, was the first of the Reeves clan to take up residence in Salzburg. No wonder Clint felt attracted to the land; it was part of who he was. Everything made sense when viewed from the rearview mirror. Clint had to admit, his was an amazing story—by anybody's standards.

Through the night, he plotted and schemed. One important issue still needed to be answered, but it required assistance. A loose end that had to be tied; he'd start at the library. To shed light on the town's history and his property was his specific aim. He wanted to know if Rod's New and Used Books ever existed. Bonnie could help him with the answer. Besides, until the curiosity seekers left town, the library was as good as any place to lay low.

At 1 a.m., Clint headed to bed before he fell asleep at the table. When his head hit the pillow, he was out like a light. No dreams, no worries, and no ghostly presence to haunt his dreams.

Saturday Morning, October 25

Bradley Abers had phoned first thing to say he'd scheduled a meeting for Monday, October 27, 9:30 a.m. at Gleason Title Company in Paoli. Kinsley, Abers & Sons, his Real Estate representatives, Jeremy Sullivan, Clint's attorney, Terence Jordan—the landowner, and, of course, Clint would all be in attendance to close on the property.

Sullivan had also phoned to assure Clint he was able to secure a loan based on liquidating a portion of his new wealth, moving the land deal to its final stage.

In his excitement, Clint decided to drive into Salzburg earlier than planned. Too antsy to sit still, he planned to stop in at the library anyhow. Clint wasn't good at computers like everyone else seemed to be. Plus, the library might not be such a bad place to hang out, considering reporters were still hanging about. More traffic than usual lingered in town as Clint drove through.

When he walked into Josie's, he was greeted by Jules' shocked expression. People were sitting in his booth. Burley men wearing ball caps. A fissure of irritation coursed through Clint. He wanted to step up, yank their hats off their heads, and tell them it wasn't polite to wear hats indoors, but of course, he did not, considering he had done the same thing only a day before. He sat down in the booth behind them, with his back to the door.

Jules walked up and put her hand on his shoulder. "Follow me," she said, leaning in. Jules put an empty coffee cup down in a separate part of the diner, where Clint had never been seated. Delighted to see him, she said, "I thought you weren't coming in this morning. If I had known, I would have saved your table."

"I didn't know either until a little while ago." He laughed, looking around at the packed house. "Surprised me too."

Jules went behind the counter to grab the coffee pot. Throwing caution to the wind, she said, "So, if I may ask, what changed your mind?"

"I wanted to ask you out to dinner for one thing. If you are so inclined to accept my offer. Thought we'd drive into New Albany."

"That sounds terrific," she readily agreed without hesitation. "Why do I get the feeling you are hiding from the press?" She laughed, realizing he was facing the wall.

Chapter 59

"Because I am," he admitted, then answered her first question. "I have a bunch of things to do. I'm headed to the library. I also have something important I need to share with you but not here. Not now." Clint's blue eyes turned cautious. "It's about the bookstore."

Jules' face went from jovial to solemn. "I won't ask, but if you want, I could come join you. My break could be moved up. We have two new girls on staff this morning. After the breakfast crowd dies down and before the lunch crowd hits would be perfect timing."

"That would be fantastic. I called to make sure Bonnie would be at the library today, and she will. She's helping me with a project. I have a few things to do beforehand, but I could meet you there between 9:30 and 10."

"You do know my curiosity is through the roof," she confessed, wondering what the project was and what he had to tell her. She suspected he might have gone to the bookstore the day before since he had mentioned it earlier. *Maybe,* she thought, *Rod, Jr. shared additional information with Clint that was pertinent to the fire.*

"I understand," Clint acknowledged. "This isn't something I feel free to talk about, especially here at Josie's."

"I'll ask Patrick about an early break."

"Perfect," Clint said. "Three heads are better than one! Bonnie's, yours and mine."

He buried his head in the newspaper, when in fact, his thoughts had traveled to an adjacent town. The trip spent over to French Lick and West Baden was expected to take no more than an hour and a half, two at the most. It was a trip he was looking forward to but could not speak with Jules about.

When Clint strolled into the library, Bonnie instantly noted his arrival. She walked to the front and gave him a hug. "Good to see you," she said with a smile. Her eyes grew large. "Although, I'm not sure how you're going to react to what I happened upon."

Clint's face showed alarm. "I'm not sure I like the sound of that."

After what you told me on the phone about the site and what happened there yesterday, I'm a little stumped. What I turned up makes absolutely no sense. Nada… zilch!"

"What do you mean?" questioned Clint.

"It's easier to show you," Bonnie suggested. "Have a seat." She pointed to an isolated table far from the main area. "I'll be back in a jiff." While it was against library practice, Bonnie offered, "Can I get you anything to drink?"

"No, thank you," Clint declined. "Thanks for asking, though."

"Okay, I'll be right back." Bonnie disappeared behind the counter into the backroom.

Clint glanced at his watch, 10:01 a.m., Jules was expected any moment. When she walked in, Clint stood, signaling his location. "Glad you were able to make it," he said as Jules neared.

"I only have thirty minutes." She touched his forearm. "Okay, Mister," she said in a sleuth like tone, "what's this about?"

"I won't waste any time," Clint stated, taking a deep breath. "Yesterday when I went to the bookstore to speak with Rod, Jr…" he stopped speaking. Clint watched Jules' face closely when he said, "Well, you were right the first time. It doesn't exist. There is no Rod's New and Used Books!"

"What?" Jules catapulted from her seat. Standing in front of Clint, she said, "But we were both in there. We went inside and walked around. Talked to the clerk." Jules lowered her raised voice. "Don't you recall, Rod, Jr. wasn't there as you'd hoped. He left a note and envelope. Your name was written on it!" Whatever Jules had expected Clint to say, it wasn't that. "That's just not possible," she insisted.

She put a hand to her mouth. "But, Clint, that doesn't make sense! Rod's New and Used Books was stamped on the *Somewhere in Time* video. The store must be there or somewhere. Don't you

Chapter 59

recall? That skinny guy with the straw hat loaned it to me, saying it was a good movie if you liked sci-fi. He said it had to do with time travel." She lowered herself back into the chair, nearly falling.

"Yeah, I know, Jules. You're preaching to the choir!" Clint could easily identify with her reaction. Over Jules' shoulder, he watched as Bonnie emerged from the back room.

She approached the table, put her computer down, and opened it. She made a few keystrokes, and then Bonnie turned the computer toward Clint and Jules. "Check this out. You both visited this place. Right?"

"Yes," Clint responded, glancing over at Jules. "We were just talking about that. We went to talk to Rod, Jr., the owner, but he wasn't there. Some other clerk assisted us."

Jules pivoted in her chair to face Clint. "But, Clint, you've been in there three or four times. Talked to Rod on numerous occasions. You bought gifts for the treasure hunt."

Bonnie's attention homed in on Clint. "You bought items from Rod's New and Used Books?"

Just then, Bonnie remembered something she'd nearly forgotten. "Do you guys recall I sent Jules that article where a building permit and license had been secured? A building was to be constructed on the same parcel of land where the general store once stood. The name registered on the application at the city county building showed Rod's New and Used Books."

"Yes, I remember," said Clint.

Jules nodded her head.

"Well, I'm glad you are sitting down. Because Rod Radcliff, Jr. did put the application in with the intention of erecting a bookstore. Bonnie's lips puckered. "You aren't going to like what I'm about to show you," she said with confidence. She clicked on a file she had prepared and turned the screen around. "It took me a while to find anything more about that place or him for that matter, but when I did, I was speechless."

Bonnie's stare was piercing when she delivered her next remark. "According to this, he was killed in a car crash on Highway 150. If you read toward the bottom of the page, it says his death came prior to building the bookstore. The year was 1981."

Clint's face turned pale, remembering Terence Jordan had bought the property somewhere around 1983. With his eyes glued to the screen, he carefully examined the image it portrayed. The face was that of Clint's Rod Radcliff, Jr. A memorial written in his honor pictured a young man with sandy blond hair, wearing what appeared to be an exquisite gray double-breasted Italian silk suit adorned with a blue flowery tie—his bright hazel eyes recognizable and familiar.

After a long silence, Clint pulled his head back and looked at the ceiling. He patted the table and said, "Thank you, Bonnie."

He glanced down at Jules. "I'll see you outside."

Clint slowly moved toward the exit. On the sidewalk, he withdrew a cigarette from the pack and lit up.

Chapter 60
Final Mystery

Jules and Clint walked back to Josie's Diner from the library, leaving the truck behind. On the way, he confessed to her the heavy burden he had been carrying since moving into Salzburg back in 1997 had dissipated. Any doubt over Rod Radcliff, Sr.'s spirit being released from its earthly plane had been removed by his recent insight.

"Hey, the kids are coming this next week. Would you like to join us?"

Jules' face brightened. After the grim news and shocking developments that had unfolded at the library, she was ready for a more uplifting conversation. "That sounds delightful. Will all the kids be there?"

"No, only the grandchildren. Lily, Trey, and Dylan are spending Thursday through Sunday with me. It's fall break. I meant to tell you, but I got sidetracked." Clint shrugged. "Tonight, I'd like to do nothing, except maybe watch a movie and eat popcorn. You up for that?"

Jules laughed. "You bet I am."

"Want to come over around 6:30 this evening. Sunday is a workday, I realize, so I thought we'd get started early. That way, you're not kept out too late."

"Perfect! What movie?" asked Jules, thinking back on the last few days. "I take it you are feeling better."

"I am. Thank you. It's a surprise," Clint teased. "You are going to laugh at me, but when I was in Paoli, I picked up an Orville Redenbacher popcorn popper. Now we can pop good old-fashion Amish popcorn to our hearts' content. Kernel popcorn is so much better than that microwave stuff. It's like what I had as a kid at the orphanage."

Final Mystery

"Sounds like great fun," Jules commented, wearing a huge grin. She didn't let the *We*, Clint had just used, escape her.

Clint gave Jules a hug when she went back inside Josie's Diner to return to work. "I've got to go get my truck." A few minutes later he honked as he drove by the diner.

Jules, on the other hand, had to know for herself. It was an enigma that was killing her. She watched Clint's truck disappear down the street. She waited another five minutes then told Patrick she had something important she needed to attend to. She'd be back in ten. When she returned, her face was ashen. Clint was right, there was no Rod's New and Used Books.

Saturday Evening

With his hands linked behind his head, Clint invited Jules to come in. He felt full of himself today. The mood of his house had elevated to new heights.

Jules sauntered into the living room. "So, you don't meet me at the door anymore?" She baited, surprised at his change in behavior.

"Not this time," he replied jokingly, "figured you knew the way." He was holding a TV remote in his hand. A huge bowl of popcorn sat on a side table between two new sienna-dyed leather recliners.

"Oh my word," she wailed. "You purchased new furniture."

Since her last visit, the living room had been completely revamped. New side tables and a sofa, plus the wall behind the television had been layered in stone. "These chairs are drop-dead gorgeous," she exclaimed, putting her hand on the back of the chair to stroke the leather.

Clint hit the control buttons to demonstrate the features of his chair. "Check this out," he said excitedly as he moved the chair's position to recline. Both chairs faced the large television on the

Chapter 60

opposite wall. The fireplace on the far wall lent a picturesque, homey ambiance to the room.

"Have a seat," he said standing and pointing to the extra chair. He gave her a loving embrace before she slid her tired body into the rocker-recliner he had clearly purchased for her. "It comes equipped with heat and a massager," Clint said proudly, eager to show off the new changes in the room. His furniture had been delivered two days prior, and the wall was finished Friday afternoon.

"Very cool," she squealed, using 1960s slang. Her pumpkin orange V-neck dress flowed around her legs as she sank deeper into the recliner. "Do you really expect me to get out of this thing now that I'm in it?" Sensing the burning soles of her feet, she added, "You're going to have to pry me out."

Pleased with himself, Clint stretched, full body, into his own chair. His next move would shock Jules more than the furniture. "You ready?" he grinned.

"Giddy up go!" she said playfully, kicking her shoes off and exposing her bare feet.

Clint dimmed the lights. The movie began to play. A familiar tune was heard, Theme of Paganini from *Somewhere in Time*. Clint leaned over and grabbed Jules' hand. "This time, I guarantee we'll see the entire movie—New television! New copy! New us!"

Clint walked Jules to the door when the film ended, promising to see her at the diner the following day.

Wednesday, October 29

The next few days passed at a snail's pace. Each minute felt like an hour.

On Monday, Lily had phoned to inform Clint that her parents' and her flight would land at 11 a.m. Thursday morning. Clint, in turn, called Rusty to arrange a pickup of his grandsons that same day.

After Wade, Clara, and Lily arrived at the Louisville International Airport, Clint planned to chauffeur everyone to Cracker Barrel in Seymour before making a return trip back home with his grandchildren the next day. Something of great importance was going to be shared. The thought of owning three hundred fifty-five acres still had Clint pinching himself. The news was expected to sweep the Reeves' family off their feet.

The property closing at Gleason Title Company was set for 9:30 a.m. On his way to Paoli, Clint phoned his attorney.

"Hey," he said when Sullivan answered, "I'd like to extend an invitation to a cookout this coming Saturday at my place. Barbequed steaks and ribs," he boasted, "and a good old-fashioned wiener roast. I'd love to introduce you to my kids if you can make it. Plus, I'll show you the infamous shack in the forest I've been rambling on about."

They covered several significant subjects in their conversation, including the financing of the land deal Sullivan had preliminarily secured on Clint's behalf until the signing. When they were about to hang up, Sullivan inserted, "Thanks for the invite. I haven't been to a wiener roast in years. I assume the invitation includes my wife, Suzanne."

"Of course, that goes without saying," replied Clint. "I'd love to meet her."

The closing went without a hitch. When Clint departed Gleason Title Company, he was walking on air. Terence Jordan had turned out to be a delightful chap. A friendly man, up in his years, he had confided in Clint about his decision to accept his offer so quickly when it came in. Apparently, he had been toying with the idea of consolidating his assets for some time. For simplicity's sake, he had started putting his affairs in order. The upkeep on the land was pushing him to the limit.

Chapter 60

"The strangest thing happened the day you put your offer in," he told Clint. "Right after I accepted yours, I had two more offers come in within ten minutes of each other. Both were greater than yours. More than the asking price, in fact."

"Is that right?" Clint said, shocked by Terence Jordan's revelation.

"Yeah, isn't that something? I wasn't sorry, though, because our agreement felt right. Like you were meant to have it. I made a vow early on not to sell to just anyone. Ownership was a deal breaker. I've put a lot of myself into that property." Jordan's face brightened. "Then, when I heard what you had in mind, I knew I had made the right choice."

"I'm glad you approve," Clint softly replied. "That means the world to me."

Later, after everyone had gone their separate ways, Clint stood on the sidewalk looking up at the sky. Reverently he closed his eyes. For several minutes he stood motionless, letting the warmth of the sun warm his face. Finally, he breathed, "No amount of appreciation will ever be enough. Thank you, God, for not giving up on me, like I did you."

"Thank you will never be enough, Mr. Radcliff! We have great things ahead of us. You and me!"

Thursday, Noon, October 30

Clint drove to Louisville earlier than anticipated to pick up his Montana family. In Jules' car, he waited in the airport parking lot for the flight to land. He wanted to formulate in his mind how much he was going to divulge about his situation. Forty-five minutes later, he was headed for the arrival gate.

On the way to Seymour, Clint hinted about a surprise. Then at Cracker Barrel, he dropped the news concerning the land purchase.

Final Mystery

When Clint finished speaking, they all sat with their jaws dropped. No one had a clue, or saw it coming.

Out of precaution, he warned his children Jules was unaware and asked they keep it that way. What they had been told in confidence was to remain a secret until told otherwise. Although the family had been filled in on the land purchase, they were not told everything. He'd held one gigantic surprise in reserve.

Clint spent the night and slept in the guest bedroom, where he always stayed when he visited up north with his son. Early the next day, the plan was to enjoy a fine breakfast before he and the grandchildren made their way back to his place.

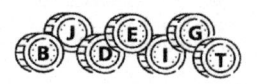

Friday, October 31
Halloween

Clint had penciled a daytrip to West Baden in for the afternoon. Jules had to work, so it would be just the four of them. There, Clint and the grandkids would tour the town and enjoy brunch at French Lick Springs.

Pluto Water and West Baden Springs' dome, and breathtaking interior, was the town's claim to fame. Replicated from elegant European spas, the hotel was once touted as the Eighth Wonder of the World. Although originally a French trading post, located near the mineral springs and a salt lick, the town had a rich history.

Lily, Trey, Dylan, and Clint stopped in at Josie's Diner before heading out of town, so they could see Jules. Over ice cream, they discussed their plans for Saturday night, probably the last cookout of the season. Everyone was excited about the gathering.

Jules warned them all, "We'd better dress warmly. I checked my weather app, and it is going to be chilly as the dickens that night."

Chapter 60

"Do you want to stop by to play Spoons with the kids and me tonight?" Clint asked Jules when she set two hot fudge sundaes on the table. "It's Halloween, in case you didn't know. Thought I'd get some extra treats today while I'm out."

Ready to retrieve the other two ice creams, she smiled pleasantly, "That sounds terrific! But only if you let me win!" She winked at the kids and grinned.

The stage was set for a pleasant Friday evening. "We'd love to have you join us," Lily chimed in, wearing a bright smile. Trey and Dylan nodded their heads in agreement. "Have you ever played Spoons before?" Lily asked.

"No, I can't say I have. However, your grandfather told me about playing it at Trey and Dylan's house on his last visit. Said it was a dangerous game."

Everyone's faces twisted, exchanging strange glances. "It's a wild game!" Lily giggled. "You're going to love it!"

Jules studied their mischievous faces, "Okay..."

After returning from West Baden, they went exploring. Since the treasure had been safely removed, Clint took the children down inside to show them where the stockpiles of stolen goods had once been hidden. The entrance, enlarged for safety, made it easier to maneuver. No longer did they have to crawl into a tiny cavity to get to the cave floor. After that, he took them underground to the living quarters where his descendants had spent time. It was an adventure they all enjoyed.

Later, before Jules arrived, Clint poured tea at the kitchen table and explained his plan for the property in more depth. He also reminded them not to speak about the additional information to anyone, including their parents. He suggested a morning drive to tour the acreage would include an early morning hike.

That night, after pizza and a rip-rousing game of Spoons, Jules left Clint's place feeling pleased to have been included in the activities.

The children hugged her when she left for home. So did Clint.

Saturday was here before Clint knew it. Only one more day to enjoy his grandchildren's company.

Jules phoned on her way to work. "I'll try to be there by six," she informed Clint. "Saturdays are crazy at Josie's this time of year."

"We aren't on any kind of a timetable." he reminded her. "Just be sure to come hungry."

"No problem there," she joked. "I wasn't planning on eating today. Need to make up for last night's pizza. Besides, I want to splurge tonight. Can I bring a dessert? I hate to come empty-handed."

"Nah, I've got everything covered," he assured her. "Just bring your appetite." They both laughed.

Clint was glad Jules had not suggested taking off early because that gave him time to spend with the grandkids alone without worrying about what might be said. By 9 a.m., they were out the door on their way to explore the new property.

When 6 p.m. rolled around, everyone was in the kitchen.

Jules knocked on the door. She didn't want to give the children the wrong impression. As she stood at the door waiting, she stared into the antique mirror Clint had purchased at Rod's New and Used Books. Although the shop later proved to be nonexistent, the mirror certainly was. The whole affair had been a supernatural experience she'd never forget.

"Hi there," Trey said, startling Jules from her reverie.

Clint came into the kitchen from the back part of the house. "Well, look what the cat dragged in!"

"Watch it!" warned Jules with a playful smirk. "My goodness, it smells scrumptious in here."

"I know," Lily said, wearing a huge grin. "That could be baked beans you are smelling or macaroni and cheese." She laid her spoon to the side and went over to give Jules a hug. "I'm so glad you could join us. Isn't this fun?"

"It is!" Jules agreed. "Though I wish your grandfather would have allowed me to bring a contribution."

Chapter 60

"No, we put together a surprise dessert, just for you." Lily saw Clint wink before turning his back to them.

"Grandpa said you are always bringing the desserts. This time we wanted to make one. He told us what your favorite would be."

Jules looked at Clint. "Is that right? And what would my favorite dessert be?"

With his back still turned, he said, "You'll find out." Then Clint went outside.

So much energy was in the house. It felt like a different place. Jules went into the living room and peered out the window to watch Clint stoke the fire. The sun had gone down, and flames flickered into the air beyond the treetops.

"Hey, need any help?" she called.

"No," he said with a half-turn to acknowledge her presence. "Just help Lily out if you don't mind. I'm glad you didn't get held over."

"Me too," Jules admitted. "I'll see if I can lend a hand."

When she walked back inside, both boys had joined Lily in the kitchen. Dylan came over and gave her a hug, just as Trey had done at the door. It made her feel like she belonged. Clint's kids and grandkids were becoming like her extended family.

An hour later, the big kids had arrived. They all carried food outside from the porch, to the firepit, to a folding table. Under the starlit sky, they placed hot foods and cold drinks.

The grandchildren and their parents all sat around the fire telling stories about the good ole days. It was delightful.

Sitting close to the fire, Clint watched their animated faces. When things quieted down, he clinked on his drinking glass and said, "I have an announcement."

Ears perked up.

Jules' face showed her surprise. Not having any idea what this could be about, she waited in anticipation like everyone else.

Final Mystery

The rest of the family looked on in surprise. Considering they had been told Jules wasn't to be made aware of the three hundred fifty-five acre land purchase, they wondered what Clint was about to say. Their eyes were affixed to him.

"Okay," he said. "Not a word until I'm through."

Jules noticed the children's expressions were not as curious as she might have expected, considering Clint had caught everyone off guard.

"As you all know, my life has changed significantly. Our lives, actually," Clint added, searching their faces for recognition of what they already knew.

"I want to make it official—here and now—I am in the process of building a structure on the three hundred fifty-five acres of land I purchased last week. The land I told you kids about at lunch on Thursday."

He turned to Jules, "I'm sorry to have kept it a secret, but I really wanted to surprise you."

The entire group searched each other's faces, totally confused as to what was going on. Clint wanted to laugh because he understood his kids thought they knew everything. They did not.

"I kept something in reserve from you children as well until tonight," Clint said as he looked at each of his family members. He had shared his secret with his grandchildren that morning, except Lily. She had been let in on the full story on Friday afternoon. He had made them all swear not to breathe a word.

"An orphanage will be built west side of Salzburg. It will be constructed on my new acreage." Clint smiled at the grandkids, knowing they were relieved not to have to keep his secret any longer. Children were never good at keeping secrets, and Clint knew that. That's why he had waited until the last minute to tell them and why he was glad Jules had not come over early.

He winked at Lily. "A children's home has been my lifelong dream. I visualized it countless times in my head. All my life. Over

Chapter 60

and over, I saw it—saw the children playing outside and on the grounds. The school rooms and the sleeping quarters. Happy faces because they had a nice place to call home."

Everyone stared at him in shock, absorbing what had been said.

Jules smiled at Clint with tears in her eyes. Her expression said it all, displaying what she couldn't bring herself to say out loud: how proud she was of him, what a wonderful man he was, how much she loved him. Everything was cleared up in a few short words. All the secrecy of the last month, succinctly explained.

"I am in the final stages of locking down the specifics. Jumping through hoops with the state, city, and county as we speak, but we should break ground before the end of the year."

Jules stood to her feet, never expecting for a moment Clint had such a lofty plan for his fortune. "Oh, Clint! This is fantastic news. I can't believe it! Where exactly is this property?"

Clint could not have grinned any bigger than when he replied, "I'm getting to that." Proudly he said, "Off Grandview and Ridge Crest. One of the entrances will be constructed where Rod's General Store had been. I've run it by my lawyer, Jeremy Sullivan—who by the way is expected here any minute to meet you guys—and he tells me some of the permits necessary for breaking ground next month are already in place."

After a few seconds, Clint added, "Where Rod's General Store once stood, there will be a historical land site describing how the orphanage came to be. Plus, a gift shop with memorabilia I believe people will enjoy and will raise additional proceeds for the Orphanage." He stopped again. Trying to collect himself. In a trembling voice and a lump in this throat, he said, "Reno Gang treasure is funding the soon to be Rod Radcliff Children's Home."

Clint fought back the tears. "An orphanage will be built, generating jobs and revenue. Let's help it send a message of paying things forward.'"

Everyone jumped to their feet in jubilation! No one was more excited than Jules.

Final Mystery

They joyously talked about the new venture that would affect each of their lives. All the many changes that would come about were a result of Clint's unexpected fortune. His endeavor would help the community, plus give orphans, like he had once been, a good home.

After a while, Clint raised his hand for everyone to still once again. "I have one last surprise. This one no one knows about." He winked at the grandchildren.

He disappeared into the pole barn. "Hey, Trey… Dylan," he called out from inside the barn, "will you lend me a hand?"

Lily and Jules stared at each other with funny faces, wondering what Clint was up to now.

Trey, Dylan, and Clint wheeled out a huge, unrecognizable contraption.

It wasn't until they were right on top of the campfire that Jules realized what they had been moving. "Good night Christmas!" She squealed. "It's a telescope!"

"Yes," Clint confessed with a grin. "A Meade 12" LX-90. It can locate over 30,000 celestial objects. At the push of a button, we will easily view the night sky."

Jules couldn't have wiped the smile from her face if she tried. "How cool," she laughed. "Now, you'll never get rid of me."

"If you give me a minute, I'll set it up." Clint offered. "We can all have a view of Saturn's rings!"

The children were beside themselves with excitement. After about ten minutes of fiddling with the dials on the telescope, Clint announced, "Okay, I think we are ready." He looked at the kids. "Let's let Jules have the first pass at it."

She moved over and put her face to the eyepiece. She tried to center Saturn, but it was too fuzzy. She squinted, trying to bring things into focus but failed. "Sorry, Clint, I can't see anything. It's blurry. It has a dark blob in the middle of the lens."

He frowned, "Really, I had it set right on Saturn."

Chapter 60

Jules shrugged. "I think it needs more adjusting." She looked at the kids and said, "User error!"

"I'll see what I can do." He had her step away. "Here, use this to wipe the lens off," he said, handing her a cloth." Maybe a bug landed it on."

Jules walked to the other end of the telescope.

A heavy silence followed, then came a scream. "Oh... My... God!" Tears streamed down her cheek, flowing off her chin. "This can't be!"

She ran back to where he was standing, arms open wide, leaving whatever it was she had seen on the lens. She hugged him like she would never let him go. "*Clint!* Is that what I think it is?" she cried openly, hardly able to speak.

"Yes, it is," he admitted and knelt to one knee. "Julie Eileen Johnes Jenkins, will you marry me?" he asked with a hopeful heart.

When she looked up, behind Clint's family came Scott, his wife Wende, David, and his wife Kim, Sean, Ivan, Patrick, Bonnie, Joe from the garage, and Jeremy and Suzanne Sullivan.

But the most shocking surprise of all was the gentle face—with smiling eyes—of Pearl Teague, who was being wheeled around the side of the house by her daughter, Georgeann. Pearl had known before anyone. As a son might confide in his mother, Clint had revealed his intentions to Pearl the day he had visited her, in Chambersburg, without Jules. He'd extended a personal invitation to tonight's celebration.

When everyone had gathered around, waiting in anticipation, Clint said with a grin, "I wanted to throw you a party!" He repeated, "Will you marry me, Jules, and make me the happiest man alive?"

A peal of laughter was heard coming from behind Jules, who was still shellshocked.

She leaned down and kissed him. "Yes, yes, yes! A thousand times over. *Yes!*"

Final Mystery

Clint got up, went back, and pulled the ring from the lens. In his other hand was a black box inscribed Baden Jewel Master. He slid the ring onto Jules left finger.

Tears of joy fell as they watched Patrick open a bottle of Dom Perignon that had been chilled and hidden out of sight in a bucket of ice. For the special occasion, Patrick had made Jules' favorite dessert and his specialty, homemade Tiramisu, covered in chocolate icing and trimmed with strawberries.

Jules clung to Clint with a heart full of joy. Then she stepped back with a broad grin, admiring her exquisite engagement ring. She moved through the crowd, proudly showing it off to everyone. The diamond sparkled in the firelight.

While Jules chatted with her future family and friends, Clint strolled over to Scott who was standing by the back door. He extended a handshake, then placed an 1861 twenty-dollar gold coin in his palm. "As a memento and token of my appreciation, I'd like you to have this. It will serve as a reminder of the extraordinary case we cracked." He grinned. "With help from an interested party."

Scott looked down and was shocked at what he saw. Their eyes met. "Whoa! Are you kidding me?" He inspected the shiny gold coin in his hand. "Your generosity is commendable." His face beamed. "How could I ever forget this chapter? The Radcliffe case was a roller-coaster ride from start to finish. One for the record books." He shook his head, "You made a true believer out of me."

Scott clutched his gold coin tight. "Saying thank you seems flimsy for such a spectacular gift, but I'm thrilled to receive it. It's a keepsake I'll treasure for life."

Clint nodded, "Me too Scott. It symbolizes our friendship, and this extraordinary episode we've come through."

Scott peered past Clint. "Congratulations, by the way. Jules is a special lady. Seems like you two were meant to find each other."

"I believe we were. Like it was written in the stars." Clint's eyes twinkled with humor when he said, "She's a gem, that's for sure."

Chapter 60

When he saw the meaning of his words were not lost on Scott, he smiled and turned toward his bride-to-be. Jules was bubbling over with excitement. "Better go. I have a fiancé waiting for me."

He took only a few steps, then stopped. In awe, he gazed up at the heavens. A strong feeling came over him. A knowingness he couldn't define. He whispered, "I know you're here."

Clint felt Jules' hand slip into his.

She tugged on his arm. "Let's study the stars together. Shall we?"

Together, hand in hand, they walked back to sit by the fire.

A new love was born.

ORDER YOUR COPY TODAY
MASENFT.COM

Shadows of December

Behind life's thin veil of the knowable, into a fissure undefined by time and its constructs, lies a place where souls move about freely without detection. A place where ghostly encounters meet angelic challenges and a desire to alter the foreseeable future is of paramount concern.

Stark changes that threaten all of mankind and what it means to be human are set into motion by a time when profit and greed outweighed concern for the future.

But none of this is known to Jay, a 14-year boy living in a rural town in 1947. Self-absorbed and mischievous, his life is upended when an angel and her constant companion interrupt his life. Soon he will be shown the future and the horrors it brings.

Provided a glimpse into a domain outside perception and beyond observation, Jay is transported from an uncomplicated life he has taken for granted so that he can see things as they really are. On his journey through layers of realities he will learn the errors of his ways and witness how his actions can influence humanities' future.

Printed in Great Britain
by Amazon